ALSO BY KYELL GOLD

Argaea
Volle
Pendant of Fortune
The Prisoner's Release and Other Stories
Shadow of the Father
Weasel Presents

Out of Position
Out of Position
Isolation Play
Divisions
Uncovered
Over Time

Dangerous Spirits
Green Fairy
Red Devil
Black Angel (2016)

Other Books
Waterways
Bridges
Science Friction
Winter Games
The Mysterious Affair of Giles
Dude, Where's My Fox?
Losing my Religion
In the Doghouse of Justice
The Silver Circle
X (editor)

OVER TIME

by Kyell Gold

OVER TIME

Published by Sofawolf Press, Inc.
St. Paul, Minnesota
www.sofawolf.com

ISBN 978-1-936689-51-4
Printed in the United States of America
First trade paperback edition: January 2016
First POD printing: July 2021

Cover and interior art by Rukis & Kenket

This book is dedicated to all the married gay couples in this country and the world, and to all the people who worked so hard for decades to make those marriages possible.

CONTENTS

Part I

Chapter One: Repair (Dev) 3

I want to crush him against me and never let go.   6

Chapter Two: Plans (Lee)..15
Chapter Three: Defiance (Dev) 33
Chapter Four: Open Doors (Lee)...47
Chapter Five: Connections (Dev) 65
Chapter Six: Signs (Lee)..77

Junior invites me to play FBA Basketball.   82

Chapter Seven: Closed Doors (Dev) 91

Is that what you want?   100

Chapter Eight: Reports (Lee) 105

Part II

Chapter Nine: Homes (Lee)..111

He freezes on the dance floor.   117

Chapter Ten: Surprise (Dev) 125
Chapter Eleven: Plans (Lee)...149
Chapter Twelve: Ups and Downs (Dev) 155
Chapter Thirteen: Thinking (Lee)...175

Part III

Chapter Fourteen: Going Home (Dev)...187
Chapter Fifteen: Emergency (Lee) 191

Dev runs into the den.   193

Chapter Sixteen: Waiting (Dev) 199
Chapter Seventeen: Conflicting Reports (Lee) 211

"If you can't answer this, I understand..."   213

Chapter Eighteen: Wired (Dev) 221
Chapter Nineteen: Old Bones (Lee)...233
Chapter Twenty: Confessions (Dev)...241

He clutches the board so tightly the frame cracks.   247

Part IV

Chapter Twenty-One: Old Haunts (Lee) 255
Chapter Twenty-Two: Brother In Law (Dev) 267

Without another word I pull him against me. 282

Chapter Twenty-Three: Back to School (Lee) 285
Chapter Twenty-Four: Homeward (Dev) 293
Chapter Twenty-Five: Old Home (Lee) 303

"You going to be okay here?" 311

Chapter Twenty-Six: Talking It Out (Dev) 315
Chapter Twenty-Seven: Talking It Out Two (Lee) 335
Chapter Twenty-Eight: Into the Future (Dev) 343

"Haven't you felt it enough?" 346

Epilogue

Epilogue: Home (Dev) 353

Afterword: A Lifetime in a Decade 357
Acknowledgments..361
Preview: Ty Game 363

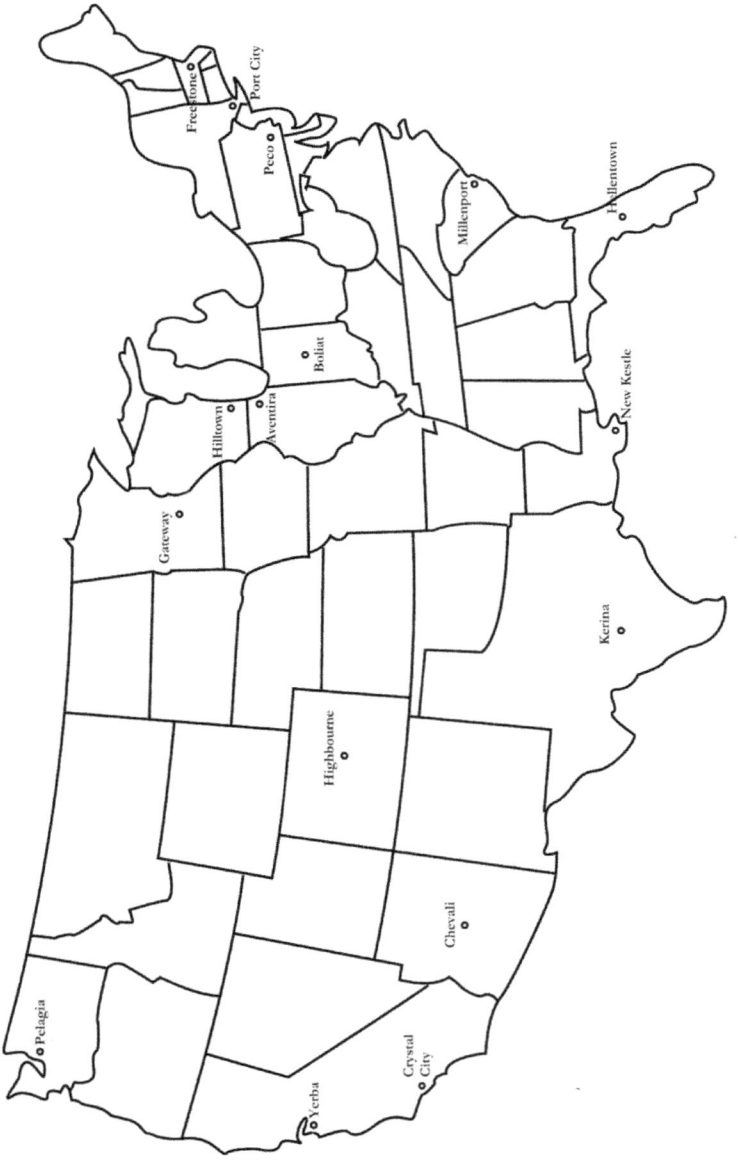

I'm not saying the Forester Universe cities are in the United States.
But if they were, this is where they'd be.

PART I

Chapter One: Repair (Dev)

Hal needs to fix the cracks in his office ceiling. I lie staring up at them and then the inside of a chocolate-brown ear blocks them from my view, followed by russet red fur and then a pair of blue eyes. I squint and re-focus, meeting the eyes as I run my paws down the naked body of their owner, feeling the warm and sleek muscled curves. His weight on me is a good pressure, like the weight of my own muscles following a workout or a football game, and the blue of his eyes is the color of a cloudless sky in summer stretching from one horizon to the other.

I stare up and feel like time has stopped. The concept doesn't bother me. If there's been any point in my life where I'd happily just hover forever, it's here, coming down from some pretty amazing make-up sex, with the fox I love on top of me. I don't have to think about what happened yesterday or two weeks ago, or what might happen tomorrow or even in five or ten minutes. I'm here in this moment, my heart full of love and peace.

The blue eyes blink. "Time to talk now?" Lee murmurs, his voice vibrating against my chest.

Time starts again. His breath ruffles my whiskers, and I snap back to reality, to the fox's face above mine, all the details of his red and white fur, his long whiskers, and the slit pupils in his blue eyes. I've seen him so much in my imagination since we fought, but nothing, nothing replaces the solid reality of him, the creases in the fur around his eyes where he smiles at me, the sharp strong scent of him in my nostrils.

I'm lazy from post-sex haze, warm down in my sheath, and the memory of our lovemaking insists that I keep this conversation at a distance. I don't want to rip the scabs off of our relationship just yet, and yet I want to have this talk with him. Sex is only half of what I've missed while we've been apart. The ache for someone to talk to, to share the highs and lows of life with, is almost as strong as my pent up physical urges. My arms lie tight across his back, holding him to me as though he might float away up through one of the cracks in the ceiling. "I think we need to fuck again," I say. "I don't have two weeks of frustration out of me yet."

He laughs and kisses my nose with a soft brush of his tongue. "My, my."

"I'm serious," I say, and the words spill out of me, giving voice to that ache in my chest. "You know how much stress I've been under? Not just the championship game, but losing it in the last minute, and defending Strike to the team and going on a double date with him…"

"Wait, what?" His eyes focus in on me now. "Okay, tell me about this double date."

So I keep my paws on his hips, take a breath, and tell him how Lightning Strike, our egocentric star wide receiver, went out with the actress from the beer commercial I did with him, "and you know he had all that tantric bullshit about not having sex during the season, but he had his paws all over her tits and he went back to her place," and how she brought a gay snowshoe hare friend who I shared a milkshake with after the fancy dinner at the exclusive Crystal City restaurant.

Lee narrows his eyes. "Is that a euphemistic milkshake?"

I don't think he's really pissed at me. "Probably. I think it said that on the menu."

The corners of his mouth twitch. "I mean—"

"I know what you mean, doc." I squeeze him. "No, it was a real milkshake, and he gave me his phone number, but only in case I wanted to talk about…gay problems with him. He has an on-again, off-again boyfriend and I think he wanted to be able to tell him he went on a date with a football player."

He relaxes, but this is close enough to the thing I do have to tell him that I better do it now. I get the words out fast. "But I did have another guy's paws on my cock."

The smile freezes and fades, and he swallows, and then nods. "I guess you had the right to," he says, but his voice is dull. "Was he good?"

"His muzzle, too," I say, "but I didn't come. I stopped."

He doesn't say anything, so I go on, aware of his sheath pressed against my stomach, mine against his thigh. "It was Argonne, the groupie who reminds me of you."

"Was it because he reminds you of me?"

"Yeah." I bite my lip.

He drops his muzzle into the crook of my neck and exhales. "Why did you stop?"

"Uh. Because he'd just blown someone else on the team and I smelled it on his breath."

That brings his head up again and his voice regains some passion. "Who was it? Could you tell?"

"Yeah." I probably shouldn't tell him, but I think, selfishly, that he'll be excited and I can win points with him if I do. "It was Colin. Can you believe that?"

He blinks and then nods slowly. "It's kind of stereotypical, right? The homophobe is the one getting the secret blow jobs?"

"Yeah. I just wish he wasn't a fox. I think…" I rub my paws down Lee's fur and rest them on his rear again. "Well, I yelled at him in the locker room."

"The locker room." He raises his eyebrows.

"The shower, actually."

"I see."

"We weren't naked. Anyway, he doesn't view it as cheating on his wife because he thinks it's not real sex. So I threaten him because I treat what we do as real."

Lee's paws find my sides and hold me, but he doesn't say anything. I rub at the small of his back. "You're not mad at me? For letting Argonne—"

He brings one paw to my lips. "I'm not that mad," he says. "But you don't need to keep talking about it. If I'm around, do you want to see him again?"

"No. Even if you're not." I pause. "Are you going to be around?"

His paws slide down my sides, gentle, conscious of my rib injury, which to be honest isn't all that bad, not now, not with him here. "I think that's one of the things we should talk about," he says. "I want to be," he hurries to add. "But I want to make sure we can be together without…you know, without betraying who we are."

"I'm pretty sure we can do that."

"Yeah, well," he nuzzles me. "I just watched my parents end a twenty-five year marriage, so forgive me for being a little skittish about things."

"Did you hear from your mother?" The words are out before I can stop them, and then I laugh and rub his rear. "Sorry. You don't have to answer that until we get clothes back on."

"Yeah." He nips at my neck, and reaches back with one paw to drag claws up my sheath, which makes me shiver. "I think most of the stuff I need to tell you is better done with clothes on."

"Sorry about saying my stuff," I say, only I'm not really, and he's getting me hard again.

His paw rubs more firmly into my hardness. "I'm not. I mean, I'm just going to make damn sure you remember how much better I am than any other fox, or any hare, or Strike's big-chested girlfriend…"

I squirm and press a finger down his rear through the lube-slickened fur until I find his entrance, which is still slick enough for that finger to slide into easily. "I think it's time to stop talking and fuck again," I say.

He pants, and thrusts his cock into my stomach fur. "I think you're right, stud," he says.

This time, I kneel and he sits in my lap. With some adjustments, he wraps both legs around me, and I thrust up and into him. Just like twenty minutes ago, I want to crush him against me and never let go.

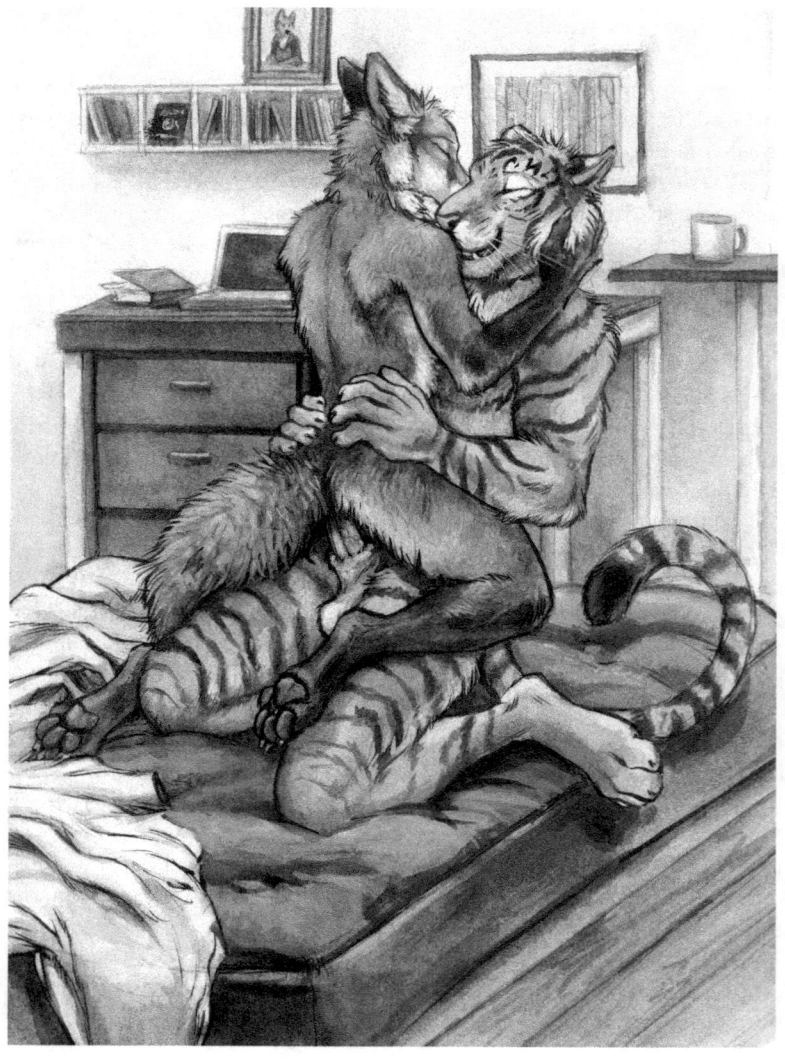

He moves up and down, slender muscled body against my chest, warm rear around my cock. I reach between us and wrap my paw around his sticky shaft, finding it as ready as I was. My other arm holds him against me by his back, and both his arms lock around my neck. I'm amazed all over again at how light he feels against me, how natural, like a part of me that had been missing for two weeks.

In this position, he's very slightly taller than me and gets to look down, which I think he's enjoying. Above and beyond the tiger cock in his rear and the paw on his shaft, that is. Because we both just came recently, the buildup to orgasm is slow and languid, until we reach the tipping point, and then I squeeze him and rasp harshly into his shoulder, pulling him tight against me and shoving my hips hard up against him, my shaft all the way inside as I shudder and come again. Once I've finished, I stroke him until he twists against me and clings to my neck and cries out, adding another spurt of stickiness to my paw and his sheath.

And then I just hold him like that, and he holds me, and I press my nose into his cheek ruff and say, "I love you, fox. I love the hell out of you. Don't you ever run out on me again."

"Never," he breathes. "Never, tiger. I love you too. I missed you so much."

I squeeze his cock and pull back to kiss him. "Yeah," I say. "I can tell."

•

He assures me Hal won't mind if we use his shower, and though I'm self-conscious about it, I squeeze in anyway to at least wash the fox jizz out of my fur. Then we're dressed, and Lee rolls up the sheets as ordered, and stands at the door with his bag packed and his tail wagging. We get into my truck and head for home.

I should be happier, with the weight off my mind, and he seems cheerful, but I can't forget that he's got things to tell me as well. "Why didn't you drive your car over?" I ask.

He leans against the door, tail flicking lazily behind him. "Hal offered to come get me, and I didn't think I should drive."

That might have been a sign I ignored, that he left his car in front of my apartment building. And I'm reassured, hearing that he was messed up, too. I've thrown out the sheets I shredded when I was crying over him leaving, so if I want him to know what I went through, I'm going to have to tell him. But not now.

Instead, I focus on the memory of him being messed up from whatever was going on in his head at the time. "Do you want to talk now or back in the apartment?"

"Oh," he says, "it's late." But his tail stills, and curls under the car seat. "Do you want to be upset tonight or in the morning?"

"Should probably get it over with. But let's wait until I'm back in the apartment."

"I'll ask you to hand me your phone before I do."

I frown. "Really? I thought you were just going to talk about why you think we should re-evaluate our relationship."

"There's that." His paws fidget. "But there's also news, and it's going to make you angry. I can't sugarcoat it and I wouldn't anyway."

"Did you..." I blink. "With Hal?"

He barks a laugh. "Hal has a girlfriend. I didn't even fantasize about him. Well...when I was really miserable I fantasized that he'd hold me. He did hug me a couple times when I cried."

I must look guilty, because he pats my knee. "I don't blame you for all of it, tiger. I mean, you've got things to feel guilty about, but me being miserable and sick and drunk—"

"Drunk?"

"One night. Maybe two." The memory flicks through his eyes and back to a twitch in his ears. "Anyway, that's not one of them. The point is, no, I didn't fuck Hal and I wouldn't have been in shape even if he did want to. Um, I did talk to my Mom, though. She apologized for burning my pride jacket and other clothes. And she's quitting Families United."

I exhale. "That's good news. So is she okay with you being gay now?"

"Well, no. But at least we can talk about it. A little bit." He leans against his door and looks at me, his big ears mostly upright, both paws on the knee closest to me. "Honestly, I don't know how to get any closer. I focused so much on getting her out of that whack-job religious hate group that I never thought she might leave it and still not be okay with who I love."

"I'm not so sure my parents still are." It's reflex, that statement, and then I review yesterday's dinner with them. "Mom is. I think. She asked about you a lot...yesterday."

I can't believe it was only yesterday I played in the UFL championship game. So much has changed in twenty-four—no, it's like nine-thirty now, so more like thirty or thirty-one hours. At three o'clock yesterday afternoon, the Firebirds still had a shot at their first UFL championship, I was the only openly gay player, and Lee and I were exchanging hesitant, broken text messages. Then we lost the game in the last minute, Aran Polecki came out to the world right after that, we flew home this morning and I met a kangaroo rat kit who told me I saved his life by coming out, and then I pushed aside all the doubt and worry, focusing on how much I missed Lee and love him, and I went to see him for the first time in almost two weeks. And now we're talking in the truck just like old times.

He doesn't say anything about my mom at first, and then he says, "I'm looking forward to catching up with her again. And seeing your dad. I respect him, and I'm starting to like him."

I laugh. "Really?"

"Well." He grins. "Once we got past the initial difficulties…"

"And you both got out of the hospital."

"…I think we both care about you a lot, and it helps that we both like football, too."

I chuckle and shake my head. "You're amazing. If you'd told me in September that you'd be looking forward to seeing my dad…"

"It's a challenge." His tail gets a little life in it. "I mean, he was ready to knock my teeth out, and a month later we were standing around at Thanksgiving."

"Well, that's Dad," I say. "He might knock your teeth out, but that doesn't mean he doesn't like you."

He rubs the joint of his thumb, the one Dad sprained. "Anyway. It makes me feel good to build that relationship. And it's good for our relationship, too."

"Is this part of the talk that was going to wait until we're at the apartment?"

He turns his head to look out the windshield. "Ten more minutes." He smiles. "Tell me about Polecki. He got in touch with you?"

"Yeah. Did you get him my number?" He inclines his head. "Thanks for that. He texted. We sat in a little gay café and formed the first UFL Gay Alliance."

He laughs. "Any other members?"

"His boyfriend is a Yerba player. Doesn't want to come out yet. Aran told me who he is, but…"

"It's okay. You don't have to tell me. Maybe I'll meet him this offseason. I'd like to meet Polecki, at least."

"You'd like him. He's very…coyote. So yeah, we just talked about being gay. He said that coming out on the podium after the championship was the hardest thing he's ever done. He was terrified they were going to turn on him and start booing."

Lee snorts. "After he brought them a championship?"

"You never know."

"True." He rubs his whiskers. "I'm glad he's a nice guy. I was worried he'd be an asshole."

"Nah." I turn onto my street. "It's been good to talk to him and Machaine about being gay, you know? Not that I can't talk to you, but you're my boyfriend, so…" It doesn't sound good when I say it like that. I stop at a light and turn my eyes on him, hoping he'll understand.

He does, reliably clever that way when he wants to be. "When you talk to me, it has weight. Yeah, I know. It was good to talk to Hal about our relationship, too. Gave me perspective. Though he was also trying to get me out of his apartment, I think."

"I'm glad you and he are friends," I say, grateful for his understanding.

"I owe him something big for letting me stay so long, and for his friendship."

My building comes into sight in the next block. "I don't think he thinks you owe him anything."

"No, but I should get him something anyway." He taps his paw on his knee. "If only for arranging to be out tonight."

I grin and pull into my parking garage. He goes quiet as I park, takes his bag out of the back while I take the bundle of fox-and-tiger-scented sheets, and is quiet all the way up in the elevator, sniffing around. When we get to the apartment, he stands there in the middle of the living room as I close the door behind him, and drops the bag on the floor.

The sheets go in our laundry pile in the bedroom, and when I come back, he's still standing there, sniffing the air, whiskers twitching. His eyes are dry, but he's got a look like they might not be for long, so I reach out and hold him, and he falls into my arms.

"I didn't know if I'd ever be back here again," he murmurs.

I squeeze him. "Really? Because I didn't think I'd ever be able to get rid of you."

That gets a shaky laugh from him. "It's easier than you'd think," he murmurs against me. "Just tell me to go away."

"Yeah?" I nose between his ears. "Since when did you ever listen to me?"

"More than you know." He presses his muzzle against my shoulder.

I'm happy to just hold him, to watch his tail swishing and to smell his fur. His ear flicks gently against my whiskers and his paws rub my sides. And I don't feel so bad then about losing the championship. Thinking about that, though, reminds me that there is something I am going to feel bad about, and I figure I should get it over with.

I rummage in my pocket and take out the phone. He steps back and looks down as I hold it out. "Ah," he says, taking it. He rubs his thumb across the cracks. "Already?"

"I didn't throw it. I dropped it when I was drunk, celebrating after the Boliat game."

"Guess you can buy another one." He slides it into his pocket and steps back again, holding my paws. "Okay, so, uh. Wow. I didn't want this to be the first thing we talked about when we got back here. But yeah, let's get it over with. You know that court case."

"The one about Vince King." I want to prove to him that I can say the kid's name without getting bitter or resentful about it. So I remind myself how happy I am to be here with him, how much I love him not only for himself, but also for the passion he brings to stuff like that court case, how much he wants to make everyone else's lives better. And I understand it just a little better after meeting the kangaroo rat kid in the airport. Saying the name "Vince King" makes me picture that kid killing himself, and cold fingers clamp my chest. I watch Lee with what I hope is understanding, and I don't grimace or turn away.

"Right." He holds my eyes with his, and I can see whatever it is tormenting him behind those blue irises. His paws squeeze mine. "Your brother is an attorney for the Families United side."

I listen to the words, but they don't sink in. "My brother—Gregory? Wait, how did he get involved in this?"

He takes another breath, holding my paws. "I think when I talked about Families United at Thanksgiving—well, I don't know. Maybe he was already inclined to work with them. I shouldn't blame myself until I know. But yes. I was writing a document to submit to the court talking about what Families United did to my family and how harmful they can be, and the attorney I was talking to said the court had to take into consideration that I had a relationship with someone related to the defense."

"Gregory?" I call him up in my mind: sullen and toothy, claws extended, shouting at me at Thanksgiving. "No, wait. I talked to Mom and Dad. They didn't say anything about it…" But they had been cagey about what kind of pro bono work Gregory was doing. Dad didn't approve of it. I thought that was just because it was free.

"I asked them not to tell you." Not even Lee's tail is moving. "I said you didn't need one more distraction. You already had—I mean—" Now he does duck his muzzle, eyes dropping to the ground. "I was trying not to be, but…"

"No, that would've been—I could've taken it." But I imagine the stags who called me "faggot" during the game, whether I would have thought of Gregory, whether worrying that my family was turning against me would have affected me. "But it's probably better I didn't have to." And then the familiar surge of anger. I try to rip my paws away from Lee, but only get one free. "God *damn* him! Did he take that case just to get back at me? All I did was be successful, but he couldn't deal with that, he has to go help some hate group?"

The fox clings to my left paw. "Dev," he says quietly. "It's not about you the person. It's about you the image, the thing you don't have as much control over. Gregory's reacting that way because, well, I don't know. With Mother, it was her looking for control in a situation where she felt helpless."

"You're *defending* him?" I stare down.

"I'm trying to help you understand him. I don't want you to get into a thing like I did with Mother that's going to take years to crawl out of." His ears are up and his eyes are sad.

His eyes are sad. That makes me stop. "What if he's just a fucking prick and I'm better off not talking to him at all?"

"Yeah." He smiles a little. "But what if you can show him that being gay isn't evil? What if you can change his opinion so he doesn't want to defend Families United anymore?"

"What if I change his teeth?" I mutter.

Lee squeezes my paw and I pull him against me. "I'm sorry, tiger," he says. "It sucks."

Breathing is easier with his body against mine, his scent in my nose. "What an asshole. Lion Christ." The anger comes in waves, beating against the bulwark of Lee's confidence. "I'm surprised he didn't call me to brag about it."

"He's probably not allowed to talk about it while it's going on."

"Well, he can sure as hell talk about it now. Give me my phone back."

He shifts against me. "No."

"Fox." I try to look him in the eye, but he's pressed his head into my chest. "I'm not going to break it."

"Tiger," he says, mimicking my tone, "that's not what I was worried about."

I exhale. "I'm not going to…"

He tightens his arms around me. "You're not going to do anything but come over here to the bedroom and take your clothes off and sleep next to me."

"But—"

Now he lifts his head. "If you call him, I'm going back to Hal's."

I stare. "You wouldn't."

His blue eyes challenge me and then his lips twitch in a smile. "Well. No. I probably wouldn't. But please, listen to me this time. Let's go to bed. You can yell and curse at him all you want. I've got some feelings about him bottled up I could stand to let out too."

I inhale and then hold him against me and press my muzzle between his ears. "So does this mean you're done with the case?"

He tenses, just slightly. "I, uh…"

"Because," I murmur against his ears, "I want to tell you that I'm so sorry about Vince King and that I want you to do whatever you feel like you have to do. I'm sorry for the times I thought you were using him as a stick to whack me into doing gay rights with. I'm sorry my fuckhead brother is involved and that your—your mom is involved, or was. I'm sorry that this guy who reached out to you is gone, and I want you to tell me that it's not your fault."

The tension drops out of him as I talk, and he shudders against me. "If I'd reached out to him, though—"

"No," I say firmly. "What he did was a sad choice, but it was his choice, and the people who made him feel that way were not involved with you either. You responded to his e-mail, you did the best you could. You can't just go up and introduce yourself to gay kids who might not want to be outed."

"All right." He takes in a shaky breath. "It's—it's not my fault."

"Good." I kiss between his ears.

"I don't know if I believe it yet."

My paws keep him against me as I push him toward the bedroom. "Then work on that. And I'll be here."

We get into the bedroom, mostly undressed and lying together on the bed, and then he's looking past me at the dresser and his paw stills on my stomach. "You put the picture away?"

My ears flush. "Kind of." I point to the corner of the wall where the framed picture hit, where jagged gleams of light show that the shattered glass is still there.

His ears dip. "I'll clean it up in the morning," he says quietly.

"No." I cover his paw with mine. "I threw it, I'll clean up."

"I'm sorry I put you through all that," he says.

A little of the anger that propelled the picture against the wall surfaces before I bury it again. "You said you'd never leave."

"I didn't want to hurt you." His fingers curl in my stomach fur. "It seemed like the lesser of two hurts."

He's just made the same promise not to leave ten minutes ago. "Next time," I begin, and he noses my whiskers.

"No next time." He kisses the side of my mouth. "If there's something so bad I'm worried it'll interfere with your job, I'll tell you and we'll—we'll figure out a way to keep it off limits."

"Me too," I say, "although what the hell could be more distracting than the last four months? If we can survive that, we can survive anything."

"Yeah." He lies back beside me and rubs his fingers across my stomach again. I've got one arm behind his head and my paw on his side, the fragile steel of him under my fingers wonderfully familiar and yet so irresistible that I want to keep exploring it over and over, his thick winter coat coming off in my claws, his muscles shifting. I think he's lost some weight but I don't want to say anything about that.

I don't want to say anything about anything, just lie here with him, and that's good enough for him, too. Vaguely I remember we were supposed to be yelling about Gregory, but that anger is now muffled by love and contentment, and I leave it lying there.

CHAPTER TWO: PLANS (LEE)

In the morning, I wake from a dream where I was searching through a desolate city and find my tiger sleeping beside me. The swelling of joy in me only grows as I slide my nose closer to him and lose myself in his scent. In all the senses of the phrase, I've come home.

He shows no signs of getting up, though he does stir when I brush his morning erection. I decide to let him sleep. It's been a long two weeks and a difficult, exhausting couple of days. But we got through it.

The sparkle of glass in the morning light catches my eye. I slip out of bed and pad over—carefully—to clean up the picture and the shattered glass. I get as many shards as I can and pad out to the kitchen to dump them in the trash. Probably should've put on clothes or at least an apron before I did this, but oh well. It's done now, and I don't have cuts on my pads or any other sensitive exposed areas.

The sensitive area is actually a little less exposed now. Cleaning up glass is not very sexy, so my erection has retreated into my sheath to await a call to action. Meanwhile, the picture frame is intact, so I take it into the kitchen, make sure I have all the glass out of it, then replace it on the dresser. The fox in the picture, lying on the cushion with his erection playfully displayed in a paw, smiles back at me. Looking at him, it's hard not to believe that everything will be okay.

Of course, the fox in that picture was looking forward to moving in with his boyfriend, never believing that he'd run out in three months. If you'd told that fox that his boyfriend would be in the championship and he'd be watching it on TV, he'd be incredulous.

Then he'd ask what he'd done to fuck it up.

I look away from the photo and back to the real tiger, here and now. Short term, I need to work through the things he told me. It bothers me more than I wanted to let on that he slept with someone else—yeah, he didn't come in the guy's mouth, but when his cock was all the way in there, does it make a difference whether he finished?

Of course it does, I tell myself. He stopped it partway through, realized it was wrong. (Not because of you, though, I argue back.) I can flagellate myself for walking out; if I'd been there in Crystal City then he wouldn't have been tempted to fuck some other fox. But if I'd been there in Crystal City, I know we'd have been arguing, and that would've been just as bad, or worse. We have to figure out a way to keep our passions under control, or at least not turn them against each other.

And Dev's going to be on the road, and I'm going to be working for another football team. There'll be more star-fuckers looking to hook up, probably a lot of them foxes since everyone knows he likes foxes (*one* fox, I remind myself with a little bit of preening). I've just told him that I wasn't that upset that he almost cheated on me; of course, we were "on a break." But how's that going to make him feel the next time? Maybe the draft's coming up and I'm stuck in the Yerba offices and he goes out to the clubs… or I'm away at the combine and he's bored and he and his teammates are hanging out…

I stare down at him on the bed and picture another fox lying in the space beside him. Cold fingers grip my heart and I shake the image away. No. I have to trust him.

So I occupy the space beside him and drive away my imaginings. I rest my paw on his shoulder and kiss his neck, and that makes me feel better. But only a little. Because the problem doesn't come when I'm here, when I'm loving him and being a good boyfriend. The problem comes when I'm an asshole, when I walk out on him, when I leave him alone. If I could be that fox lounging in the glassless frame all the time…but below the sexy and attractive surface of the picture there is a lot of ugliness: vanity, mistrust, insecurity.

Dev snorts sleepily and turns, but doesn't wake. I'm still too awake to just lie here next to him, and the specter of the other fox is gone for now, so I put coffee on and then curl up on the couch. I plan to call Hal, but there's a voicemail on my phone that must have come in sometime yesterday.

"Hi, Mister Farrel," a young male voice says. There's a whistle in his voice, so maybe a rabbit or squirrel? "My name is Elmsley Chatten, and I'm with the Chevali Firebirds…"

Another job offer? Did they hear I was hired by Yerba?

"I'm sorry to have been so late getting in touch with you, but I'm brand new here, just taking over from Lake. Did you ever talk to Lake? Anyway, you weren't on the list of player wives but I've read about you, and Vince had your number, so I wanted to call you and introduce myself. Which, ah, I did. So I'm Elmsley and this is my number. If you have any problems with…with Devlin, or, you know, with any of the team, please call me first and we'll try to work it out. Okay? Call me if you have any questions."

O-kay. That was a little weird, but I guess not completely so. At least he explained where he'd gotten my number from. I wondered if this was something that was brand new, or if the previous person—Lake, was it?—just hadn't ever contacted me because I'm not female.

Well, I don't need to call Elmsley just yet. So I go ahead with my original plan and call Hal.

"By the state of my shower," he says when he picks up, "and the smell in the office, I'm gonna say your date went better'n mine."

"Did yours not go well?" I ask quietly.

"It went okay, but I didn't stay the night." He chuckles dryly. "What d'you think? Things going to work?"

"They worked pretty well." I grin, resting a paw on my tail. "We tested them a few times."

"What'd I tell you about details?"

I lean against the sofa back and laugh, rubbing the arm where weeks ago, an age ago, Dev pushed me back and jerked me off. "Thanks."

"Don't mention it. No hurry on returning those sheets, either."

"I'll wash 'em today. But I mean it. Thank you, not just for last night, but for—y'know, for letting me stay with you and for not letting me give up on us."

He coughs, or scoffs. "Ah, you wouldn'ta given up. Not in your nature. As for the rest of it, well, you got me into the championship game party at Yerba and I made a couple connections there and had a great time. So let's say we call it even."

"It's hardly even. I owe you..." I can't even think of what to say.

"How about we *call* it even and say that in the future we do what friends do when other friends need something from them?"

"All right," I say. "So things with Pol are good?"

"We got another date." He sounds pleased. "At this stage, I just want every date to end with 'see you next time.'"

"Glad to hear it," I say. "Hope there keeps being a next time."

"Hey." He taps his phone with his claws. "Come to think of it, there is something you might be able to do. I don't wanna get you in trouble or nothing, but I know you were talkin' to Kingston's wife about visiting them soon. If you could scope out whether Kingston would be willing to talk for the story I'm doing...that'd really give it a boost."

I drop my tail and go a little cold. "Fisher? Uh, well..."

"I know you're friends," he says. "I don't wanna mess with that. But maybe if the Firebirds cut him, if he can't catch on anywhere else next year, maybe he'll want to talk about it."

"Free agency is a month away."

"I can wait a month."

I take a breath. "Okay. I'll see what I can do. But I think even if the Firebirds release him, even if nobody picks him up, he might want to wait and see if anyone needs him in pre-season. Guys get injured, you know? Teams might want a veteran."

"Lee." Hal's patient. "Don't screw up your friendship, and don't press him if he doesn't want to. But can you figure out if he might?"

"Yeah, sure." I relax.

"Honest, the story's going to work either way. But with a player just coming off the championship game—a game where he got injured—it'd grab a lot more eyeballs." He clears his throat. "A *lot* more."

"Those contacts in Yerba, do they know what kind of story you're writing?"

"Believe it or not, some of the guys running teams want this stuff out there. The owners, the suits up top, they want it to go away. They want to expand the league in a year or two, and they think if the public's worried about long-term injuries to players, they'll lose some of the millions and billions they stand to make. But the guys running the teams, the ones who see firsthand what this does to players, they think the sooner it gets talked about, the sooner we make the game safer."

"Huh. Well, I'm all for that." I think about Dev in the next room, wondering what damage might already be done below that tough exterior.

"You should be."

My tail curls around me, and my gaze stays on the door of the bedroom. "Dev's never had a concussion. He plays smart, with his head up."

"One of the things the docs are telling me in this article," Hal says slowly, "is that with the head, it ain't just the big hits. It's all the little ones, some that might not even register. They accumulate over time. The one that causes the concussion might not even be that bad."

That fits with what happened to Fisher, but I don't say anything about that, wary of even the slightest mention of his situation until I get permission. The other thing complicating Fisher's situation is his use of illegal substances to speed his recovery. In my mind, I roll around a question about whether steroids could make a guy more likely to suffer a concussion, but Hal's a sharp fox and he would understand what that meant immediately.

So I just say again that I'll ask Fisher. Hal thanks me and then says, "Good luck with Dev. I think you guys got a real shot."

"Thanks." I smile. "We just have to figure out how we deal with life, you know? I don't think it's likely to throw a shitstorm at us like it did this year, but we can't just ignore how we responded to that."

"The more you stay together, the better you can deal with it."

I think of him and his ex-wife, divorced after about ten years; about my parents, divorced after twenty-five. My tail uncurls to hang down to the floor. "Maybe."

"Definitely." That dry chuckle again. "Just the shitstorms get bigger. You think a little argument about whether to film some gay rights spot is bad? Try arguing over cubs."

"I know, I know," I say, "though I have to add in his brother and my mother and Vince King and…yeah, I know, compared to the issue of having a family, it's different."

"At least you don't have to worry too much about that yet. He's got football, and if you want a cub, I'm sure he'd support you, but you've got football too."

I hear rustling from the other room. "We have years to talk about it," I say. "Hey, speaking of which, sort of, I got a weird call yesterday…" I tell him about the call from Elmsley. "You know this guy? Or Lake?"

Hal clears his throat. "Don't know any Elmsley. But Lake…I think he was the lion worked with Vince the media guy behind the scenes. He'd try to smooth things over with the wives when they caught their guy cheating or something. So maybe this guy is the new Lake."

"What happened to Lake?"

"No idea," Hal drawls. "But if you're on that list, that legitimizes you, don't it?"

"I guess so. I'm glad they reached out, but I'm also wondering why now."

"New guy, new philosophy. Maybe Lake wasn't so keen on your relationship. Or maybe he was leavin' his job and didn't feel like reaching out to someone new. Dev didn't say anything?"

"No." I glance toward the bedroom and rest my free paw over my sheath. "But I should get back to him."

"What," Hal says, "you're not in bed right now?"

"Would I do that to you?" I ask innocently. "Again, I mean?"

He snorts, tells me to arrange a time for us to have lunch or dinner, and hangs up.

Carrying my phone, I slip off the couch and pad back to the bedroom. Dev is in the same position I left him, but his gold eyes shine up at me in the darkened room.

"Who were you talking to without any clothes on?" he rumbles.

I set the phone by the naked picture of myself. "Hal."

"Again?" He shifts and reaches out a paw. "Would've come out if I'd known."

And just like that, my nakedness is sexy again. I step into his paw and he pulls me to the bed, and his fingers trace my body through the fur and he kisses me, and the conversation with Hal goes to where all the other nonessential thoughts go.

Later, as we're washing each other off in the shower, those thoughts filter back through the pleasant ritual. "Hey, Gena asked if I'd call when we got back," I say, scrubbing shampoo into Dev's back while he leans against the wall.

"Mm." He half-turns. "I haven't checked up on Fish. Probably should."

"Also," I say, "Hal asked me to feel out Fisher to see if he'd want to be interviewed for that story he's writing."

He tenses under my paws and then relaxes. "You're not going to demand that he talk or anything." It's not a question, nor is it a command. He's talking out his reaction. His tail lashes against my legs, and I keep my paws on his back. "You're just going to see if he's open to it."

"Uh-huh." I resume scrubbing, and slide up a little closer behind him. "Hal understands that we're friends first and he says that while it would help his story a lot—and help the league, ultimately, because it would draw attention to a problem—he doesn't want to insist. But he's a journalist. He can't leave an opportunity like that unexplored."

"Mmm." He stretches as I scrub down to his rear and legs. "All right. Leave me out of it, though."

The words hang there, and then he turns and looks down at me. "I should say: do you need my help? Do you want to do this together?"

I reach up and give his sheath an affectionate squeeze. "Thanks, tiger. No, I think it's best if you stay out of it. If Fisher wants to talk to you about it, just be honest. This isn't my crusade and I'd rather keep our friendship than steal information to report to Hal."

"Fair enough." He takes the shampoo as I stand and applies it to my fur, strong fingers pressing through my winter coat to my muscles. "And Gerrard wants to hold workouts after a week or so."

"A week?" I stretch and close my eyes to focus on his paws.

"Maybe two."

When my wet tail wags, that's a workout, dragging all that water around. "Want to come to Yerba with me and look for a place to live?"

Now his paws still, right there on my sides above my hips, holding on to me. "You got the official word?"

"Well, no. But Peter said if I didn't hear today, to give him a call. It's pretty much done."

His fingers squeeze. "I just got used to you living here."

I reach down to cover one of his paws in mine. "I know. But I can't commute from Chevali. I mean, I guess I could, if you want to pay my plane fare and get up with me at five a.m. to catch the flights…"

"No, I know." He goes back to soaping. "At least we'll get a little time together."

"We'll have more than a little. We've gotten through two and a half years living separate, and Yerba's closer than Hilltown."

His paws regain some of their life as they move down my legs. "That's true. Hey, Polecki said he and his boyfriend fool around during halftime of their games."

I turn and grin down at him as he finishes with my feet. "You want me to come down during halftime next time you play Yerba?"

"Maybe." He flashes a grin up. "Doesn't seem to've hurt Polecki."

We rinse, and Dev says, "Oh," as I'm wringing out my tail. I look at him and his ears are down. "There's another thing."

"About Polecki?" I rinse my paws and shut off the water.

"No." He leans against the wall of the shower. "The job you were offered with the Firebirds."

"What, the one you asked them to offer me?"

He looks startled. "Who told you?"

I reach out my arms and hug him. "You did, just now. But I guessed. I mean, why else would they call me out of the blue? The Firebirds barely know I exist. They only got around to having their player relations liaison person or whatever call me yesterday." He doesn't know what to say, so I poke my nose at his chest. "Plus, when I told you I wasn't taking it, you looked like I'd returned a Christmas present you got me."

"Yeah, uh…" He hugs back and presses his nose between my ears. "I thought it was a good solution and I was being sneaky. Like you."

"Yes, that's kind of what I figured." I smile and step back. "I mean, I wish you'd told me, and I was upset at first that you were going behind my back."

"If I'd told you, you would've thought that I was doing it just to get you out of my fur, or like, implying you couldn't get a job yourself, or something."

"Well?" I flick my ears, spraying his muzzle with drops of water.

He shakes his head, his whiskers still dripping. "Yeah," he admits. "Some of that, I guess. But I just wanted you to be happy and you were driving me crazy."

My smile falters, because now I'm going around from "he did a dumb thing" to "I drove him to do a dumb thing," and it's back to being my fault. But I keep my ears up and say, "I know. I'm sorry. It's cool."

"Really?"

I slide the shower door open behind me and step out. "Yeah. A lot of stuff happened in the last month and we're still sort of processing it. Compared to almost sleeping with someone else…" His ears flatten. "Or, y'know, walking out on you…that's pretty minor. I think."

"All right." His ears come back up. "What's this player liaison guy thing?"

I hold his towel out to him. "I guess the phone was off. He left a message." I tell him about Elmsley, and what Hal said about Lake.

"Huh," he says, rubbing his head dry. "If you need to call him, go ahead and do that."

"I'll tell you first." I hold a paw over my chest, fingers flat against the damp fur. "Promise."

"Speaking of family drama…" He rubs his head dry and meets my eyes. "I'm going to call Gregory."

I'm not thrilled, but he's cooled down enough, and I can't keep him from talking to his brother forever, so I go into the other room to sit by the window with my laptop and wait for my fur to completely dry. He closes the bedroom door, but after thirty seconds I can hear his raised voice, so I flip my ears away and focus really hard on the computer.

And when I open my mail program, it becomes a lot easier to shut him out. I'm staring at the e-mail from Peter Emmanuel, GM of the Yerba Whalers, offering me a position in their scouting organization. Actually, he's asking for Dev's address so he can have the job offer couriered over, but basically I've got the job.

The glow from that e-mail gives me enough confidence to open the second one I should read, from Brian. Because of course he can't shut up, even when I buy him off with a bottle of wine and a good-bye that (I thought) leaves no room for rapprochement. "My dear Tip," he writes, "*An there were two such, we should shortly have none, for one would kill the other.* We hope of course that Polecki and your tiger will not come to that, but I do suspect that we shall be left with one. Now that there's a championship-winning gay football star, your tiger will be free to recede into the background and, how did you so charmingly put it, focus on football. You can stop agonizing about getting him to work with Equality Now, or any other organization, because Polecki will happily reach out to all the young gay athletes. Your tiger will be first, and I suspect that's enough for him and you.

"I suppose you'll expect me to apologize for hounding him on Media Day, and you'll likely think that his outburst about wishing he'd never come out was solely my doing. But of course, Tip, thou art deceived. And yet, and yet, if that be your lot, if you are *shot through the ear with a love-song*, the very pin of your heart *cleft with the blind bow-boy's butt-shaft*, then well, there's no more for me to say on the matter. Or at least, I can't think of any more of Mercutio's lines to say. Our show starts next week, if you'd like to come see me without having to talk to me; of course, *anyone that can write may answer a letter*. Ah, look at that, I found one more.

"My work here is done, Tip. I would like to say I still hold out hope for a reconciliation, but I do not expect one. Fare well, dear friend."

Dev yells, "Fine!" from the bedroom and then there's a thud like a tiger's fist hitting drywall. I close the e-mail and try to put Brian out of my head, to prepare myself to be the sympathetic guy my tiger's going to need.

He comes out of the bedroom quiet and sullen, so rather than ask him about it (I'll do that later), I call him over to read the e-mail from the Whalers. It works: the anger and stress vanish from his face and muscles, and he gives me a powerful hug and a kiss that almost distracts us both, never mind the three times we've had sex in the last twenty-four hours. "So proud of you," he murmurs.

"And you too," I say, though I leave it there. Probably he's still not ready to hear how amazing it is that he came within a point of being a world champion, when the loss is so fresh.

"The year's turned good." He mouths my ear, and I twist away and grin.

"If you keep that up, we'll never get anything done. We'll just stay in the apartment and fuck until my job starts."

He purrs, keeping hold of my wrist. "And the problem with that is...?"

My tail is only damp now, easier to wag. "At some point we'll run out of lube and have to go out to get some."

His hold doesn't lessen. "Maybe if you stretched more, you wouldn't need so much."

I laugh and step in toward him, kissing the underside of his chin. "You'd be more convincing if you'd bottomed even once."

His purr gets stronger, and so does his hold on my wrist. "I'll come to Yerba with you next week. Like I said a while ago, I hope you still think of this as your home too. Maybe it'll be like we have two homes."

"Yeah." I rub into his chest fur, feeling his sheath just above mine, neither of us getting hard. Pressing close, just being together is nice. But I think of some of the things Hal said, and the idea of having two homes with Dev, and my ears flick around against his muzzle.

"What'cha thinking about?" He slides paws down my sides.

I hold him. "Well, not that the last, uh," I check the clock, "fourteen hours haven't been amazing. But you know, we keep fighting and making up, and...I think we need to really, seriously talk about our future."

His tail flicks, and he bends his head to meet my gaze. He doesn't relax his arms or his paws, doesn't let me fall away from him. "Wow, I've been wondering for two years when we were going to have the 'where is this going' talk."

I smile and put a paw on his side. "I mean it. I want us to do it together, but...I was telling Hal that I don't think we'd have to go through anything as stressful as the last few months—I mean, your family, my family, the Vince King suicide and the trial and Gregory and..."

"I remember," he says lightly.

I want to ask him about what Brian said, whether he's still going to resist helping with the gay rights movement, but the fact that Brian said it makes it a lot harder for me to bring up. And anyway, it's about us first and foremost. "Yeah. But Hal said not to underestimate the ability of life to throw shit at you. So I don't think we can ignore it and just keep going. If we're going to really do it, really go through life together, then we need to be ready. This fighting and making up makes for great sex, but it's exhausting, and we both—again—have careers that mean a lot to us, where a couple weeks of emotional stress at the wrong time could wreck a once in a lifetime opportunity." Which is way more true for him than for me, but then, I'm really editing this to make it seem like it's about both of us, when it's really about whether he can stand to live with someone who might ruin his foot-ball career with an ill-timed outburst.

He doesn't say anything, so I reach out and grasp his paw. "I want this to work, I really do," I say, meeting his eyes. "I love you, tiger, and I've never been happier than when I'm with you." He nods and squeezes my paw; I see the echo and affirmation in his eyes without him having to say a word. "But I don't know if I could live with myself if our relationship ends up holding you back."

"Why isn't that my decision to make?" He rubs the back of my paw with two fingers. "What if I wouldn't be as happy being a lonely great football player as being a pretty good one with a boyfriend?"

It's a good point. "You have such a passion for football, though."

"And a passion for you."

I take a breath. "But have you really sat down to think about whether we can have both? I'm not saying we break up and go figure it out separately. I want to figure it out together."

His serious expression curves up into a smile. "You're the smart one. Can't you just figure it out for me?"

"Cut it out." I lean forward to kiss him. "Look, even if we decide we want to focus on our careers, we can still be really good friends."

He considers that, and lets go of my paw to rub my ear. "Really good friends who fuck once in a while?"

"Or more frequently." I squirm a little against him. "But you know, if one of us meets someone else…down the road…maybe you'll find a boyfriend who doesn't carry drama with him like fleas."

"Hah." His purr comes back as he crushes me against him. "What fun would that be?"

"Urgh." I try to hug back as tightly, but it's like hugging a pillar of iron.

Then he lets me go, and reaches down to cup my sheath in a paw. "Well," he says, "since you don't want to fuck all day, let's go get some breakfast so you're at least ready again tonight."

My tail is drier now, and wags still harder.

•

Over breakfast at a diner, Dev mumbles around a mouthful of steak and eggs, "So how do we have this talk? You're the only real relationship I've ever had."

I swab up maple syrup with a bit of pancake. "Peter said they want me to start March 1. Well, officially in the office. I guess after I sign the job offer, there's a bunch of paperwork they have to file, and then Jocko's on vacation until mid-February, and we might talk on the phone when he gets back, but anyway. Yeah. So I start March 1, and you can stay with me in Yerba for a couple months if you want."

"Got workouts with Gerrard," he says.

"Right, so maybe split your time. Anyway, you think maybe we can figure this out in a month?"

He muses, rubbing the last piece of steak around his plate. "So until then, what are we?"

I reach across and rest my paw on the table, halfway between us. "Just what we have been. Boyfriends. Partners. Just because we're thinking about the future doesn't mean we stop being what we are. After all, I mean…" I lick the sweet taste of maple syrup from my lips. "We both want—I mean, one possible outcome is—"

He laughs at my discomfiture. "Right now, doc, yeah, I know which way I want us to decide. But…" He lifts the fork, eats the steak delicately off it, and chews, looking thoughtful. When he swallows, he reaches out and rests his paw on mine. "You're right. The last couple weeks were…yeah. I think we should really talk about it. Not just assume things are going to be okay from here on out."

"Okay, then." I realize that he hasn't looked around the restaurant at all to see if our public affection will be noticed, and that makes me the one to do it. Nobody's looking our way. Wait, scratch that: one teenager is, a chubby mouse who's tugging at his father's shirt, trying to get his attention. He sees me looking at him and looks down at the table, at which point I turn away.

Dev's followed my gaze, and then comes back to me. "Don't worry," he says. "If they try to pour maple syrup down your back, I'll protect you."

I try to grin at his joke and manage it for about a second before the memory comes flooding back: the lukewarm beer splashing down my back and rear, the wolf's paw grabbing my tail, the slow flush of shame sitting in the Boliat arena's security office. I'm sure that me not telling Dev about that fight right away—even though it wasn't my fault, even though I was just humiliated, not hurt—was part of the atmosphere of mistrust that led to us splitting for two weeks.

Dev sees my ears flatten and his smile goes the same way. "Aw, sorry," he says. "Man, I'm getting our month off to a great start."

"It's okay," I say. "I should be able to joke about it, but…"

He tightens his paw over mine. "That kid at the airport, the kangaroo rat…I keep thinking about him. His dad beat him up, he said, but they were there together and it looked like things were getting better. And he said I did that. Maybe…" he searches my eyes. "Maybe he's my Vince King?"

I nod, slowly. "I want you to tell me about that, too." We've only brushed over the highlights of our two weeks apart, but they sound pretty eventful. "I'm glad your Vince King survived."

"Me too."

We pay (he pays), but before we can leave, the mouse kit runs over to Dev with big eyes and asks if he's Devlin Miski, and Dev says he is, and the kit produces a scrap of paper and a pen. His paws are shaking so much he drops the pen, and Dev picks it up and signs the paper for him. Meanwhile, the parents come over to me where I'm standing a little apart.

"You must be…Lee, was it?" The father catches me by surprise.

"That's right." I curl my tail away from them, but they seem pleasant, and there's no hostility in their scent. Anyway, who could be upset in a diner that smells of pastries and fried eggs?

"We're pleased to meet you," the mother says as the kid is gushing to Dev about the championship game. "You must be very proud of him."

"I am." I incline my head and smile. "And thank you."

"We read the profile on you," the father says. "Sounds like you had a pretty rough time."

"I've got a new job," I tell them. "I'll be working with the Yerba Whalers."

"Congratulations." The mother gives me a toothy smile. "Though we've been Firebirds fans since the team started, so we won't wish you luck."

I return the smile. "Only if we're not playing you."

By then, their kit is back with his paper and Dev's standing up, so we say our good-byes. They thank Dev for taking the time and he tells them it's no problem, and we walk out.

"When do you want to go to Yerba?" he asks as we walk back to his truck through a warm Chevali morning. His tail flicks at the back of my leg.

"I need to stay here to get the official offer, so why don't you give Fisher a call and see if we can come visit tonight or tomorrow?"

"You actually talked to Gena. Maybe you should call her."

I squint into the sun, waiting for him to unlock the truck doors, and then clamber in when he does, tucking my tail behind me. "Sure, I can do that. And Hal wants to do lunch or dinner with us. Maybe I can get him to bring his girlfriend along."

"Girlfriend?" Dev asks, so I tell him about the coyote Hal's dating, and how I don't really know much about her except that she doesn't take Hal's bullshit and threatened to break up with him when he spent one of their dinner dates on a phone interview for his story.

"Supports his passion but won't let it get in the way of their relationship," Dev says. "Sounds like my kind of girl."

"We're not even an hour into our month of figuring things out." I glance forward and see a high-end shopping mall. "Give me a chance. Oh, and can we stop here?"

"You're a fox," he says, then turns obligingly and looks ahead at the huge complex of stores. "How much time do you need?"

"Tigers are complicated." I grin. "Or did you mean at the mall?"

He huffs and reaches over to grab my thigh while making a turn with one big paw on the steering wheel. "What's complicated about wanting to live with a fox and play football for a living?"

"You can keep both paws on the wheel." I grip the door handle with one paw and his wrist with the other as the truck careens around a corner. "Also careful of cops."

"I just played in the first championship game in over twenty years for this town." He does slow, though, and finds us a parking spot. "No cop will give me a ticket for at least a month."

"Yeah, but don't press it." I let go of the door as the truck rolls to a stop.

"What are we here for, anyway?" He turns the engine off and we both get out.

I point to the big iconic logo. "I want to get one of those new iPhones for Hal. As a thank-you for putting me up. And putting up with me."

"Oh, cool. I can see if they can fix my screen."

"At this point you should get a warranty plan," I tell him, and he growls but doesn't gainsay me.

We pick up a phone for Hal (Dev offers to pay for it, but now that I have a job, I feel better about using some of my savings), and the store manager authorizes a new one for Dev even though he doesn't have the receipt. I think it's because they recognize him, but then one of the employees asks for his autograph as we're leaving, and the manager looks surprised. Anyway, it's a nice visit and puts me in the mood to do some clothes shopping, so I indulge myself.

We walk back through the parking lot in the warm sunshine. Dev swings bags off his fingers like he's a carousel ride. "You're just going to have to buy a bunch of Whalers gear when you start your new job."

"I'm not going to wear Whalers gear when I go out for a nice dinner. Which I'm going to do with you." I heft one of the bags over my shoulder and look up at him. "A lot."

He stares back. "As long as the portions are big."

"Order two entrees, then."

"Hey, I'm still only drawing a rookie salary."

"Yeah, but you have a million in beer money coming."

He gets quiet and I'm worried for a minute that he's thinking back to the PSAs. But as we toss the bags in the back of the truck, he says, "Shit. I forgot, I fired Ogleby."

I stop, the iPhone bag still hanging from my paw. "What?"

"Over the phone, Sunday night. But I'm not sure—I mean, he pretended not to hear me, and he hasn't called me since then. He was going to line up some deals, but—shit, he was going on about Polecki stealing my endorsements or something, and I was fried from the game, and I just blew up."

We get into the truck, and I hold the phone bag in my lap. "I'm not going to pretend I think that was a bad move. The guy was holding you back."

"I know." He grips the steering wheel but doesn't turn the key. "I just feel weird about it."

My turn to put a paw on his thigh. "I know you might view your explosion as an overreaction, but that doesn't mean it was wrong. I mean, you've exploded at me, too, and you weren't necessarily wrong those times. I really think you can do better, and you owe it to yourself to do better. You've got a contract negotiation coming up…" I trail off for a moment, remembering the veiled hints from Peter that Yerba might be interested in trading for Dev. "…anyway, negotiating commercials is one thing. Do you really want Ogleby determining how much you get paid for the next five years?"

He lets out a long, slow breath. "No. When you put it like that, fuck no. I don't want him anywhere near my next contract."

"So."

"Yeah." He shakes his head. "Doesn't mean I have to like it."

"No, but you have to do it. Another reason to call Fisher—his agent was one of the ones who called you. Damian, I think his name was."

"I know." He sighs. "What did you think of him?"

"From the phone message, he sounded stable. What did Fisher say about him?"

"I don't know. Never mentioned him all that much."

"That's a good sign, then."

We do call Fisher that afternoon, but Gena answers and says he's asleep. "At three in the afternoon?" I hear Dev say into the phone, and then, "Uh-huh," and then he hands me the phone.

"Gena. She wants to talk to you." He scratches his ear when I take the phone, looking puzzled, and then gets up from the couch. He hovers a little ways away while I lean against the couch arm.

"Lee?"

The strain in Gena's voice comes through loud and clear, and my ears go down over the phone, which has the unintentional consequence of making it harder for Dev to overhear. "What's wrong?"

"He hit Bradley," she says. "Not hard, and they've roughhoused before, but…it was different."

"Oh boy."

"He said he had a headache when he got home, and then the boys were talking about how good he was in the game, and he said that Kerina was just a little bit better."

It takes me a moment to remember that Fisher's Highbourne team lost to Kerina the year before they won their first championship against those same Knights.

"And Bradley reminded him it was Crystal City, and Fisher got upset, and when Bradley told him to calm down, he smacked him in the chest. Junior got between them."

"I'm sorry," I say, wishing I could do more.

"Then he said he wanted to lie down and he fell asleep. I told the cubs he's on pain medication, but I think they know something's wrong. I don't know who else I can talk to."

"Dev and I wanted to come visit anyway," I say. "Would that be okay?"

"Yes." She replies so fast that I know she wanted to ask. "When can you come over?"

"Tomorrow?" She doesn't say anything. "Dinner tonight?"

"I've got enough steaks," she says. "Thank you."

"Oh," I say, remembering, "did you call Elmsley about it?"

"Who?"

"The guy with the Firebirds, said to call him if there were any troubles..."

She sounds more confused than upset now. "I thought that was Lake."

"I got a call from an Elmsley who said he was taking over. Sorry, I didn't know if you knew yet."

"No." Gena sighs. "I haven't called anyone. It wasn't that kind of trouble."

"It sounds like it is," I say. "What if he hits you next? Or what if things escalate?"

"I don't want to think about that." Her voice gets shakier and worse. "Please, I know Dev can help."

I'm feeling uneasy about the whole thing, but I let it go for now. When I hang up, Dev waits while I just hold the phone. He reaches out to take it. "What's wrong?"

So I take a breath. "I didn't talk to you about this before," I say, "because Gena asked me not to. But Fisher was behaving erratically after his injury, and she found some somatotropin in his room. That's a hormone that's usually used to aid recovery time."

He goes really quiet then. "It's not illegal, is it?"

I wiggle my paws. "It is, but he wouldn't go to jail or anything. He'd get suspended by the league for sure. The thing is, it's often used in conjunction with steroids. And Gena said Fisher's been angrier, more touchy, ever since the injury."

There's a long silence. "Look," I say, "I don't want to know what you know about anything Fisher or anyone on the team is using. Hal doesn't either. The story he's working on is about injuries that accumulate over a career, not about banned substances."

"I'm not using anything."

I hadn't even considered it, but the words trigger a blossom of relief in my chest. "Good."

"Fisher isn't—he wasn't when he was with the team."

"Dev—"

"No. I'm sure of it." The words are clipped, hard.

"All right." I don't want to get into how easy it must be to sneak an injection here or there. I don't want to speculate on whether the trainers might be complicit in it. I want to focus on us. "I just want to be clear, when we go over there, I'm not trying to dig up any steroid use or anything. We're going to ask about his injuries for Hal, about his agent for you, and we're going to let Gena know that we're here for her, because she sounded like she really needed that."

Dev backs down from his aggressive stance. "Do we have to ask him about his injuries?"

I weigh the question. "Not right away. But if he's losing his grip on reality after two concussions in a month, then yeah, I think that's something worth asking about."

He sits back down on the couch next to me and stares down at his knees. His tail curls between us. "I never had a concussion," he says finally. "I got hit in the head a couple times in high school. Never in college."

I reach over to pat his knee. "Good."

He turns then, his gold eyes meeting mine, and they're calm, but the stripes around them are creased in thought or worry. "You think I might end up like Fisher? Not knowing where I am?"

"No," I lie, and he puts an arm around me, and we hold each other.

Chapter Three: Defiance (Dev)

The shit about Fisher really throws me for a loop. He was disoriented during the Boliat game, sure, but that was just a one-time thing. That evening, he was fine. I think. From what I remember, anyway, which isn't a lot. He'd shaken it off, though, and he'd been fine until he got knocked down in the championship. Maybe it's just the hangover from that close loss that's got him riled up.

Lee didn't tell me exactly what happened, just that Fisher didn't seem to know what year it was, and that he hit Bradley. Which doesn't sound like him. He loves those cubs. Though also he believes in discipline, so maybe it was just discipline, and Gena read it wrong.

Argh, I don't know. I don't know if I want to know. As we're getting ready to go over there, I form the words, "Why don't you just go without me?" half a dozen times and never say them.

Because Fisher is my friend, and Lee is my boyfriend, and I'm not going to send him over to face Fisher alone. At least if I'm there, I know there's someone on his side in a fight.

The ride over is quiet; we're both tense, not knowing what we're going to find. Lee navigates me to the address Gena gave us, a three-story house with a large yard, neighbors on either side.

Despite the fact that I'm sure Fisher's made more than Gerrard over his career, his house is much more homey and inviting. Gerrard's is like the dream house I wanted when I was ten, a sprawling mansion with enough room for three families and a whole raft of servants, with extra bedrooms and a backyard basketball court and a pool. Fisher might have a pool in the back, which I haven't seen yet, but judging by the size of the houses around it, it's not going to be Olympic-sized or anything.

Fisher Junior answers the door. He's fifteen, if I recall, two years younger than Bradley, but he's much more his father's size. He can look me in the eye, although his shoulders aren't quite as broad as Fisher's, or even mine. "Mom!" he yells back into the house. "Dev's here with Lee."

He leaves the door to us and just walks back into the house, and then he stops halfway across the broad living room and turns back to me. "You played good," he says. "You guys coulda won."

"Thanks," I say. "Your dad did great."

I guess that wasn't the right thing to say. His eyes slide away and then he turns, slouches to the couch, and picks up a video game controller. Basketball, I see: FBA '09. Not football.

Gregory and I used to play video games: Hedgehog Adventures 2 was the one I remember best because it was the first one I could play as well as he did. Up til then, we'd play two-player games and mostly I tagged along with him while he solved the puzzles and fought the fights. In Hedgie, he kept getting killed while I was the one keeping us alive. And he lost interest in it. I finished it myself, without him, so proud of my accomplishment that I called him back to watch the ending movie with me. It was pretty fun then. My fists tighten now, remembering his silence watching the movie and the way he just left the room after, without even saying, "Good job," or, "Cool."

At the other end of the living room is a bright doorway with white appliances and black granite counters. The smell of steak and butter and potatoes rolls out in waves toward us, and then Gena steps out, smiling. She holds out her paws and gives Lee a hug, and then does the same for me. "Thank you for coming. Dinner's about a half hour away. Fisher's in the den if you want to go talk to him."

Lee and I exchange a look. "Can I help in the kitchen?" he says. "I'll let the players talk for a while."

"Sure." Gena ushers him into the kitchen and then points me to the den. I cross behind the sofa where Junior is playing, pause by the end table to look at a photograph of the family at the Grand Canyon, and then walk to a large framed picture hanging on the wall beside the door to a short hallway.

The 1998 world champion Highbourne Rocs stare back out at me, all smiles. I pause and find Fisher in that picture. He looks a lot like Junior, but thicker and more filled out. How old was he then? That was ten years ago—they won the championship in January 1999—so he was close to my age. Of course, he was drafted after his sophomore year, so by '98 he had four years of experience, not my two. Or, really, two thirds of one year, if you're only going to count starting.

In the hallway, the door to the den is partly open. Everything is so still that I can hear the noise of the video game from the living room clearly. So I tap at the door and step into a room with a small liquor cabinet to one side and a bookshelf full of model trains on the other, a room that carries an undertone of locker room smell. I suspect Gena isn't allowed to clean in here often.

Fisher's sitting behind a large wooden desk staring down at one of the side bottom drawers, but he looks up as soon as I spot him. His whiskers twitch and he slides the drawer shut easily. Silhouetted against the window and the stark branches outside, he cuts an imposing figure. So do I, I remind myself. I examine him casually, looking for any evidence of the steroids Lee suspects. Does he look bigger than in the championship picture? Bigger than at the beginning of the season? He looks bigger than Junior, and I remember thinking that during the Christmas party, but that was just a month ago. How quickly do effects show up?

Fisher gestures to the armchairs in front of the desk. "Gena told me you were coming. Want to talk about the game, I guess?"

"Yeah, a little." I sit in one of the leather-upholstered chairs and keep my claws carefully retracted, though it feels like the leather is treated. "Also wanted to ask you about your agent."

His ears perk in surprise. "Sure. What do you want to know?"

"I need a new agent. Is he any good?"

"He's great." Fisher goes on to tell me about some of the deals his agent got him, and I listen pretty attentively, but I'm also trying to figure out how to ask him about his injury, how he's feeling, and...maybe, if I get the chance, whether he'd be willing to talk about it.

"Cool," I say when he finishes talking about his agent. "I think I have his contact info, but can you give it to me? I'll call him up."

He pulls open the shallow central drawer and comes out with a business card, starts to copy it on a piece of paper, and then just pushes it across the desk with a wave. "Take it, I got his number in my phone anyway."

I pick up the card and glance at it before tucking it away in my pocket, and then I look at it again. "Lee was right. His name's Damian."

"It's Leroy," Fisher says absently.

I show him the card. "Says Damian here."

"Oh." He squints. "That's right. Leroy was my agent before...No, it's Damian. He's great."

He's tense; I can see that. So I start talking about the championship game, about how we couldn't hold their offense when we needed to. "We held them plenty," he says. "If we play that game ten times, we win five of them. At least four."

"I'd settle for one more." I lean back in the chair and look at the model trains across the room. My tail flicks.

"Next year." He sets a huge paw on his desk and stares down at it. "Next year."

He's not wearing his championship rings. They're in a large display case to the right of his desk, along with pictures of him holding the '98 and '99 championship trophies. "You guys got to the game the year before you won it, right?"

"Yeah." He doesn't need to look around. "Kerina was loaded that year. We couldn't do anything against 'em. They lost Krapinski next year and Jones was hurt and Trig and Lombar just had lousy years. Didn't even get back to the championship game." He flexes the paw on the desk. "Wouldn't have mattered. Nobody could touch us that year."

"You think Chevali'll get better next year?"

He looks up, and exhales. "You'll be better," he says. "Gerrard…maybe. Those corners need to tighten up some, but maybe that Colin kid will be ready for prime time. We need someone who can give Aston time to throw, and need to keep that fuckin' cheetah around."

"He's not that bad once you understand him."

"I understand him." Fisher glares down at his desk. "Doesn't give a shit about football except as a way to make money for himself."

Strike would probably say that we're all in it for the money, but I can't think that about Fisher, sitting hunched over his desk with his two championships in the past and that burning in his heart to get just one more, to go out on top, to be a winner. I shift in the chair, thinking again about all the things I could have done differently, how if I could have stopped the Sabretooths just one more time, we'd be having a much different conversation. Fisher might be thinking about retirement.

"How do you feel?" I ask, because my thoughts are going in that direction anyway and because I'm trying to come around to helping Lee. I guess it's really helping Hal, but I won't think of it like that until I talk to him myself.

Fisher just laughs, sharply. "How do *you* feel?" he counters.

"My ribs hurt, my legs hurt." I hold up one paw. "This hurts. But I feel pretty good overall. How's your leg?"

"You're young." He snorts. "My leg's fine. I…" He lifts his head, looking at the door behind me, and then shakes his head slowly. "I'm fine. I feel five years younger. I can squeeze another year or two out of the uniform before I have to hang it up."

I flex my claws, wondering how to go on, if I even want to go on at this point. "You were kinda groggy after the game," I say.

His head snaps up. "Yeah. I got my bell rung. I shook it off, I'm fine now."

He's louder, and when I glance down at his paw, I see claws digging into the scarred wood of the desk. "Okay," I say. "Just checking. I mean, uh, I was pretty down on Monday."

"Yeah, that happens. Takes at least a couple weeks to shake off a big loss like that. Months, years for some guys." His claws retract and he looks my way again. "You seem better now."

I nod and flick my tail. "Talking to Lee helped." Hell, just being close to Lee again helped. "And Polecki, actually. He's a good guy and you know, much as I'd rather be in his place, I was happy for him too."

"Happy for him." He levels a finger at me. "Goddamn kids. You don't get happy for the other team. You get jealous; you get angry. You get so worked up that you can't wait to get back to camp for the chance to be where they are. You drive yourself until you think you're going to break, only you don't break. You make it the next year, or the year after."

"Or both," I say, looking at his trophies, because I don't want to start another argument by telling him what a great guy the coyote was, how his brilliant smile made it easy to like him, how his casual acceptance of being gay put me at ease. How we posed for a photo outside the café and laughed when the picture-taker asked if we were dating.

"Yeah, or both!" My tactic doesn't seem to have worked. He's just getting more agitated; he picks up a pen and plays with it. "You think we'll be able to beat Kerina next year if we sit here thinking about how *happy* we are for them?"

I don't want to point out that he's just said "Kerina" instead of "Crystal City." It's an easy mistake, except that it's really not. He's just emotional, I think, and so I say, "That's not what I meant, Fish."

"Then say what you goddamn mean," he says.

Damned if I can think of anything to say to that. I stand up and raise a paw to him. "I'm gonna see how Lee's doing."

"Hey!"

As I half-turn, something hits me on the shoulder. Did he just throw a pen at me? Yep, there it is on the floor of the den. I pick it up and stalk forward to the desk, tail lashing, where I brandish it at him. "What the fuck is this?"

He stands too, facing me across the wood. "Don't walk out on me. I'm tryin' to tell you something important."

"Then say it!" I drop the pen between us with a thunk.

"I said it." He's a foot from me, and we're both breathing hard. "I said it. You just…"

He flinches and puts a paw to his temple, and then he sits down in the chair. I lean forward. "You okay?"

"I'm fine," he growls. "Get the fuck out."

First he doesn't want me to leave, now he does? I turn and stride to the door, out to the hall, and into the living room. Junior's still playing basketball, so I watch him for a few minutes, trying not to worry about Fisher.

He's always been volatile and passionate. He's getting toward the end of his career and he knows it, and he doesn't want to leave anything on the field.

Hah. That's what Strike told me on the phone the last time I talked to him. Fisher'd be annoyed if he knew how similar the two of them really are, which is almost enough to make me go back into the den and tell him that. But I don't want to goad him, especially if he is still suffering from a concussion, and that paw to his temple worries me. So I go into the kitchen, where Lee and Gena are talking about cookie recipes.

"Dev likes chocolate chip," Lee says when he sees me.

I walk over and put an arm around him. The phrase is casual and really means nothing, but it makes me happy because after the conversation with Fisher, it's normal and friendly and intimate, and it reminds me of the other world I'm part of. "Love it," I say, partly in response to him.

I don't want to talk about Fisher's erratic behavior in front of Gena, even though I'm sure she knows, but I don't have a chance to get Lee alone before Gena declares the steaks almost done and calls Junior in to set the table. I do hazard a low whisper saying, "He's touchy," which I hope is too quiet for Gena to hear over the bubbling of the water under the steaming vegetables. Lee flicks his ear, then nods and reaches over to take my paw.

Gena asks Lee to pick a wine, so we wander into the dining room, where Junior is setting forks beside plates. "How much do you think a house like this in Yerba would go for?" I ask Lee as he peruses the wine rack.

Junior stops and looks right at me, his ears up. "Are you getting traded to Yerba?"

"Uh, no." I gesture to my fox, who's pulled a bottle out to examine the label. "He got a job there with the Whalers."

"Oh, cool." Junior goes back to setting the table.

Lee slides that bottle back, pulls out another, and keeps that one. "You guys have had to move a few times," he says with his eyes on the teenager as he sets the bottle on the table. "Pretty tough, huh?"

"It's okay." Junior gives a very teenaged shrug.

"I just moved down here, too." Lee leans on the table, his forearms reflected in the polished wood. "And now I have to pack up everything again and move to Yerba." Junior doesn't say anything, so Lee goes on. "It's different when it's my choice, I know, but it's still a pain. I have to make all new friends and stuff. You play football down here?"

At that, Junior does nod, and when he finishes with the silverware, he looks up at Lee. "I made junior varsity. I'll be varsity next year. If we stay here."

"You play end?" Like your dad, Lee doesn't say.

Junior shakes his head. "Tackle."

"Oh, hey, that's a hard position. Left or right?"

"Right." The young tiger perks up a bit.

Lee talks about some of the great right tackles in the league. One of them, a cougar named Mosely who plays for the Devils, is Junior's favorite. I didn't see much of him in the game we played against them, but I know Pike squared off against him a bunch. Fisher would have if he hadn't been injured. I wonder idly if Junior ever practiced against his dad, if Fisher would've made him, if he'd have wanted to.

Gena brings the steaks in about ten minutes later, and Junior stops talking as soon as she comes in. "Go tell your brother dinner's ready," she tells him, and he slouches out of the dining room.

He only goes about five feet, though, before yelling, "Brad! Dinner!"

"I could have done that," Gena says when Junior comes back and plops into his chair. But he doesn't respond, and after an awkward silent moment, Lee asks her where we should sit. She points to a chair at the foot of the table and one just around the corner from it. "I'll get Fisher," she says, and walks out of the dining room.

Lee asks Junior about his other favorite players, but he just says, "I dunno." So I chime in about Mosely and say how tough he was to play against, and when I mention the way he always set his feet and stayed low to the ground, harder to budge (the only thing I can remember Pike saying about him), Junior does perk up again.

Bradley comes in a minute later. As tall as his brother but more slender, he moves with the same athletic grace. I try to remember if Gena's told us what sport he plays; I'm sure it's not football.

He pulls out his chair and then spots us and freezes. "Oh, hey," he says, whiskers flaring. His eyes register me and then linger on Lee. "Mr. Miski and…"

"Mister Farrel." My fox smiles. "You can call me Lee."

Bradley slides into his seat. "I was working on homework," he says.

Lee asks what classes he's taking, and he says it was math homework but refuses to elaborate, and silence grows again. It's not helped when Gena returns alone. She looks around the room and I see her stop and pull herself together because she comes in behind the boys. By the time they turn, she's got a bright smile on. "Your father will be here in a minute," she says. "Let's eat."

She serves us all steak and hesitates before leaving Fisher's plate empty. The steak is as good as we'd get in a restaurant, and I tell Gena so after a couple bites.

I'm almost done when we all stop at the sound of footsteps in the living room. Fisher kicks something plastic and curses loudly, and because I'm looking past the boys at the living room door, I see their ears flatten. A moment later, Fisher fills the doorway, but he doesn't come in. His eyes light on me. "Dev," he rasps. "C'mere."

Gena looks up and says, "Don't you want steak?"

"Later." He doesn't look away from me. "Come on."

I look guiltily at Gena, but what am I going to do? I mumble, "Excuse me," and get up, walk around the table behind the two silent boys, and follow Fisher through the living room back to his den.

"Shut the door," he says when we're inside, and I comply while he crosses to his desk. There's a laptop on it now that wasn't there before, and he just stands there staring down at it.

"What's going on?" I say finally.

He growls something unintelligible and spins the laptop around, pointing down at it. As I step forward, he turns and looks out the window, then up at the glass case holding his championship memorabilia.

There's an e-mail program open to a message that it looks like just came in an hour ago. It's from David Rodriguez, the Firebirds' General Manager. I feel weird about reading the e-mail, but Fisher clearly wants me to, so I skim the paragraphs that are showing, and then I slow down and read them more carefully, because holy shit.

"Because the Crystal City staff are involved, we can't just keep this in the organization. I've talked to the team's doctors and they say that your return next year was 50-50 anyway. If you retire, we'll make sure you get some of the money left on your contract, and you get to keep your reputation."

"Fisher, you've only been a part of the family here for a couple years, but John feels very strongly that we should take care of you. If you choose not to retire, then we won't be able to do that effectively and John may opt to just cut all ties at that point. I'm not saying that would definitely happen, but if I were you, I'd retire. You've had a great career, and I'm sure next year Highbourne will want to bring you in for a celebration of the '99 champions just like they did with the '98 team this year."

"Give me a call tomorrow and let me know what you're thinking."

"What's this about?" I scroll up the message, but there's no indication of what Rodriguez is talking about. He just makes allusions to something that happened in Crystal City.

Fisher turns and glares. "They're forcing me to retire. Can't you fucking read?"

"What happened in Crystal City?"

"What the fuck does that matter? They're just using it as leverage, trying to get out of paying me. I'm gonna call Leroy—fuck, I mean Damian—and get him to lean on them."

He sweeps the air with his paws as he talks, something that isn't familiar to me in all the time I've known him. Then he slams a fist down on the desk so hard the laptop jumps and rattles, and that tightly bottled frustration, *that* is familiar and oddly reassuring in a way.

"It matters," I say, trying to keep calm but at the same time bracing myself for a fight, "because the kind of leverage matters. If they're pulling up some bullshit thing to get you to retire, you can fight it. You can play another season for sure, I don't give a shit what the doctors say."

"Damn right." He stalks back and forth behind the desk, coiled energy, tail lashing like he's about to pancake a tackle and leap on a quarterback. "I should just tell Damian to start looking at other teams. I bet Pelagia would give me money, no questions asked. I used to play with a couple of those guys."

"Pelagia stinks," I say. "You don't want to go there."

"Better than here." He hits the desk again, though not quite as hard. "I thought this team was different, but they're just like everyone else. Who gives a fuck if you've won a championship? It's all about money."

"Well, yeah. I mean, you told me that when I came here." I glance down at the message and the numbers catch my eye. "I can't believe they're making up that 'fifty-fifty' bullshit. Your leg was fine." But then I remember what Lee said about the somatotropin and the steroids and an ugly suspicion crawls up my gut. I can't ask him flat out about it, though. I can't.

He kicks the desk then. "That fucking boar. I'd like to rip his tusks out and shove them up his ass." Another kick, harder. "I could've made it through the season, could've made it through the championship. What the fuck do I do now?"

"You know injuries are part of the game. Sometimes you get lucky and nothing comes along for years. You got a bad break and you know, you just deal with it."

"I *was* dealing with it!" He drops both paws to the desk, leans on them, and glares at me.

Time to back off. "What…" I take a breath. "What kind of 'reputation' thing are they talking about that might happen if you don't retire?"

The intensity of his glare does lessen. "Doesn't matter. It won't be news. Who the fuck cares about it? Everybody has shit they don't want out in the open."

"But—"

"Hey!" He narrows his eyes. "What if the team told you to retire or they'd announce you're gay? What would you do?"

"They already know." I'm trying to keep calm, but it's hard to follow the thread of the argument. "And I'm not at the end of my career."

"No," he says, "you're not at the end of your career, so maybe you should just shut the fuck up with the advice. You have no idea what it's like because you got another ten years ahead of you at least. You don't have the curtain staring you in the face. What am I gonna do if I'm not playing football, huh?"

His tone keeps rising, getting more and more belligerent, but at least he stays on the far side of his desk. I'm tense, ready in case he doesn't. We've scrapped a couple times before, but always in the locker room. I don't want to fight in his house. So I say, "Relax." It's both an answer for the future and the immediate now.

"Relax. Relax? What does that mean?" His claws are out again, but he's just swiping at air. "How am I supposed to do that when they're attacking me like this?"

"Look." I try to stay calm myself. "I know you can still play. But maybe take a year off? Lots of guys retire and then come back. It sounds like Rodriguez is offering you an easy way out."

"Easy." He stares down at the laptop, then swats the screen closed, picks it up, and looks like he's going to drop it in the garbage. He thinks better of it, though, and just puts it into one of the drawers of his desk. His voice rises as he shuts the drawer. "It's never easy. You know what people say about those guys who come back from retirement? 'Courageous,' and 'battling age,' and all those other shit words you say about people who are going out when they shouldn't be. Once you retire, that's fuckin' it. You can come back and have people laugh at you. Otherwise you're done. I'm not ready to be done. I'm not!"

He yells that last bit, swipes impotently at the air, and then, before I can say anything, collapses into his desk chair rubbing his head.

"You don't have to be," I say, thinking about maybe coaching or commentator positions, but he's not looking at me. His eyes are shut and his fingers press against his head like he's trying to hold it together. "Hey, you okay?"

"Fine," he snaps.

"Fisher."

He doesn't stop rubbing, but his eyes open, and the anger is gone. They're just tired. "Don't tell Gena. I get these headaches now."

"You should see a doctor."

It's the wrong thing to say. He starts up out of his chair and yells, "Doctors! If I tell them, they'll just force me to retire. They'll…" But the pain overwhelms him and he drops back into the chair, pressing paws to his head. "Fuck."

"Jesus, Fisher, how bad is it?"

"It's just a fucking headache, okay? I got knocked in the head, I get headaches. It happens."

How many other retired players have recurring headaches? Hal might know. I shift on my feet and shelve the question. "Is that why the doctors think you shouldn't come back?"

"Hey, mind your fucking business. I didn't ask you here for a medical opinion." His growl still has force, even when his body is slumped in the chair.

"Why did you ask me here?"

He opens his eyes and looks up from between his paws. "What should I do?"

"You're asking me?"

"You see anyone else here?"

I shake my head. "I mean, Lion Christ, I don't know. What comes out if you don't retire?"

"I told you it's no big deal!" He lifts his head long enough to roar it at me, and then winces like he's hung over and just heard himself shout. "It's…it's no big deal," he repeats, more quietly.

"If it's really no big deal," I say, "then ask them if you can be traded. But if it is a big deal, then maybe you should take the retirement."

"Oh, what the hell do you know?" It's still soft, but there's a growl behind it, that same force that intimidated tackles for a decade and a half.

It doesn't intimidate me. "You asked me here."

"And now I'm asking you to get out." He reaches for his phone. "I'm going to call Damian."

I leave him sitting behind his desk, and return to the dinner table. Lee is keeping the conversation going, but it stalls when I come in. "What was that about?" he asks. Gena clearly wants to know but isn't going to ask.

"The team's, uh." I look around at the three other tigers at the table, all staring at me. "They sent him a message about next season and he's trying to figure out what to do."

Junior throws his fork down. "I'm not moving again," he says. "I'll stay with George. He said I could."

"Calm down," Gena says. "Nobody's talking about moving."

"We could all just stay here and Dad could go live in another city." Bradley sounds more reasonable. "A lot of players do that."

"Just settle down." Gena tries to follow her own advice. "I'll talk to your father and we'll figure it out. We want you boys to stay here and finish high school if at all possible. We've already talked about that."

That calms them down, but their fur stays prickly. They ask to be excused when they're done, and both run off upstairs to work on homework. I take Junior's chair, across from Lee and next to Gena, and we drink a little more wine because Gena's still hoping Fisher will come to dinner.

"What was it really about?" she asks in a low voice, when we all have full glasses again.

"The team wants him to retire," I say. "He doesn't want to."

"Oh." She relaxes and smiles. "That's not so bad. If he retires, we can just stay here."

"He's not really interested in retirement." I weigh how much of our conversation to tell her. "He thinks he can play another couple years."

"Why does the team want him to retire? His contract's not that bad." Lee, ever sharp, leans forward across the table.

"There's some…" I look between the two of them, then at my fox. "She knows what you told me about, right?"

"She's the one who found it."

"Yeah, well…it's just a guess, but I wonder if the team found out about it somehow. Rodriguez's e-mail sounded like there'd be a media thing, something embarrassing, if Fisher doesn't retire."

Gena sags and drops her head into her paws. "Oh, no," comes muffled between her fingers.

Lee rubs his whiskers. "Would retirement be so bad right now?" he says quietly. "Gena, you have enough money set aside, right?"

"He's going to hate it." She lifts her head and steeples her paws in front of her nose. "He's already hit Bradley, and this won't make anything easier. At least the boys are at school most of the time."

Lee and I exchange looks, but can't think of anything to say. His ears perk a moment later, and then I catch Fisher stomping through the living room again. He comes in and sits down at the dining room table at the far end from Gena, eyes the steaks, and grabs one. Without saying a word to any of us, he cuts and eats a bite, then another.

"How is it?" Gena asks.

Fisher takes another bite. "Lukewarm," he says while chewing.

Silence sets over the table, broken only by Fisher's eating. He eats about half the steak and then looks up at us. "Well?" he says. "What were you talking about? It was me, wasn't it?" He glares at Dev. "Just came in and told them right away, huh?"

"I told them you were offered retirement by the team." I bristle back at him. "They asked why you wanted to talk to me. What was I supposed to say?"

"You coulda said it was private."

"Yeah, well." Gena looks even sadder, and it makes me angry even though I know it's not my place. "I assume you woulda told Gena eventually, and I tell Lee everything. We waited 'til your cubs were upstairs."

At the mention of the boys, he stops eating. "Good," he says. "They don't need to know about this yet."

"They're afraid we're going to move." Gena says it slowly.

We all wait for Fisher to say that they're not going to move, but he just takes another bite of steak. "If another team makes me an offer…"

"We can't move the boys again. If it comes to that, maybe we could stay here and you could go—"

Fisher shoves his chair back. "Yeah, maybe that would be better. You think? You going to live without me while they finish high school? That's…" He snaps his jaw shut, stands up, and walks into the kitchen.

Gena glances at us and then stands. "Excuse me," she says, and hurries after her husband.

Lee and I look at each other across the table. "Maybe we should go," I say.

My fox nods, but bites his lip. "I hate to leave Gena," he says softly. "She's having a really hard time."

"What can we do?" I spread my paws. "If there were some way we could help, I would, but…"

"Fisher seems more willing to talk to you," he says. "Maybe you can see if he wants to get together at a gym or something, somewhere he can open up without the family around. Look at how he keeps retreating to his study."

"Yeah." I think about the championship rings there, the photos, the things he keeps obsessing over. "Maybe that's not the best place for him."

"I guess that's our best—"

Fisher's voice echoes from the kitchen. "I *know!*" he yells, and then there's the sound of something breaking.

I jump up and head toward the sound without even thinking. If he's hurting Gena...

But Gena appears in the kitchen doorway as I get there, one paw out to my chest. "It's okay. It's okay." She's breathing heavily. "He just got..."

We look at each other. Fisher steps into view behind her. "I got a little excited," he growls. "I'm cleaning it up."

"Ah, look," I say. "It's getting late."

Fisher comes out to shake my paw and Lee's. Then he goes back into the kitchen and there's the scrape and clink of shards of something.

Gena walks us to the front door while Lee murmurs apologies and I stay quiet, trying to figure out if Fisher's just upset at the prospect of retirement or if there's something else going on. I mean, he does keep kind of messing things up, like the name of his agent and the team we played, and there's the headaches, which are pretty worrisome. But heck, he was always kind of a volatile guy, and if you'd told me the team was trying to force retirement on him, well, I'd have been able to tell you he wouldn't take it well.

At the door, Gena hugs me and says thanks for coming, and then she hugs my fox. He murmurs, "It'll be okay," as she bends down, and then she shakes and seems to lean on Lee. He supports her well enough, and she gasps out something next to his ear that I don't catch.

I reach out, uncertain what I can do, if anything, but a moment later she's standing up and wiping her eyes. "I'm sorry," she says. "I'm sure I can..."

I put a paw on the door handle, feeling like shit, but what can we do?

Chapter Four: Open Doors (Lee)

When I tell Gena that things will be okay, she chokes out, "I hope so," with so much pain in her voice that I stop, searching my memory for anything else we can do to help. She told me in the kitchen that she was checking around for some live-in help, and at the time I thought that I could've called her instead of Hal when I ran out on Dev two weeks ago, that at least I'd have had a proper bed to sleep in (not that I regretted staying with Hal).

And thinking about Hal reminded me again about his article, and then I felt bad for thinking about that when Gena was hurting. So as Dev moves to open the door, impulse seizes me and I ask Gena the only thing I can think to offer. "Do you want me to come by tomorrow and help out with things?"

I'm serious, but I expect her to laugh and say, "Oh, goodness no," and at least I would feel good for offering.

Instead she looks at Dev, and then back at me. "Would you really?"

"Uh." Dev's kind of caught by surprise and so am I. "If you need me to, of course."

"I don't want to separate the two of you. I know you haven't had a lot of time together the past two weeks."

It's hard, because I do want to go back and cuddle up to my tiger; more than ever, in fact. Watching Fisher's arguments with his family makes me even more aware of how special Dev is and how much I love him. Still, the desperation in Gena's eyes doesn't leave me a way out. Not one that leaves me feeling good about myself, anyway.

So: "No, it's fine," I say. "I can help with the cooking and shopping and let you worry about Fisher while he figures out this retirement thing, and maybe in a couple days you can find someone you can hire to help out. I can help with that, too."

She starts to smile, then looks up at Dev. "Fisher won't like it. Especially if he thinks you're there because he's being a problem."

My tiger puts a paw on my shoulder. "I don't like it," he says, but before either of us can say anything, he squeezes my shoulder. "But I think you should do it. Just don't tell Fisher you're there because of him."

I nod. "If it comes up, we can tell him you're going out with Gerrard and I'm here to visit Gena."

Gena breathes. "That would be wonderful. I can handle things tonight and I'll tell Fisher you'll be coming by tomorrow."

"Right." I keep the smile on. Maybe I can use the time to get closer to Fisher and tell him about Hal's story.

Dev stays quiet as we get in the truck. When he pulls out onto the street, he says, "That's a nice thing."

"She needed someone." I uncurl my tail, relieved he's not angry. "And you couldn't stay there. Fisher would figure that out and might feel threatened. You never know."

He nods. "I'm glad you're coming home with me tonight, though. You're still not finished making up two weeks."

"Still?" I laugh softly. "How much more do I have to do?"

He purrs and looks sideways at me. "How much lube do we have?"

"Not *that* much."

"Well, you can use your mouth when it runs out."

I chuckle and lean back. "Happy to."

On the highway, he drapes one paw casually over the steering wheel and keeps looking forward, but his tone gets more serious. "It's hard to remember the things we need to think about when we're getting along like this."

"And when we're distracted with other people's problems. I mean…" I spread my paws. "We're doing something constructive. We're trying to plan our future. We're not watching our relationship fall apart."

"Already did that," he mutters, maybe so that he thinks I can't hear him, but then he turns slightly and the corner of his mouth lifts in a grin.

I'm glad he can joke about it. "But Gena and Fisher…they're trying to plan a future too, only one of them doesn't want that future at all. He keeps reaching back for a past that—well, I don't know the details, but it sure sounds like it's gone."

"Yeah." He exhales, and I can see as clearly as if it were one of the road signs that flashes by that he's looking into his own future, to a time when age or injury or both takes football away from him.

"We've got a long way to go to get there," I say. "And I plan to stick with you, FYI."

"Well, yeah." He taps the wheel. "Who's going to remember the names of the championship teams I'm on when I can't?"

I don't know what to say to that, and a moment later Dev hits the steering wheel, his smile gone. "Sorry. That wasn't funny. Shit, what a—I'm sorry."

"How bad is it with Fisher?" I ask, to avoid having to think about Dev losing his memory.

"Not bad." He sounds relieved, either that he's not thinking about himself, or that I didn't jump on him for a bad joke. "Just seems like sometimes he's flashing back to ten years ago. He got the name of his agent wrong, and I think once or twice he was confusing this year with '97 when they lost the championship game."

I try to remember what happened with my great-grandfather—Father's grandfather—when he started to lose his hold on reality. Did it start slowly? I wasn't there, so I don't really know. "Doesn't sound that bad. And it's been a stressful weekend, and he doesn't have a fox to release stress with."

The smile comes back across his striped muzzle. "True."

"Maybe he just needs to rest up." But even as I say it, I'm not convinced. I don't think this is just the end of Fisher's football career. I think he needs more help than a live-in maid.

By the time we get home, it's not so late that we have to go to bed right away, but we also don't want to talk about Fisher anymore. So I get some ice cream out of the freezer and make up a couple bowls, and we sit on the couch and throw in a short movie. It's the perfect distraction, and snuggling together on the couch makes me feel warm and safe.

In the morning, I do a load of laundry while I pack up some clothes to go to Gena's with. I also call my father while I'm down there. I'd tried to call him Monday, but he had meetings, and he'd said Tuesday or Wednesday morning would be a good time to call. Sure enough, he picks up the phone on the second ring.

"You talked to your mother?" is the first thing he asks.

"Yeah. She said I finally convinced her of the error of her ways." Into the silence on the other end I add, "maybe not in those words."

"Right." He coughs. "What about you? How are things with you and Dev? Are you talking again?"

I rub the base of my tail. "Uh. Yeah."

"Good."

"And other things too."

"Wiley. I didn't ask."

I lean against the washer, tail swishing. "I thought you were concerned about me."

"This conversation alone makes me feel better about how things are going for you. I'm just going to assume that along with 'talking' goes all the other things couples do."

"We had to do the other stuff to get to the talking part."

That startles him out of his cynical tone. "What?"

"It was very romantic," I tell him. "Hal went out on a date but told Dev that I'd be at his place alone, and he showed up without telling me."

"Okay," he says, but I don't stop.

"He said he didn't want to give me time to prepare. And he said we had to get the physical needs out of the way before we could talk about our relationship without just wanting to jump into bed."

"That's…" He chuckles. "That's pretty smart. I remember when Eileen and I were that passionate for each other."

"He's a smart tiger." I look up as though I can see through six floors to where he's sitting in his apartment. "So we're talking. We're going to spend a month figuring out if this is going to work long-term. But even if it doesn't, we'll still be friends."

"That's good. Why a month?"

"Oh." So I tell him my news about Yerba, and he's excited for me, more so than for me getting back together with Dev, but I guess if you look at it objectively, this is probably more surprising. "We're going out there in a few days to look for a place to live."

"Rental or purchase? In Yerba, you'd be better off buying if you can. Property there is a great investment as long as you're going to live in it for a few years."

"I plan to. I don't really know what I'm looking at, though. Isn't property crazy expensive there?"

He launches into a discussion of investment and rental prices versus interest and reminds me that mortgage rates are pretty low at the moment. "Okay," I say, "so I'll send you the info before I make any purchases?"

"I don't know the area, but I can probably point you to someone who does. Or I'm sure your new bosses can, too."

"Probably. I'll give them a call. Though…I wouldn't be able to buy a house without Dev's help, I'm sure."

"And?"

"Well, that might complicate all the thinking we're doing about our relationship."

He thinks about that for a moment. "The house would be a good investment out there. So even if you break up—"

"We're not talking about breaking up. Just maybe scaling down to 'friends with benefits.'"

"Okay…there are plenty of people who would buy a property for an investment and rent it to a 'friend.' It'd be fine."

I'm not sure, but that's a conversation to have with Dev. "Speaking of investments, how's work? Have you started with the Firebirds accounts yet?"

"I don't have the whole team," he says. "Vonni DiCarlo's wife has their money all taken care of, and Fisher Kingston seems pretty set too. But I sent contracts out to Gerrard Marvell, Carson Omba, Jorge Lopez, and of course Winston Porter."

Lopez is Pace, a jaguar who plays safety, and Gerrard and Carson are Dev's fellow starting linebackers, but… "Porter? Oh! Charm. I don't think I've ever heard anyone use his legal name in front of him. It's not even on his jersey."

"Probably not." Father sounds amused. "He didn't want to give it to me until I reminded him I'd seen it in the media guide anyway. There are three more players who were interested, but I haven't heard back from them yet."

"Dev's interested. Did you send him something?"

"No. I was waiting to see what happened with you two. I can send him an e-mail today."

"Just send the contracts. He'll sign 'em."

"They're not contracts, technically. They're agreements and legal documents conveying—

"Whatever. He'll sign 'em."

He chuckles. "Thanks."

I pause until he asks what else is going on, and then I take a breath. "When your grandfather had Alzheimer's…"

He fills in the silence when I pause. "That was twenty years ago. Wait. Thirty, now."

"Do you remember how it started?"

The silence stretches on longer. "Not particularly well. I wasn't living with them. I got a phone call from my father saying that he—my grandfather—wasn't remembering things so well and that I should come see him. I went a few times. Early on it didn't seem like much was wrong. He'd forget names, you know, or dates. But he still seemed sharp. After a few months, it got worse. He'd forget things you'd just talked to him about, and then… well, you know how it goes. He never forgot my name, but he could never remember my age or what I was doing." He exhales across the phone mic. "I stopped going to see him around then. It was just too hard."

"I can understand."

"I wish I'd gone to see him one more time." He sighs again. "But I presume you didn't ask just to make me feel bad about missing my grandfather. What's happening?"

"It's Fisher." I tell him about the anger and the small slips and the concussions, though I leave out Hal's report for the moment.

Father absorbs that. "It's pretty soon after the concussion," he says finally. "I'm not a doctor, but I presume the team has one. If he's home, they can't be too worried about it."

"Maybe. I was talking with Gena in Boliat after his concussion there, and she said he was dizzy and forgetting things there too. She mentioned his father, who had Alzheimer's."

"I guess she would know better than I would. I hope not, though. He's so young."

In the world at large, he is. In football terms, he's old. Not ancient yet, but definitely old. "Was there anything your father did with his father? I mean, things that could maybe help a bit?"

"I don't remember any. Wait—I do remember the nurses saying that if you ask him about memories, make him try to remember things, that that can help. If he's accessing the memories, it stabilizes them. Not a lot, but every little bit helps."

"Did he get angry about losing his memory?"

"Sometimes." Father says it slowly. "Sometimes. But your great-grandfather wasn't that kind of person. He was pretty calm. There was one time…I was visiting him, and he was trying to tell me the story of how he'd helped the union stand up to the factory he worked in. He remembered the dates but he couldn't remember any of the names of the people who'd stood with him. 'Bren,' he said, 'I worked alongside those foxes and wolves and rams and deer for thirty years. I can see their muzzles and I remember their scents as clear as yours. But the names are just gone.' And he put a paw over his heart then and he said, 'I remember the love, the passion we all felt. God might take the details, but He leaves the important things.'"

That sets my tail swinging against the washing machine. "That's pretty inspirational. He sounds like a great guy."

"He was."

"I don't think Fisher has that zen of an attitude. He tends to want to tackle problems."

"I can see that. Hang on." He types for a bit. "I just got the e-mail confirmation from Angela Marvell. Hey, I normally don't travel to clients, but since I'm setting up several new ones, I think the firm would pay for me to go down to Chevali to do some setup in person. When will you be back from Yerba?"

"I don't know. We haven't even bought flights or anything."

"You know how much more expensive it is last-minute…" He laughs. "For normal people, I suppose."

"It's more expensive for Dev, too," I say. "Just not so's he'd notice. He hasn't even asked about his forty thousand dollar playoff check."

"Were you going to donate that to Equality Now?"

"I was. I still might. I haven't decided yet. I want to give it to a good cause, but I've been…kind of distracted the last couple weeks."

"You should invest it in the meantime. Hold onto it until I come down and we'll work something out."

"We can just take you out to a nice dinner for the amount of commission you'd be losing."

"Ah-heh. It would have to be a *very* nice dinner. But that's not the point. The point is, it's not doing anybody any good just sitting there."

"All right. I'll deposit it today before I go over to Fisher's."

"What?"

So I have to explain that to him, and he says it's a good thing to do but be careful, you know, in a house with a football player who's violently coming to terms with his loss of memory, and I say I'll be fine. "I have experience with football tigers," I remind him.

"Somehow I don't think Fisher or Gena would appreciate the kind of experience you have."

I laugh. "You never know. Maybe it would calm him down. No, no, I'll be good, I promise. I'm just going over to help Gena out today."

We say good-bye after I promise to keep him updated with my itinerary. Then I head back upstairs and find Dev sitting on the couch staring at his phone.

"Having trouble setting up the new one?" I ask, going over to sit beside him.

He shakes his head. "I got the number of Fisher's agent. How do I fire Ogleby?"

"I thought you already did."

"Sort of. Over the phone. But he pretended not to hear, and god, I don't want to call him…"

"Call Fisher's agent." I point to the number on his phone. "Tell him you want to hire him and ask him how to proceed."

"Yeah." He taps the phone. "I guess I can do that."

I lean against him. "You want me to do it for you?"

He holds out the phone. I reach for it, and then he laughs and grabs my paw. "Nope, I can do it. You're just taking charge of everyone these days so I thought maybe I'd let you do it all. You can call Hal and set up lunch and I'll call Damian."

"Deal." So I go to the kitchen and ask Hal if he's free for lunch, and he says he can clear time off his schedule.

"How'd it go with Fisher?" he asks.

"I'm going to see you in two hours," I say.

"I know. But Miski'll be there. So tell me privately, how'd it go?"

I sigh. "Well, we didn't ask him. But I'm going back tonight so I'll see if there's a chance. He's…the loss hit him pretty hard."

"Imagine so. Pretty near the end for him. What's the team say about the concussions?"

He's sharp, Hal is. I start to tell him and then catch myself. "Don't know." I keep my tone bland. "Not sure they've said anything."

"All right. See you in a couple hours."

I hang up and wait in the kitchen. Dev's still on the phone with Damian and it seems to be going pretty well. He'd sounded tentative when he first called, though I was talking to Hal and didn't catch most of the words, but now he sounds at ease, and he's talking about the Firebirds. "…it's a great group of guys, and it's a great situation for me, honestly." He listens. "I think they do. But…" Another pause. "No, nobody. I mean, we talked about wanting to stick together and win a championship."

Leaning against the kitchen door, I watch him. He relaxes back in the couch and laughs. "Yeah, for sure. You think I'll be able to…?"

He listens intently and nods for a bit. There's a few more words and then he says, "Sounds great. Yeah. I'll do that and I'll call you tomorrow. Thanks, Damian. Yeah. Me too."

When he turns around, he sees me, and he gets up off the couch and stretches. I walk toward him. "Can't think when I ever heard you that relaxed talking to Ogleby."

"Can't remember the last time I didn't hang up on Ogleby. Damian is, like, a professional. It's weird." He scratches behind an ear. "He says he can get me a good five-year deal if I want it, but he's also not sure it wouldn't be better for me to play out my current deal. He wants to look into my situation more closely once we're officially in business."

"Is he going to fire Ogleby?"

"Ah." His ears fall. "No. No, he said I have to do that, because if I decide to terminate *his* services in a few years, he doesn't want to get a call from some other agent. He'd want to hear it from me."

"Good point." I look at the phone he's still holding. "When are you going to do it? Can I listen?"

"I'm not happy about firing him," he says.

"I don't think you should be." I reach out and take his wrist. "But you have to do it. Do I need to read off the list again?"

He says no, but I do it anyway. "The press conference. The Ultimate Fit contract. The fake engagement."

"I know, I know."

"Your upcoming contract negotiation."

He sighs. "How do you tell someone they're not good enough for you anymore?"

"Tiger," I say, "if you could do that easily, you wouldn't be the tiger I love."

"So why do you want to listen?"

I grin. "Because I want to be able to tease you later about what a softie you are."

He growls as I poke his stomach, and he grabs me and shoves his muzzle at my ear. "I'll show you how hard I can be," his bass voice rumbles through me.

"N-not now." I twist away from him. "You have to fire Ogleby first."

"Now?"

"Well, before we go to lunch with Hal. So you have two hours to work yourself up to it."

He lets go of me and walks to the kitchen. "I need a beer."

"It's ten-thirty in the morning."

At the door, he turns. "So think of something to do until noon. Then I'll fire Ogleby and we can go."

"Well," I say, "you could tell me about the conversation with your brother."

He glares at me. "Look," I say, "I heard the yelling. I just want to know what happened and if there's any way I can help."

"I don't want to talk about it now."

"Okay," I say. "I can tell you I got an e-mail from Brian."

"Ugh." He grabs my paw. "Later. Let's just walk."

As we get to the door, he says, "I will talk about it, I promise, and I want to hear your e-mail. But let me get through one thing at a time. I think talking about Gregory and Brian will just get me worked up, and I'd like to relax."

"Fair enough." I kiss him. "It's a nice day out. I'm up for a walk. You want to go to the gym? Miss workouts yet?"

He rolls his eyes. "Sex is about the most intense workout I want for a couple days."

So we go out and walk in Chevali for an hour, and he gets recognized and asked for autographs. We don't talk about Ogleby or Brian or Gregory, and probably as a result, we return to the apartment around quarter to noon in good spirits.

Once he's cracked open a beer and drained half of it, he sighs and picks up the phone to call Ogleby. I gesture to the couch. "Don't you want to sit down?"

"I don't want it to last that long," he says.

We'd discussed some of the things he could say, and I'm pleased that he starts out all professional. "I've been evaluating my needs over the last year and I don't think that our relationship is the best thing for me at this time. I really appreciate all that you've done for me in the past…"

There's silence while he listens and then tries to break in. "No…Yes, of course, but…no. I haven't forgotten…but…Ogleby, just…Ogleby…" He shoots an exasperated glance at me and mimes a mouth chattering with his free paw.

"Ogleby, listen. I appreciate the Ultimate Fit deal, but I would appreciate it more if I didn't have another commercial to film with them for no extra money. I know. I know contracts are hard. Yes…okay, but you didn't get me that deal. Strike got me that deal and you made *me* read the contract!"

He paces around the room, his tail lashing now. "No! I will not…" He comes up face to face with me. I put my paws up to try to calm him, but he rolls his eyes and turns away. "I'm getting new representation, Ogleby. I'm sorry. No. No. No! We're done."

His thumb cuts off the call and then he stands there staring down at the phone in his paw. After a moment, he drops it and looks up, trying to muster a smile. "Did we really think it would end any way other than me hanging up on him one last time?"

"Do you have to do anything official?"

"Yeah, I have to fax him an official letter of termination. I'll do that after lunch." He sets the phone down and stands there.

I walk over and hug him. "You had to do it, you know. He drove you crazy and he wasn't good for you."

He presses his nose down against my ears. "That doesn't make it easier."

"No, I know." I hold him and rub up and down his back. "Like I said, I love that about you."

He holds me tighter. "Thanks."

The letter of dismissal is easy because Damian sent Dev a template to use. We modify it slightly—I hold back my suggestions to fill in the whole section about "reasons for termination" and allow Dev to type in "different philosophies." We print it out and then meet Hal at a brew pub downtown with great old wood beams and the smell of malt and hops mixed with burgers and fry oil.

The swift fox is sitting in a booth; we slide in across the dark wood table, me on the inside so Dev has room to stretch out. While he picks up a menu, I pass Hal a pile of folded sheets with a gift bag on top.

His nose twitches as he takes it. "What's this?"

"Just a thank-you gift. I really appreciated you letting me stay with you."

He peers inside. "Aw, dammit. It's too much. And anyway I told you I didn't need one of those."

I flick my tail and wink. "I thought Pol might be impressed if you had one. It makes texting easier, you know."

He grumbles at me, but he does take the iPhone box out and turn it over. "You gonna help set it up?"

"If you want, sure."

"Well." He puts the phone back in the bag and sets it and the sheets on the seat beside him. "Thanks. Wasn't necessary but it's nice of you."

"You put up with a sick, mopey fox for the better part of a week. It's a fair trade."

Dev lowers his menu as Hal starts to protest that it wasn't that bad. "I've seen him mopey," he says. "It's from me too, for taking care of him and putting up with him."

"Oh, well," Hal says, and his smile widens. "Thank you, then."

"Oh, it's okay from him but not from me?" I put on mock annoyance. "I have a job now too, y'know."

"Yeah, don't rub it in. And congratulations. I guess it's official?"

I tell him about the offer letter, which should be coming in today, and after we order, we talk a little about the Whalers. When he finally gets around to asking about Fisher, Dev and I go quiet and look down at the table, at the burgers we haven't started eating yet.

Hal looks between us. "What, things not going well?"

I get Dev's nod of permission to answer. "We didn't really get to talk about the injury much. It was just a social visit. But I'm going back there today to help Gena with some stuff, so I'll see if I can ask him then."

"Right." Hal looks up at Dev. "Championship loss hit him hard, huh?"

"It hit all of us." Dev takes a big bite of his burger. "Fucking sucked."

"Sure." The swift fox nibbles on his chicken sandwich. "He's been through it before, though. Shouldn't he be the one with the perspective? Lose it one year, win it the next?"

"Most championship-losing teams don't make it back to the game the next year," I say, and then wince as Dev glares at me. "That doesn't mean there can't be exceptions."

"Most championship-winning teams don't make it back the next year either," Hal points out. "People remember the old dynasties like Kerina's four straight or Hilltown's four out of five, but those were thirty, forty years ago. Highbourne was the last team to get to the game three times straight and they only won two of them."

"So what kind of perspective should Fisher be offering?"

"Well." Hal puts down his sandwich. "You don't start the season assuming you won't get back. You tell yourself and your teammates you're going to be the exception."

"We are." Dev sinks fangs into his burger.

"Course y'are," Hal says. "I'd put down money on it."

We eat a few more bites, and then Hal says, "Course, I'd also put down money that Fisher Kingston won't be with the team when you do."

Dev puts the burger down. "What do you mean?"

Hal faces him with the composure of a guy who's been through a lot of press conferences and maybe locker rooms, facing much bigger guys. "Just that they gotta figure out if they're gonna commit to a 36-year-old defensive end who can still play, or if they're going to go with a 25-year-old polar bear who's got his best years ahead of him. You want one more year of Kingston, maybe? Risk another concussion or another injury? Or you want a young, healthy guy who's maybe not as fast, but with a summer to prepare you can build your plays around him?"

Dev scowls, and I don't want to say anything. "It's a business," Hal goes on. "I know you been kinda shielded from that, being on the bench."

"I got traded."

I rest fingers on his wrist. "But you didn't really ever feel like part of the Dragons. They had you on special teams, on the bench the whole time. You told me you hoped you'd be traded, even."

"Yeah, but…" He shakes his head. "I know. I know he probably won't be back. I just kinda hoped we'd keep all the guys together. I know it never happens to those other teams, but I thought…I thought we had something pretty special here."

"You do," I say. "And you will again. Because the thing that's special, it's partly you. You mesh with your teammates, you bring out the best in them and they bring out the best in you. This isn't a once-in-a-lifetime opportunity. There's a lot of good guys out there. Yeah, you might get on a bad team once in a while, but you," I poke a finger at him, "won't let them stay bad for long."

He looks startled and then hmphs in a way that I know means he's more pleased than he wants to let on. "Just so we don't lose Gerrard."

"Oh yeah," I say. "If you lose Gerrard, you're screwed."

Hal laughs. "Marvell ain't going anywhere, not with his contract. Look, I don't mean to put down Kingston. For his age—for any age—he had a pretty good season. But the team won most of the games he didn't play last year. Yeah, that was a lot of things: you, Lightning Strike, Marvell, whatever. Point is, when they look at people who were essential to the team's success and people who're worth investing in, you probably got two dozen names come up before his."

Dev sighs. "He was talking about maybe retiring."

Hal pauses to evaluate that while I register some surprise that Dev told our friend the reporter. Dev goes on while we're both silent. "What do you think? You think he should?"

The swift fox shakes his head. "I can't answer that. Sure, financially he's probably fine. But I don't know how he feels, what passion he's got inside him to drive him to keep going. If he's ready to hang 'em up, then yeah, this is a good time. If he's not, I'm sure he can find another team to take him on if the Firebirds really don't want him."

Silence ends that conversation, so after a little while, I ask, "How's Pol? When do we get to meet her?"

"When you set up a dinner date. She works out in Yellow Springs. Can't come into the city for lunch." He finishes off his sandwich and takes a drink of beer. "Pity though that is."

"Okay, well." I tick off nights on my fingers. "I'm busy the next couple nights, and we're going to Yerba soon after that. Maybe when we get back? How about Wednesday night?"

"Sure. No rush."

I grin across the table. "Things going that well, huh?"

"They're stable. We're just having fun for right now."

"Good." I wag my tail. "How's the article?"

He raises an eyebrow in Dev's direction. My tiger rumbles, "I already know about it. I was trying to get Fisher to talk to you. Well, I was going to try. If he—anyway." He stuffs his mouth full of fries.

"Yeah." Hal grins. "Appreciate it. Article is fine. It's hard to get people to talk to me about it. Y'know, the league got wind of it and they're trying to stop it."

"Can't imagine why." I growl. "Protecting their brand, not their players."

"Basically." He rubs his whiskers. "Also, well, you'll probably read this in a couple weeks anyway, but they're looking to expand next year. They want to add four more teams."

This is something I've read about for a few years already. "It's going to happen next year? Where are they looking?"

"I don't know exactly, but…" He ticks off on his fingers. "Mostly mid-west. Big opportunity there—college ball is huge and they think they can get more pro teams going. So Cuyahoga, Crockett, Cansez—they're really building up the C-cities—and either St. Clair or Deleon. Both of them have bids in and I think the owners are leaning toward Deleon because they'd like to be able to head down there for vacation."

"Better than St. Clair. It's colder than Hilltown." Dev finishes off his burger. "I played a college game there. Run down city."

"They're hoping the team would revitalize it." Hal flicks his ears. "Anyway, they don't want anything coming out that would harm the league."

"Coming out, eh?" I elbow Dev. "Too late for that."

"I didn't know!" he protests.

"Hey," Hal says with his paws up, "you and Polecki, that's been terrific for the league. You might not've got that, but they love it. It's positive publicity outside the game—usually that's charitable foundations and that stuff is boring like a town without a sports team. It's got lots of attention focused on the league and they can show how progressive they are by how accepting they are and how homophobia is down and all that shit. No, trust me, the league loves you, Dev. Don't know about the individual teams, but at the top they are all on your side."

"Loves me, like, big bonus to my salary love?"

"Good luck with that." Hal laughs. "Leave it to your agent to work out, which means probably not."

So then we tell him about firing Ogleby, which Dev is still flat-eared over, and Hal nods when we're done. "Good for you. From what I saw, you deserve better. That guy Fisher's got—I don't know much about him, which is a real good sign."

"Yeah." Dev toys with his fries. "Still feels crappy, you know? Disloyal."

"Business," Hal reminds him. "Do you get all weepy when you cut up a credit card, too?"

Dev's eyes go wide. "I don't know. I never have."

"Okay, well." The swift fox takes out a credit card and taps it on the table. "When I cut up the first credit card I ever got, I got kind of emotional about it. It was dumb. The company didn't give a shit. But I made it emotional. It's what we do: we like to put emotion and feeling into our lives. You have to recognize when it doesn't help you."

"That's what I've been telling him," I say.

"Yeah, yeah." Dev points at both of us. "When you have to fire someone you've done business with for years, who gave you your first break…"

"Don't have to," I say. "They fired me."

"Ditto."

We both look smugly back at him and he growls. "Foxes."

"People," Hal says. "Also, your Dragons basically fired you, too, only they set you up with another job when they did it. So it all works out. Your ferret'll find another client, and you've got a new agent, and the world keeps turning. Nothing's irreplaceable."

It's a good lesson to learn, although as we drive back from lunch I wonder how much it applies to our relationship. Could Dev replace me? Well, that's a stupid question; of course he could. There's no shortage of gay guys out there who'd at least be interested in a relationship with him. I'm not that vain, that I think I'm the only guy, or even the only fox, who'd be able to live with him. Would someone else be better for him? Maybe. Probably in the world there's at least one guy who'd challenge him without sparking fights so furious that they endanger his focus.

At least, I think, I'm not the Ogleby of relationships. Sure, my list of missteps is nothing to be proud of, and I recite them to myself whenever I need to feel humble or ashamed of myself. And then there are the things that aren't isolated incidents, like the way I can't seem to keep my muzzle shut around him. I've always been able to fool people and lie to them or tell them only the right parts of the truth, but I can't do that with Dev. Things would be a lot easier if I could, that's for sure. But I always want to tell him everything on my mind, and while sometimes it's to produce a desired effect, most of the time it's just to share myself with him.

That's why I found it so difficult during the playoffs not to talk to him all the time about Equality Now and Vince King. Not because I wanted him to do anything about it, but because I wanted him to know what was on my mind. I'm not sure he understood that, or understands it now, so I file it away for something to discuss during our month of relationship examination. It gives me hope; maybe if we just sit down and affirm where we are with each other, we can keep going.

Back at his place, I throw my stuff into a bag and he walks me down to my car. "You're packing a bag?"

"Yeah. I called Gena. She's setting up a spare room for me just in case she feels like she needs help tomorrow too, and she talked to Fisher."

"He's okay with it?"

I make a noncommittal head movement. "She said she told him. I don't know what he thinks about it."

"Well, take care of yourself, fox." He wraps arms around me, right there on the street.

I hug him back. "I'll either come see you for dinner or invite you over, if Fisher wants to talk to you a little more. And if you want to go out tonight, I can stay there. If not, I can come back." I poke him. "Don't call Gregory."

"I was trying not to think about that."

"I know." I nuzzle him. "But sitting alone in the apartment, you were going to, and then you might call him. So call me instead and talk about it."

"Or," he says, "I can start our month of thinking about our relationship."

"Even better." I grin and try to pull back, but he doesn't let go.

"Hey, so…where should I start with that?"

His ears are askew, so I squeeze his arm. "Well, you know what our problems are, right?"

He raises his eyebrows. "Mostly you?"

I laugh to cover up the sneaking suspicion that he's right. "Okay, then, figure out what you'll need to do so I don't drive you crazy."

"I was teasing." He pokes me back. "I know I got to work on stuff too."

It's a nice retraction but doesn't make me feel a hundred percent better. "Let's start with…well, I think we both feel like the relationship is worth working for. So let's think about the problems we've had, and how we can avoid them if they come up again."

He squints. "Like if Brian threatens to out me to the league that already knows I'm gay?"

"Brian has moved on to sending me good-bye e-mails," I say.

"Do you have other friends who will threaten me about other things?"

I glare. "I was thinking more about family issues—"

"You told me not to think about Gregory."

I put a paw on his arm. "But think about how it affects our relationship. Like, do you want my help with whatever you're going to do, or do you want my advice, and can you not blow up if I tell you things you don't want to hear." I clear my throat. "Whether or not they're my fault."

"All right." He smiles at me. "I'll give it a shot, and maybe go out with the guys, too. Go see what Gena wants you to do." He looks around and then ruffles between my ears. "Don't cause too much trouble there."

I wiggle my thumb at him. "I've been practicing my aikido."

He snorts. "What, while you were sick with a cold at Hal's?"

"It's congested style aikido. I blow my nose on my attacker and run away while he's wiping mucus out of his fur."

That makes him laugh, and I smile and wag my tail as I get into the car and head off to another house full of tigers.

CHAPTER FIVE: CONNECTIONS (DEV)

True to Lee's prediction, once he's gone off to Fisher's I try to think about anything but my brother, and I fail. I keep replaying the short, harsh phone conversation we had this morning.

"You're defending a hate group?" I yelled.

"Whoa," he said, "they're not a hate group, and—"

"They killed a kid," I growled, "and you're defending them."

"I don't get to pick my cases."

"You can tell your company you don't want to take one."

"And anyway," he said, "they didn't kill the kid. They tried to help him, but he was already pretty fucked up in the head."

"Why, because he was gay?"

"Your words, not mine. I think the evidence is that he ate a shotgun, but I won't argue with you."

"He killed himself because bigots like you convinced him he couldn't have a life!"

"So can I talk to your husband directly or are you just going to spout his words at me all day, Devlina?"

"Fuck," I snarled, "you."

"Now *those* sound like your words," he said.

"If you're not going to talk seriously about this, then just hang up," I said, and he did.

So nothing really got resolved except I yelled at him and he put me off and I didn't feel any better about it. I sit and think about Lee and Gregory, and what Lee might say, what he might want to do that would piss me off.

Lee might want me to make a statement about my brother representing Families United, so that we could call attention to the case. How would I feel about doing that? Well, Dad wouldn't want me to pull our family business out in the open. I could say something about this tragedy, but it's not my family. I guess the kid did write to me, so maybe I could do an interview with Hal about it, but I still feel like it's not my place to do it.

Lee would understand that, I think. And if he didn't...well, I would have to do a better job of explaining to him what was important. And if it was really more important for him than for me, then...I could talk about Vince King if I left Gregory out of it.

Even if he agreed about the statement though, Lee would want to go have a conversation. He'd tell me that the best way to change Gregory's mind would be for me to let him get to know us better so that he wouldn't have these conceptions of what gay people were. And he isn't necessarily wrong, only with me and my brother it's more complicated than that. I honestly don't think Gregory's issue is that I'm gay. I think it's that I'm winning.

Gregory is at the same point in his career that I am in mine: just about two years in, enough to know how the system works, enough to know where his place in it is. We should be talking to each other, sharing our discoveries like we did back in middle school.

But that changed when Gregory hit high school. He was a tough tiger then, didn't want his kid brother tagging along with him. I had just started playing football, and Gregory was too smart for sports; he was on the debate team and taking advanced placement tests and talking about going to Whitford and those fancy East Coast schools (eventually he went to the U of Aventira, which is still a good school). I had football friends and football games that he wasn't interested in attending, and so even though we had adjacent rooms, we didn't talk much his last few years of high school. When I came home proud of a two-interception game, he said, "But you didn't really have to think. You just went where the coach told you and caught the ball." Not in front of Mom and Dad, of course; there he limited his comments to "Good job" as he artfully turned the conversation back around to his accomplishments.

I went to his graduation and he came back for mine, but the couple times I wrote him to talk about problems I was having in high school, he just wrote back with quick, short messages. School was hard, taking up a ton of his time, he was busy, he was rushing a fraternity or planning his fraternity's rush calendar or studying for finals. When I told him I had a sort-of girlfriend, he said lazily that he wasn't going to tie himself down to any one girl, that college was a time for exploration.

He spent one summer back home, but even then I spent a lot of that summer in football practice and I barely saw him. After that, he stayed the summer down in Aventira with some friends, and then got an internship at a law firm one summer.

He attended law school in Gateway, and my parents were thrilled. At the time, I was just a junior in college, and my football career wasn't going anywhere. That was right before I met Lee, that Christmas that Gregory came home brandishing his acceptance to law school. "Well," he said to

Dad, "if you get sued because Dev breaks something on someone's car, I'll be able to defend you."

Didn't matter that I was getting a basic business degree or that Dad was thinking I'd work in the office, not on the cars. He showed off pictures of Marta then, and when I told him that I had lots of different girls, he patted me on the shoulder and said, "Someday you'll meet the right one."

Like that was all there was to it. Meet the right one and everything works out. I wonder if he and Marta fight about things like whether he should take the case. Probably not; Marta seemed happy to go along with whatever her husband wanted to do as long as she got a family to take care of. As far as I could tell, she doesn't challenge Gregory at all, not like my fox does me.

Which makes me a better person, I know, even if it also makes me an annoyed person. But the point is, he's the one who comes up with the ways to challenge me. If I could imagine the things he'd say to me, then he wouldn't be challenging, would he? He'd just be saying things I already knew.

Ugh. It's complicated, thinking about this relationship stuff. I pull up my e-mail on the off chance that there's another kid sending me a desperate attempt to connect. There isn't; just the usual parade of fans and crazies. I get bored of it after twenty minutes and nostalgic for my team.

So I put the computer away and pick up the phone. Gerrard and Ty don't answer, and Carson's out of town, but Charm and Zillo both pick up and say they'd love to get together. "I can squeeze in a couple hours before my date," Charm says.

We get together at the bar we went to after games, and the first thing Charm asks me is how Lee—"Mrs. Gramps"—and I are doing. I scowl at the big stallion, who's got his date clothes on already: silk shirt over black jeans with his mane artfully styled between his ears into a kind of wave. Zillo's just wearing a Firebirds t-shirt, cargo pants, and a wary expression at the discussion of my love life. "We're doing better, *Winston*," I say.

"You're the one who called me," Charm says. "You want me to go home, I'll go."

I shake my head. "Sorry. It's fine. We're talking."

He elbows me. "*Just* talking?"

I'm comfortable with him and he clearly wants to hear it. I'm surprised and pleased at how easily the response comes to me. "And fucking, okay?"

The coyote looks mortified, ducking his long muzzle behind the big glass of beer he got, but Charm just laughs and punches my shoulder. "Good," he says.

"You really want to hear about it?"

"Not more than that," he says. "I mean, I could tell you about the gal I'm taking out tonight." Both of his massive hands come out to cup imaginary breasts a foot in front of his chest. "But I guess you'd be about as interested."

I snort and turn to Zillo. "What about you? When do you leave for that island with your girlfriend?"

"Oh, uh." He shakes his head. "Couple days, I think. Maybe next week."

"You don't know?"

"She planned it." His big ears flatten out. "I'm just goin' along, you know?"

"How come we never met her?" Charm leans forward.

Zillo snorts. "You think I'd introduce her to you?"

I'm remembering Zillo going to the strip club in Crystal City, and maybe Charm is too, because he meets my eye and raises an eyebrow. "Hey, I don't hit on my pal's gals," he says. "Sometimes they hit on me, though."

"That's what I'm worried about." Zillo looks away and waves. "She's not that into football anyway."

"So why the hell is she going out with you?" Charm gulps down half his beer and signals the waitress that he'll want another one pretty soon.

I clear my throat and step in before Zillo can answer or punch Charm. "So is she off somewhere tonight?"

"Yeah, she's got her own friends, and I was at my folks' place anyway."

He tells us a bit about his older sister, who's a nurse, and then we start talking about siblings and Charm mentions his two younger brothers, one in the army and one still in college.

"Oh hey," he says to me. "I was gonna tell you. My brother in the army called me up yesterday and came out. Told me he's gay."

"Wow." I stare.

"Said he heard about you and then Polecki and he figured he could tell me now because I know you, but he always kept it hid."

"Yeah, being gay in the army kinda sucks." I flick my tail. "Poor guy."

"That's what he said."

"But hey, on the bright side," Zillo pipes up, "he's a horse."

We both stare at him. He grins. "So he doesn't give a shit. Isn't that what you always say?"

Charm laughs and slaps a huge hand on the table. "That's right. Only his problem is, if he came out, he could get all the guys he wants, but he can't, so he can get the girls, but he doesn't want 'em." He holds up his glass. "It's like me at a wine bar."

Zillo and I exchange looks. "Because...there are no girls at a wine bar?" he says.

"Or all the guys at a wine bar are gay?"

Charm snorts at us. "Because I drink beer, not wine, and they don't serve beer at a wine bar. Jeez, I thought you guys were s'posed to be the smart ones. Well, coyote over here anyway."

"Ah, whatever." Zillo sticks his tongue out and drinks. "I told you 'bout my cousin, right?"

"The gay one? Yeah." I look at both of them. "Am I the only one who doesn't have a gay relative?"

Charm points a finger at me. "You *are* the gay relative."

I consider that and it seems a fair point, so I nod and toast him. We shoot the breeze a little more, and I worry that Zillo feels left out because Charm and I just joke back and forth a bunch. But he sticks around and puts in a comment here and there, and when Charm leaves, he says he'll stick around if I do.

So we say goodbye to the stallion, making sure he's okay to drive (he says he's fine, with two light beers over two and a half hours), and then order one more round. "Look," Zillo says, "if you called me to make sure I'm coming to the workouts, don't worry. I will."

I frown. "No. Just wanted some company tonight. Lee's busy and..." I lap up a little beer. I could never say this next thing in front of Charm; he'd tease the hell out of me. "I miss you guys."

His ears go up. "Really? I mean, I miss you guys too, but I figured you got your fox and Gerrard and all them."

"I haven't seen Gerrard since Monday morning. I just saw Fisher yesterday, but he's...he's not doing so great. I wanted to talk to someone." I squint at him. "And hey, you can always call me if you want to hang out."

"Yeah, okay. I wasn't sure, you know. I mean, season's over, contracts are getting tossed around. If you're going to another team..."

"We been through a lot this season," I say. Sometimes I forget that it's Zillo's second season too, and he came out as a sophomore, so he's two years younger than I am. "We're not gonna just say goodbye and never talk again."

"I know," he says.

"Anyway, you've got lots of other friends on the team, right?" I think of who else I've seen him palling around with. "I know you and Colin aren't, but..."

He shakes his head slowly. "Nah. My roommate last year is in Peco now, and me and Marais kind of talk, but he's back home, and I mean, I know a bunch of the special teams guys, but not, like, to go out for drinks with. And nobody else really went out of their way to hang out." He tips his glass to his muzzle. "I was one of only two guys my year from Candleton to be drafted. My old college teammates are all, I dunno, selling real estate or cars or boats."

"Oh. Well, like I said, anytime. Did you ever meet Lee?" I can't remember if Zillo was at the Christmas party at Gerrard's.

"Just saw him for a minute at the Hellentown dinner." We both go quiet as I remember Colin yelling at Lee there, and I'm not sure what he's thinking of. "But yeah, I'd like to meet him."

"He might come to Gerrard's workouts. So you'll see him then."

He chuckles and elbows me. "I told you, I'm comin'."

I lower my head. "Didn't mean it like that."

"Nah, it's cool." He takes a drink. "I never had someone nag me about getting better before."

"Not your family or anything?"

"My dad just thought it was cool that I was playing. My folks are old hippies that way."

"Coaches?"

"Oh, sure, coaches." He waves a paw. "But they nag everyone, right?"

"Didn't realize you wanted personal attention." I grin and elbow him. "You made it to the league. Weren't you a star in college?"

"Enh." He sets his elbows on the table and cocks his ears. "Like I said, Candleton isn't a high-profile program. The coaches had a real team spirit philosophy, since most of us weren't going to be drafted. Still, three of us got to go to the combine and I blew away the numbers there. I got drafted in the fifth round, and the other guy from Candleton, a right guard, went sixth."

"Seventh." I hold up a paw to his and he slaps it. "But look, you can play for sure. I've seen you. Don't you believe you can?"

"I thought I'd get a shot with Gerrard, you know, coyote bonding and all. Then they moved you over...I was pissed about that, but I'm over it." He frowns slightly. "Why you wanna help me, anyway? What if Gerrard sees I can be better than you?"

"Then I need to step up my game." I take a drink, trying to hide the fear that this coyote will replace me, that nobody else will want me, that I'll be out of football in a year. "That's what happened with Corey."

"True." He pats my shoulder. "I don't think I'm as good as you. Not yet."

"I think you can be." I point a finger. "Just wait 'til I'm gone, okay?"

"No promises." He leans back in the chair and his tail wags. "You really think I can be as good as you?"

"Well, different. You're a coyote, so you have to play to your speed and smarts. But hell, yeah, I mean, I mainly got where I am by studying hard. And, uh…" And having Lee push me, inspire me. "Lots of practice."

"Mmm." His eyelids droop down. "You think I can be as good as Gerrard?"

I snort. "You think *I* can be?"

He laughs. "Yeah, I dunno. That guy's driven."

"Sure is." He hesitates, and I remember the couple times he's mentioned knowing something about Gerrard's private life. I don't want to press, though, and after a moment he goes on. "I never had the fire in me like he has. Colin has it too, this like giant chip on his shoulder to prove to everyone he can make it. He's gonna be really good."

Much as I hate the idea of bigoted fuckhead hypocrite Christian Colin doing well, I can't disagree. So I just don't talk about him. "Fisher's the same way. Can't imagine not playing, can't stop chasing one more title."

Zillo nods. "I love the game, but you know, I think I could hang it up if I needed to. I'd hate it, I'd miss it, but…I'd find something else."

He looks at me, asking without asking, and I wonder. What motivates me? Could I hang it all up if I needed to?

"Not me," I say. "I need a title. A lot of people believed in me—and didn't believe in me." I tap my chest. "Starting with me."

"Yeah." He grins. "I see that a bit. Some guys it's money, you know?"

"Some guys it's fame." I think of Lightning Strike and his last words to me. They weren't about winning. They were about people knowing who he was. "I didn't always have that. Not the fame thing, the motivation thing."

"What turned it on for you?" His ears are up, and he's curious now.

I start being evasive like I always am when people ask me about my relationship, and then I look into his eyes. Zillo's a friend, and he knows about Lee, and I have no reason to lie. "Lee did it. I'd kinda bought in to all the stuff everyone said, about how I'd never make it playing football, not from a Division II school. He said I could be more. Then he made me believe it."

He gets a smile, and with the paw he's using to lift the beer, he points a finger at me. "That," he says, "I would go gay for."

While he's drinking, I chuckle, and then I feel Lee beside me and I feel obliged to say, "It doesn't really work that way."

"Yeah, I know." He looks abashed again. "Sorry, I mean, I *know* this shit, but I just don't always remember it. Didn't mean nothing by it."

"I know you didn't." I toast him with my own beer. "You're a good guy, so don't worry about saying the wrong thing out of habit. Around me, anyway. It's cool."

"I know. I appreciate it." He sets his glass down. "Maybe I'll pick up some new habits, too. Anyway, I just meant it'd be nice to have someone who cares about me like Lee does about you. Not in a lovey way, but, like, someone who cares about making me better."

"You can make yourself better."

"Yeah, I know. So could you."

I have to laugh at that, and he does too, and we chill a bit longer until we're good to drive on home. I promise him we'll get together again, for the workouts with Gerrard if not before.

On the way home, my stomach rumbles. I call Lee to ask how he's doing with Fisher and Gena, and to see whether I should come over for dinner. "Yeah," he says. "Fisher wants to talk to you. It's going okay. I'm mostly taking care of house chores. Gena and Fisher were talking and he got angry again and broke a picture. Gena won't call anyone about it, even that Firebirds guy who called me. And Fisher talked to his agent. Have you?"

"I had an e-mail from him this afternoon. He said he was going to file the paperwork with the players' association and that he'd get back to me within a couple days."

"Good. I'm anxious to hear what he has to say."

"Me too." I smile just from hearing his voice. I tell him about drinks with Zillo and Charm, and he asks if I got his offer letter from Yerba yet. I say I'll look when I get home.

We stay on the phone while I park and head up to the apartment, and there's a note from the courier that they needed a signature and they couldn't leave the envelope. So I tell Lee I'll pick it up on the way over; it's five-thirty and they'll be open for another hour.

Talking to him reminds me of my thinking that morning, of what he'd ask me to do about Gregory. Once I've gotten his letter, I take out my phone and call my parents from the truck. It's not calling Gregory, but maybe the subject will come up, and then it won't be my fault. I've been meaning to call them anyway to let them know I'm changing agents. That seems like a bit of a big deal.

"Why change agents?" my father wants to know, so I explain all the problems with Ogleby and then he says, "Why wait so long to change? You never told us these problems."

"He gave me my first break," I say. "I mean, when no other agents would take a chance on me—well, anyway, I felt loyal to him is all."

Dad thinks that's all right, and he talks about one of the mechanics in his shop whom he kept around even though his performance was slipping. He retired when I was four or something. And then Mom gets on the extension and asks about Lee, and I tell her he's fine, he's spending the evening with Fisher and his family. "He and Gena are friends," I say when Dad wonders why Lee's hanging out with my teammates.

"So now that there is this coyote," Dad says, "will you play football?"

"I was always planning on playing football."

"You do not have to film these commercials that talk about your private life."

What? I'm racking my brains to figure out whether I talked to them about the Equality Now stuff—I don't think I did—and then Mom chimes in. "They did not *talk* about his private life."

"I have not seen other football players filmed in..." Dad clears his throat.

"The clothes are sports clothes," Mom says. "They have to be tight."

"Or with his arm around a male wolf."

Mom doesn't say anything, and I want to laugh. They think the Ultimate Fit and Strongwell commercials are gay activism, are distracting me? Perspective, I guess. Lee got mad at me because they weren't activist *enough*. I clear my throat. "I got paid a million dollars to put my arm around that male wolf."

As soon as I say it, I know it was the wrong thing, because they both stay quiet. "You know, I'm getting a new agent. He's going to get me some better deals."

"One million dollars." Dad rumbles it.

Mom steps in. "That's a lot of money."

"Well," I say, "Ogleby took fifteen percent or something, and then there's taxes..."

"We paid ninety-two thousand dollars for this house," Dad says.

"I'm not saying it's not a lot of money. But you know, a lot of the guys are making a bunch more. That's just the way the business is here."

"I know." He pauses. "Perhaps you could help your brother."

"What?" I can feel the chill in my voice and I try to warm it up. "He's doing fine with his law job."

"Alexi is having some health expenses."

"He never mentioned that."

"It is not serious," Mom says. "Infants have seizures and it may be nothing. But there are tests, and the doctors recommend he stays in the hospital."

"How long—I mean, when did this start? Alexi seemed fine at Thanksgiving."

"After that," Dad says. "One month ago, perhaps six weeks."

I hold the phone to my ear and can't think of what to say. Off to my left, a half mile from the highway, a large white building with a red cross on it catches my eye, and I imagine Gregory's family in there. Alexi's my nephew, even if right now he's just a little white bundle of crying and eating. "But you said it's not serious?"

Mom comes back on. "The doctors say that many infants have seizures and often they stop before they grow up."

"Usually they stop." Dad's tone is casual. "The doctor says even if they do not, they are easily controlled with medication."

"All right." I shake my head. It's still a little weird to process. "I'm not playing football for a couple months, so…keep me posted."

"If you could spare some money for hospital expenses," Dad says again, "I am sure Gregory would appreciate it."

On the face of it, that sounds reasonable, but when he says Gregory's name, I hear again the sneering voice saying, "Devlina," and the click as he hung up on me. "Lee's father wants me to invest my money," I say. "And Gregory just yelled at me on the phone. I don't think he'd want my gay commercial money." As soon as I say that, it sounds harsh, and I feel bad. "But yeah, if he asks me for help himself, then sure."

They're quiet. "I will talk to him," Mom says after a moment.

"Say, what case has he been working on lately?"

The quiet lasts longer this time. "A pro bono case his company assigned…" Mom trails off.

"Lee told me," I say. "It's okay, I'm not playing football anymore. Did you guys know what this case was about?"

"Gregory tells us only that it is a faith-based group under attack, that his company assigned the case to him." Dad has that sharp, loud voice that indicates that he's getting defensive.

"Lee told us," Mom says, more gently. "He asked us not to tell you. He cares a lot about you."

I think Dad makes a grumbling noise there, but I ignore it. "I know," I say. "He didn't want me to be distracted before the big game."

"That should not matter." Dad is softer. "Alexi is your nephew, Gregory is your brother, and they need your help."

"Yeah," I say, "and like I said, I'll be glad to talk to Gregory. Directly."

Both of them seem to know how difficult that'll be, but I don't think it's unfair, and neither of them accuses me of that. I've arrived at Fisher's, so I tell them I need to go, and I'll talk to them soon. It's only as I'm walking in the front door of Fisher's house that I realize that neither of my parents told me what *they* think about Gregory's case.

Chapter Six: Signs (Lee)

When I pull up outside Fisher's, I call Gena to let her know I'm here. She meets me at the door, looking more together than she was yesterday. "Fisher slept in," she says, which explains it. "He just got up an hour ago."

"You want me to make up lunch? Anything else I can do?"

She laughs. "You're not a live-in maid. Come on in. You can keep me company for a little while."

So we hang out in the kitchen and talk about little things: Dev signing with Fisher's agent, the news that morning about the new president's first actions in office. I guess I missed the inauguration while I was sick.

Fisher shoves open the kitchen door as we're starting to make up sandwiches. "Gena—" He stops and stares at me. "What's he doing here?"

"He's helping out around the house." Gena shakes her head. "I mean, he and Dev are—"

"I'm visiting," I say. "Just getting a little bit of time to visit Gena before I move to Yerba."

He grumbles and walks toward the refrigerator. "Is Dev here, too?"

"No, he had a thing to do this afternoon."

Gena and I look at each other as he rummages in the fridge and then takes out a plate of leftovers. He heats it in the microwave, watching the plate turn, while the numbers count down to zero and Gena and I curl our tails and examine our claws. I know I should be thinking about a way to bring up Hal's article, but in the tension of the moment, my throat is dry and none of the words in my head sound right.

When the microwave beeps, Fisher takes the plate out. He finally faces us and says, "I haven't decided yet." Then he walks out the door.

It's a little scary watching Gena's shoulders sag. "I thought you talked to him about me last night," I say.

Her voice is small and she stares at the floor. "I did."

"Oh." I don't know what to say. "He might've just for—he has a lot on his mind."

She walks over to the counter. "I'm going to start making dinner."

I ask if she needs anything, but she says she doesn't, and so I guess it's up to me to go talk to Fisher. I step out of the kitchen and sniff around the house, following Fisher's scent back to his den. I don't really get anything from him other than his regular scent, which feels aggressive and territorial here in his home. My fur prickles with a little bit of worry, but I press on. Nothing's going to happen.

At the den, I knock, and when he makes a grumbling sound, I walk in. He's eating slowly from the plate on a large wooden desk, model trains on one wall, championship pictures in a glass case against the back wall. "What do you want?" he says without looking up.

"I never really got a chance to talk to you one on one. I wanted to ask you a bit about the championships you won, and this year's playoffs."

"Ask Dev." He's still angry, but simmering, and he hasn't asked me to leave. "He remembers the games better than I do."

I ignore all the layers of that statement for the moment. "I've talked to him a bit. But he doesn't have as much experience. I want to hear your perspective. I know you're facing some tough decisions, but I thought it might help if you didn't have to think about them, just remembered the good times for a little. Can you tell me how you beat Hellentown?"

"I don't want to think about the Firebirds." He picks up another bite of food. "Doesn't look like I'll be there next year, and I sure's hell don't want to think about them winning it all without me."

"Fair enough." I sit in the chair, and he doesn't object. "How about the Highbourne games? Any good stories from there?"

He pauses, and then grins. And then he tells me stories.

That keeps us occupied for about an hour, and though I enjoy the stories, I can't find an entry to talk about injuries. There's one point where he talks about a safety who was knocked out of the game, and I ask about the rest of his career. Fisher pauses and just says, "He did okay."

After that I take his plate back to the kitchen and find Gena in a better mood. She asks what we talked about, and at first I'm reluctant to bring up his memory loss. Then I think, hell, she's been living with it, so I can at least mention it in an upbeat way. "He seems to remember the Highbourne games really well," I say, rinsing the dish in the sink.

"He should." She smiles slightly. "He always said those years were the best of his career."

"Were they good for you, too?" Too late, I catch myself reacting to the tone of her voice and the slight emphasis on 'he' in the second sentence.

But it turns out she doesn't mind so much talking to me. We sit on the couch in the living room with a pitcher of iced tea and she curls her tail into a tight spiral, the kind I can't do with all my fluff. Her voice stays low. "Well, of course the championship was wonderful. Both of them were. But…I told you about how he used to play around on the road?" I nod. "Those years were the worst. I found out about one of them, a gazelle…" She waves her glass. "And then there were others. He claimed he needed it to keep his focus, and I said he could either have his focus or his family, and we went back and forth on it."

"Clearly he made the right choice." I sip the cool, slightly bitter tea.

"It's nothing more or less than most wives go through. I didn't know it then. I thought I was special, and I was ashamed to talk about it with the other wives. We weren't all that close anyway. It wasn't until a couple years later at Pelagia that I found out that it happens a lot with football players." She sips and looks over her glass at me. "That's where I met Felice, my friend who's coming in Friday for the weekend. She's Alex Forcetti's ex-wife—he was cheating on her, too, and—sorry. It doesn't happen with everyone. I'm sure Dev won't…"

But I'm already remembering Vonni and the blow job he got at the club just months after his wedding, how it wasn't a big deal for him. I'm remembering all the groupies sitting in the lobby of the hotel and how improbable it would be that all of them would be only going to the single guys on the team. That lifestyle is something that comes with the money and glamor of being an athlete.

Dev is different; he never came up as a star, and so he doesn't have the entitlement complex that a lot of his teammates do. By the time a guy gets to the UFL, he's been one of the top players in college and probably in high school, and he's used to getting anything he wants. Sometimes, like Fisher, they grow up—sooner or later. Sometimes, like Lightning Strike, they never do. Dev, I think, has grown up a lot, but has he grown up enough?

Well, maybe in a month it won't matter. Maybe we'd be better off if we just agreed we would fuck when we're together and when we're not, all bets are off. That thought doesn't sit well with me, though, so I change the subject. I feel a little uneasy discussing Fisher when he's right there in the den, so instead I ask Gena how she likes the Firebirds wives after two years.

We both like Angela, Gerrard's wife, who is a sweet homemaker. "I know what it's like raising two boys," Gena says, "and she's just getting to the hard part."

I chuckle. "One was enough for my parents. I think if they'd had another they would've killed one of us."

"Oh, no. Angela and I both feel that two is the right number. They get each other in trouble, but they also look out for each other."

Of course, Dev has a brother, and the two of them don't exactly look out for each other. But I just go on making conversation with Gena until Fisher comes out of the den. "Where's Dev?" he asks, interrupting our conversation. "I thought he was going to be here."

"He's coming later." Gena scrambles to her feet. The change in her demeanor makes my ears flatten. From the relaxed, confident lady I'd been talking to, she's transformed in a moment into a tense, worried wife with wrinkles along her forehead and a twitch to the end of her tail. "Is there anything you need?"

The big tiger's gaze drops to me. "No. I just want to talk to Dev."

"He signed with Damian," I say, trying to be friendly.

The words have the wrong effect. "Damian! That asshole. I should never have—" Fisher swipes at a curtain, tearing it. Gena winces. "I should go back to Leroy. That guy knew how to take care of a football player."

"He was cheating you out of hundreds of thousands of dollars," Gena says steadily.

"Who? Leroy?" Fisher looks confused. "The hell he was."

"You fired him for it."

"*I* fired him?"

Gena nods. "Your last year in Highbourne."

The big tiger's eyes widen and he looks out at the patio as though just now realizing where he is. He growls and kicks at a nearby side table, sending it toppling over. The picture of their family that was resting on it hits the carpet at the wrong angle, and a sharp crack announces the shattering of the glass. Gena jumps and I startle, my tail bristling up.

"Shit." Fisher stares down.

Gena holds up a paw. "I'll clean it up. Just…go back to the den. I'll bring you some iced tea."

"I want a beer."

"All right. I'll get you a beer. Just go sit down and we'll figure out when Dev is coming."

He goes back to the den. When the door closes, I say, "I can clean up the glass."

I think Gena would normally refuse, but she just says a distracted, "Thanks," so as she gets the non-alcoholic beer from the fridge and pours it into a glass so Fisher won't see the bottle, I spend a few moments picking glass out of the carpet. There are only a few pieces, and when I'm done I ask Gena for the vacuum and run it over the spot to make sure. She stands to the side, her tail twitching.

With the vacuum running and the den door closed, I'm more confident about talking. "That guy from the Firebirds…Elmsley. You ever think about calling him?"

She shakes her head. I can't read her expression. "Maybe you should," I say. "Just in case. I mean, he told me to call if things went bad with Dev…"

"Every team has a Lake, or an Elmsley," she says. "I called the one at Highbourne. Fisher had been cheating and we'd fought. He threw a lamp at me."

I stop moving the vacuum and just stare at her. She nods slowly. "It didn't hit me, but still, I was scared. But that was the first time, and the last. He came back and apologized the next day. I think he scared himself, too. He promised to stop cheating, to never hurt me, and I told him the next time he threw something or hit me that I'd call the police. And he hasn't. Until now. He's scared again."

"So what did the Elmsley at Highbourne say?"

Her tone sharpens. "His name was Jake. He told me not to call the police, that the team would talk to him and they'd work things out. And he told me that if I called the police, then things would be out of the team's hands and I might lose a lot of friends."

I suck in a breath. "Seriously?"

She nods. "And it worked, too. I was too scared to call the police, worried about everything I might lose. Looking back...I should have called them anyway. There was no way I could've known he'd actually change. What if he kept doing it and getting worse? I know a couple wives that happened to, until they left. They never called the police either." She meets my eyes. "You're lucky with Dev. I don't think he'd ever hurt you."

"No," I say, and I go back to vacuuming. But Dev did hit me the one time, years ago at the combine. He hasn't since, but if he did, if the stress gets to him and that ugly side comes out again, I won't have the team to count on. As long as it took them to embrace me as his boyfriend, they'll drop me in a second if I'm a threat to the image of one of their players—and by association, their team.

Still, I'm not nearly as worried about Dev as I am about Gena. Fisher's a good guy, but just because he's been restrained thus far doesn't mean he'll continue to be, especially as the stresses of his memory loss and the situation with the Firebirds continue to get worse. I had planned to go home with Dev, but now I wonder whether I should try to stick around for a night until she finds a live-in nurse. I'm not under the illusion that I can do anything other than call 911 if Fisher becomes violent, but maybe my presence as a guest will give him an extra incentive to behave well.

The boys come home as I'm finishing up, and everything is chaos for a while. They're not sure why I'm there or why I'm vacuuming, but once Bradley goes up to his room, Junior invites me to play FBA Basketball with him.

I'm not very good, which is perfect, because it gives him the chance to teach me some of the game. He's a nice kid; he gives me the Bikers, a great team, and he coaches me on how to play. I still don't beat him, but we have a couple fun hours.

That's when Dev calls and I tell him to come over for dinner. I think it would do Fisher good to have someone else to talk to. I'm curious about Dev's agent, too, wondering what's going on with him and Fisher.

Gena comes out into the living room as I'm wrapping up the call and puts her paws on her hips. "If you boys have nothing better to do than play games, you can help me fix dinner." To me, in a less sharp voice, she asks, "Is Devlin coming?"

Junior gulps and mutters something about homework and runs upstairs before I finish nodding my head. I smile and get up from the floor in front of the couch. "I'll help. I like cooking."

She puts me to work cutting green beans while she seasons ground beef. In the middle of that, Dev shows up with my offer letter from Yerba, so Gena and I wash our paws and the two of them crowd around me as I open it. I show them the signature from Peter Emmanuel and the one from the owner, Michaela Martinet, and they can't help but see the salary offer as well.

"That's all?" Dev wrinkles his nose. He's been a little quiet since he arrived.

"It's a good salary." I shove the letter back in the envelope. "It's enough to live on in Yerba. You do know that not everyone makes athlete salaries, right?"

"Yeah, but…" He scratches his ear. "I thought you'd be making…well, you're part of a football team."

"Sure. And I'm not the part that gets on TV or gets merchandise sold or gets his picture on banners outside the stadium. 'Wiley Farrel, new,' um," I pull the letter out to check the title. "New College Scout, Southwestern Region. Whoa. They put me in the Southwest?"

"He was Eastern Region with the Dragons," Dev tells Gena.

"Maybe they did it so you could be closer to Dev."

My tiger and I edge a bit closer together, our tails touching behind us. "Maybe. Peter didn't talk about that. I thought they only had one opening."

Still, money aside (it is a good salary, really, and more than I was making with the Dragons), I feel warm and bouncy and wanted all through dinner prep and the dinner itself. There's a lot of talk and joking about me helping the enemy—Yerba lost the championship game just a couple years ago and I say I'm going to get them back there again, but only after Dev gets a couple rings. Fisher comes out and actually makes conversation throughout the dinner without getting too angry, though we keep the topics away from football. I find myself watching him as subtly as I can, tensing slightly every time he picks up a knife.

The dinner passes without incident. As soon as we're finished, he grabs Dev and pulls him off to the den. I help Gena wash dishes and our spirits remain pretty high. I'm reminded of Dev's family in the way Gena's just accepted me as part of Dev's life and a friend of hers, and so when she asks me about my own family, I speak pretty frankly.

She's sympathetic about my mom, saying that sometimes it's hard for someone to recognize change in the people close to them and even harder to accept it once they do see it. I agree, even though Father did an admirable job of changing along with me and we've grown closer than ever these past few months.

When the dishes are done, Gena goes upstairs to check on the boys' homework and I go sit in the living room. To pass the time, I take out the laptop and look for flights to Yerba, and grab a couple for Friday even though they're more expensive. Thursday—tomorrow—is cheaper, but I told Gena I'd be around one more day if she needed someone until her friend Felice gets here Friday.

That reminds me that I still haven't talked to Fisher about Hal's article. I bite my lip and wonder whether I want to broach that subject or let Dev do it. My tiger has a better in, but also a lot more to lose if things go south. Probably better that I do it. Maybe tomorrow. I'm sure I can bring up some way to work it into a conversation.

Gena comes back down as I'm pondering how to do that, and it strikes me that I could ask her about it too. But I don't want to jump into that because she looks relaxed and relieved as she plops down on the couch, so instead I tell her about our upcoming trip to Yerba. She promises to give me the name of this restaurant she and Felice found when they traveled down there for a game one weekend.

I'm just about to work my way delicately to Hal's article when there's shouting from the hallway, only it's not Fisher this time. It's Dev. My ears perk up reflexively and I catch most of the words. "...can't believe you would do that! You told me not to!"

The door opens, and now we can hear Fisher as well. "...my age, your priorities change. Call me in ten years and then we'll see who's the asshole!"

"In ten years, if I've gone through what you have, I'll hang up the uniform, and you should too!" Dev stomps out into the hallway and stands at the entrance to the living room, staring at me.

I shoot a look at Gena as I stand. "Hey," I say. "You okay?"

"Yeah, I—sorry." He gives Gena a shake of his head. "I think I better go. You want to come?"

I pack up the laptop under one arm and turn to Gena. "Are you going to be okay if we go?"

"I'll be fine." She looks toward the den, then at my tiger. "Is he…"

"He's stubborn." Dev's tail lashes.

"I can come back tomorrow," I offer.

"If you want." She stands up and straightens her back. "Don't worry. I know you have to go with Dev. I can handle this."

She sounds tired, but confident enough that I really believe her. So I give her a hug, and I say, "Call us right away if you need anything at all. Promise."

Dev doesn't say a word as we walk out to our cars. "What happened?" I say, dropping the laptop into mine. "Or should it wait until we're home?"

"Home." He talks tightly and shakes his head. "I can't believe he'd— what an *idiot*. Like nobody would—Lion Christ!" The words explode out of him like fireworks.

I grab his paw. "You okay to drive home?"

"Yeah. I'm fine." He exhales. "I'll see you there."

I follow his truck all the way home trying not to think about what he found out, and the CD in my car doesn't really help. I end up tapping my paws on the wheel and thinking a lot about Dev and football players in general. Fisher isn't just Dev plus twelve years, I remind myself. He's a different guy, rated highly enough by scouts (*like me, again!*) that Highbourne grabbed him in the second round. He had a big salary and bonuses from the beginning, the full entitled lifestyle, and he's been fortunate enough to have had a career that includes two championships and relatively little injury. Two of the years in Pelagia, he was hurt, but only pulled muscles and sprained ankles, things that heal relatively quickly on their own. Not until the Millenport game last year did he have anything serious, and a boar's tusk tearing up your calf muscle is pretty damn serious.

Gena and I both thought he was taking steroids to keep up his muscle tone, but Dev wouldn't have reacted so strongly to Fisher confirming that. It saddened him, but he understands it. Probably a third of the guys he knows take them, and for the guys on the line who have to get bigger, they're almost an unspoken part of the job. Dev always looked up to Fisher, though, called him a good guy who did things the right way.

The thing about good guys, moral guys, is that it's easy to do things the right way when everything works for you, when you win championships and get endorsements and accolades and big eight-figure contracts (and a pretty, compliant wife). A lot of lucky bounces start to look to you like things you deserve. Then when the breaks don't go your way, when "the right way" doesn't heal your torn calf muscle (or when your pretty wife becomes less compliant), you…you what? What's worse than steroids?

The growth hormones I've read about, maybe. For years, people have known that cubs produce hormones that help the body accelerate new cell development; cubs heal quickly partly because their bodies are working overtime to turn this little infant into a full-grown person. A scrape here or there isn't much more than a speed bump.

So science, in the enterprising way it has, set about trying to isolate the growth hormone so they could give it to adults to accelerate healing. The article I read on it said that a lot of this was happening in Sonora, just south of where we were in Chevali. Easy for Fisher or someone close to him to get access too: the Sonoran border was only six hours by car.

If someone found out he was doing that, then yeah, he'd be in big trouble. That's illegal importing of drugs, possession and use of a controlled substance…that's potentially jail time, even if the league gets involved. But Gena never said anything about trips to Sonora or shady meetings or anything. She just found the bottle labeled Somatotropin and that was it.

So when I meet Dev in the parking garage, I'm still trying to figure this all out. He doesn't say anything until we get up to the apartment, where he twists his key in the lock savagely, then kicks the door open.

"Hey," I say as I ease it shut behind us. "Calm down. You're reminding me of Fisher. What's going on?"

He closes his eyes, breathes, and collects himself. "You know, he always told me to keep my nose clean, that nothing was worth breaking the law, that I had a promising career that I shouldn't throw away. And then he goes and…"

I pull him over to the couch and sit down, surrounded by our scent in our place. "Was it the growth hormone?"

He shakes his head. "He had a friend, wouldn't tell me who…I can't believe he'd do this to himself!"

"Can you tell me about it?"

His golden eyes meet mine, and at the pain in them, I just want to hug him. "I gotta tell someone," he says. "Okay. So when Gena found that bottle? He'd stopped taking it. He took the somato-whatever for a month and then went to the doctor and got the same return schedule he'd had. So he got impatient. He wasn't sure he'd be at full strength for the playoffs."

"Oh, no." I can already feel how bad this is.

He takes another breath. "So I guess there's this new kind of growth hormone shit they're doing over in Xiaqin. It combines regular growth hormone and growth hormone from wild animals."

Ah, shit.

Not all the species in the world have extant ancestors close enough to do that with. Wild foxes are all over, of course, and coyotes and mice and rats.

"The first experiments used wild rat hormone with rats—person-rats— and got improved results. So they started making them with other ancestors."

"And there are wild tigers in Xiaqin." I can't even imagine putting animal hormones into myself. It just sounds insane.

He nods. "So Fisher tried these treatments and they seemed to work. He came back a couple weeks early, enough to help with the playoff push and the championship game. And then he was supposed to stop taking it. It was already messing with him, making him more aggressive, but he thought that was okay for playing football, you know?"

"Sure. Help him chase down the quarterback, right?"

"Then he got the concussion in Boliat."

I read his eyes and see what happened before he tells me. "Oh, fuck, and he went back on the stuff."

"Uh-huh. And then, because he got another concussion in Crystal City, he forgot he had it in his locker. Someone on the cleaning staff found it and reported it to C.C. management. And they called the Firebirds."

"That's why they want him to retire." Jesus Fox, now I understand how agonized Fisher was. How must he have felt listening to me and Dev talk about our new jobs, our new lives?

"He wouldn't even admit he'd done anything wrong. He just yelled at me about how precious the remaining years were and how everybody's doing what they can to get an edge, and how I'm not qualified to judge him. Like he hasn't judged me plenty." His muzzle twists into a scowl.

"Leaving that aside." I slide closer to him and hold his paw. "He's not really thinking of trying to fight it, is he?"

"He doesn't want to retire. He wants to fight something, but Damian convinced him that fighting the Firebirds or the league is a bad idea. I hope."

"Poor guy."

Dev scoots away from me and glares down. "Poor guy? He did this to himself. He always told me, 'don't fuck around with steroids or any of that shit because it's not worth it,' and now he's just a fucking hypocrite, that's all! What am I supposed to think? 'Poor guy'? No. Asshole, that's what he is."

"Okay." I pull my legs up onto the couch and hold Dev's paw. "He's hurting. He's being forced to leave the game on a sour note—and this after he risked so much to hold onto it. Can you see how hard that must be for him?"

"He did this to himself." But he's softening.

"Granted. Yes. But we can still pity him. And we should help him if we can."

"What?" He stares down. "Like, help him get out of it?"

"Help him come to terms with the decision. It's going to be a big change for him and it won't be easy."

"Huh." He leaves his paw in mine and holds my gaze. "So you don't think he should go to jail?"

I think about that. Do I? If Fisher had robbed a bank or assaulted someone, would I be sitting here talking about helping him adjust to it? "He did break the law," I say carefully.

"Uh-huh. And the league's just going to cover it up. They don't want the embarrassment."

I sigh. "What do you think?"

He shakes his head. "I asked you first."

"All right." I curl my tail into my lap. "I don't think athletes should be held to a different standard. If he's suspected of a crime, he should be charged with it and they should try him in court."

I don't know how he's going to react at first, because he doesn't change his expression. But then he gives me a slow nod. "Okay," he says. "That makes sense to me."

"I'm sorry. I know he's a good friend."

"He was."

"Okay, hold on there." I squeeze his paw. "Maybe he has to go to jail, but he's still your friend. He didn't throw that away. I know it feels shitty that he went and did the things he told you not to, but…he's still the guy who helped you get oriented on the team, who helped motivate you, who accepted me. None of that changed because he committed a crime in a desperate attempt to get one more shot at football."

"For *two weeks*!"

"He didn't know you'd make it to the championship. What if you'd lost that first playoff game to Hellentown while he watched from the bench and that was it, that was his season?"

"He'd have two fewer concussions," Dev growls. "Maybe he'd be able to remember what fucking year it is."

I bite my lip again, because that's the worst part of it all. Who the hell knows what this animal hormone shit did to his system? "Sometimes it takes a few weeks to heal from a concussion," I say. "He could be better by March."

"Or maybe he won't."

"We can't know any of that now."

He stares off into space. "If I couldn't remember things like that…"

"Hey." I slide closer. "You're not there yet and hopefully won't ever be. Not all football players end up with concussions, and if you do suffer one, I'm sure as hell not going to let you go out and play two weeks later."

His eyes catch mine. "You think you can stop me?"

It's playful, but I'm dead serious and I don't smile. "Yeah," I say. "I do. Because if it's a choice between you getting a ring to wear on your finger and you having forty or fifty more years of good quality life, I don't even have to think about it."

"So what would you do if I did go back in and play?" Quietly, because I think he knows, but he wants to hear me say it.

"You think I can't distract you for two weeks?" I say, and now I'm trying to be playful. "Let's worry about that when it happens, which will hopefully be never."

Gold eyes search mine, and then he gives a quick nod and a smile. "Thanks, fox. I don't think a lot of people would make that choice for me, but maybe someone should."

And he pulls me into a hug, and I think about saying that I'm not condemning Gena for not doing the same for Fisher, because I'm not sure she could. I guess she put her foot down about him fooling around, but that's not the same as football. If she'd forbidden him from playing in the championship, would he have left her? Would he have done it anyway? Was she scared he might throw another lamp at her, or worse?

I shove those thoughts aside, because I'm in the arms of my tiger and it's warm and nice here, and things might start moving along to the bedroom in a moment, except right then his phone rings. He glances at it, then at me, and I nod and wink. "Go ahead. We can pick up again when you're done."

He returns my wink and picks up the phone. "Oh, right," he says. "Good to talk to you again. Is anything wrong?" He glances toward the computer. "Oh, no. I got caught up in stuff. I'll go look at it now?" He starts to get up, then settles back down. "Sure. Tomorrow? That works. Okay. Oh, yeah, I've been talking to him too." He starts to get more animated, and then shuts down. "Right. That makes sense. Sorry. Okay, so tomorrow at two? Are you going to Fisher's house? We could meet you there. Lee's been helping out Gena. Okay, sounds great."

At the mention of Fisher, my ears perk up. When Dev hangs up, I raise my eyebrows and slide closer to him again. He curls an arm around me and purrs. "That was Damian."

"Kind of late for him to call, isn't it?" Dev's phone as he puts it away reads 11:19 pm.

"Yeah, but I didn't respond to his e-mail. He's coming into town to meet with Fisher about the situation, and he wanted to take the chance to meet me too."

"Wow, an agent who actually travels to his clients for important meetings. Imagine that."

"Ogleby came down for the press conference." His ears go down.

I rest my muzzle against his neck. "Yeah, he did. He's a good guy at heart. Just not a very good agent."

His breath washes down my cheekfur and neck, and he kisses me. "No. Anyway, he wants to meet you, too. He's going to Fisher's house to meet him there, so he said we could just come over there again if we wanted to."

I nod and flick my tail across the couch. "As long as Gena's okay with it."

"She loves you. It'll be fine."

I look up at his striped muzzle and grin. "She loves me?"

"Yeah." He reaches up a paw behind my head and rubs at the base of my ears. "You can see how relaxed she is around you."

"Well, that's nice." I rest my paw across his chest and rub through his shirt.

"She doesn't love you like I love you."

"Mmm. That's probably good. Fisher'd be jealous." He chuckles, and then I reach my fingers up to his throat and rub where I can feel him purring. "Why don't you show me how you love me?"

CHAPTER SEVEN: CLOSED DOORS (DEV)

Thursday morning, I wake to an empty bed and the smell of coffee. A moment after I roll over and set the bedsprings creaking, a fox muzzle pokes around the bedroom door, followed a moment later by the rest of the fox, naked, holding a cup of coffee. "Morning, sleepy," he says, and sits at the edge of the bed. "When you don't have practice, you sleep late."

"Mmm." I reach out for the coffee. "Is that for me?"

He laughs and gives it to me. "Sure. I'm just using your fax machine to officially accept the Whalers' offer. I already called Peter and I'm just writing up the letter now."

"Talked to Gena yet?" I sip the coffee and wait for it to wake me up.

"Not yet. When was Damian supposed to be down? Two? So we have a morning together and then lunch, then head over there. Sound good?"

"Uh-huh." I put the coffee on the nightstand and pull him down atop me, and while we might not get all messy and sticky again, we enjoy just holding each other and having nothing in particular to get out of bed for.

During that time, I tell Lee that I started thinking about our relationship, and about what he would tell me to do about Gregory, and I end up telling him about Gregory's call and the call to my parents. He lies in my arms, big ears perked, and when I'm finished, he exhales across my muzzle.

"Sorry to hear about Alexi," he says.

"Yeah, I dunno, my dad says it's not serious but apparently it costs a lot of money to find out it's not serious." I pause. "Was it unreasonable? Saying he has to ask me himself?"

"Keeping in mind that I'm extremely biased..." He rubs a paw up my chest. "I don't think it was unreasonable. I think it'd be a nice thing for you to do, but at the same time, it feels like he resents your success, and giving him money isn't going to solve that problem."

"It might make it worse. Like I'm rubbing it in his face."

He nods. "So yeah, waiting until he asks you directly is probably a good idea."

My tail curls and thwaps the bed, and I hug him. "Okay. I feel a little better about it. Still pissed at him, though."

"Mmm." He slides his arms around me. "Yeah. So what did you think I would ask you to do about him?"

"Oh, just…" I try to remember. "Talk to him. Confront him directly. I thought you might ask me to make a public statement, but the trial isn't public and that'd be weird."

He shakes his head. "No, I think I'd ask you to try to convince him to drop the case."

"Dammit." I smack my head. "I didn't think of that one."

He kisses my nose. "But I'd understand if you didn't want to get into a whole thing."

I press my fingers into his back, rubbing down his spine. "Thanks, fox. I'm going to try not to."

What I don't tell him because I haven't quite finished thinking it through yet is that that conversation with Fisher rattled me. Right now, sure, I don't want to take any illegal chemicals, but what am I going to do in five years, or eight, or ten? What if that title is tantalizingly close and I twist an ankle, or get gored like Fisher, and someone tells me I just take this one injection this one time…? What if I think I can control the side effects and I lash out at Lee, hurt him even? He trusts me, and I don't want to let on that I'm scared I might be tempted.

Eventually we shower, and Lee starts packing for our trip to Yerba tomorrow. I ask if he's got a hotel reserved, and that sends him to his computer to make those reservations, but before he does that he has to sit staring at real estate and apartment listings to figure out what areas he wants to look at.

I sit with him, though to me the areas are just names on a map. I keep pointing at places that sound cool or goofy and saying, "You could live there," or "I've always wanted a house with a Mountain View. You think there are mountains there?"

"Hey," Lee says after about half an hour of this, "wasn't Polecki's boyfriend a Yerba player?"

"Yeah. The mule deer."

"Why don't you text Polecki? See if maybe he'll be up in Yerba when we are."

"Sure." I nod and take out my phone, with one last glance at his screen. "Are you just trying to stop me from telling you that you should not even be looking at Coyote's Point?"

"Depends which coyote," he says, and grins.

So I text Polecki, *Hey, I'm going to Yerba with my boyfriend. Any chance you'd be in the area?*

Lee's now figured out where he wants to look and is finding hotels in the area. His phone rings in the middle of it and it's his new boss. So I go to the kitchen, find eggs in the fridge, and heat up the stove.

And that's how our morning goes: making plans, making coffee, making breakfast. We avoid thinking about Fisher's problems and Gregory's problems, and for a few hours, the world cooperates. There are no phone calls, no arguments, no practice; an island of peace in our lives, even though the waves of future dramas lap at our shores. Polecki texts back to say that he and his boyfriend are in Crystal City but were heading up to Yerba this weekend for a family thing and would love to meet up. Lee's boss promises to bring along housing recommendations to the welcome meeting. Gena calls to tell us that she's ordering out from a barbecue place for lunch if we want to join them and Damian. We offer to pick up the food on our way over. Gerrard calls to ask if I'm free this weekend and I tell him I'll be back from Yerba in a week, that I thought the workouts hadn't started yet. He says they haven't, that he was just watching film of the championship game and wanted to talk about a couple things.

My instinct is to offer to go over there tonight, after Fisher's, because I want to please him and make sure we keep our good relationship. Then I think, hell, I've proven myself on the field and I deserve at least a week of relaxation away from football and Gerrard's unquenchable fire. I don't quite have the confidence to tell *him* to lay off the film, but I do say, "Hold those thoughts until next week. I'm just taking some time off, trying to relax."

"Enjoy that," he says, and hangs up.

"You know," I say to Lee, staring at the phone, "outside of football, Gerrard is kind of a dick."

"Passionate about the game," Lee says. "Hey, we have an hour and a half before we have to go. I've been wanting to see this movie you rented. Want to pop it in?"

I look at the envelope from the movie-delivery place that I requested like a month ago. "Sure."

So we sit and watch a movie, lose ourselves in gunshots and explosions, and don't worry about anything else for a while. It's a nice feeling, but my muscles feel bored and restless with inactivity when the movie's heroes are running around, and my mind feels bored when they're not. It's weird that there isn't a game to prepare for this weekend, nor next weekend; no plays to go over, no offense to prepare for. It's my second off-season, but this past season was so intense as a starter on a playoff team that I'm used to a whole different level of adrenaline now.

Even so, I don't really want to think about football specifically. Which makes me wonder, am I passionate enough? If I were going to be one of the great football players, would I be already reviewing film of the championship game like Gerrard is? Maybe I should be, but right now I don't even want to think about it. I'm enjoying relaxing and being Dev Miski, not number fifty-seven. Does that mean that if I were in Fisher's situation, that I wouldn't be tempted to break the law? That the title doesn't mean as much as I think it does, not enough to risk my future?

I'm twenty-four years old. I have a long time to figure out what my legacy is going to be. I don't want to get to the end of my career and find out that I don't have a life. I tell myself those things in my head, but still the itch remains.

•

The boxes of barbecued chicken and ribs from Uncle Bob's Southern Kitchen fills my truck with amazing smells, and by the time we get to Fisher's and bring it into the kitchen, my stomach's growling and I'm licking my lips compulsively.

"Patience." Gena's laughing as she takes it from me, watching me lick a bit of the sauce from one finger. "I'll have it on plates in a minute. Go meet Damian; he's in the living room."

Lee follows me in. Fisher's sitting on the couch staring out at the patio, and on the other side of the couch, holding his PDA-phone, is a pudgy tiger about a foot shorter than either of us. He stands and smooths down the light grey suit jacket he's wearing over the lime-green tie, and then I don't notice the pudge as much. His voice is the same as it is over the phone: deep, smooth, and confident.

"Dev? Damian. And you must be Lee." He grips my paw firmly, then releases it and takes Lee's. He's only a little taller than my fox, so they can almost see eye to eye, and he gives Lee his full attention when they shake paws.

Lee smiles, his tail swishing. "I am. Pleased to meet you."

"Dev tells me you've taken a position with the Whalers. Congratulations. I've worked with Peter quite a bit. Good fox, good organization. Big change from a few years ago. And I'm glad you're working again. What the Dragons did was wrong."

"Well," Lee says. "Technically it wasn't."

"Perhaps not." Damian releases his paw. "But it was unkind and unnecessary. You could make an argument that it was homophobic."

"Oh, I…" Lee flicks his ears back. "I didn't…"

"No, because you wanted to work in the league again. Smart choice. The league isn't ready to handle that kind of publicity yet. You'd have been given a settlement and never gotten a phone call returned again."

It's the first time I can remember someone beating Lee to the gay rights punch, and one of the few times I've seen my fox speechless. "Uh, yeah," he says.

"But anyway." Damian turns back to me and lifts his ears and whiskers with a warm smile. "Business can wait until after lunch. Is that Uncle Bob's I smell?"

His nostrils flare, and Gena beams. "I wouldn't get anything else for your visit."

"Delicious. Have you had it before?"

He's addressing me, and I shake my head. He claps me on the shoulder. "Best barbecue in Chevali. You'll see."

I haven't had a whole lot of barbecue in Chevali, but the ribs Gena serves us are pretty amazing. The meat is smoked and tender and the sauce spicy-sweet. Lee grabs one of the chicken pieces, which is so juicy it stains the white fur under his muzzle. We're all licking our fingers and reaching for more, and there's not much conversation other than praising the barbecue. The side dishes go neglected until the meat is gone, and then we start, slowly, on the black-eyed peas and the potato salad, and by the time the carryout boxes have been reduced to a pile of glistening brown-stained cardboard, I'm stuffed. I lean back in my chair and watch everyone else do the same. Even Gena is slow to start cleaning up.

Lee helps immediately, springing up with energy that makes me feel queasy. He and Gena clear the table as Damian, Fisher, and I talk about other restaurants in Chevali—rather, they talk and I take mental notes. And then Damian says to Fisher, "You ready to talk?"

"No." Fisher hunches in and stares down at his paws. "But I'm running out of time, right?" Damian nods. "Fine, then."

He shoves his chair back hard and then gets up and stomps toward the den. Damian rises more gracefully and nods to me. "Sorry. This shouldn't take more than half an hour or so."

I sit at the table, wondering what I'm going to do for half an hour, and then Gena comes out of the kitchen wiping her paws and sits down next to me. She looks toward the den. "Would you retire?" she asks softly.

In Fisher's situation, she means, and I've been thinking about just that so I have an answer ready. "I think so. I mean…" I rub my fingers over her yellow-checked tablecloth. "I don't know if I would have made a lot of the choices he has, so maybe I'm not the best one to ask about it. But I think I'd retire. If I had two rings and this family…or even my family."

" 'Even'?" Lee smiles from the kitchen doorway.

"You know what I mean." I lift my paws and notice brown smears on the tablecloth. "Oh…" I rub at them. "Sorry."

Gena frowns and then sees what I'm rubbing at and laughs, a little shakily. "That's what the tablecloth is for. Don't worry about it. Look." Even hers and Lee's, the cleanest spots, have some sauce spilled around them. "I'll throw it in the wash later."

Lee sits down with us. "Life after football is hard."

Gena's quiet for a moment and then says, "I worry about Junior."

Neither Lee nor I is expecting that. Lee leans forward. "Because of how he views his father?"

She shakes her head. "You've only seen him the past couple days. Usually when Fisher's around, he spends time with the boys. He's coached Junior with his football, he's talked about the things he does with the team. But now…"

"Well," I say, "he has a lot on his mind. It's only been a couple days." Lee nods in agreement.

"It's not just the last few days." She rests her paws on the table. "It's been ever since the injury. He's been brusquer. He spends more time just sitting in the den. Bradley's off to college in September; he can't wait to be gone anyway." Her voice gets wistful at that. "But Junior has two more years at home, and if his father is distant…"

"He'll snap out of it." Lee's voice has more confidence than I—and, I think, he himself—feel.

In the lull of conversation, which isn't exactly racing along anyway, we all hear raised voices from the den. Lee's ears go up, and Gena and I both look toward the living room and the hallway beyond. All the doors are open, and the sound carries.

Lee folds his ears down with a guilty expression. "If you don't mind," he says gently to Gena, "I never asked you, but do you have any idea where Fisher would have gotten the somatotropin? It's not exactly something you can walk over to the drugstore and pick up."

Gena shakes her head. "I thought about that, but I never heard anyone else mention it. There was one player, on the Rocs, an older one who used it, we think. There were reports later…Fisher might have called him. He's retired now."

"That was before…" Lee stops. "Well, it's a possibility. There could also have been players on the Manticores. Or on the Firebirds, for that matter. Just because they haven't been caught yet doesn't mean they're not using."

I think about Gerrard and his passion for the game. But he's a few years younger than Fisher, and he's still in excellent shape. He probably hasn't had to face those decisions yet.

"Why does it matter?" Gena asks. "Is someone else going to get in trouble?"

Lee shakes his head, and I notice he still has a spot of sauce on the white fur of his chin. "I don't know if anyone's going to get in trouble," he says. "I was just wondering."

I reach over and clean up his chin, and he smiles at me. I think again about poor Fisher, and then about Hal's article. "Gena, do you think it would help Fisher to talk to someone? About life after football?"

"You mean like a counselor? I don't think so. He's enjoyed talking to you, but I don't think he'd talk to anyone official."

Lee meets my eyes and his eyebrows rise as I go on. "Lee's friend Hal— our friend—is writing an article about players living after football." I take a breath. "He's kind of focusing on the damage done by the game. If Fisher would talk to him, maybe he could tell Fisher how some of these other guys deal with it. Maybe put him in touch with them."

Gena's ears go back when I mention writing an article. "He has friends who have retired. I don't think he would want to talk to the press."

"Sure," Lee jumps in, "and Hal doesn't want to pressure him. But the reason he's writing this article is not to tear down the league, but to make the game safer for the people playing it now."

Her eyes widen, but she shakes her head again. "I don't think…I mean, I would love for him to have someone to talk to, but…"

"It'd be his decision, of course. We're just trying to figure out how to approach him so he doesn't immediately shut it down." Lee talks carefully, earnestly. "And if you think we shouldn't approach him at all, then we won't."

"For sure not when he's upset," I say.

She holds up her paws. "Okay, all right. I think it's a good thing, but…I don't know how he'll react. I really don't."

"For what it's worth," Lee says, "I think the article is going to do a lot of good. It'd be important to have someone as recently active as Fisher contribute, especially if he retires. Maybe next week, once the emotions have cooled down."

"And we don't have to talk about it again until then." I feel bad for bringing it up already, and not only because I'm back to wondering if Fisher is my future. When I'm on the threshold of losing football, will I grow sullen and withdrawn? And then I think about something else: what if Lee's stress and anger and all the things that made the last few months difficult stemmed from losing his job and his parents, losing his direction in life, and I reacted like he was specifically trying to inconvenience me?

I'm glad to change the subject to Bradley's college; he's going to Fort Green about an hour north of Highbourne with a lot of his friends from ten years ago. They got back in touch on ScentBook and visited the college together. He's not going to play football and he might not even play basketball. "He wants to be a doctor," Gena says with fondness, "Specializing in orthopedic surgery. He wants to fix up football players."

"That's great." Lee starts to add more, but then the den door is yanked open and slammed shut.

We all turn to look. Fisher stomps through the living room, stops just long enough to call to Gena, "I'm going for a walk," and then another door slides open and shut.

A moment later, the den door opens again. Damian walks into the living room on soft pads. He stops and nods to all of us, letting the silence linger for a moment before he breaks it. "He's going to retire. We were just working up the official statement. I'll call the Firebirds with it, and then Dev, I'll sit down with you."

He disappears into another room. We stay silent, and even my tiger ears hear Damian on the phone. "I'm calling on behalf of Fisher Kingston. I'm faxing over a statement now. Can you confirm that you're receiving it? Yes, he's announcing his retirement. He wants to thank the Firebirds organization for providing him with three years of unparalleled experiences and one more taste of the championship game, but with his sons growing up, he wants to spend time with them during their last high school years and their college experiences. He will always treasure the friendships and memories from his time in Chevali, and most of all the passion of the fans here. Yep. Uh-huh. Sure. Well, do you want to highlight it or bury it? Or don't care? Okay, then let's say Monday at nine a.m. We can do it at the Firebirds offices, right? Great, thanks."

Gena and Lee and I all stay quiet around the table. "I found a couple good services that provide live-in help," Lee says when Damian finishes talking and still hasn't come out. "I'll send the links along."

"Thanks." Gena's eyes slide toward the door where Fisher left. "Felice said she's got a couple friends who have needed help, and she's bringing some phone numbers."

"He'll be over the concussion in a few weeks." I don't know if I believe it, but I want to make her feel better.

The sentiment lands awkwardly, because neither Lee nor Gena really believes it. I can see it in the splayed ears, the eyes that won't meet mine. "I hope so," Gena says finally.

"This week'll be hard." Lee reaches out a paw to her.

"Oh, God, yes." Gena exhales and looks between us. "You know, I met some other players who looked forward to retirement. The constant pounding of the season got to them. Maria Johnson in Highbourne said her husband promised her they'd travel when they retired. I got an e-mail from her last month from Firenza. Ally Porter and her husband talk about their cubs on Scentbook all the time. He doesn't talk about missing football. But Fisher…Fisher only ever talked about it as 'the day they make me quit.' He never wanted to."

I try not to plunge back into that morass in my own thoughts, even though Lee's looking at me and probably wondering what those thoughts are. "It had to happen sometime. He'll get used to it."

It sounds lame, so I'm glad when Damian comes out to talk to me. Lee flashes me a smile as I get up and follow the short tiger into the den.

He sits on Fisher's desk, which is a little weird, but I guess there aren't many places to sit, and it lets him be at about my height. I glance around the room; my eyes skip over the trains and settle on the championship display case.

Damian starts out with a "nice to meet you" and regrets that it's under these circumstances, and then he turns his head and follows my gaze to the rings. "Is that what you want?"

"Well, uh. Yeah. Who wouldn't?" I grin.

He stays serious. "I mean, what drives you? Some guys want the rings. Some guys just want all the money they can get. Some guys want fame. Some guys want girls."

I raise an eyebrow. "You get girls for guys?"

"No. But I can get them money and teach them how to use it effectively."

"Wow, agent and matchmaker." I flatten my ears. "Sorry, that came out wrong. I just mean…"

"It's okay." He smiles briefly, then returns to being all business. "A sense of humor is a good thing. It'll keep you sane. Football's a tough sport. That's why I encourage my clients to focus on their goals."

"Wouldn't you prefer I get the most money?" This is such a different philosophy from Ogleby, who never even discussed any goals other than "make all the money you can," that I'm having difficulty processing it. Like

if my English teacher had shown up one day in high school and told us we were only going to read sports magazines for the rest of school.

Damian nods. "Of course. That's my job and it's how I get paid. But I'll be honest with you: even if money isn't your primary goal, you're still going to make a lot of it. And so will I. We're talking maybe a difference of ten million over a career where you'll make sixty."

I gape at him. "Sixty million dollars?"

"Quick math." He holds up three fingers. "This is the number of years an average UFL player plays. It's also the length of your rookie deal. A little over a million total from the team over three years, I'm guessing. I don't have the file from them yet."

"Right," I say.

"How much was the Strongwell commercial?"

"A million."

"Okay." He holds up all ten fingers on both paws. "This is the average length of a career of a player who's made the starting lineup in his second year. So we've got seven more years to work with. Marvell's making about twelve million this year; Omba's making three and a half. Let's say we can get you four in your fourth year and it never goes up beyond that. It will, but just as a minimum. That's 28 million over the rest of your career, thirty total. Now salaries go up by a little each year. I'm not saying you'll be getting Marvell's salary by the end of your career, but if you just play the kind of football you've been playing and you stick with teams and so on, probably that number goes up to..." He waggles his paws. "Forty-five, let's say. There's a renegotiation of the agreement between the players and owners coming up in four years that might bump that number up or down slightly, but I'm pretty confident that if you play ten years, you'll have pulled in forty-five million in team salaries, and that's not including playoff bonuses. You know those go up when you have more experience, right?"

"Uh…I didn't. I thought everyone got the same."

The fur around his eyes wrinkles when he smiles. "Marvell got more than a forty-thousand dollar check for making the playoffs."

"But…everyone got the same check. At the banquet, I mean." And mine is still at home somewhere.

"Sure." He flicks his tail against the desk. "Owners do that to make everyone feel the same. The other checks get sent out privately. Anyway. Not important. The point is, forty-five. And with your recent championship run, you can get at least ten million in endorsements even if you don't stay in Chevali. If you stay, hometown hero. If you leave, you'll be the guy bringing the championship experience to a new town. And as the first gay player out, you can probably get at least another five, and that's a conservative estimate because it's never been done and I have no idea what the market is like for it."

"Wow." I'm as impressed by his breakdown of the numbers as I am by the numbers themselves.

"Which reminds me, I meant to add one more potential goal: do you want to be an ambassador? I can set up speaking engagements—paid ones—and I'm sure there are other opportunities if I look around."

He has his paws clasped in his lap, and my first thought is, Dammit, Lee got to him already. But I feel bad thinking that and dismiss it. Damian's very businesslike and clearly is just running through my options. "Lee's the ambassador," I say. "I know he's just starting a new job, but he's the one who's all passionate about gay rights and stuff. And he's way better at speaking than I am. He was an English major."

"Okay. Look, we can do all of this stuff. Focusing on winning a championship doesn't mean you won't make money. Aiming for the big payday doesn't mean you can't do some outreach stuff on the side. At least you and Polecki can talk to some owners about how to make their teams more accommodating to gay players."

I tilt my head. "People want that?"

"Some owners do. Or at least, they say they do. I'm new to this. But you can do stuff within the league too, and you probably should. It'd be good for your image behind the scenes, which counts for more than you know." He grins at me. "And it's a good thing to do."

"I got enough of the image talk with Lightning Strike," I say. "But yeah, I get it."

"So? What do you think your top goal is? Off the top of your head. Don't think too much."

"Championship," I say. "But not to the exclusion of everything else. I do want to do some ambassador stuff, and I want to earn my pay."

"Sure, sure." He smiles and turns his head to look at Fisher's memorabilia.

I look, too. "You can't guarantee a championship, though."

"Dev," he says, turning back to me, "if I could, you'd have one. No, I know you weren't my client this year, but Fisher was. Couple other Firebirds too, but Fisher was the one I wanted to take care of."

I raise my eyebrows. "You got Fisher to go to the Firebirds when they were terrible because you thought they could win a championship?"

He ticks off points on his fingers. "Most of the pieces of a good defense, but a need for a defensive end. Competent quarterback, borderline star running back. Good wideouts. Most importantly, a GM in his third year who'd been successful elsewhere and had been building the team according to a philosophy I believe in. And it helped that New Kestle and Kerina were going to be terrible, and Hellentown was taking a step back. Well, two out of three, anyway. I thought there was an opportunity last year, but it turns out Coach Samuelson, and maybe you, were the missing pieces."

"So would you recommend I stay in Chevali?"

He considers the question. "Let me see what else is out there. There are a half dozen teams with strong management in place where I could see you contributing to a championship. It depends on which of them need a line-backer. If you're more focused on a championship than fame or money, you could potentially land as a strong backup to an established squad."

Go back to sitting on the bench or sharing time? My paws tighten. "If I win a championship, I want to be part of it." Like Polecki said when I talked to him, he barely played the year he won his first ring, and this recent one meant so much more.

"Of course. But would you rather start for ten years and not win, or start for seven and back up for three and win one?" He waves a paw. "It's a hard question. Never mind. I'll do some research and see who's willing to pay what. For the moment, let's assume you're going to stay in Chevali, because they have the most invested in you. They may be willing to offer an extension this year, but more likely they'll want to wait one more year and see."

"Gambling that I won't do as well next year."

"With some teams, yeah. With Chevali, I think I would view it as being very cautious with their investment. Lots of teams throw millions at guys who were very good for a quarter of a season and then never get that good again. Rodriguez doesn't like to play that game, which is why I like to get my players to work with him. I think you'll command more money next year than you would this year, but I'll still sniff around for you."

I'm going to thank him, but the den door bangs open then and Fisher stalks in. He stops and stares at the two of us, and then his gaze settles on Damian. "Did you send it in?"

"Yep. Nine a.m. Monday."

"Huh." Fisher's tail snaps back and forth. "I have to go down there?"

"Ideally, but you can do it on conference call if you want. These things go better in person." Damian talks about ending Fisher's career with the same poise with which he discussed planning mine. "You need help writing something else to say, or you just want to read the statement?"

"Do I have to do this?"

The room goes still. Now Damian's voice is gentle. "It's the best way."

"But is it the only way? Dammit, you promised me you could find me one more ring! You promised!"

Damian looks at me and licks his lips. "Dev, do you want to give us a minute?"

I get up, and Fisher says, "No. Both of you get out. I'll write something."

Both Damian and I pause. We look at each other and then at Fisher. "You, ah, want to talk?" I ask.

"Get out!" he yells, and then presses a paw to his head and stumbles toward the desk. Damian hops off it and scoots out of his way before the big tiger gets there, and joins me at the door.

"If you need anything…" I say, hesitating with Damian already out and heading for the living room.

Fisher slumps into his desk chair and waves a paw at me. "I'm fine. Just leave me alone."

I close the door slowly. I'm not thinking about the end of my career anymore. I just wish I could do something to help my friend.

And Damian stops and rests a paw on my arm. "Listen, Dev," he says. "Can you be around for Fisher's retirement?"

"I—" Lee pokes his head out of the kitchen just then. "Lee and I are going to Yerba to look for houses. I don't know when we're getting back."

"Tuesday morning," Lee says. "It was a cheaper flight and I wanted to spend Monday there in case I need to do some legal stuff about the housing."

Damian considers that. "How early? We could do a Tuesday noon thing."

"I think we get in around ten." Lee pulls out his phone. "We can move it to earlier if it'll help Fisher."

"Yeah," I say. "Anything to help."

Chapter Eight: Reports (Lee)

Damian seems like a good guy. At the very least, he's a competent agent, which is going to be a great change for Dev. I ask Gena a little about him to pass the time while he's in Fisher's den with Dev, and she tells me he suggested Chevali for Fisher because he thought it'd be the best fit. "At the time, we thought, 'Move to the desert, to a terrible team?' I think they were 3-13 that year. But he told us they had a good organization." She laughs. "Of course, he said that about Pelagia too, and they were terrible the whole time. But Fisher didn't have a good coach, and the workouts they did, well, he ended up tweaking muscles almost every year he was there. He didn't complain, just played when he could, but it showed."

"I remember, sort of." I didn't follow Fisher specifically, but I remember how Pelagia always seemed to have worse luck with injuries than the rest of the league.

"I didn't believe Chevali would be different, and uprooting the boys…" She sighs. "It almost worked out. One point."

"Would it have been more worthwhile if we'd won?"

She looks down at the tablecloth. "Can you help me clear the table?"

While we do that, she says, "I don't want to say that coming to Chevali was all bad. The boys were frustrated, but they made friends here. I like it better than Pelagia. I know some people like the northwest, but it really does seem like it was grey or drizzling just about every day even though I know that isn't true. And the other wives…" She shakes her head. "The older I get, the less I have in common with them. I thought when I was in Highbourne that we would all age together, but a lot of them, their husbands aren't playing anymore, so they just fall out of the community. They go to picnics and Rotary with their neighbors, and their husbands only made hundreds of thousands instead of millions, so they resent those of us who made more. And a lot of the younger players coming in now aren't getting married early like our generation did, so they don't have wives." She meets my eyes. "Or spouses. They have groups of college friends who don't want to hang out with other people's spouses."

"That's frustrating. I thought I'd always be friends with my college friends, but…things happen." I think about Brian, and about the less dramatic drifting apart of Salim and Allen, Daniel and Liz. Everybody went their separate ways; it wasn't just me retreating into my football world, because I know Salim doesn't talk to anyone outside his family, mostly, and Daniel broke up with Jake and moved to Anglia, and Allen is still living in Hilltown probably hitting on college students, and nobody's heard from Liz in forever. Even Brian's and my strained relationship was more than he or I had from anyone else once we'd graduated.

"They do." We move the last of the dishes to the kitchen, and Gena gathers up the tablecloth. "But it was in Pelagia that it first hit me. I didn't know it was going to happen. If not for Felice, I don't know what I'd have done."

I follow her to the laundry room and lean on the door as she throws the tablecloth into the washer. "For what it's worth," I say, "I know Dev and I still want to be your friends, retirement or no."

"I know." She starts the machine and smiles at me. "I'm grateful for that, believe me."

"I think Angela will, too. Are they the only other family with two boys?"

Gena nods slowly. "Angela's already talked to me. I should call her and tell her about Fisher. Gerrard will want to know." She rests her paw on the machine's lid, feeling the vibrations, and looks down at it. "I hope she's doing all right."

"Angela?"

She takes a moment, thinking something over, and then she looks up. "Oh, she told me Gerrard is annoying in the off-season. Always stalking about the house, reviewing film, wanting to play football with the boys."

"Playing doesn't sound bad."

"Hah." She leads me into the living room, where we sit on the couch much as we did yesterday. "He wants them to run routes and he yells at them when they don't do it properly. And they aren't old enough to tell him to shut up and have fun."

Fisher opens the patio door and stalks in, tail lashing. "Where are they?" he demands when he gets to the living room.

I feel again that tension of not knowing what's going to happen next, of the potential for something bad to erupt. Gena stands and holds out a paw, then gestures to the den when he doesn't move toward her. "Honey, we'll get through this. You'll be fine. It's bad now, but—"

He ignores her, crossing the living room in long strides. "Can't wait to have all these people out of the goddamn house," he growls, and then disappears into the den. A moment later, we hear raised voices.

Gena sits and looks awkwardly at me. "I'm sorry," she says.

"Don't even worry." I raise a paw, letting the tension drain out. "It's a stressful time. Maybe Dev and I should leave when he's done with Damian."

"Who's done with Damian?" The tiger himself comes down the hall from the den and brushes his suit jacket down. Dev walks up behind him, towering over him. I know Dev's taller than me, but it's slightly odd to see him so much larger than another tiger.

"We were just talking about Fisher." Gena turns to greet both tigers.

"You're not quite done with me yet." Damian walks over to sit in one of the chairs near the couch. "There's still a lot an athlete can do after retirement. If you need advice on post-career management, I can help with that. He can still do endorsements and coaching or broadcasting if he wants. Take a year off, maybe two, see the cubs off to college, then think about the next phase. He and I talked about all that."

Gena perks up. "Did he say what he wants to do?"

"Well, no." Damian ducks his head. "He's very focused on not being able to play anymore. But if you have those possibilities in mind, you can discuss them with him when this has worn off."

Dev comes over to stand behind the couch where I'm sitting, and rests his paw on the arm I have draped over the back. I smile up at him, but his return smile is distracted. "Thought about what you want to do when you retire in ten years?" I ask, jokingly.

"Roll around in my seven championship rings," he says, and everyone chuckles.

Damian leaves a little while later. Dev and I talk with Gena a little longer, and then just as we stand to make our good-byes, a car screeches to a halt in front of the house. Gena folds her arms and glares at the door, and as soon as Bradley comes in, Junior trailing behind him, she reprimands her older son for his driving.

"Sorry," the teenager mutters, and makes a beeline for the stairs to his room.

I say good-bye to Junior, and he says, "Mom, can I play one game of FBA with Lee?"

Gena tells him it depends on whether we want to stay, so I say that of course we will. So we all go to the living room, where three of us talk about the movie Dev and I watched that morning and two of us play video basketball (me being the one doing both).

When the first game's over, Junior checks to see whether Gena's paying attention, and then quickly starts another one with the same players. I don't say anything, just keep going, both of us cross-legged on the floor in front of the couch.

We're in the second quarter of that game when Fisher emerges from the den. "I'm going to sit on the patio for a bit," he says, and his eyes slide over me and Dev. "I'm looking forward to a nice quiet family dinner tonight. Dev, Lee…nice to see you."

"Yeah," Dev says, raising a paw. "See you Tuesday."

But Fisher's already on his way out, and slides the glass door closed without any indication that he heard.

Dev and I look at each other. Junior pauses the game and glances back at his mom. "I guess we should go," Dev says.

I put down the controller. "Sorry. Can I get a raincheck on the game?"

"Sure," Junior pauses it and gets up to say good night.

We say our good-byes and Gena wishes us luck in Yerba. And Dev and I stay quiet in the truck for the first half of the way home. Then he clears his throat. "Damian seemed cool with setting up, like, outreach stuff."

I perk my ears. "Oh?"

"Yeah. So…what outreach stuff do you think I could do? I know you wanted me to do those spots for Equality Now, but you're not working with them anymore." He steers with one paw and rests the other on the dashboard. "Also, I was thinking…I'd like to do something that helps kids, you know?"

"Uh-huh." I think about that, and then think again about my friends from FLAG. "I guess I could reach out to Forester, see if maybe you could do something with them."

"Like what?"

"Ah, I dunno." I watch the highway roll by as we go up to our exit. "Maybe just come and talk to the team? It'd be good for Forester too. They still get mentioned now and then as the place the gay guy got beaten up."

Dev grimaces even though I didn't mention Brian by name. "Maybe Damian can talk to them. I trust him a lot more than Ogleby already."

"Good idea." I smile. "And I won't bug you to do more than he advises you to."

"Does this count as figuring out relationship stuff?" He turns toward me and raises an eyebrow.

I pat his thigh and leave my paw there. "Absolutely."

PART II

CHAPTER NINE: HOMES (LEE)

The whole way to Yerba, Dev complains about the flight not being first class. I booked it in coach out of habit, and his knees are right up against the seat in front of him when the flight attendants bring the drink carts through with their repeated warnings of, "Please clear your tails from the aisle." When they pass, he can stretch his legs out, but there's always someone walking up and down, and he has to move his feet or they trip over them.

"You should be more flexible, like me," I tell him, sitting in the middle, even though the cougar in front of me has his tail hanging down and constantly flicking back and forth around my legs. At least I'm keeping my own tail curled under the seat like a polite passenger.

"It's not about flexibility, it's about size," he grumbles.

I don't say anything until he looks at me, and then I raise an eyebrow and grin. He plays back his words in his head and then rolls his eyes. "Foxes," he growls.

"See, this is what you have to get used to when you don't have a private jet to fly you everywhere. Anyway, it's only a two-hour flight. When I was working for the Dragons, I flew minimum three hours every time, coming down to see you or going out to the East Coast for work."

"Don't know how you managed it." He opens up the in-flight magazine and tries to read again, just as someone else nearly trips over his feet.

"Lots of Neutra-Scent," I tell him, and take one of the tissues out, because even though the newer planes have pretty good air circulation, I can still smell everyone crammed into the seats around me and it's giving me a headache.

We land and rent a car, and with him navigating, I find the hotel with only a little trouble. The room is nice, though the view isn't as nice as the last time I stayed here: it looks out onto the parking lot.

"Bed's firm enough." Dev jumps onto it and sprawls there. "Feels good to stretch my legs."

"I got a full size car." I check my phone again. "You think I should call Gena?"

"If you want, but she's probably busy with her friend showing up today and all." He stares at the ceiling.

"Yeah, I know." I put the phone into my pocket and sit on the bed. He doesn't move as I rest my paw on his stomach. "Thinking a lot about you and how your career's going to end. I hope it won't be like that."

"Not if I can help it." His other paw covers mine.

"Also wondering if Fisher's going to be charged with a crime."

"All right." Dev squeezes my paw. "Look, we're here to find you a place to live, so if you want to talk about Fisher some more, you've got five minutes. Then we're going to go out, see some places, go to one of those nice lunch spots you found, and we're going to have a good day."

I smile at him and turn around, lying down and pinning his arm to the bed. "Fair enough. What if I want to talk about our relationship?"

"We can do that over lunch." He draws his paw along my tail. "Anything else?"

I sigh and nestle against him. "How much time do we have left?"

"Hmm. Four and a half minutes."

"Okay." I rest my muzzle against his shoulder and exhale.

We rest there for a little longer than four and a half minutes, but in the end his stomach growls, and I laugh and pat it and then he rolls on top of me and kisses me, holding my cheek ruffs in his paws. "You ready to go out?"

"Uh-huh." I stroke claws down his sides. "Sounds like you're good and hungry."

"Maybe we'll hit the lunch places first." He purrs against my chest.

We do, checking out the sushi place that Peter Emmanuel took me to for my interview with the Whalers. I don't take Dev to the back room, but the sushi is just as delicious in the front near the windows. The only problem is that Dev thinks the pieces are really tiny, so he orders about six rolls, gets through four of them, and then stares down at the plate. "How can I be full already?"

I laugh. "It's a lot of rice. Also you're not working out so much."

He frowns and growls. "Can we take this with us? It's really good."

I swish my tail, smiling because I'm glad he likes it as much as I do. "We can stop back at the hotel to put it in the room fridge."

So there's only time to see three of the apartments on my list before the rental offices close for the day. After that I suggest we stop at a Starbucks to have a drink.

"I thought you hated Starbucks." Dev squints up at the sign as we go in.

"Their tea is all right," I say, holding the door for him.

I get iced tea and he gets coffee, and we look at the info for the three places, comparing them. None of them really jumps out at either of us. "Maybe you should buy a condo. It's a better investment."

"That supposes I'll be living here for a while."

"I have confidence in you." He sips the coffee. "I don't see why you don't like this."

I stick my tongue out. "I could always rent for the first year and then buy."

"What did your dad tell you?"

"He wants me to buy, but he also wanted me to graduate college. Some things aren't realistic."

A smile creases his striped muzzle. "I like that I'm the one with a college degree."

"Yeah, yeah. I'll go back and finish it sometime. When Professor Shithead dies."

He snorts and takes another drink of coffee. "I liked the second apartment. It had a nice big patio."

"The first one was closer to the downtown."

"And how often are you going to be home and able to walk down there?"

"I walked lots of places from your apartment in Chevali."

It had all been very comforting, this talk of me being busy with a job and Dev visiting, and then I had to go and bring up the time I walked out on him. My good mood fades and I bury my nose in my tea.

"Well," he says after an awkward pause, "the third one was cheap and functional."

"Hey," I say, "while we're thinking about how busy I'm going to be all the time, what do you want to do tonight?"

"Dinner?"

"And after?"

He leans forward and makes a low purr in his throat. I shift in my seat. "Okay, and before that?"

"Does there have to be something between bed and dinner?" He waggles his eyebrows.

As tempting as it is to think about rolling around with him in bed, I kind of want to unwind a little and I feel like going out with him. "How about some dancing?"

"You mean going back to Korsat Street?" He frowns. "Isn't that sort of out of the way?"

"Yeah." I lean back in my chair and uncurl my tail, swishing it to fluff it out. "I could use a little unwinding after this week."

"But dancing?"

"Sure." I lean forward and widen my smile so my cheeks fluff up. "I want to go out with you and I don't feel like finding a new place to go where we can dance together."

"Aw. Yeah, okay." His smile gets pretty wide and he taps a rhythm out on the table, matching the music that's going throughout the shop. "I'm still not that good a dancer, though."

"Hey, neither am I. We'll just have to watch the people who are good. Can't you take lessons from Ty or something?"

"There's not a lot of time during football season. Mostly our lessons are focused on, you know, winning games." He finishes his coffee. "So where's dinner?"

Dinner is a really nice Sonoran place, which I pick even though we have a lot of them in Chevali. It's a fusion kind of place, so the food might not be authentic, but it's really good, blue corn tortillas and octopus ceviche and lamb shank marinated in Muscat wine wrapped in banana leaves and carnitas, which I know is traditional but this one has a different kind of salsa with it than what we get at the taquerias in Chevali.

Dev is wary at first, but he trusts me and soon enough is devouring everything and ordering seconds. We're pretty stuffed by the time we stagger out to the car. "You sure you want to go dancing still?" Dev asks.

"We've got to work out that meal somehow." I elbow him. "Since you don't have workouts anymore. Come on, I'll drive."

And actually, as it takes us half an hour to get up to Korsat Street and about twenty minutes to find a place to park, we're feeling more able to dance by the time we roll up to The Floor, the club we went to last time. Because it's Friday night, there's a bunch of people waiting to get in. "Can't we just walk in?" Dev asks, following me to the back of the line.

"It moves fast, and I'm not trying to impress your friends this time." I tug him back into line. "Besides, this way we attract less attention."

"I guess that's a good thing." He still fidgets as we shuffle our way forward.

It takes us only about fifteen minutes to get to the door. The bouncer is a big polar bear, and I think it's the same one we had last time. Sure enough, when Dev gets up to him, he says, "Wait. Miski? You know you can just come right to the door, right? Owner's orders."

"Didn't want to presume." Dev glares at me.

"You should be grateful," I say after we thank the bouncer and walk in. "Now you look like a nice guy."

Dev's reply is lost in the rapid percussion and shouted conversations of The Floor. It takes me a moment to adjust to the rainbow strobes and fog of noise, but the gyration of bodies is familiar, and as soon as I see it, I get excited.

It's not that I'm a great dancer. I danced a bit in college, then gave it up when I started dating Dev, mostly because I didn't have anyone to go with anymore. When I went with the football team a few months ago, I had a lot of fun, although I lost sight of that in the enjoyment of setting up Vonni to get a blow job from a star-struck leopard femme. Well, I meant it for Ty; how was I to know the married guy would swoop in?

Anyway, it's a part of gay culture I hadn't lived in for a while and it was fun, so I was excited to come back with Dev when I could just enjoy it. There weren't too many moments like that with the playoff pressure and then our problems, and maybe I originally thought that coming back here would, like, reconnect us or something. But now it seems like a great ending to a great evening, another way to clear away the stress of the last few days, to give us a glimpse of a more or less normal life together. Once I'm living here, maybe we can come here regularly.

We both dance stiffly at first, trying to loosen up. It takes him about twenty minutes and most of a beer before his smile becomes genuine and his movement gets more of that fluid grace he has on the football field. I match his energy, glad he's enjoying himself.

A couple guys dance up near us and one puts his paw on my tail. Dev scares him away pretty quick with a glare that melts into a smile once the guy's gone. Then he takes my paws and spins me around, and we keep on dancing.

"All right," he says when we take a break. "This was a good idea. I'm having fun. The music is pretty good, and I'm not worried about how my teammates are going to react."

I laugh and lean back against the bar, my muzzle right up against his shoulder so we can hear each other. "It's really nice to have time with you away from your team. Although here, there's a lot of big guys around. Check out that horse. He's not much smaller than Charm."

He shakes his head. "No way. Charm's got better shoulders and his mane's different. Now, let's see…oh, that fox over there could be on our team. He reminds me of Ty. His ears have those narrower points and he kinda moves like…"

He trails off. I follow his gaze and see a tall fox tearing it up with a shorter wolf. They're part of the thickest crowd, over by the DJ, and the only reason they stand out is because the fox is so tall. He shakes his head back and forth, and then a bright yellow light catches him as he turns in profile.

Dev makes a noise, and when I turn to look at him, he's just staring. "It's not Ty, is it? Dev?"

"I…I'm not sure…" He frowns.

"He does know the club, and maybe he's in Yerba to talk to the team or something? Does he live around here?" I watch the fox. I don't know Ty as well as Dev does, so I have no idea if this tall fox is him or not. He's got on a silk shirt that gleams under the lights, and a low-collar tank top underneath it. The wolf has on a similar shirt but a darker t-shirt under it, and something that glitters around his neck.

"I don't think so. He's from around Pelagia." He keeps staring. "Wait, it's not him. No, it is. It definitely is."

"We should go say hi." I start to walk toward the fox, until Dev grabs my shoulder and pulls me back.

"No. If he doesn't want people to know he's here, then I don't want to go over."

I fall back into my spot right next to him. "He doesn't know you're here. Okay, fine, wait until he sees you then."

So we stand by the bar and watch Ty, or the fox who looks a lot like him, as he and the wolf dance through that song, their shirts flowing around them the way their tails do (at least when I get a glimpse of them through the crowd). At the end of a song, they walk toward the bar, and I'm waiting for them to look our way, but they're deep in conversation, laughing and bumping each other back and forth, and then the fox grabs the wolf and kisses him on the lips.

"I guess it's not him," I say to a staring, silent Dev.

And then the fox looks up from the kiss and sees Dev. He freezes on the dance floor, and even a wily fox can't hide the shock of recognition. The wolf says something to him, then looks ahead, and recognition dawns there, too, if a little slower.

"What the fuck is going on?" Dev growls beside me.

•

We find a corner that is marginally less loud than the rest of the club. Ty and the wolf, who introduces himself as Arch, get beers while Dev and I point out where we'll be.

"If he was fucking gay this whole time and didn't say anything, if he let me take all of that and all this time he could've…"

"Maybe he just hooked up when we went to the club? Or just came back and…" I struggle.

"He asked me if I was on top!"

I fold my ears down. "What?"

"Ty! He was the one—one of the ones—who said 'you're the guy, right?' He was all worried about who was doing the fucking." He growls. "I'm pretty sure it was him…I guess it might've been Vonni."

"Okay, look." I put a paw on his arm. "Let him talk. Don't get all worked up like this. It's probably really hard for him." I'm thinking of the other teammate of Dev's that I know is gay, the bear Kodi. If this is how Dev reacts to Ty, I can't imagine how he'd have reacted if Kodi had told him, which I'm assuming Kodi hasn't, because Dev hasn't said anything to me about it.

"He's probably ducking out the back." Dev stares in the direction of the bar. "He's probably not even going to come over."

But Ty does come over, with Arch trailing behind him, and they set down their beers. There's a moment of silence, or at least of uninterrupted club noise, and then Ty takes a breath. "Hey, Dev. Didn't know you were in town."

"Lee got a job here with the Whalers. I was looking at apartments with him." Dev's voice is low and hard to hear over the music. "I didn't know you were here, either."

"Right." Ty looks down. "You won't tell anyone else on the team, will you?"

Dev's ears don't come up and his brow stays lowered. "I'm not here with anyone else on the team." He realizes that doesn't really answer the question and catches himself. "I won't tell them."

"Thanks." The other breathes out and grins, and his eyes flick over to the wolf. "So, uh, this. I met Arch when we came here in December. We talked—just talked—and after the game I hung out with him a bit more. And we just kept texting, and look, it was because I knew you that I thought hey, what's the harm in trying?"

"Trying? What are you trying?" Dev leans forward. "Trying being gay?"

I catch Arch's eye. He's relaxed, doesn't seem offended. So it's not serious between them. Ty confirms that a second later.

"I'm not gay." The wolf stays quiet, but Ty's ears and eyes flick toward him. He clears his throat. "Maybe a little bi. I like girls, but it turns out I don't mind doing stuff with the right guy either. Arch is pretty cool, but I haven't been, like, checking out other guys or anything here."

"Oh, my fluttering heart," the wolf says.

"So this has been going on since December?" Dev's still worked up, trying to figure out how mad he should be with Ty.

"Oh, hell no." Ty grins back at the wolf. "I mean, he flirted with me over text…"

"Me?" Arch shoves the fox's shoulder. "You're the one who asked if I'd blow you."

Ty's ears go flat and he looks guiltily at Dev, but he's still got a wide fox grin on his muzzle. "How else was I supposed to find out?"

"Fuck," Dev says. "I can't believe you didn't come talk to me."

"Really?" Ty says, nodding his head toward me. " 'Cause I figured Lee wouldn't be too happy if I asked *you* to blow me."

Dev just stares at him while I break into giggles and then clamp a paw over my muzzle. Ty leans across the table, more serious now. "It's a joke. Hey, seriously, look, I'm sorry, but you were—we were all just up to our fuckin' ears in the playoff shit and I figured I'd sort it out myself and then I promise I was gonna come talk to you about it." He turns his head slightly to the wolf and his ears splay a bit. "I mean, I can't really talk to the other guys about this nice piece of ass I found if there's a cock on the other side of it, right?"

"Oh, is that how it is?" Arch folds his arms. "Maybe I'll just go back to my place tonight."

"Yeah, maybe," Ty says cheerfully. "Until I remind you about the fluffy robes and the bread pudding and the view at the hotel."

"God dammit." The wolf shakes his head and meets my eye. "Rich guys, what the fuck are you gonna do?"

I clear my throat. "Hey, you wanna leave these two to chat a bit?"

"You don't have to go," Dev growls.

"It's okay." I raise a paw. "We'll just hit the, uh, bathroom or something."

Arch gets up to join me, and we walk along the wall toward the bathrooms. "Hey," he says, "I figure you're not going to the bathrooms for a quickie, so…I don't do anything stronger than weed anymore, and I don't do other people's weed."

I shake my head. "No, I really meant to just let them talk a bit. I don't even do weed anymore."

"Really?" We find a little alcove and stand there talking. I expect it looks like we're getting ready to make out or something, from the outside. "Why'd you stop?"

I shrug. "I never really started. I tried it a couple times in college, then I drifted away from my group of friends and didn't have any way to get it. Never missed it."

"Each his own." He swigs his beer, looks back toward Ty and Dev. I follow his gaze.

"So is this serious? I know, I know, it's only been a couple months, but sometimes you know."

"Honey." The wolf pats my arm. "He's a football player. I don't expect this to last beyond—well, honestly, I'm ready every night for him to say, 'That's it, I'm going back to the girls.'"

"Don't you want anything more?"

"Oh, sure. That's why I'm not worrying about him."

I glance at the other fox, leaning in, talking earnestly with Dev. My tiger looks a little more relaxed now. "He's not a bad guy."

"He's a great guy. But he's a football player. It'll never work." He sees my expression. "You hit the lottery. Don't ever let that one go. But if he packs up tomorrow and I never see him again, I've still enjoyed the few nights I got. And not just physically. He's a sweet guy and a hell of a dancer. Now, I will say that whenever I do have a permanent partner..." He looks over at Ty, and there's hunger in his eyes, but I think there's affection, too. "He's going on the list. He would totally do a three-way."

"Ty?"

He laughs. "That fox is a freak. Not just athletic, either." His smile widens. "Look, I appreciate the concern, but I'm okay. And hey, I get to say I got laid by a guy who caught a winning touchdown in the championship."

"Semifinal," I correct. "He didn't catch a touchdown in the championship."

He waves a paw. "Whatever. Point is, he's famous, at least in some circles. But," he holds up a finger, "he's not a complete asshole about it. He's still surprised when people recognize him."

"Yeah, I don't know him that well, but most of Dev's friends on the team are pretty good guys." I survey the club, now half-expecting to see Pike or Vonni. "At least, the ones I brought to this club that night."

"Oh, you brought him? I don't know if he told me that. Well, thank you. I'm getting a nice break from the scene. And some good sex thrown in too."

"The 'scene'?"

He leans forward on the table and his ears flick around. "You know. No? Well, around here, it's kind of a big community and everyone sorta kinda knows each other. So you might go on a date with Jack, and then find out the next day that he dated Jorge, the rat you went out with last year. And then if you don't get naked with Jack, the next date you go on with Zach might start with him saying, 'I hear you don't put out.' And we're all the same here, twenty-something or thirty-something, or fifty-something, spinning the wheel every night to look for a place to stick your cock, or a cock to stick in your places. Some of us don't want more than that. Some of us want to meet the guy of our dreams and settle down. Some of us want to be part of the scene forever."

"Wow," I say. "How old are you? Because you sound about fifty."

Arch laughs. "I'm twenty-six. But I've been living up here since I was nineteen. It gets old, you know?"

"I don't." I take a drink of my own beer. "I did the gay activism thing in college and then met Dev…and he wanted to keep it secret, so I did. Never really found a 'scene.' And my best friend from college has spent the last six months trying to break us up."

"Huh." Arch flicks his ears. "What do your enemies do?"

"Break my thumb," I say flippantly, and then dismiss the question. "It's complicated."

"The tiger's worth it, though, huh?"

"Yeah." My smile curves up. "And then some."

Arch gestures around the club. "It's not all bad around here. The community is awesome. Found me a job, found me a place to live, found me a roommate. I just like a little change once in a while."

"And The Floor is great."

"We like it." He smiles.

"So…" I hesitate. "You don't have to answer, I guess, but…he's not just doing the 'gay tourist' thing?"

The wolf's eyes drift over to Ty, and his smile fades. "I don't think so. But maybe. He says he's not, but when we first met, wow, I can't remember the number of times he told me he was straight."

"Protesteth too much?"

He focuses back on me. "I didn't go to college."

"They teach Shakespeare in high schools, too. Anyway, sorry."

"Whatever." He waves a paw at me. "But I guess it was the night after the game here, he spent the night—long story," he interrupts himself at my expression, "he was kind of, uh, drunk and didn't think he should go back to the hotel. But we didn't do anything then."

I can't help myself. "So he slept on the floor?"

The wolf's tail wags. "No. But we kept some clothes on. We texted after that, on and off. I started watching his games, he told me when he got laid, I told him when I did, and he invited me down for the championship game and got me a hotel room. We danced the night before, and then the night after, I guess he didn't want to be around any of his teammates, so he came over and I," he pauses for effect, "helped him take his mind off it."

"Seems his mind is still off it."

He chuckles. "Aw, yeah, it's fun, I'm not gonna be a dick about it. It's kinda like when I was seventeen again and just finding out all the things you can do with other guys, y'know? I'd forgotten how much fun that was, but for him it's all new."

"Does he like it better than straight sex?" I chuckle and hold up my paw. "You don't have to answer that. Not relevant."

"No, no." He takes the question seriously. "I asked him that. He just says it's different. He's a boobs guy and there are things he misses, but he also likes the, I guess, casualness of it? He says he's always worried when he's with a girl that she'll want it to be more serious and then he feels like a dick when he tells her it's not. I told him I know plenty of straight femmes who just want a fuck every now and then and aren't husband-crazy, but it sounds like his folks are working overtime to set him up with a wife."

After all his talk about the scene, I'm glad he's not one of the girl-hating gays I met back in college. "Athletes have that problem. I guess anyone with money does."

"I sure don't!" He tips back another drink of beer with a short laugh that makes me think there's a story there. I'm about to ask about his family when he cuts things short. "You think they're done hashing it out yet? My feet are itching to get back out there."

I turn and look. Dev's fur has settled down some, and even though he's not smiling, he does have his beer in one paw and he looks more relaxed. "Yeah," I say. "I think we can head back over."

"Oh, hey," he says, and stops me as I turn to go. "Is there anything I should know about football players? I mean, like, that I don't already."

I shake my head. "Well…I mean, you're not angling for anything long-term. So just appreciate the amazing body and take some pictures."

Arch drapes an arm over my shoulder. "Oh, I took care of that already. He let me take a pic of me sucking him off. Something for my scrapbook."

"Anything you can share?" I give him a conspiratorial grin.

He grins back. "Mmmm, maybe. Depends on what you got to trade."

"I don't have pictures. I took one of me, but Dev's kind of paranoid about that. How about as a thank-you for bringing him to the club in the first place? I made this all possible, y'know."

He rolls his eyes. "Foxes. I'll think about it, hon."

"Would you believe I've never been with another fox? Well, another red, anyway. I dated an arctic fox for a while, but…"

"They're about as far from foxes as I am," he says.

"*Thank* you." I exaggerate my reaction, sweeping my paws out. "I have a swift fox friend who keeps giving me a hard time about being a red."

"Oh, hon, red is the only way to go. Although I would totally do an arctic sometime. All that fluff."

"It's nice in the winter, but they get really fussy when they're shedding."

We've gotten close to the table now, and Ty's ears flick back as we approach. Dev's already looking up at me. "What was that about an arctic?" the fox asks, turning.

"Nothing." Arch looks down and holds out his paw. "Wanna dance?"

"Yeah. I told these guys we'd have coffee with them after." He takes Arch's paw. "But it's not 'after' yet."

They wave and disappear into the crowd, leaving their beer bottles behind. I stand up next to Dev. "You okay?"

CHAPTER TEN: SURPRISE (DEV)

It's not that it's Ty, specifically. I mean, I remember him being all worried about whether I was on top or not (yeah, I'm 90% sure it was him), and I went to a strip club with him, and now that I think about it I remember him talking to a wolf at the bar when we were here last time…but really the thing is just finding someone I know here in the club kissing another guy. All of the relief I felt at not being the only one when I talked to Polecki gets turned on its head, upside down and inside out.

Of course I knew that there were other guys playing who were gay, and I couldn't really fault them for not coming out. Everyone has to make his own decision, all that. But that Ty didn't even come talk to me about it has my claws out and my ears flat. It must be really obvious, because he starts out all apologetic when my fox takes his wolf away from where we're talking.

"I promise I would've come to talk to you," he repeats. "I was actually just thinking that when I get through with all the shit happening with the folks that I should look you up in Chevali. This all happened kinda fast."

"Over months," I can't help saying through gritted teeth.

"Yeah, but…" he grins, making it hard for me to stay mad. "Well, at first it was just teasing around. I hung out with him, he was cool, and I said, 'so would you do me?' And he was all coy about it. He's not really impressed with football at all. So I kept texting, and he texted back, and it was fun, like this little secret life. And then after that game, that fucking game, I didn't want to be around anyone from the team."

"Being around the team helped me, sort of." Except when they were all being shitty about Strike. "I mean, everyone felt the same way."

"That's what Rodo said. But you know, none of them had the ball on the last play."

"I kinda fucked up toward the end, too."

"Ah." He waves a paw. "You did what the coaches told you to. You did good."

"You were fine on the plane home."

"Yeah." He ducks his head. "Kinda wish I'd talked to you then. But…" He glances at Arch. "Thing is, y'know, I know this can't be serious. I can't be gay like you can."

I clap a paw on his wrist. "Sure you can," I say. "I'd like to have another friend who's out."

"No, I mean—" He sighs, and the grinning, relaxed fox is gone. "I ever tell you about my folks?"

I shake my head. He searches his memory, eyes drifting up to the ceiling as he scans back through time. "Traditional Yamatase family even though Mom was born here and Dad came over when he was five. But that's why I started in football, because it kept me after school, kept me away from home. I mean, I love them. But they have this idea of life with lots of patterns and places for me and football kinda screwed up some of them. I liked being able to do that."

I squint. "They're okay with the money, though, right?"

"Heh. Yeah. We're starting a charitable foundation in my name that will at least let my mom say, 'Yes, he plays sports, but look what he's doing for the community.' And they're lining up a parade of Yamatese foxes for me to interview for potential wives."

"You get more than one?"

"Oh, God. No, but I had dinner with like four this week already and I had to get away and come down here and, uh, I didn't sleep with any of them, so I was sort of worked up, and…"

I hold up a paw. "I get it. So…" I look over at the wolf, in animated conversation with my fox. "He's just a…a pressure release valve?"

Ty follows my gaze, and his whiskers flare up and then settle down. "He knows it's not serious. Anyway, I just thought, you know, I'll come down to Yerba and I'll dance and I'll hang out with Arch and…y'know."

"Seriously? It was that easy? You went from straight to bi in, what, two months?"

He grins again, a long red fox smile that reminds me of Lee when he's just pulled one over on me. "Honestly? It was more like two weeks. I was taking a shower, I looked around at the guys, and I thought, these are some good-looking guys. And I don't want to get on my knees or anything, I don't want them to jerk me off, nothing like that. I just didn't feel that at all. But when I thought about Arch, I'd get…you know, I'd be more interested."

"Huh." I know what he means; it's like me with Lee. "Why, you think?"

"Damned if I know."

Oh well, it was worth a try. Ty goes on: "Maybe that he can dance, or that he's interested in me and I know I can do stuff with him. I mean, at first I was like, it's not right, it's not the way I am, but then I thought, well, hell, Dev seems to manage okay. And who the fuck cares if I am into him? Arch, I mean, not you. It's not going to hurt anyone." He takes a drink of his beer. "Except my parents. It would kill them."

"Heh. I know what you mean."

"No, I mean, like, literally. My dad would have a heart attack and my mom would probably stick her head in the oven like she always says she will."

I stare, but he looks dead serious. "Wait, really?"

"Ah, I'm sure it's just an expression. I don't think she'd ever do it. I was a good cub, growing up, and my sisters were too, but she'd still threaten us with it. After a while, you just get numb." He rubs his whiskers and takes another drink. "Though she did have a screaming fit when my younger sister brought home that kinkajou."

"Anyway," I say, because we can talk about Ty's family later, "you just said, 'who the fuck cares' and then it was over?"

"More or less. I mean, it was this whole series of little events that led me to the edge and I looked down and it wasn't as scary as I thought. Like you know, the high dive looks way more scary from the bottom than the top." He leans forward. "How bad was it for you?"

"Lion Christ," I say, "It wasn't a high dive, it was a base jump from the Sentra Tower. I spent a whole goddamn summer freaking out about Lee and what it meant that I fucked a guy, and worse, that I wanted to go back and do it again. I thought I might not be able to play football anymore, I thought I might get kicked out of my house, I thought I might get some stupid disease but I was too scared to go get tested for anything…God, that whole summer was a nightmare."

"Wow. Sorry." Ty folds his ears down. "If it makes you feel better, though, I mean, like I said, part of the reason it wasn't so hard for me was because I knew you."

"I wish you'd just fucking *talked* to me."

"After you said you wished you'd never come out?"

That kind of stops me cold. "I did say that, didn't I?" Ty nods. "Fuck. I apologized for it, too."

"I heard that. It just didn't feel like the right time to have the conversation. But I swear I would've come to you. Especially after this week."

I look past him to where Arch and Lee are talking. "Really? You're into him?"

"Not like you and Lee. It's…it's fun, you know? We hang out, we dance, I tell him about sports, he tells me about clothes and tech companies, and then we go back to my hotel and…"

"So," I say, raising my eyebrows, "you're on top, right?"

"Hell yeah." He frowns at me.

Now I'm in the lame position of having to explain a joke. "It's just… you asked me that when I came out. I was just…" I wave my paws, trying to show the whole turnaround is fair play thing.

"Oh." He snaps his fingers. "I did, right? Well, you know, to be honest, I'm wondering about that a bit. He gets so fuckin' into it, I'm starting to wonder. You, uh…you ever?"

"I told you, no." It's not even a joke anymore.

"I know you said that in the locker room, but I mean, I get it now, it's not…it's not a big thing." He squirms though, so I know this is more something Arch has told him than something he one hundred percent believes right now.

"Look," I say. "For the first year we were dating, I wasn't even sure how to do things with a guy. He had to teach me how to give a blow job. And then we only saw each other every week or two, with his schedule and mine, so we…y'know, stuck to what works."

"Makes sense." He clears his throat and lowers his voice. "You do suck him off, though?"

"Uh. Yeah." I duck my head and rub at my cheek ruff.

"That was weirder than fucking him, for me. I mean, I put my own in my mouth when I was growing up, but someone else's? That's weird."

"It is. I mean, it was. It's totally natural now."

"Cool."

We stare at each other across the table and I realize that my upended, wrong-side up relief is reversing, slowly. I give it a nudge, force a wider smile, and reach around to slap him on the side of the shoulder. "You guys want to get coffee or something later?"

"Sure." His smile broadens. "We cool, then?"

"Yeah, sorry. It was just…I wasn't expecting it."

He nods and pulls at one of the lapels on his shirt. "Sorry. I know you were going through a lot of shit. I wish I'd been able to help more. Better late than never, though, right?"

I can feel how sincere he is, and it's nice seeing this side of him, too. So I push aside the weak impulse to be snarky, and say, "On the bright side, I never had a teammate I could talk to about blow jobs before."

He laughs. "Really? Charm didn't want to hear about them?"

"He didn't want to hear about giving them. You remember him in the club."

Ty leans back easily and laughs, his tail swishing. "Yeah. That guy. You know he wanted both waitresses?"

"Doesn't surprise me." I gulp down the beer, which is getting warm fast in this overheated club, and I remember wondering whether Zillo cheated on his girlfriend. "Wait, so did you end up with the other one or did Zillo?"

He snorts, but right about then is when Arch and Lee come back, and Arch is saying something about doing arctic foxes that distracts us all. Then they're gone, and it's just me and my fox again, and he asks me if I'm okay.

"I'm good," I say. "Got over that first reaction."

"Good." He slides an arm around my side, and it's nice that we can stand like this, arms around each other in public, and nobody really cares. "When is Polecki coming into town? Was that Saturday? You think Ty might want to hang out with him too?"

"Er…he didn't seem all that anxious to be out. Like, he didn't want me to tell anyone on the team and he was really afraid of what might happen if his parents found out."

"Maybe not, then." He leans his head against me. "I'm glad he's willing to come out and have coffee with us. Hope he stays on the Firebirds."

"Hope I do, too," I say, and then, because he reacts right away, I put my arm down and hold his shoulder. "I haven't heard anything from Damian. Just thinking."

"Okay." He relaxes again. "So, ready for more dancing?"

There's not much else to do in The Floor, so we head back out to the dance floor. It's easier this time to slip into the rhythm of the music, and I feel more comfortable. When we first arrived, I was pretty self-conscious, remembering how all the other guys there danced, and this time I'd be coming in without fellow terrible dancers Pike and Vonni. But I guess I was only remembering the good ones, because I don't think I'm that much worse than about a third of the guys on the floor. I'm never going to be like Ty and Arch, the kind of dancer people make room for so they can watch them, but at least nobody laughed openly at me and Lee.

And Lee's not much better than me, but he really enjoys himself, and that's fun for me to watch. I like playing off his movements, and he notices and plays back off mine, and there's music and light and maybe it has something to do with the beers, but I forget about Ty and his wolf and just enjoy the beat.

Until Lee grabs me and says he needs another break and a drink. "Maybe I should dance with Ty," I say. "He wouldn't need to take a break every fifteen minutes."

He sticks his tongue out at me. "I have a desk job."

"You don't have any job right now. You can't spend a couple hours at the gym?"

"Hey." He grumbles at me. "I've been sick. And broken-hearted."

"That was your own fault."

And for the second time in an hour, a joke I try to make falls flat. He flips his ears back and says, "Yeah," and I curse myself.

"It wasn't all your fault. I was pretty single-minded about the football."

"Nah, you had to be. You have to be." He pokes my chest. "But if you promise to come out dancing more often, I'll make sure to hit the gym. I'm sure the Whalers have a good facility. Maybe I can train with Polecki's boyfriend."

He's shaking it off, but the reminder of what we're supposed to be thinking about this month stays with me.

We dance for another fifteen minutes and then go for coffee. Ty and Arch aren't ready to leave, so Lee tells them where we'll be and we walk off through the refreshingly cool night. My fur clumps a bit from the close humidity of the club and the night air, not nearly as dry as I've gotten used to, but it's also not the humidity of Hilltown. There's a salty tang to it, a reminder that the ocean isn't too far off, and there's another tang to it as well, although maybe I'm just imagining that as we pass two shadowy alleys where guys are making out.

At the coffee shop, Lee combs through his tail, his fur as sticky from the humidity as mine is. The place is small but crowded; we're lucky enough to walk up just as another couple was leaving a sidewalk table. Those are less popular because it's still chilly outside, but our breath steams with the heat of the club and we don't mind at all. Lee has longer fur and I've got a jacket on, so we sit with our backs to the café's glass and watch the people walk by along the street.

"So," he says finally, "that was a surprise."

"Don't know if 'surprise' is a big enough word." I shake my head. Now that I've sat and talked with him, of course it feels less surprising, but that moment when I saw him kiss the wolf...on the *lips*...

"You think they're telling the truth about it being casual?"

"Huh?" That was one question I hadn't even considered. "Why would they not?"

He shrugs. "I don't know either of them well. I was just curious is all. It could be casual just like they say."

"You know what? I'm going to assume people tell me the truth until I find out they're not. Ty said his parents are lining up vixens for him to marry, so I'm guessing he was telling the truth."

We order coffees and our talk turns to the next day. Lee wants to look at more houses and also to go into his office to meet up with his new boss and his boss's boss, the fox. I probably shouldn't go, but I figure I'll call Damian and ask if meeting another team's executives socially is considered tampering. In the process, maybe I can get more information on how Fisher's doing.

"And we should call Gena," Lee says, as if reading my mind.

"And then dinner with Polecki." I lean back and extend my legs out. "And here I thought this trip was going to be like a little vacation."

"Hah." Lee grins. "I'm gonna run you all over this city. But right now I'm going to get you a coffee."

"If you're all worn out from dancing," I say as he gets up, "I can go."

He sticks his tongue out at me again and walks around the table and into the café.

So Ty has a boyfriend. Maybe not a serious one, but enough that he came to Yerba to see him. I'm glad I'm already friends with him, because otherwise he might be afraid to hang out together a lot when the season starts up again. Hell, we all went to a gay club together and nobody thinks any of us but me is gay. So he'll be fine, and maybe we can all go dancing every so often.

He and the wolf walk up while Lee's still in the café, and cram in around our little table. I ask what they want and text it to Lee, and I notice there's a text message from Gerrard. This new phone, I think as I call it up. Either he texted sometime during the day and I didn't notice, or it didn't beep when the message came in.

I can't deal with this bullshit, is all it says.

I guess maybe he heard about Fisher. I check the time, but it's way too late to call him. I'll figure it out tomorrow.

But it reminds me to tell Ty about Fisher retiring and to keep it quiet until Tuesday. "Sure," he says. "Was it the concussions? I thought he had at least another year or two left."

"His kids are finishing up high school," Lee says smoothly, putting down four drinks: black coffee for me and Arch, a cappuccino for Ty, and a latte for himself. "He wants to spend some time with them before they go off to college."

"Wow, kids." Ty shakes his head. "We got Pike, so I guess we'll be okay." He grins at me. "Maybe we'll pick up another tiger in the offseason."

"Hey," Lee says, sitting down, "if he's a rookie, you could mentor him."

"Yeah, I was sort of bummed when they traded Ford." Ty sits back, then turns to Arch. "Ford was the other wideout who's a fox. Now if I want to hang out with the foxes, they're all cornerbacks."

"Is that a big difference?" Arch looks around at the three of us.

"Well, it's the reason I'm hanging out with Dev here," Ty says. "I mean, I never really hung out with the defense too much in college, but—"

"Cornerbacks are defenders," I say, "like me. Wideouts are offensive players."

Lee turns to the wolf and says, "Enough football. Arch, what do you do?" and we hear about his data entry-slash-customer service job for a small tech firm.

"Just a mile that way," he says. "The owners and my boss are gay, and it's a really friendly workplace."

I nudge Lee. "Maybe you should be looking for a place a couple miles from your office so you have to walk every day. Build up your endurance."

"Oh," Arch says, "you're moving up here?"

"Not to the city." Lee gestures vaguely southward. "Down by the Whalers office."

The wolf grins. "I don't know where that is."

"Down the peninsula, maybe forty minutes?"

"Ah, gotcha. Well, too bad. If you ever want to go dancing, just give me a ring. I'll be glad to show you around." The wolf sips his coffee and then looks around at the quiet table. "Just dancing," he says.

"Oh, seriously." Lee snorts at my expression. "If I were going to fool around with another guy, dear, I would invite you, too."

I grin, and then that image pops into my head and the grin wavers, and then I think about Ty coming to terms with his interest so easily and wonder if I really would be into that, and then I shake my head. "I wasn't thinking that," I say, mostly truthfully. "I was thinking that if you go dancing with him, you better bring a couple energy drinks along."

He gives me a baleful look, and Arch says, "Hey, I can tone it down to whatever you're comfortable with," and that earns him the same look.

"I'll train up for next time," Lee says finally, and sips his latte so that when he exhales, his warm breath shows white through his teeth.

"Ah, you weren't that bad," Ty says. "Foxes can't look bad on the dance floor."

"Did you *see* Vonni?" I ask, not because Vonni was that bad a dancer, but because you make fun of guys behind their backs, and also to make Lee feel better if he really is feeling bad, which I'm not quite sure of.

It works; we all laugh, and Ty makes a comment about foxes from the northeast being an exception. Arch asks for a demonstration, and Ty and Lee both try to imitate Vonni's jerky arm movements while seated. We all laugh, and then Lee asks Arch about the Korsat neighborhood and we finish our coffees over some of his stories of things that have happened here.

There are more people standing around waiting for a table, and Lee and I at least have a half-hour drive back to our hotel, so we stand up and shake paws. "Hey," Ty says as I clasp his paw in mine—he's a fox, but he's got the biggest paws of any fox I've ever met—"I'm glad you ran into us here. It's cool, right? We're cool?"

"Yeah," I say, because you can't be mad at Ty for too long. He's not quite got Charm's slippery good-natured humor, but he has an infectious grin and he doesn't let anything rattle him. "We're cool. And hey, have fun. He seems like a cool guy."

He winks at me. "Thanks. Hey, when I get back to Chevali, I'll call you."

We wave and head our separate directions. In the car on the way back, Lee chuckles and shakes his head. "So it worked after all. Wonder if we should check up on Pike. Maybe he hooked up that night too."

"Ty didn't hook up that night," I point out. "He just met a guy he liked and got to know him better."

"I know, I know." Lee leans back with an expression as satisfied as when we'd finished that sushi, keeping one paw casually on the wheel. "I'm taking some credit for this, though, and you can't stop me."

"I wouldn't." I open the window on my side, enjoying the warm, humid air that casts a haze around the glowing names atop the buildings. "No, it's totally cool. Because he's happy, because he's having fun, because Arch doesn't seem to mind."

"Hope it works out." Lee squints ahead. "Do you remember what exit our hotel was off of?"

I pull out my phone, which has a map program on it. "I think it's working out about as well as it's going to. I mean, they don't want much more than what they're doing now, right?"

"Sure, but I mean, eventually they're going to get more serious or stop seeing each other, aren't they?"

"What was our hotel's name?" He tells me and I put it in. "I don't know. I think they're both getting something they want."

"They can't keep it casual forever."

"Okay, take exit 440b. And why not?"

"How far is that? People change, you know. You get older, you want different things."

"How old is Arch? It's in nineteen miles."

"Twenty-six." Lee grips the wheel and grins. "He was the oldest guy in our group."

"Acted like it, too. Stayed quiet, didn't try to push himself into the conversation. Ty was the one all chatty."

"Arch is a nice guy. If anyone was going to be Ty's first gay experience, I'm glad it was someone like him."

I turn and grin. "Not me?"

He just laughs. "Jesus Fox, can you even imagine feeling up one of your teammates? How awkward that would be?"

"Yeah, you're right. Anyway, you're cuter than Ty."

His tail swishes. "Well, thanks for that. I don't know if Arch would really be interested in me if you decided to go off with Ty."

Staring down at my phone, I remember Gerrard's message, and I call it up again. "I guess Gerrard heard about Fisher. I should call him tomorrow."

I show Lee the text, and he frowns. "'Bullshit' is kind of a strong word to talk about a friend retiring."

"That's Gerrard." I shrug. "It doesn't have to do with football, therefore it's bullshit."

"Give him a call tomorrow maybe."

"I was thinking that." I put my head back and close my eyes.

I half doze off in the car, so I'm groggy when we pull up outside the hotel, and I think we probably will just go to bed, but when we do get up to the room, maybe the coffee kicks in or something, because when Lee strips to his boxers and gets into bed, I climb in and crawl on top of him. He squirms, but I press him to the mattress, purring down against him.

"What?" He grins up at me, and I know he can feel what, pressing against his leg. I can feel him getting harder against my stomach too. But I just lean down and kiss his nose, and then his lips.

"Thanks for taking me out dancing," I say, and slide my arms around behind his shoulders.

"Aw," he says, "you don't have to thank me. But thanks for coming."

I squeeze him and press my nose into his fur, breathing into it and inhaling his scent. "You'll be saying that again in about fifteen minutes."

He works one of his paws between us, manages to bring fingers to my erection. "Oh, you think it'll take that long?"

My length stiffens further under that touch. "Well," I breathe next to his ear, "I'm counting the time it'll take you to go get the lube out of our luggage."

He pushes me up very slightly, enough to get his other paw down onto the other side. His fingers stroke up and down. "You think we need lube? I think you might be ready just like this."

"Uhhh." I can't argue too much, especially when his paw curls around me and starts to stroke. "You sure...you want your fur all sticky?"

He chuckles throatily. "It'll get sticky one way or another. Just depends where. Hmm."

His paw tugs forward more, and his left paw reaches back behind my thigh to pull me forward. I scoot up and end up kneeling astride his shoulders, gripping the bed's headboard as his tongue meets the end of my shaft, which somehow along the way got worked free of my underwear.

Then I just stay there, trembling and restraining the shudders as he opens his whole muzzle around me and I drive forward, panting. His right paw stays around my base, while his left pushes my boxers even farther down and then trails back up under my tail.

It's nothing he hasn't done before, sort of playing with my rear. Once when we were messing around with lube, he asked if he could push a finger in, and I let him. It wasn't great, but it wasn't too bad. Now I'm thinking about what Ty said and whether it means I'm a bad boyfriend that I haven't even been curious about that.

Tonight, though, Lee doesn't insist on anything. He just teases the fur around there, which is nice and arousing, and he plays around my cock with his expert tongue, his fingers reaching down to brush my sac. Meanwhile, I thrust gently against his muzzle and then I thrust a little harder, and then my hips start to shake and I gasp out some incoherent moans. He answers below me and pushes me deeper into his muzzle, and when I come, it's all the way in, against the back of his throat, and I feel him swallow around my cock, which just makes the orgasm more intense. I end up panting against the headboard, my cock so deep in his muzzle that his lips are actually around the tip of my sheath and his nose is buried in my stomach fur.

"Mmmmmf." I rest there, and he doesn't seem to mind. I feel the warmth from his breath as it ruffles my fur.

He breaks the moment before I do, twisting his head to let my cock out from his lips, though he presses his muzzle into my stomach. "Sorry," he says, muffled. "I need to breathe."

"Yeah, yeah," I murmur down, and let myself fall to one side, scooting down on the bed so I land facing him on the pillow.

Our muzzles meet, and then our lips, and then our tongues, and there's not much taste of me in his muzzle. Must've been all the way in him. I reach down and find his erection, the smooth, hard skin, and he squirms as I stroke it.

Ty might be further along than me in thinking about letting his boyfriend (or whatever) fuck him, but at least I have more experience in blow jobs. I roll onto my back and pull Lee on top of me, pushing his underwear all the way off and then pulling him up my chest. He lets me move him around without objection, and arches his back when I bring my soft paws to either side of his shaft. "Your turn," I murmur, even though my eyelids are heavy and I want to sleep.

I can close my eyes once his tip is against my lips, though. I inhale his scent and lick at his cock, my paws steadying his hips and at the same time feeling the waves of tension that travel through him each time I slide my muzzle down or curl my tongue around him. Sometimes I like to push him into my muzzle, but tonight I just hold him and let him find his own rhythm, as his long tail swishes over my legs and his paws press down on my shoulders.

Such a light body, such a warm touch, and it's so nice to give him this pleasure, bucking against my tongue. His fingers curl into my shoulders and his blunt claws press against my skin, but he can't hurt me. I can't quite take him as deeply as he takes me, but it's deep enough.

As he did, I tease the fur under his tail, but I go farther than he did, pressing against his opening with a finger. He moans and tightens up, and as I rub, he gasps. It's not long after that that his body jerks and he thrusts his cock against my tongue. His muscles shake in my paws, and then I feel warmth spurt into my mouth. I hold it while he comes, then purse my lips and swallow, making him squirm as I lick his sensitive shaft.

"H-hey," he gasps, but my paws hold him tightly, and he can't get away, until finally he does, wrenching out of my grip and falling atop me with a silly grin. He kisses me again, and we exchange the taste of each other, arms circling one another's bodies.

"I don't need a month, fox," I murmur. "I want to be with you. I know we can make it work. We just need to keep talking to each other, right?"

"Mmm. Right now that sounds awesome," he says. He rubs his paws over my ears. "But if it's so certain, you'll still feel that way in three more weeks, right?"

"Don't you feel that way?" I turn so I can see his eyes.

"Right now I do." He licks my nose. "But what happens when we're not naked? Or when we're naked and arguing?"

"Our naked arguments usually all end the same way." I reach down and squeeze his still-hard shaft.

"Nnnf. Yeah. But...you see what I mean? We haven't really talked about it."

I want to tell him that I don't think we need to talk that much. But now I'm remembering him shrinking in on himself back in my apartment, afraid to talk to me, trapped between me and the shit the universe likes to dump on him. I think about Fisher barricading himself in his den, yelling at his wife about how much football means to him and to me. My certainty wavers.

"Okay. But now, you feel like that now, right?"

He meets my eyes and smiles. "Well, yeah."

"That's good enough for me." I pull his body against mine, every curve of sleek ivory, every muscle rippling below fluffy russet fur, every little sound of breath and contentment, every scent of fox and come and shampoo, and every movement of his arms and hips and tail, and for this moment, all my wants and needs sing in sweet harmony.

•

It doesn't last, of course. It never does. The chirp of a cell phone ring wakes us when it's still dark out Saturday morning, and Lee shifts in the bed and then mumbles, "Yours."

"Fuck it," I say, looking at the number, which I don't recognize, and the time, which is 6:37 a.m. I decline the call and set the phone back on the nightstand. A moment later it chirps with a voicemail, then chirps again with a text, and Lee places it on my paw.

I blink at the number and then at the small preview of the text message: "This is Dax from AltSports.com. Do…"

I swipe the message and it comes up in full. What Dax from AltSports.com is asking is whether I have any comment on the statement made by my brother. "Fuck," I mumble.

"Mmmrr?" Lee burrows his muzzle into my shoulder.

"My asshole brother said something."

While he levers his head off the pillow, eyes shining at me, I listen to the voicemail. "Hi, Devlin, this is Vince from the Firebirds. I just wanted to ask if you were aware of your brother's statement about this case he's involved in, and if you have any comments. I know it's early there but give me a call so I can get ahead of this if there's any blowback. It's pretty low-profile at the moment, but we're in the off-season so you never know. Call me back." And he leaves his number.

"Shit." I turn to Lee's shining eyes. "Let me call Vince and find out what's going on."

He rests a paw on my stomach as I make the call.

Vince is a weasel, but unlike Ogleby, he's mastered the art of harnessing his energy. His words come in short, economical bursts, and then he gets you off the phone. So when I tell him I haven't seen what Gregory did and in fact didn't even know about it, he says, "Hang on," and ten seconds later, he's reading it.

"I'm proud to have reached a settlement that reinforces the value of traditional families and the good work done by the Christians of Families United. I look forward to continuing to support them against all the intolerant people who wish to encumber their freedom of expression in this country." He stops. "He doesn't mention you directly, and this wasn't flagged by any sports media yet. One of my interns came up with it because of a match on the last name. You know what this lawsuit was about?"

"Yeah," I say. "A guy from AltSports already texted to ask me for a comment."

"I'd advise 'no comment,' of course, but it's up to you. Just let me know if anything's going to happen."

"Fuck," I say. "No, I'll send him a 'no comment.' Just...that fucking..."

"Also," Vince says, "Let me know if you're going to assault him."

"No, no." I press my other paw to my eyes. "I might call—"

"I was kidding. Okay, Dev, you've got my number if you need anything, right?"

"Yeah." We hang up, and I turn to my fox. "Gregory made a public statement—I guess the Vince King case came to a settlement. He talked about how great it was to be working with Families United." My paws are squeezed into fists.

"Did he mention your name?"

"No." I tell him about Vince's intern and the message from the AltSports guy.

Before I can go on to tell him Vince's advice, he says, "I think you're right about the 'no comment' route. If he didn't mention you personally, then you don't have to wade into the fight."

"Really?" I push my nose up against his. "You don't want me to get up on a big stage and yell about him?"

He kisses me. "I want you to speak out and encourage gay kids. And this is the kind of thing you don't need to get involved in."

"What if people find out my brother is in league with those assholes?"

"Remember Ogleby? If you make a big public statement, people will find out. Right now it's just a minor press release about an otherwise unremarkable case. Only people following the case or looking for information about people named 'Miski' will find it."

I know he's right, but I think about Gregory saying those words all smug—I can hear his voice—and when I don't say anything, people assuming I must have known about it, or I condone it. I think about that kangaroo rat kid hearing my brother say that people who speak out against homophobic assholes are intolerant, and wondering what I really stand for. I wonder what Polecki would say about it, and that actually calms me a little. I can ask him tonight.

"It's just different," I growl to Lee, "when you know someone who'd be disappointed if he heard your brother say that, and you didn't respond at all."

"Polecki?" he guesses.

"Him I can talk to. No, I mean that kangaroo rat I met at the airport." I haven't actually told Lee the whole story. "He said his dad kicked him out when the kid came out, but they bonded over football and uh...the kid got to go back home and the dad went with him to the airport."

"That's great." He slides his arms around me and hugs me. "I'm proud of you. Have I said that lately?"

"Mmm." It feels good, but doesn't stop my worrying. "But if that kid doesn't see me come back..."

"Tiger," Lee says, and rubs his muzzle against mine. "Think about why Gregory's doing this. Either it was his idea, or it was Families United's idea. If it was his, then he's trying to needle you, to draw you into a public confrontation. If it was their idea, then they're trying to draw attention to the division in your family. Either way, if you respond publicly, it's just playing into their paws."

He's right, I know he's right, but I can't just do nothing. Can I?

"Tiger."

I turn toward him and find his eyes creased with concern, but his muzzle slightly curved into a smile. "Ow."

"Oh, shit." I retract my claws where they're pressing into his back. "Sorry!"

"It's okay. I know it's emotional, I've been there."

"Yeah." I nuzzle him. "And you got through it with your mom. But Gregory's not...I mean, he's..." I take my paws away from my fox because my claws are threatening to come out again.

"Why don't you book a trip home to talk to your parents? And maybe we can go by Hilltown if you're still interested in talking to Forester about doing something with them."

"Sure," I say, and feel a little better. Having a plan, a play I can follow, makes everything easier. "I'm going to check into tickets back from Chevali this week. We fly back, what, Tuesday?"

"Yeah," he says, and then I'm climbing out of bed even though he scrabbles at me with a paw trying to keep me there.

"Can I use your laptop?"

He sighs and flops down. "Sure."

I turn it on. "What's your login again?"

He tells me, then pulls the blankets up around his shoulders. I log in and find the browser, and dick around for a bit before I say, "Fox?"

Nothing. Pretty sure he's not asleep, though. I clear my throat. "Fox?"

"Mrrf."

"What site do you use for tickets?"

He turns his head. "Fastflight.com," he mumbles.

I find it. "Do you have a log in for it?"

There's a moment of silence, and then he gives a long, exaggerated sigh and rolls out of bed. "I can do it," I protest, but he walks over to the desk, gives me a kiss, and logs in to the site.

I wrap an arm around his waist and nuzzle his chest. "Thanks."

"When do you want to go?" He types in Chevali to Hilltown.

"I can do this." I push him back toward the bed, getting my paws on his bare rear as I do. "Go."

"It's okay," he says, but then I push him harder and he lands sprawled on the bed.

"Oh," he says, staying there, "Tiger and bed working together to keep a fox down." And he arches his tail a little, the white tip waving back and forth over that rear.

"Mmm," I say. If I were less focused, or if we hadn't just fucked last night, I'd jump on him, but right now I want to get that ticket bought. Then I can tell Mom and Dad I'm coming home and I can talk to them about Gregory.

It takes me a while to find the right flights, and then I have to go find my credit card to make the purchase. While I'm doing that, Lee's phone rings, and he gives another tired, exasperated sigh and grabs it.

As soon as he sees the number, he clears his throat. "Hi, Peter," he says. "No, no, just talking about breakfast. Sure. Uh-huh. Yeah, noon is fine. We have a couple places to look at. Should I bring Dev? Right. Yeah, okay, I can see that. Okay, just send me the name of the place and I can find it."

He puts the phone down. His eyes gleam in the shadowy darkness as he looks in my direction. "Well," he says, "I guess we're up."

"I got tickets," I say. "Leaving Thursday, coming back Saturday. I got you one, too. Um. You don't have to use it."

"I don't mind going with you." He sits on the edge of the bed. "But ask me, next time."

"Yeah, I know. I just want you with me is all."

"I'm glad." He pads over and puts his arms around me. I lean into him from the desk chair, my muzzle against his chest. "It's going to be all right, tiger. Nobody's going to notice and you'll work it out with the family."

"I should get back to that AltSports guy," I mutter, catching sight of my phone.

"After we shower." He kisses my ears. "Then we have time to look at apartments for a couple hours until I meet Peter and Jocko for lunch. You're not invited. Tampering and all—you can't meet with another team's officials."

"I know I'm not supposed to discuss football with them. Does that mean I can't meet them for lunch, too?"

"Definitely. Sorry. Hope you can occupy yourself for a couple hours."

But all during the shower, I'm thinking about Gregory still. That'd be more of a problem if the shower were big enough for two, but alas, I'm showering alone. When I get out, Lee gropes me and then hurries in himself. I let the pleasant feelings of the grope fade and then I call my parents.

Mom answers and I tell her quickly that I've booked a flight to come back up there. "Oh," she says, "of course we will love to see you."

"And I want to see Gregory, too." I manage not to growl as I say it.

"Did you call him?"

"I'm not going to call him."

Mom sighs. "Your father will insist—"

"He made a public statement this morning, Mom. After settling that case, he said—" Dammit, I can't remember everything Vince said. "Something about a victory for traditional families being oppressed by the forces of intolerance." She doesn't say anything, and I realize that maybe the rhetoric of gay rights hasn't made it up to Lake Handerson. "Basically he was saying that gay people are trying to oppress straight people by insisting that they have basic civil rights."

"I'm sure it was nothing like that."

"Mom, I heard it."

"You heard him speak those words?"

"No, I mean, my team's press liaison read the statement to me. I don't know if it was on TV anywhere. I don't think it was that important." Anger makes me toss in that last snide remark.

"If it was not important then why do you need to fly here to talk to him?"

It's my turn to sigh, though there's a lot of growl in it. "Because he took the case in the first place. Because he was trying to make it more important with that statement. It's a shot at me, Mom, he's trying to get me to respond because he's angry that, I dunno, I'm happy or something."

"I'm sure he is not angry at your success." Now she sounds scolding.

That's exactly what he's angry about, I think, plus some other stuff, maybe issues around me being gay that took a while to boil over. "We'll see. Just—can you call him and ask him to come over? Because if I call him, I'll lose my temper and yell and then he'll never come."

"You should call."

"Did you hear the last conversation we had? This is worse, now. If I call, I'll end up calling him a bigot and an a—" I catch the profanity. "And worse."

"Then you should control yourself."

"How is this my issue?" I'm starting to raise my voice. "He's the one who took that case! He's the one who made a completely unnecessary statement—"

"Devlin." She cuts me off. "Ever since high school, you and Gregory have taken every opportunity to be offended at each other. We hoped that would end when you both graduated college, but perhaps it only ended because you live apart."

I'm so sure I'm right that I can't say anything for a minute. Finally I compose myself enough to hide the seething. "All right, Mom. Just call him, please?"

"No." She's firm. "You say you will consider giving him money for Alexi if he asks directly. How can you expect him to do that if you will not ask him directly when *you* want something?"

I know she makes sense, but I also know I'm going to have difficulty controlling myself if I do talk to him. "Fine," I say, "I'll call him. But if we start yelling at each other…"

"If you don't start yelling, then there will be no yelling."

"He starts things too," I point out.

"Gregory says things to make you lose your temper. So don't lose your temper."

"You say it like it's so easy." I grit my teeth. "Maybe I'll call him tomorrow."

"Sunday he goes to church in the morning, so don't call early. And they may be going to the hospital soon. Alexi's tests require an overnight stay, so they have been going in on Saturdays because they both want to stay with him."

"So I should call him now."

"Or you could call him in the hospital."

"I'll call him now. Thanks, Mom."

I hang up and stalk back and forth in the hotel room as the sound of the shower is replaced with the loud whirr of fur dryers. They're taking Gregory's side again. I should've just booked a ticket to Gateway and gone to his house directly, had it out without our parents being around. It's going to be all of them against me again, and they'll guilt me into giving him the money for Alexi.

I really don't want to call him, but I also don't want it hanging over my head the rest of the weekend. I've got probably ten minutes before Lee's fur is dry. So I pull up Gregory's number and call.

My hope that he won't answer is dashed in two and a half rings. "Hi, Dev. What can I do for you?" he purrs.

"I'm coming to Mom and Dad's place next weekend. I want to talk to you."

"We're talking now." He knows I've seen the statement, or he's guessing. He's too smug to not know.

"Nose to nose." I take a breath. "Saturday or Sunday, whichever works better for you."

"Can you tell me what this is about? Even a lawyer defending a murderer gets to prepare his case."

"Well, you'd know, wouldn't you?"

"I've no idea what you're talking about."

I take another breath. "It's about the statement you made at the settlement of that case you were working. Defending murderers, by the way."

"Mmm, a settlement specifically excludes any admission of guilt or wrongdoing. It's simply a considerate gesture on the part of my client to avoid extending this painful experience for the family."

"Wow," I say. "I mean, I should have known that becoming a lawyer would accentuate the worst parts of you, but somehow I'm still surprised."

"And likewise for the brutal game of football." A little snarl creeps into his voice. "I shouldn't be surprised at how well you're doing in it, and yet I still am. Of course, it helps when you make yourself a celebrity."

A hearty "fuck you" builds in my chest, but I remember Mom's words. "Yeah, it's too bad you couldn't make yourself a celebrity the same way."

That gets to him. His voice chills. "So what about this statement? It's too late to retract it. What exactly do you want to talk about?"

"I just want to understand why you said it. And I want you to promise you won't do it again."

He laughs, sharp and bitter. "Of course you do. And why would I promise that? You think family comes before God? You think Dad will take your perverted side in this argument?"

"God hasn't done your cub any favors, has he?"

It slips out, mean and off-topic, but he's so fucking smug and I can see the smile I want to smack off his face disappear as I say it. "That is not relevant to this discussion."

"It could be. He's my nephew. Maybe I want to help him."

"Oh. Oh, now I understand. You want to bribe me to be silent, to keep your image all pure. You're using my son's problems as leverage against me."

"What?"

"This is low and disgusting, even for you. Don't bother. I don't want your homosexual money."

I can't make words get past my throat. Gregory goes on. "If Mom and Dad want me to come talk to you, then I will for their sake. But if they don't want anything more to do with you after hearing this conversation, then that's not on me."

"You just better fucking hope that a week is enough time for me to cool down," I say. And then the fur dryer stops, so I hang up the phone in the middle of his reply. Wow. Our relationship is as bad as ever. He just brings out the worst in me and I can't stop myself from being a dick. It makes me angry and kind of sick at myself.

Lee comes over to me with his fur all puffy from the dryer. I respond to his questioning look with a kiss on his damp ears, then let him get dressed. He stays quiet, sensing my mood, and then when he's got a shirt and pants on, pulls out his map.

My temper subsides and my thoughts crystallize as he's talking about where to go for the apartment search. "No," I say as he mentions one neighborhood.

"Uh." He looks down at his paper. "I thought you liked this one."

"I mean, no, let's not look at apartments. I'm going to buy you a house."

His ears go askew and his newly-dry fur fluffs up around the collar. "Don't we have to…I mean, that's a big thing."

"It's an investment. Your dad said it'd be good to do, right?"

"Well…" He puts the paper down and reaches up to scratch behind an ear. "What's this about, tiger? You haven't been thinking about investments all morning."

The actual logic behind my decision sounds petty and childish, so I go with something a little more adult. "It just doesn't make sense. You're going to be a lot more stable in this job than I am in mine, so why would you pay rent when you could be living in an investment?"

"Of your money. Wouldn't I still be paying you rent?"

"We could work that out." I flick my tail. "Anyway, if we're together, it's our investment, right?"

He breathes in and then nods. "If."

"I have faith," I say.

He doesn't respond, just gets that look that means he's turning things over in his head. "You talked to your parents just now?" I nod. "And…?"

So I tell him about the call with Gregory, and he winces. "Ah, I'm sorry he was a dick about it."

"It's what he does." I rub my muzzle and grab my jacket.

He thinks a moment. "And if your money is all tied up in a house, then you can't help him even if he does come around and ask."

I shrug the light mesh fabric on around my shoulders, wishing he weren't so bright. "I guess not."

"Don't buy a house out of spite." He smiles. "The house will last way longer."

My paws find his shoulders and I stare down at him. "Look, doc. The house is a good investment. I'm buying it with the Strongwell money. I have the chance to buy it now, the money to buy it now, and you need it now."

"I don't *need* it—"

"If I'm going to be coming to stay with you, I want it. Next year if I get a long-term deal with Chevali, I'll buy a house there. But I know you'll be here for a while."

"You can't know that." He places his paws on my waist and looks up.

I squeeze him. "You're good. You'd still be with the Dragons if it wasn't for me, and the Whalers know about me."

"What if…" He looks down, away from me. "What if they're just hiring me to try to get leverage to bring you here in the off-season? And you end up not coming?"

"Uh." The question catches me off guard. "Do you think that's what they're doing?"

"No." His eyes slide sideways, toward the bed. "But you know, when you're lying around late at night and your mind is trying to list out all the things that might go wrong with your life…"

"Listen, doc." I slip a paw under his muzzle and lift it. "You got the job here because you're a good scout. You know football. It doesn't matter where I am or what I'm doing."

"Mmf." He smiles.

"And you're going to be here for years, and I'm going to buy you a house to live in and for me to live in with you."

"If…"

I stop him with a hug. "Yeah, I know. But even if we don't decide to be together, we'll be friends, right? And a friend can buy a house to rent out to another friend cheap? Ty has a whole pawful of friends living in his house rent-free."

He shakes his head. "It does make sense, I guess. But shouldn't you ask your parents about the money first?"

"Lee." I leave pet names aside and stare down at him. His eyes widen. "I don't want to talk about my brother and the money. I just offered it to him, okay? Let it go."

He nods and then shakes his head. "Tigers."

"Yeah, if you had a brother, you'd be worse. Look at how you are with your parents. You'd be having yelling fights on the phone and calculating ways to get back at each other."

He's quiet for a moment, then raises his eyebrows and says, "Maybe you're right. Okay, how about if I ask my boss where to look for houses when we have lunch?"

"Good thought." I pull him closer to me and force thoughts of Gregory away, focusing on the slender body against me, his warmth relaxing me enough to purr. "And if we don't have to go look at apartments this morning…" My paws slide down his back.

"Mmm." He hugs back and nuzzles at my throat. "How about we go look at apartments anyway? Just in case. We can look for houses for sale in the area too."

"Oh, fine." I let him go. "Can't believe you want to go out rather than stay here in bed with me."

He steps back, tail flipping from side to side. "Oh, I want to stay here with you. But it's a nice day and we'll have plenty of time in bed tonight."

Two hours and three apartments later, when Lee takes off for his new office with a kiss on my nose, I've pushed that morning's conversations into the past. I was going to call Damian and ask him his thoughts on the Whalers, so I park myself at a sandwich place that calls itself a deli café, get a thick roast beef sandwich, and call him up.

"Afternoon, Dev," he says. "What's on your mind?"

I still can't get over that this guy with the assured, deep voice and the confident manner is my agent. "Lee's having lunch with his Whalers bosses. They thought I shouldn't go along."

"Definitely not, even if they weren't one of the places that I think might have some interest in you."

"Have you had a chance to call around?"

He chuckles. "I've been on the phone non-stop for the past week. Not just for you, of course. I have a lot of clients I'm taking care of. So far I've had one team other than Chevali tell me they'd like to take a look at you, but we haven't talked numbers yet. I want to wait and see what the market is."

"Okay. Is there anything I should do?"

"Enjoy your time off. I think probably by this time next week I'll have a much better idea of what's going on. No firm numbers, but as teams start to re-sign their current players, we'll have a framework to plan from."

"Thanks." I lean back in the chair. "Have you heard anything from Fisher?"

He's quiet for a moment. "Professionally, I shouldn't say anything, but you're a friend of his too and you know his struggles."

"Yeah?"

"I just want to make it clear that I'm not asking you to talk to him or intervene."

"Ah, fuck, what's he doing?"

Damian sighs. "He's called me twice to tell me that he's not retiring, and I've had to talk him back into it both times. I'm worried that he's going to get up there and refuse to read the statement, or not go at all."

"We'll both be there with him, right? I mean, I'm still coming?"

"If you're willing. I think it would help him."

"Yeah, for sure. I know he wants to play longer, but if this serum thing gets out, he'll never play anywhere anyway." I catch myself. "Ah, shit, did you know about that?"

"Yes." Damian sounds distant. "That's not strictly true. There are teams who would take him. But in Fisher's case, he's just afraid, and I keep telling him he can do things after football." His voice sharpens and slides into what sounds like a well-rehearsed speech. "My clients who have retired from football go into coaching, Cub League or high school or college, some in the pros. Some of them cook or build houses for homeless people or go to law school or write books or play guitar. They travel around the world and visit national parks and help hungry people. They can do whatever they want except play football. And they've done that."

"Law school?"

"Sure." He huffs into the phone. "Brandt Merchant, know him? Seven-year career, retired two years ago. I made him twenty-four million dollars, and even after taxes and taking care of his family, he retired with eight million in the bank and two properties. He's in his first year of law school now. Wants to do sports law and work for the players' union."

"Impressive."

"You want to go to law school?"

My jaw tightens. "God, no. Never."

"Well, you don't have to think about what you want to do after football, not for a while. You're going to be playing next year, that's for sure. We just need to figure out where."

"Thanks, Damian. Should I call you, or…?"

"Let's set up a time to talk. When are you back from Yerba?"

I shake my head, impressed. Ogleby never even thought to set up a schedule, and he could barely remember what day it was, let alone what I was doing. "We fly back Tuesday, but then we're leaving for Hilltown Thursday morning."

"What's in Hilltown?"

"Family. Oh, and…speaking of that. Lee had an idea that I might be able to do something with my college, Forester University. What do you think about that?"

I'm just looking for his advice, but he says, "It's a good idea. Let me give them a call and I'll see what sort of thing they might be open to. College speaking events are good because you're raising your profile while also doing something charitable. Double-win."

"Also," I feel compelled to say, "Forester had an incident while I was there where a gay guy was beaten up by a couple football players."

"Ah-ha, the redemption angle. I'll hit that with them. Anything else?"

"No, that's it. Thanks."

"It's what I'm here for. I'll see you Tuesday with Fisher, but it might not be appropriate to talk business then. How about Wednesday morning I'll give you a ring and we'll catch up? If I get some news, I'll call you, but don't pick up if it's not convenient. I always leave a message."

"Great." I hang up, reassured that I made the right decision about changing agents, and take a bite out of the sandwich, which also proves to have been a good decision. If the cloud of Gregory weren't looming over me, it'd be a pretty good day overall. Maybe when Lee gets back from lunch, it still can be.

Chapter Eleven: Plans (Lee)

I call my father on the way to lunch to ask if he knows any real estate agents I can talk to and end up telling him about Dev's brother's statement. He asks if I want Mother to call Gregory, and that at least makes me laugh. I can't even imagine how that would go.

Peter and Jocko meet me at the Whalers offices, a different building than the one I watched the championship game in. It's mostly deserted except for some administrative assistants, one of whom greets me and sends me back down a hallway. The distinct smells of fox and bear lead me to a conference room with a big maroon-topped table in the middle and a window looking out over the parking lot. Peter and Jocko sit at the window end of the table with a pile of papers and a plastic bag between them, and both the red fox and black bear turn muzzles my way as I knock on the door.

"Come on in," Peter says, gesturing to the dozen or so empty chairs. "Have a seat. You want a drink?"

He and Jocko both have silver beer cans in front of them with an artsy design on it, probably some local microbrew. "You have Diet Coke?"

Jocko raises his eyebrows. "Don't drink?"

I smile and shake my head, taking a seat. "Not at a meeting with two people who are going to be my bosses at a job I haven't started yet."

He snorts and heads for the door, looking across at Peter. "Foxes. Always thinking, calculating, worrying. Y'ever just let go and do what you want?"

I'm well-behaved enough not to say that I did last night with my boyfriend, and anyway, Peter's eye glints and he shows his narrow canines. "You ever actually think about anything you do?"

"Sure. I think about enjoyin' myself. Worrying all the time leads to heart attacks." The big brown muzzle turns back to me. "You don't have to worry about that for a few decades yet."

"Aw," I say, "and here I thought I was going to work hard at this job."

Peter laughs, Jocko squints. A moment later, though, the bear laughs. "Fair enough," he says. "Don't you worry, you'll work plenty. I'll be back in a minute."

"Here." The other fox pushes the pile across to me. "Your official contract, your starting paperwork, and a polo shirt and jacket to get you started. I guessed at your size, so if they don't fit, you can exchange them at the store."

I smell new cloth in the bag and pull out the jacket, a light windbreaker, to try it on as Peter watches. "I figured since you'll be working in the southwest, you won't need one of the heavy ones," he says. "It never gets really cold here."

"Fits great." I slide it off and hold up the polo shirt to my shoulders. "This one looks good too. It's a medium, so that's perfect. Thanks."

His whiskers and cheek ruffs rise and his ears perk up. "We're glad to have you aboard."

Jocko comes back then and plunks down a silver can of Diet Coke in front of me, filmed with condensation. "Break room's down that way." He jerks his thumb as he takes his seat. "When you're officially working here, you can get your own."

"I will." I look around the walls at the pair of plasma TVs on each side wall, the posters of the Whalers' top draft choices of the last three years—no, three of the last four, I note, missing the one who's no longer with the team. "So is this the scouting team's conference room?"

"Yup." Jocko swigs his beer. "Month or two and you'll know it real well."

"I bet. I've been through two drafts," I remind him. "And been to three combines."

He nods at me, and Peter speaks up. "That's one thing we wanted to talk to you about," he says. "We said unofficially a month, but the combine starts on the 19th, and Jocko would really like you there."

"That's fine. Only can you put me up in a nice hotel this time?" I tell them briefly about the fleabag hotel I stayed in when I was an unpaid intern with the Dragons.

"Can't promise you your own room," Jocko says, "but yeah, we stay at the Circle."

I recognize the marquee from looking longingly at it on my way back to the fleabag. "Nice."

Peter asks how the house hunting is going, and I tell them about some of the apartments I've looked at. The one I liked from yesterday they both shake their heads at. "You'll get your car busted into," Jocko says, and Peter agrees.

"As a matter of fact," I say, "Dev kind of wants to buy a house in the area for me. I mean, with me. So I was going to ask if you guys know of any good real estate agents we could talk to, where I should look, and so on."

Jocko's big bear claw taps the table. "My sister-in-law's a real estate agent. Let me give her a call. She can probably find some houses for you to look at tomorrow."

"But…" I look back at Peter. "I heard property here is insane. Can I afford it?"

He grins as Jocko takes out his phone. "If you're going to buy, this is the time to do it, and there's not a bad place to own property in this area. It's all constricted, so they can't just build out the suburbs like they do down in Chevali."

"And the more relevant question," I say. "Is it worth buying a house?"

The other fox raises his eyebrows and ears with a smile. "Are you good at your job?"

"Yes."

He clasps his paws in front of him. "Okay, then. There's no guarantees in this business, of course, especially when you're depending on all those youngsters on the field." His paw indicates the posters on the wall. "They might have an off year, we go 5-11, and ownership decides the front office needs a sweeping. You know how it works."

"At least I know I'm not going to be fired for my relationship again." I lean closer to him as Jocko starts talking to his sister-in-law on the phone.

"Not unless you're dating another one of our players on the side."

"No," I say, "but I'm in a foursome with a couple guys from Port City, is that okay?"

"Sure." He waves a paw. "Anyway, I have a good relationship with the owner. She likes how quickly we turned things around and she's inclined to give us at least a year or so of leeway. Which is usually all we need. If we go 5-11, which we won't, then next year we get a softer schedule and better draft. Should be easy to add a few wins to the total and look good while building up the team. Coach Gonzalez is a good guy, too. We're still figuring out our relationship, but I trust him and he trusts me."

I take mental notes. "Sounds good."

"So I think I can guarantee you at least five years. And honestly, probably longer if you want. Half of the guys here on the scouting side are from the previous management. Good scouts don't change much."

Jocko puts his paw over his microphone. "Less they want to," he says, and then goes back to talking to his sister-in-law.

"Plus you'll be working with Morty again. He won't be at the combine, but he asked me to get you an office near his, so he must still like you."

"Great," I say, "I'd just gotten used to clean air."

I smile to let Peter know I'm teasing, and he acknowledges that with an answering smile, but says, "Whole building is non-smoking, actually."

"Wow. How did you convince Morty to come work here?"

"Didn't tell him." His smile turns into a sly grin. "I'm actually looking forward to seeing his expression."

Jocko hangs up and says, "She's showing a house but she'd love to talk to you. I told her you'd want a two to three bedroom, near the office, price no object. With that new agent, Miski can cover the mortgage with the spare change from behind his couch."

The table is silent for a moment, but Peter doesn't glare at Jocko or do anything overt to let me know that the bear shouldn't have said that. I only pick up on it because of the momentary silence and the twitch of Peter's ears. It's easier to pick up on a fox's mood cues when you're also a fox.

Peter goes on to talk about the area and the renovations they've been doing near the team headquarters, the couple little downtown areas near it, pointing to one or two things visible from the window. I follow his pointing black-furred finger while I figure out silently that what upset him was that Jocko shouldn't have revealed that they knew about Dev's new agent. Means they've talked to him or at least have shown some interest in Dev. I hide my inner smile. Maybe it's worth buying a house here after all. I find myself eager to have a larger place than an apartment, a place I can own.

When Peter sits back down, Jocko takes the stack of official welcome papers from him and slides them over to me. "I'm supposed to be on vacation," he says, "and one rule I have is that when you're on vacation, you're on vacation. We work hard enough the rest of the fuckin' year that when you get time off, you take it. So go off to Gay Springs or whatever with your boyfriend and enjoy the time. When you come in the week of the combine, though, bring a case of Blitz Star because we're gonna be up all night looking at these guys."

I just stare at him when he says that, and after a second he checks himself. "Their stats, I mean. God dammit."

"Hey, it's okay," I say. "You should've told me you like looking at guys all night. I wouldn't have worried so much about working with you."

He snorts and points up at the screens. "We do have porn in the room sometimes. That gonna bother you?"

I shrug. "You guys jerk off to it? Just getting a handle on my work environment here."

The bear laughs, and Peter mock-groans. "Seriously," the fox says, "if anything this guy does feels harassing to you, don't hesitate to report him. He has a crush on the harassment seminar leader."

"Right." I grin and shake his paw, and then turn to shake Jocko's.

"Don't worry," Jocko says to Peter, "we're cool. I'm just gonna show him lots of T & A pictures. Figure he probably hasn't seen enough in his life."

"Perfect," I say. "Since we'll be spending the weekend looking at athletic guys in skintight suits. Fair's fair."

Peter shakes his head. "I guess I shouldn't ever have worried whether you can handle Jocko."

"You should've worried that I can handle him," the bear rumbles. "I'm just a *straight*-forward guy."

"All right, all right. You guys can work on your puns over the next three weeks." Peter sighs and rubs his ears. "Lee, we'll be in touch about travel arrangements for the combine. If you've moved in here by then, we can fly out of Yerba, but we can also fly you out of Chevali if you prefer. Now… you hungry?"

There's a gourmet brew pub called Brown's in walking distance, where the hostess recognizes Peter and takes him to a booth with a bunch of pictures of famous Whalers around it. We have a pretty good meal, and then they say good-bye and send me on my way feeling pretty good about how my life is going.

Dev's waiting in the hotel lobby for me, so we don't even go up to the room. On the way to the car, he tells me about his talk with Damian. I recap the lunch for him, leaving out the part where they let slip that they know about Damian, and end with Jocko's sister in law. "So we have a connection if you still want to buy a house. I mean, if you really want to do it."

Part of me is hoping that he'll back off, because there's that additional element of commitment to me living in a house he owns, and we haven't, after all, figured out our relationship yet. But he looks me in the eyes and says, without hesitating, "I want to do it."

"All right, then." I squeeze his paw and firm up my inner resolve, telling myself that this isn't really deciding anything. "I'm on board."

CHAPTER TWELVE: UPS AND DOWNS (DEV)

We go to meet Lee's boss's sister-in-law, a black bear named Clara who's almost as tall as me. The house she's showing is big and a bit out of my price range at a million two hundred thousand, but she points us to a few listings that might be good, and we visit one of them on the way home.

I'm pretty excited as we walk around the place, a townhouse near a main street with lots of restaurants and shopping. I like the idea of buying a place up here that he could live in and I could come visit, and after Ogleby's percentage and taxes out of the Strongwell check, I could pretty much pay cash for this one. The townhouse might not be anything special, but as I'm looking around, it's special in my mind because it's the place we live, and it's got his paintings and my posters on the walls, it's got our food in the kitchen, it's got our scent in the air. I stand on the staircase and look up toward the bedrooms and think about how apartments feel temporary and houses feel permanent and settled, and the thought of a place like this being home, with Lee, is a warm, happy thought.

Lee doesn't seem quite as excited. When I say, "This place looks pretty cool," he just rubs his feet through the carpet.

"I don't know about 'cool,'" he says. "It looks like a place where people sleep and keep their stuff."

"That's what a 'house' is, doc," I say. "I was imagining it as our house."

"Okay," he says, and then his smile brightens.

•

Polecki gave us an address that Lee's map on his phone says is a little over an hour away. It doesn't seem to be in any city, a ways northwest of Yerba proper, but we check the address twice and the directions come up the same both times. The countryside is really pretty once we get out of the suburbs, and we get to take a bridge across the bay and catch a glimpse of the ocean, which for a couple Midwestern guys is pretty cool.

I think about owning a house here, maybe retiring here, with Lee. In the best case scenario, nothing goes wrong in my life and I have a couple rings and Lee is a head of scouting or even more maybe, and I can talk to him about his job and we can drive down to the ocean on weekends.

And on the other side of the Bay we run into traffic, and I'm reminded that nothing ever follows the best case scenario. Except maybe me hooking up with Lee. I look over at his orange fur and chocolate-brown ears silhouetted against the blue sky and light clouds. I'd be an idiot to throw that away, I know that. But what if Lee ends up like Gena, taking care of a sullen, resentful Dev who never got to a championship game, maybe becoming forgetful and violent in his late thirties? Could I do that to him?

To stop that line of thought, I ask him about the movies that are out and which ones he might want to see before we head back to Chevali. I don't talk about Fisher or Gregory or his mom. Or—dammit, I forgot to call Gerrard. Well...after this dinner maybe.

As we get out of the suburbs, the gentle green hills give way to low mountains and then fields full of low wooden racks on which leafy vines curl and cling. "Vineyards," Lee says. "This must be some fancy restaurant."

"You couldn't tell that from the name?" I read it off again. "Royaume Perdue?"

He snorts. "Not the kind of place I'd expect a couple football players to go."

"Hey..." I try to think of a counterexample. "I'd go. If you took me. Maybe Polecki's boyfriend..."

"Who is also a football player."

"All right, all right." I check the map again. "Another three miles and then a right turn, it looks like."

And two minutes later, we see a sign for Royaume Perdue. "It's a winery," Lee says.

"Maybe they also serve food?"

He flicks his ears. "Did he say 'dinner' or just that we'd get together tonight?"

I check my phone. "We just said getting together."

Lee makes the turn down a gravel drive and then stops. "This is the turn," I say. "The sign was back there."

He points to the other side. A large sign reads, "Closed for a private party."

"Oh. Well..." I pick up my phone and call Polecki.

"Hey!" He sounds cheerful. "Are you guys on the way?"

"We're here. But it says it's closed for a private event?"

"Yeah, that's us! Come on back!"

"All right. Be there in a minute."

Lee looks at me. I point ahead. "We're the private event," I say.

He just shakes his head and drives forward. "Football players. He rented out an entire winery just to hang out with us for an evening? How much…"

"Don't ask."

"Yeah." He laughs and rests a paw on my thigh. "I can't wait until a few more years when you get a new contract."

I drape my arm over his shoulders and lean in. "I'll rent out any winery you want when I win a championship."

The winery itself is a gorgeous old mansion, green moss on the shingles and old maroon and black stones in the walls. It's bigger than Gerrard's house even, and there are two buildings farther down the driveway, one of which looks to be a four-car garage and the other of which is a big barn-shaped thing.

We park next to a shiny black truck—football player truck for sure, I think, looking at the extras on it—and walk up a smooth stone walkway to the stone patio out front of the house itself, past a flower garden around a fountain and a stained wooden sign with the name "Royaume Perdue" lettered in gold. The "RP" monogram is there in gold again on the keystone over the door, which Lee hesitates at. The large wooden doors are closed, with elaborate iron handles, and there's no door knocker or doorbell visible.

So I try the handle and the door opens, letting onto a cool, dark foyer that smells strongly of wine and wood. There's light and faint noise from an open doorway ahead of us, and also from one to our left, and in the light from the doorways we can see framed pictures all over the walls.

Lee lifts his nose and turns toward the left. "I think this way?" he says, and just then a large-eared canid silhouette appears in that doorway.

"Hey, Miski!" Polecki's cheerful voice echoes in the dark room. "C'mon in here, we've got some wine pouring." He stops in front of Lee and extends a paw. "Hey, you must be Wiley."

"Lee," my fox says, shaking the offered paw. I can't help but notice the glint of a ring on his finger. He can't have gotten the championship rings already—no, that's right, he has one from his rookie year.

"Aran Polecki, but you know that." His smile is bright in the room, and when he comes over to hug me, I can smell the wine on his breath. "Dev, it's great to see you again. Thanks for coming all the way up here."

I hug back. His tail wags enough that I can feel it in his body against me, and for a moment I forget the jealousy over the championship ring. "Did you rent out a whole winery just for dinner?"

"Ha!" He punches my arm. "When you get out of that rookie contract, you won't be so surprised. Place like this for an evening…twenty grand, including the wine we're buying for everyone. I earned that in the first five minutes of the championship game."

The jealousy spikes and then I stifle it. I made a million dollars on a commercial and Damian's going to make me sixty million over the rest of my career. "You're buying wine?"

He grabs my arm to steer me into the next room. "Jay's parents love this place. They used to bring him here, and he started bringing me here. So we're celebrating the championship with a dinner and I'm buying everyone a case of their wine. It's only his parents, his brother and sister, one aunt and uncle, and a cousin. You two are welcome to stay if you want."

We get through the doorway, Lee trailing behind, and the coyote turns to him. "Sorry! Jay's my boyfriend. He's right here."

The room he guides us into is a large room with French doors that open onto a terrace, and beyond the terrace is a vineyard and a hill glowing with the last light of the day. I stare out at the view and think about Polecki renting out this whole winery for a dinner. Not just for a dinner—to celebrate a championship. My claws flex out and back in, and I rub one paw over the other. I want that ring. I want the feeling of being on top of the world, of knowing that I am, for at least a few months, the best in the game.

The voice of my fox pulls my attention back to a long wine bar, behind which a tuxedoed white-tailed deer stands at attention. Lee is in front of it shaking paws with a mule deer and introducing himself.

"So," Polecki says as I turn to them, "this is Jay Cornwall."

Yerba player, mule deer…"I know you." I stick my paw out. "Tackled you a couple times."

"Missed me a couple times too." His hand clasps my paw, strong and sure, and we trade smiles.

"Yeah, well, we went to the playoffs." Then I turn to Polecki, who's just watching the two of us with his ears perked up, a smirk building on his muzzle. "And I know how that came out, so I'll stop talking about that now."

Lee smiles and wags his tail and says, "Thanks for inviting us up here. The place is gorgeous."

The coyote and deer exchange looks and smiles, and Polecki puts his arm around Jay's waist. "We like it a lot. We talked about maybe buying a vineyard down the road."

"And thanks for coming up all this way," Jay adds. "I'm glad to meet you two finally. Well…" He ducks his head shyly. "You know, meeting you with Aran."

Lee glances at the wine bartender (is that what they're called? I'll have to ask him) and Polecki sees his look. "Don't worry. The staff here knows us. They're cool."

So I go and put my arm around my fox and I say, "I didn't realize you guys had all this planned."

"Oh, we didn't." Polecki laughs. "It's been non-stop. Interviews, travel, all that shit. When I got your message I thought it was a great chance to finally turn my phone off and get away from people."

"And to see Jay?" I ask.

"Oh, I was down there with him." The deer elbows Polecki. "Someone has to cook or else he'll talk on the phone until eleven at night and then order some shitty takeout pizza."

"Hey," Polecki says, "our pizza beats the shit out of your pizza."

"We have Solitaire Pizza up here, too. We just don't eat it."

"I only ordered that once."

I squeeze Lee. "He cooks for me, too. I go out all the time when he's not around."

"But," Lee says, "his place is downtown so he's got a good Etruscan place and a burger place, a sandwich shop, and so on. So he's not ordering crappy takeout."

"Oh, sure," Polecki says. "Take his side. Look, I'm classy." He turns to the attentive white-tailed deer. "Can you start a tasting for these two, and then pour us another each of the cab sauvignon?"

"I won't have any." Lee holds up a paw as the bartender guy takes four glasses out from under the counter. "I'm driving. Unless you have a chardonnay."

"That is our first wine." The deer holds the bottle over the first glass, eyes on Lee.

"Oh, all right." He nods, and then looks at me. "I'll just have a mouthful, and we'll be here for a little while."

"Where did you go to school?" I ask Cornwall while the deer is pouring.

"Hoffridge. Total party school, but the football team was pretty good."

Polecki elbows him. "You got some action there, you said."

The mule deer grins and ducks his head. "Yeah, there were a couple guys who'd make out under the bleachers."

"Dev and I never tried under the bleachers at Forester." My fox leans against me.

"Well, it was winter. I wouldn't want to risk frostbite…down there."

Polecki laughs. "I went to U of Crystal City, warm weather too."

"Hey," I say, "I just talked to my agent about maybe doing an outreach event at my college. Maybe U of CC would want you to do something?"

The coyote nods slowly. "Maybe. I can have my flea give 'em a call. If not, you think your school would want me to come along too?"

"I don't see why not." The offer takes me by surprise.

"Two's better than one, right?" His muzzle slides up into a grin and he turns to Lee. "You coming, too?"

Lee nods. "I'll be there, though I don't know whether I'll be a speaker or anything."

"Lee is about to start a job with Yerba," I tell them both, especially Cornwall.

The mule deer perks up at that. "Awesome."

"Yeah," Lee says. "I'll keep in touch. Maybe we can grab lunch a couple times."

"Maybe." Cornwall shuts up as the white-tail pushes our wine glasses across the bar.

Just then my phone rings, but I don't do more than glance at the number to make sure it's not Fisher or Gena. It's Zillo, which is a little odd, because he's supposed to be on an island with his girlfriend now.

Polecki toasts the first meeting of the "UFL Gay Alliance," which makes Lee wag at being included, and Cornwall look kind of abashed. Polecki sees it, and after we drink (the chardonnay is pretty good, I think, and Lee's smile and closed eyes confirm that he likes it too), he puts his arm around the deer.

"Hey," he says, "you don't have to come out at all. It's cool."

"Yeah, but you guys are all out, you're talking about doing these cool programs, and I'm…I'm not."

He stares down at the table. I look at Lee, and we keep quiet as Polecki keeps his arm there. "You don't have to be. You'll figure it out when you're ready. I know how you feel about the team, and about your friends and all, and believe me, we were all there. I wouldn't have come out if Miski here hadn't."

They both look up at me, and I turn to Lee. "Well, I wouldn't have even figured out I was gay if not for him. And I wouldn't have come out if not for his friend leaking things on a blog and my idiot agent telling everyone about it."

"Ex-friend," Lee reminds me. He rests his paws on the table next to his glass. "We all have to make the best of whatever situation we get ourselves into. I didn't come out at work, either. I got outed by his father." He nods toward me.

Cornwall raises his head and looks between the two of us. "Do you guys actually live in a soap opera or does it just sound that way?"

Lee laughs. "We're trying to get out of it."

"Although," I remind him, "we did just run into a teammate of mine in a gay club who said he's been messing around with a guy."

Polecki grins and leans forward. "Who was it? Was it Omba?"

"No." I shake my head. "Carson? No, it—well, he doesn't want to come out either. He's worried about his family and he says it's not serious, and... you know, the point is, there are a bunch of other gay guys in the league who haven't come out. I got pressured into it, he," I punch Polecki's shoulder, "won a championship..."

"Right place, right time," Lee says. "Don't worry about it."

"Yeah," Polecki says, and nuzzles the deer. "I love you anyway, ya big lug."

"Get off." Cornwall pushes his muzzle back against the coyote's, but he's smiling now.

"All right, if you promise to perk up. Come on, eventually someone will take a pic of us together and then you'll be outed, so don't worry about it."

Cornwall shakes his head. "I guess so." He sighs. "Then there'll be all the jokes about getting tackled and how I let you grab me..."

"Yeah?" Polecki chuckles. "And they're all true. So?"

The mule deer leans his head back. "I'm just being stupid, I know."

"Yeah, you are. It's okay, we've all been there." The coyote nuzzles him again.

I'm enjoying watching them. It's funny, but I haven't really hung out with another gay couple. Seeing him say "I love you" to the deer feels a little weird to me, until I think about how it feels when I say it to Lee. So that's how it looks to other people, and the more I hear it, the more I get used to it, the more it'll feel as normal to hear it as it does to say it.

"So your family's coming up?" I ask Cornwall. He nods. "I guess you're out to them?"

Another nod, a bit more hesitant. "He is." Polecki scruffles his boyfriend's head where the antlers probably just dropped, and Cornwall squirms away from it. "It wasn't as dramatic as with you guys—they didn't learn about it from TV, obviously." He gives me a look.

"Oh, you told him about that?" Lee shakes his head. "Did he tell you his dad broke my thumb?"

They both stare, and Polecki shakes his head. "Well, that didn't happen either. No, he came out to them in college, but they didn't really believe him, and then it was hard when he was dating me because he couldn't tell them it was me."

"We know that routine." I look down at my fox.

"But they'd met him is the thing." Cornwall picks up the story. "Last off-season, he came up and spent a week, and I thought that would make it easier to tell them."

"Or that they'd figure it out without you having to." The coyote laughs. "But they didn't, or at least they didn't say anything. They're definitely not coyotes."

"Jenny figured it out. She asked and I told her."

"But when I came out at the championship…" Polecki pauses for effect and holds up a finger. "Then they figured it out."

"So they did learn it from TV. Sort of." I'm a little over-anxious not to be alone in this, and I take another drink of the white wine.

Cornwall's ears flick down. "I was watching with them and we talked about it right then."

"Anyway," Lee says, "deer aren't tigers, either. Is your family generally mellow?"

"We're quiet," the mule deer says, "and we don't talk about stuff a lot."

"Wow." Lee turns to me. "I wonder what that's like. Hey, where's the restroom?"

They point him to it, and when he's gone, Polecki leans in to me. "So I guess you guys worked things out."

"Yeah, sort of." I look after Lee, and then bury my nose in the wine glass again, finishing it. "We're trying to figure out if we can be together without driving each other crazy."

The wine bartender reaches for my glass with a look to me. I nod, and he pours a red wine into it and hands it back.

"Sometimes you need a little crazy," Cornwall chimes in as I sniff the wine and take a sip.

I look up at the deer and he turns fondly to Polecki. "I mean, for Stag's sake, I ran into this guy in a bar. We have sex in supply closets at halftime. I would never have done that on my own."

"Oh," the coyote says, and gives his glass to the wine deer for a refill, "but sex under the bleachers in college, that's okay."

"It's college!" Cornwall leans into Polecki. "That's different. This is, like, our professional careers."

"That's what makes it exciting." He gives me a big coyote grin that reminds me of Zillo, because Gerrard doesn't grin like that, but Polecki has more of Gerrard's intensity than Zillo does. "What are they going to do, fire us for having sex in the stadium?"

"Maybe."

"Anyway." Polecki turns back to me. "I hope you guys work it out. He seems like a really cool guy. You know, for a fox."

"Seriously, foxes." Cornwall rolls his eyes.

"I know." I laugh. "But he's mine, you know? He kinda puts all that—all that foxishness into us, and I love that." I pause. "I love him."

"Awww." Polecki takes his glass back and mock-dabs at his eyes with his free paw.

"Oh, come on." I wave my glass at the two of them. "You guys were all lovey before."

He chuckles, and then Lee comes back, and Polecki leans in conspiratorially. "Hey," he says, "did you know that Miski loves you?"

Lee's ears perk and he gives me a look. "He tells me that from time to time."

"When you've been good," I say.

"I cause trouble," Lee says like he's explaining something to our friends.

They laugh, and I take another drink of my wine, almost finishing it. "So," Polecki says, "Jay's family will be getting here pretty soon. You guys want to stay for the dinner? You're welcome, honestly."

Cornwall nods and adds, "Definitely. My family's mellow." Then he takes a drink of his wine and half-turns toward his boyfriend.

Lee defers to me. I consider it, but I don't really want to intrude on this dinner. I'm sure it would be okay with them, but celebrating Polecki's championship—am I up for that already?

"I don't know," I say.

The mule deer wipes his mouth. "I'd actually appreciate it. I mean, you guys are a really nice couple, and it'd be good for my family to see another example…especially another football player, you know?"

"If you're okay with it," I say to Lee.

"Yeah, I think so." His tail swishes. "I'll try to be at my most charming."

We try another one of the wines and chat, and then I feel the weight of the phone in my pocket. "Oh, Zillo called," I say. "Mind if I call him back?"

I'm excused, so I head outside. The sun is setting on the mountains across from the road we drove up on, turning the sky into a red and gold painting, and the air is cool with a slight breeze that smells of earth and vegetation. There's a little bit of auto exhaust, too, and I can hear some cars, but most everything around is quiet.

The first thing Zillo says when he picks up is, "Christ, poor Gerrard, huh?"

A million thoughts flash across my mind in a second: shit, did he get cut? Was he using what Fisher was using? Was he in an accident? "What happened?" I ask.

Zillo whistles. "Angela kicked him out. He's crashing at a hotel for a couple days and he asked me to go back and pick up some of his stuff."

First thought: thank God he's okay. Second thought: wait, Angela kicked him out? "He called you?"

"Yeah." He draws it out. "I guess his real friends were out of town so he called me next because I was going to come to workouts. He said he wasn't going to bother you or Carson when you were out of town and I said you at least would want to know, and he said he'd call you, but I guess he hasn't yet."

"He sent me a text. I got distracted, hadn't gotten around to calling him back. What the hell happened?"

"Ah, yeah. Well, uh." I picture Zillo scratching his ears. "He didn't tell me, but I got a pretty good guess."

He hesitates so long that I say, "Do I get to hear the guess?"

"Yeah. Okay, look, you know how we were talking the other day about having girls on the road and shit and how it doesn't mean anything?"

He pauses again, so I say, "Uh-huh?" to prompt him.

"I was in Hellentown last year with the team. I was a rook, and the guys made me carry their bags in from the van. So I was carrying them in and I stopped in the lobby to rest."

I have no idea where this story is going. "Right?"

"Anyway, Gerrard has these old beat-up bags, you know, the old Firebirds duffel bags from whenever, the 90s or something, and that was the first one I picked up. And suddenly this little cub comes tearing across the hotel and wraps herself around my legs and says, 'Daddy!'"

And now I know where the story is going, where it already has gone, and I'm way ahead of him. "Shit. Angela found out?"

"Yeah, uh." He finishes the story quickly and lamely. "Uh, the cub's mom came and took her away and said she was making a mistake, but then I saw the mom later with Gerrard—you get it already. So yeah, I guess Angela probably found out."

"Of all the stupid-ass things to do." I glance over at Polecki and think about all the secrets football players can have on the road. And how my "almost getting a blow job from a groupie" is pretty boring compared to a secret boyfriend and a secret family. "So is he going to Hellentown?"

"I don't think so. I mean, Carson's up in Peachtree, which is only like, what, six hours away from there, but I think Gerrard's planning to stay around Chevali. He can afford the hotel. I just hope the news doesn't get hold of it."

"Yeah. Shit. Should I call him?"

"Up to you, but, uh. I thought he was going to call you. So maybe wait? Or I dunno, give him a call. You know him better than I do. I never really talked to him much."

"I'll figure it out. Thanks for letting me know."

"Sure," he says. "So how's Yerba? What are you guys doing there?"

"Lee's looking for an apartment. Or maybe a house."

"Cool," Zillo says. "Say hi for me and I guess I'll see you in a week or so. I mean, if we're still doing workouts. I dunno where we'll do them now."

"Gerrard can probably get us into the stadium," I say. "Wait, so you're around? Aren't you on an island somewhere?"

"Oh." He pauses. "No, I'm back in Chevali."

"What happened?"

"Ah…I'll tell you more in person. Long story short, we get to the island, I go for a swim, come back, girlfriend's fucking this otter, I slept at the airport and got the first flight back."

"Jesus."

"On the bright side, y'know, I didn't have time to get jetlagged."

"I'm sorry."

"It's okay. I'll talk to you when you get back. How's Yerba?"

"Great." I tell him where I am and that I'm hanging out with Polecki, and he says a couple profanities, but amiably, and then a car comes rumbling down the drive, so I sign off.

When I go back in, the other guys have moved to the dining room, so I warn them that the family is coming. Cornwall's parents walk in a few minutes later with his siblings; Lee and I are introduced and then mostly sit quietly while the older mule deer talk to their son, and his brother and sister talk to each other. Then more relatives arrive and we're introduced again, and Lee starts talking to Jenny Cornwall. The other brother, Josh, joins in, and the four of us have a pleasant dinner while Jay talks to his older relatives and Polecki basks in the compliments over his championship.

Okay, to be perfectly fair, after the first one, he gestures down to me and says, "Let's have a little consideration for my friend Miski down there." And then they just congratulate him and me on coming out. Everyone seems really friendly and even Jay's brother and sister only have nice things to say about him.

Josh is a professional surfer, it sounds like? I'm not really clear; I ask him what he does and he says, "I surf," and he talks about competitions. Jenny is studying for her MBA (advanced business degree, she clarifies for me), and though I like Jay, she's definitely the brains of that generation of the family. I ask indirectly how they feel about their brother's career in the public spotlight, and they're both super-supportive of him, which makes me think about Gregory. Why did I have to have a competitive asshole lawyer for a brother? Why couldn't I have had a surfer? I guess not living near the ocean, but still, there was one guy in my class who just skied all the time. That would've been nice, to have Gregory be a ski bum.

We wrap up after a pretty terrific dinner, just standing around and drinking wine, until a boar in a deep blue jacket and a gold "RP" nametag reading "Corinne Stiles, Manager" comes up to Polecki and tells him they have fifteen minutes left. "Keep it open another hour," he says, but the elder Cornwalls tell him they need to be leaving soon anyway, and the party breaks up.

Polecki and Cornwall bid us good-bye, exchanging phone numbers and promising to stay in touch. Lee and I maneuver the car around the other parked cars and get back on the road.

"So what was the call from Zillo about?" Lee asks as we get back onto the main road.

I push my thoughts back through the evening to the other coyote, and summarize the conversation for Lee. Briefly I wonder whether I should filter any of the news, whether it'd be considered private by the Firebirds now that he's working for the Whalers, but it's late and I'm tired and he hasn't officially started.

He listens, and when I run out of words, he sighs and exhales. "Sorry to hear about Zillo," he says. "That sucks. For Gerrard too, but…another family? He had to know that would catch up to him sooner or later."

"Probably he was figuring he'd have until his football career was over. Or maybe he just thought he could keep it going forever. Or…" I shake my head. "You know what, I don't know. I have no clue. Gerrard is all about football. I can barely picture him as a father anyway, you know?"

"Yeah." He slides me a look and taps his paws on the wheel. "I can see you as a father, though. If there's some cute tigress in Port City or something, you'd tell me, right?"

I sputter. "First of all, you were with me all the time in Port City. We went out with your aunt. And second of all, I couldn't even let another fox blow me. You think I could have an affair and a cub?" But I don't know what was going through Gerrard's mind, either. Maybe he considered sex before games as part of his preparation, something necessary for football, and he didn't discriminate about where to get it. Maybe he and Angela had been fighting and he slept with a coyote who reminded him of her.

"Easy, easy." He reaches over to rest a paw on my leg. "I'm just saying, you could tell me and we'd work through it. And I'm sure Gerrard didn't plan for it. Maybe he just picked her up one night and then a few months later she decided to keep the cub and he didn't have a choice."

"I should call him." I take out my phone, but I just stare at it. "Shouldn't I?"

"Your call," Lee says. "You know him better."

"Well, what would you do?"

His paw tightens on my thigh. "You're asking my advice in a touchy personal situation?"

I poke his shoulder. "I'm not asking Lee of four months ago. I'm asking Lee now."

"Fair enough." He nods. "Wait for him to call you. He probably knows Zillo would call you, but maybe he didn't, so give it another day or so. If he hasn't called by the time we're back in Chevali, then you'll have to call him anyway to see about the workouts."

"Right." I put my phone away. "Besides, there's better ways to spend the rest of my evening. Once we get home."

He doesn't change expression, but his foot presses down harder on the accelerator, and the car speeds up.

•

In the morning, Lee checks his e-mail, which reminds me that I have an e-mail account that Gerrard might have sent something to. It's a long-shot, but if he didn't want to contact me by phone, he might have tried my e-mail, the private one I hardly use. Not the Firebirds one—none of us use those because they get flooded with fan mail.

So while Lee's showering, I log in and check it. Not many messages, mostly spam and a couple from the Forester alumni association. There is one from Caroll saying I looked good in the championship game and can she meet my fox next time I'm in Crystal City? And then, scrolling back, there's one from Gregory, dated a week ago. He must have sent it right after the game. With some trepidation, I open it.

Dev,

Tough breaks. Good game though. Marta and I are real proud of you.

It's not signed. It just makes me mad; I wonder if he was working on that Families United case while he typed this, defending the people who want to tear me and Lee apart with one paw and typing out his grudging praise with the other. What a fucking piece of shit.

I start a reply with lots of colorful language in it. I'm on the second paragraph when Lee comes back to the bed, brushing his tail out, and looks over my shoulder.

"Whoa," he says. "You didn't accidentally re-hire Ogleby, did you?"

"This is to my brother," I say. "He sent me a message after the game."

"Huh." Lee reads more of the message. "You sure you want to send that?"

"No." I type a little more. My anger's running out, so I call up his message. "Look what he e-mailed me."

He reads it. "He's real proud of you?"

"He's a fucking hypocrite! Sends me this message and then goes out and talks about traditional families a week later? I bet Marta made him type this out, that's why he didn't put his name after it. She probably even typed it for him. No, seriously, I've had it with him. He can stay home. I'm done with him." I smack the laptop screen.

Lee rests a paw on my wrist. "Not arguing that he's an asshole, though you know him lots better than I do. But you're going up there to talk to your parents. You don't have to send your brother a message that includes more 'fucks' than I've seen in most Internet comment threads."

He's right, of course. I get up and wave at the screen. "Go ahead and delete it." While he does that, I stalk over to the window and stare out at the parking lot.

Lee finishes, shuts the laptop, and comes to stand beside me. He rests a paw at the base of my lashing tail. "Look," he says. "When you say you're done with him…"

I gesture, swiping the air and imagining it's Gregory. "Don't worry, doc, I'm not going to cut out part of my family, even if he thinks I'm trying to bribe him."

"I was going to say—what?"

So then I tell him about the phone conversation that I somehow screwed up, Gregory's cold attitude. "But I didn't start yelling. Mom said I would start yelling."

"I dunno." He scratches behind an ear and then slides that arm around my waist. "Sounds like maybe you should have. He was being a grade-A dick."

"I've had a lot of practice in keeping my temper the last few months." It comes out a little sharper than I mean it to, so I drape an arm over his shoulder. "Which I'm grateful for."

"Uh-huh. I just mean, I basically avoided my mom when she was caught up in Families United, but I had to go deal with her eventually because she's my mom. Your brother—well, you don't go home for Thanksgiving and Christmas really anyway because of football, so you could probably…"

"What? Cut him out of my life?" I stare down at the parking lot and think again about the Cornwalls, the quiet mule deer family: shy, loving Jay; casual, fun-loving Josh; bright, driven Jenny. Maybe they have tensions simmering below the surface or maybe they just always get along. "He's the one who keeps trying to get a rise out of me."

"With what? That public statement that nobody heard? Pretty lame." His fingers rub along my side and the touch in my fur is lulling, reassuring. "I'm not saying you *should* cut him out. I'm saying it's an option you can consider."

"Maybe." I bring him closer, wanting that reassurance to continue.

"Conversely…maybe you drifted apart because of our relationship, because of the secrets."

"No." I squeeze him to shut that thought out.

"Have you two always fought?"

"Not really." I sigh. "But pretty much since he started high school. All my teachers would tell me how well he'd done in class, what a high standard I had to live up to. I never did, except in football and baseball, which he didn't even play. But he wouldn't help out and he didn't want to hang out with me anymore. He had his older friends, his girlfriend…"

I go quiet, and after a moment he says, "I always kind of wanted an older brother. You know, someone to team up with me against my parents. But my dad was the one who showed me the ropes, who taught me about football, whom I really looked up to. So I don't really know what to tell you. I only know how to deal with parents and ex-boyfriends and cousins. And boyfriends, sometimes."

"You do pretty good at that." The anger's draining away from me, but I don't really want the sadness that threatens to replace it, either. "I had my football friends in high school, and you know, once we went out to see him at college, my folks and me. We met him at his dorm and he came to dinner with us, but he left early because he had to meet some people. He said he might hook up with us later, but he never did. We ended up walking around the campus all the next day." I rub his side. "It was pretty, anyway. Dad was mad and called Gregory to yell at him, but Gregory I guess said something about his classes and a study group and apologized, and Dad dropped it. He could always talk his way around Mom and Dad better than I could."

"You're more honest." Lee leans against me, tail brushing my legs.

"Yeah, that and twenty thousand dollars will rent me a winery."

He laughs and pushes his nose into my shoulder. "You'll get there, tiger."

"The championship or the money?"

"Both."

"Heh." And the sadness lifts a little, too. There's a vicious little needle of pride at the thought of rubbing a championship in Gregory's smug muzzle, but that's only a small part of why I want it. I imagine Lee's eyes after winning, the way he beams at me with pride. "I'll need to work at it a lot."

"Yeah." He tilts his muzzle and looks up at me. "Speaking of, do you want to call Gerrard?"

I shake my head. "I don't know. I mean, I'm still mad at my brother, and we have to go look at houses and then I'm worried about Fisher and all. Do I need one more thing to stress about if it's not urgent?"

He makes sympathetic noises. "You miss football season, huh? Only one thing to worry about?"

I turn, and he's tilting his head, eyebrows raised, lips curved slightly upward. For a second, I want to yell at him because he's not understanding how I feel about Gregory, and then I realize that he understands perfectly. My anger at Gregory slides to the back of my mind, because he's not here and my fox is; I redirect it to a mock-growl down at that fox. "Shut up." I push him over onto the bed and pin him down when he struggles. "Jock smart! Can understand many things at once!"

"Yeah, I see that." He raises his eyebrows up at me. "You going to shut me up like you did last night?"

"Tempting," I say, grinding down against him, "but we've got houses to look at and I wanted to see if we could get together with Ty again before we go."

"We've got two more days. I'm sure he'll be free."

"I'll text him now." I lean down and kiss Lee on the nose and then muss up all his fur so that he gets mock-pouty and has to fluff it out again while I get dressed and text Ty. Then I tease him for taking so long to get ready, and he growls at me and says he'll get me back.

It's probably just a way of keeping my mind off my brother and my family, but it works. We go out and get a breakfast at some place that smells like it was run by hippies, all wood and flower-patterned wallpaper and signs that proclaim "organic" and "locally sourced" food as well as "fair trade" coffee. It's got a weird underscent of patchouli that bothers Lee, but I barely notice it. The place was recommended by online forums and it turns out the omelettes are actually really good. Lee gets one with fresh spinach and peppers and ham; mine comes with sliced steak and I order an extra side of potatoes, and we get one of the place's famous cinnamon rolls too, thick and chewy, dripping with sweet icing and bursting with spice.

Then we work off that breakfast running around the neighborhood looking at the houses Clara recommended to us, and we find two that look pretty likely—good location, and a price that will take all of my Strongwell check and then some if we pay cash.

There are still half a dozen houses we could look at, but that night over dinner we talk about it, and Lee says he can stay in a long-term hotel for a couple months until the house purchase is settled. But we're both warming up to the idea of a house, more and more so as we talk back over the two we liked.

We've made it back to the hotel and are lying in bed just talking and holding each other, the idea of sex present but not immediately so, and Lee's been quiet for several minutes, so I ask what's on his mind.

"Well," he says, "what if we buy a house and then we have a fight again? Or we break up, or think we'll break up? Am I going to have to pack up all my stuff and go sleep in a hotel and just leave the house empty?"

I snuffle his ear. "Doc, I don't want to plan for a breakup, okay?"

"That's what we're doing this month. Part of it, I mean."

"Sure," I say. "But people buy houses all the time together. Married people buy houses and get divorced."

"Or get kicked out of their houses."

I rest an arm over his side and rub my fingers through his fur. "So we sell the house then, if it comes down to that. That's what guys in the league do when they move from one city to another."

"I guess." He scoots closer to me in bed and rests his head against my shoulder.

The idea of owning a house in Yerba that has no fox to live in it feels really empty to me. The idea that I might lose him because of football feels very real and very terrifying to me at that moment. "Fox," I say right into his ear, "we're not gonna break up. We've already been through about the shittiest stretch of four months that could happen, and we're here together still. I want to buy a house with you and come here for two months and live with you, and see you on weekends during the season and whenever we can until our careers are over. I know you want to wait a month, but we've been together close to three years, through football season and off-season, and I don't know how much longer we need to wait to figure this out."

He exhales into my fur. "I know how we feel now," he says, and I cut him off.

"If you feel it too, then why is this a problem? Why can't we just say we want to be together? Do I have to ask you to marry me?"

I don't know why I said that. Probably because we've been walking around Yerba, where gay couples are more normal, where Clara doesn't bat an eye at two guys who want to buy a house together, where Ty can kiss a guy in a club and it's nothing at all that a hundred people around him aren't doing, where Polecki and Cornwall can stand in a winery and say "I love you" without caring about the wine bartender. And it's desperation, frustration that I still don't quite understand what we're supposed to be thinking or talking about.

He pulls his head back. Our noses almost touch; his eyes stare into mine. "Are you asking me?"

Heartbeats in my ears. I part my lips and then I start thinking, dammit. About my parents, and about his parents, and about whether or not it would be viewed as a publicity stunt. Marriage is only just starting to be an option, with Freestone currently the only place it's legal, although it's going through the courts here in Yerba as well. I get bogged down in all those thoughts and I shake my head slowly. "I'm not asking," and then I feel shitty about that, like he'll think I would never ask him, and so I say, "yet," and I kiss his nose.

His ears flick upwards and he kisses me back, a gentle affectionate kiss with a brush of his tongue over my whiskers. "Okay," he says. "Because I don't think we should get married if we haven't figured out if we're going to stay together."

"Doc—"

"You want to know what I've been thinking about?"

"Um. Sure?"

He reaches up to rub behind my ears. "I'm thinking about what happens in ten years. What if you end up with multiple concussions like Fisher? What if you can't remember things like what year it is, or the names of— well, maybe we'll have pets. Or our friends."

I blink. "Lots of guys retire without those problems."

"What if it's five years down the road and I'm busy with the Whalers, or what if I get let go and I end up on the staff at Port City or Peco or something, or in one of those new places they want to put a team? And we can't see each other as often, and you're on the road in some restaurant and a cute fox comes up and you start thinking, 'That's how Lee used to be.'"

"Wait," I say, "Why is it always me who's the problem?"

"Okay, fair enough." He flicks his ears. "What if I'm going out here during football season and there's a guy who reminds me of you, only he's local and he's not busy for nine months out of the year, and his family's okay with him being gay and he wants me to meet his parents?"

"You met my parents." I poke his side through the soft russet fur. "They like you."

"I know, I know." He sighs. "But more than that, I'm worried about me. What if I get some crazy ideas about something I think you should be doing—anything, not just gay rights—and I can't keep those thoughts in? What if I start screwing up your life every time something happens? The gay rights movement has years, decades left…"

"Hey." I put a paw on his muzzle. "You're smart, right?"

He gives me a questioning look and doesn't answer. So I go on. "You're smart. And we've been through that shit already. We're going through different shit now. You're telling me you didn't learn anything from the last couple months?"

Slowly, he shakes his head. I remove my paw, and he kisses it and sighs. "I know you're right. But…I'm not sure I can change. You get what I'm saying?"

"Of course, doc. I'm not a dumb jock."

He smiles. "No, you're not." His paw reaches up to brush my whiskers back. "You're a very smart jock, and I love you so much."

I wrap my arms around him and hold him, and murmur, "I love you, too, you silly fox. So why is this so hard?"

"I think that's why." He wiggles his hips. "Also because you're pressing it into my leg, probably."

"Grrrf." I mouth his shoulder. "Don't change the subject."

"All right," he says, though he does reach down and brush his fingers along my rear. "How about this, then: I agree with you, but I still need time to sort out my own thoughts."

"That's fair." I press fingers through his fur, down his back. "So enough thinking for tonight?"

"Yeah," he says, and he kisses me. "I think so."

Chapter Thirteen: Thinking (Lee)

Those days in Yerba are about the happiest I've had with Dev in a while. We do everything together, laugh about the hippie restaurants and savor the delicious food and wine and beer, enjoy the amazing February weather, talk about Polecki and Cornwall and Ty, and behave like a couple. It makes his argument more compelling: we really are a couple, so why not just decide to be one?

I'd been holding back telling him my hesitations, but then I thought that wasn't fair to him, so I just let it all out, and he surprised me by accepting it. I'm sure he doesn't want to think about ending up mentally unstable like Fisher, or philandering like Gerrard, but the fact is, nobody sets out to lose their memories or to cheat on their families, or, for that matter, alienate their boyfriend by getting fanatical about a cause. Well, maybe some people do, but not as many as it happens to. It happens because you get hit in one game and you feel fine and you come back for the next one and get hit again. It happens because you had an argument that morning and you're feeling unappreciated and there's a guy (or a girl) standing there who adores you. It happens because when you're an athlete and you're famous, you start to believe that you deserve everything you have and everything you want; you start to believe that nothing will ever happen to you. It happens when you get caught up in ideas and everyone else who might need you, and you lose sight of the person next to you in bed who also needs you.

And then you can't remember your cubs' names. You get a message from a coyote you hooked up with telling you you're a father again. You dance in a nightclub and a guy comes up and dances with you. And none of these things happen all at once. They happen as a series of events over time, and you might look back and wonder how your steps took you to this place, but the path is right there and it's easy to see—looking back.

It's not so easy looking forward. Buying a house: how would that change our relationship? Would I be resentful that he'd bought me a house? Or would I come home every day and smile because he bought me a house? How much of that is up to me? How can I guarantee that our ending will be different from Fisher's or Gerrard's, from Hal's or Mother and Father's?

I roll those thoughts around on Monday, when we take a break to drive out to the coast and see the ocean, actually get out and walk on the beach rather than just look from the car. It's an amazing thing to both of us, brought up where trips to the beach were things that happened in movies. We play in the sand and get silly, take pictures and sit in the sun and watch the waves. It's still a little cold for swimming, but we get our feet wet, and because it's a Monday, the beach is barely populated, so we can even hold paws as we walk, which feels very romantic and movie-like and keeps my tail wagging even when we're back in the car.

After a meeting with a mortgage broker, a slightly-manic tiger, I call Father sitting on a coffee shop's patio in the sun (which I make sure to describe to him), and he says if we need someone to talk to the mortgage guys that I could call him in. I also tell him I'll be up in Hilltown with Dev next weekend, though I don't mention Dev's family troubles, and he says he'll plan his flights to Chevali accordingly.

On the way to dinner, Dev and I talk about the house purchase and the houses we visited. It feels very grown up, very mature, and very couple-y to be discussing finances and houses and all, and it erodes some of my objections. The more time we spend being a couple, the more it feels right, and I can't ignore that. But I also feel like I can't just give in to it. The last four months have been up and down and I'm scared that as soon as I commit, it'll all go downhill again—*I'll* send it downhill again. I love him so much and I want this to happen, and in a way, buying a house with him feels like support, like maybe it'll be harder to storm out of a house we co-own than out of an apartment and that, if nothing else, will keep us together. But I know I can't rely on that, that the strength has to come from inside me, and I just don't know if I have it.

Monday afternoon, Damian calls Dev to tell him Forester loves the idea of having him back for an LGBT day. I listen in as we're driving up to meet Ty in Yerba proper. Mostly it's Dev listening, but occasionally he says, "Sure," or "Sounds good," and, "Sure, I'd love to see Coach again."

"So when are they planning it for?" I ask as he puts the phone away. We're crawling along the highway because I'd forgotten to account for rush hour. "And tell Ty we'll be a little late."

He takes his phone back out. "I told them we can't do it after mid-April so they're shooting for March, the week after spring break. The football team's not in practice but all the students will be around and we'll be able to get a good turnout. They're checking with the local LGBT group to see if they can get other people to show up as well."

"Nice. I can talk to…" I pause. "Well, no, maybe I can't."

He pats my leg, his claws just unsheathed enough to snag my pants. "I think the gay rights movement will move forward without Brian."

"I could call some of my ex-FLAG friends." The thought brings a pang, as I remember the camaraderie of those meetings and briefly wonder where they all are. "But I'm sure the current FLAG people will be involved. Maybe there's not much for me to do."

He retracts his claws and squeezes. "You can stand up there as my boyfriend. That's pretty important."

The memories fade before the power in those words, and my muzzle creases in a warm smile.

We'd heard a lot about the piers that used to bring all the business to Yerba, lined up between the two big bridges and crammed full of tourist spots. Mostly we want to walk along them with a view of the water, and we meet Ty at the end of one of the piers standing next to an old lion whose mane is braided into dreads with beads at the end, streaked with grey. "There are my friends," the tall fox says as we come along. "But I'll take your advice about the basketball."

He comes over to us and shakes his head. "High as a kite. Almost asked him for a hit, but my agent told me to lay off." He scowls. "How are you guys doing?"

"Good. Sorry about the traffic." Dev clasps Ty's paw. "It's almost as bad as Crystal City."

"I wouldn't know. I just take taxis everywhere and chill out to my music." Ty shakes my paw, too. "Nice view, eh?"

"Gorgeous." Clouds have rolled in for the evening, but the low grey light still glimmers on the water. A bunch of small boats skid and glide about, and from this pier we can see the stately Golden Bridge spanning the strait that leads out to the ocean, and in the other direction, the longer, lower Buena Bridge crossing the bay. Out in front of us is De Ayala Island and its famous prison, dark and gloomy without the sunlight on it. I turn to the taller fox, whose ears are partway down like mine against the breeze that ruffles our fur. "No Arch?"

Ty shakes his head. "He's gotta work in the morning. Said for me to pass on his apologies for missing you guys."

Dev says we're sorry to miss him, too, and I nod toward Ty's shirt, an aquamarine silk/linen blend with nice stitching and patterns inside the cuffs. Even the low-necked t-shirt under it looks fancier than your standard jock underclothes, and it's light enough to flutter in the wind. "Nice shirt," I say.

He reaches up and fingers it. "Arch took me to the fancy shopping area here," he says, his ears splaying out, and then he grins. "You like it?"

"Yeah," Dev says, and turns to me. "Why don't you take me shopping?"

"We've got an hour maybe tomorrow morning before our flight," I say, so Ty gives us the name and some vague directions, and I note them down on my phone.

"You've been shopping for apartments, though," he says. "Way better than shirts. Find a place?"

Dev tells him about the house we saw on Tuesday that we liked, and Ty says, "Oh, going to buy? Smart. Maybe you can find something with a view like this. So are you buying together, or Dev, are you buying—?" Before we can answer, or even look at each other, his eyes widen, remembering something. "Shit, you heard about Gerrard, right?"

"Uh." Dev's ears go a bit flat. "Yeah. How did you hear?"

"Vonni called me. He said he heard from…" Ty's ears go a bit askew as he concentrates. "Zillo, maybe. I figured you'd already know, though. What the hell, huh?" He shakes his head and then grins at Dev. "Better watch yourself on the road or you might get kicked out of that house you're gonna buy, right?"

He elbows Dev, who looks uncomfortable for a moment but recovers quickly and says, "Hey, at least I won't come home with another cub."

The other fox double-takes. "God damn, he had a cub? Did he know about it or was it like, someone shows up at the door and tells Angela this is her husband's cub?"

"I don't know." Dev keeps himself from showing his annoyance, but I see the flicking of his tail tip and I know it's taking an effort. "I mean, from what Zillo said, it sounds like it. But I haven't actually talked to Gerrard yet, so I'm not sure exactly what happened."

"Oh." Ty frowns, looks at me and then Dev, and for a split-second I see the question in his eyes: *why haven't you talked to Gerrard?* But he figures out that Dev doesn't know why he hasn't talked to Gerrard either, and his muzzle settles into a smile. "Like you said, guess you don't have to worry about that."

He raises his glass. Dev raises his and says, "Also I don't cheat on Lee, so I wouldn't have to worry about it anyway."

"Aw," I say with a smile. "You guys want to walk around some more? Anything else to see here?"

"Up there," Ty points toward the Golden Bridge. "There's street performers and a chocolate shop."

"We haven't eaten yet," Dev says. "But it looks like there are plenty of restaurants around."

I take out my phone to see what I can find online, but Ty waves a paw. "Let's walk around and see what we find." He starts off, and we follow.

He's heading back up to his parents tomorrow, he says; it was supposed to be Monday, but he decided to stick around because we were in town. Dev accepts the explanation but I think that probably the absent wolf is more responsible for the extension than we are. I don't know if Ty is always happy and tail-waggy like he is at this dinner, but I can't attribute all of it to our company.

He also seems a little nervous, but I only pick up on that the second time he glances at me and seems about to say something. Walking with three people is tough on sidewalks meant for two abreast, especially when two of the three are bulky football players, so mostly I let the two teammates walk ahead of me and I trail behind in the middle, listening and chiming in when there's something for me to say. But twice Ty looks back at me and meets my eye and then responds to whatever Dev was saying.

We find an Etruscan place that smells of melted cheese, marinara sauce, and fresh basil, and crowd around a tiny wooden table that's barely large enough to contain the baked ziti and the pizza we all get to share. The house chianti is okay, but to my surprise Dev tells Ty how much better the wine was up at Polecki's winery, which leads into the whole story of that evening. "Fuckin' Sabretooths," Ty says. "Can't wait to get my next contract and a championship. Maybe we'll rent out this place."

A tourist restaurant on one of Yerba's busiest piers might, I ponder, cost more than the winery. But I keep my muzzle shut and laugh with them, and limit myself to half a glass of the chianti because I'm driving. And also Dev's right, it's not as good as the wine we had with Polecki.

When Dev gets up to use the bathroom, I say, "I'll go too," and Ty coughs. Dev and I both stare at him.

His ears splay and he says, "Uh, Lee, can I talk to you for a couple minutes?"

"Sure." I stay in my seat and Dev lingers for a moment. "I'm just warning you, though, Dev and I don't keep secrets from each other."

"Yeah." Ty fidgets, which is kind of funny, this big athletic fox who's at least a foot taller than me, six inches sitting down, and he's all nervous. "I'll tell Dev tomorrow or Friday, I promise, it's just…I need to ask you something."

Dev grins. "All right," he says, and reaches down to tease one of my ears. "I can always work it out of Lee later."

As he walks away, I lean forward to Ty. "He can't really. Well. Probably not." I grin and brush my whiskers back. "What's up?"

He takes a breath. "I was thinking about trying…uh…letting him fuck me." He drops his voice to a fox-whisper, not that anyone would hear him over the crowd here. "I just wanted to ask how your first time was, and, y'know, any tips?"

"Oh." I scoot my chair closer. "Well, basically, use lots of lube—*lots*—and go really slow."

"Did you like it right away?"

It's surprisingly easy to talk about personal details because he's a fox and he's at least exploring his gay side. I try to ignore the fact that he's really hot and I'm about six inches away from him and we're talking about sex. I am mostly successful. Mostly. "Well, yeah, but you gotta understand I'd played with myself a lot before I had a first time."

He considers, takes another sip of wine, and then says, "You think I should wait?"

"Nah." I push away the image of his wolf mounting him, attractive as it is. "Trust me, if I'd had anyone in high school willing to play with me, I'd have done it. But also, some guys just like that more than others. Polecki says he and his boyfriend—" I remember in time that Cornwall's identity is still secret. "They switch back and forth. Dev and I don't. You might try it once and think, eh, not for me."

"Yeah." He taps the table. "I kinda feel like that's what's gonna happen. But you know, just looking down at him when he's taking it, and he gets…" The corners of his mouth curve up. "Mmm. He gets loud like a girl, and I'm thinking, wow, I should try that at least once. Maybe it's awesome."

For all his size and confidence, it's hard to remember that Ty is a couple years younger than I am. "You're exploring. It's cool." I wag my own tail because I'm thinking of Dev under it now, which is better than thinking of Ty under it, or his wolf, or… "How are things going with him?"

"Good. But you know, it's not really a relationship or anything. I mean, I'm gonna have to get married and have cubs; that's how my family is."

"He knows that?"

"Yeah. He doesn't want anything long-term or serious either. So maybe this is it."

Which is why he wants to try getting fucked tonight. Might be his last chance. "Who knows," I say, "maybe in ten years your wife will be kicking you out because she found out about him."

"Ah, shit, I hope not." He gets serious. "I like to think I'm better at keeping secrets than Gerrard. Dude just lives football year-round. Probably he sent the cub a football or something. But that's the life, you know? You get laid on the road because there's all this tail hovering around waiting for you. Like," he waves a paw around the restaurant, taking in the decorative wine bottles and the pictures of old Etruscan crooners and the delicious smells. "Say you're on a diet and you walk into this place and they tell you that you can have anything on the menu for free. And you think, well, I can cheat on my diet this one time and nobody will care."

"But eventually you get fat," I say. "And also then you're only cheating yourself, not someone else who trusts you."

His ears splay out a bit and he grins. "We took Dev to a strip club once. Charm and I banged a couple waitresses there, but he just went home. Didn't really care about any of it. Don't know if that's because he's gay or because he was thinking about you, but…I don't think he ever did anything. Not that I heard about, anyway."

"Thanks," I say with a smile as Dev comes back across the floor.

"I took as long as I could," he says, dropping his bulk into the chair. "But there's only so much writing on the wall in there. Secret fox conference over?"

"Yup." Ty punches my shoulder. "Lee's helpful."

"Ask him about running your routes sometime," Dev says. "He's helpful like that too."

"I don't watch the wideouts," I protest, but Ty laughs and says something about how he's got plenty of coaches already and he's okay, and then he and Dev talk about one of the coaches on the team.

They get a big serving of tiramisu for dessert, and the one bite I take makes me seriously consider Ty's diet-cheating example. But I'm really full, so I savor the taste of my one bite while the two football players devour the rest.

Ty pays the bill, insisting on it, and Dev and I walk him outside back along the pier. The sun's set and the water looks different in the night, flashes of white as the wind-blown whitecaps crest and disappear. We can't see De Ayala anymore, but both bridges are lit up and glowing through the twilight. The street performers Ty talked about before have tripled in number, buskers with guitars and jugglers and living statues. We enjoy them and walk around the crowds of tourists until we get to Ty's car.

The air has a little chill to it and a drizzle has started up, so we don't linger long. "Great to see you guys," Ty says. "I'm glad you came to the club."

"Me too," Dev says, and they squeeze paws.

Then I lose my paw in Ty's huge one and he says, "Good luck with the house and all."

"Thanks," I say. "Good luck to you too."

He winks and then gets into the car, brushing the rain off his ears, and Dev and I hurry back to ours.

"So," Dev says when we're inside and I have the heat on, "do I have to work it out of you, or are you going to tell me what he said?"

"He said he'll tell you tomorrow," I say.

Dev's paw creeps around to my tail and starts to tease around the base. "Maybe I don't want to wait until tomorrow."

"Not while I'm driving!"

He relents, laughing, and lets me get us back to our hotel. There we play prisoner and interrogator, an informal game that I win based on not giving up Ty's secret, although I'm amused to think of how close Dev's methods of interrogation actually come to the secret itself.

•

Early Tuesday morning we call Clara and give her a firm list of our top three houses and she promises to get more info for us. I've got an application from the apartment complex I liked in case I change my mind, but the prospect of the house is more appealing, despite (because of?) the weight of the relationship it carries with it.

In the city, we spend an hour shopping and I get Dev a half-dozen really nice shirts, plus some pants and ties while we're at it. Rather, I team up with the salespeople in three different stores to pick out some clothes and Dev buys them. Same difference, right?

And then we return the car and deal with airport hassle and this time I upgrade our tickets to first class at the counter so that Dev won't complain all the way home. "But we should watch our expenses if we're going to buy a house," I say.

He frowns. "It was what, three thousand? What's the big deal?"

It's not worth arguing about. I'll let my father talk to him this weekend or whenever Father's coming into town. And when we're sitting in first class, stretching out, and I'm plugging my laptop into the power port, enjoying a complimentary wine, well, it's hard to argue with how much happier he is. Three thousand, to me, is an immense amount of money. It's three months rent (or was; in Yerba it'd more likely be two, or one and a half), it's half a dozen round trip plane trips, all squandered on one flight so that Dev can stretch his legs out.

But it's his money, not mine, and he's earned it. So who am I to tell him how to spend it?

When we land in Chevali just after noon, there's a message from Damian asking Dev to be at the Firebirds offices at 3 pm for Fisher's retirement, so we have time to stop by the apartment.

There we collect all our mail, and there are a couple things for me, including something from the Superior Court of Boliat. "Oops," I say, opening it with a sinking feeling. If it's a summons that arrived last week and I missed it, I could be in actual serious trouble.

But no, it's only a notification that my presence isn't required. "What's the matter?" Dev asks, sifting through credit card pre-approved applications and dropping them in the trash.

"Oh, nothing, it turns out. Remember that wolf I got in the fight with in Boliat?"

He growls. I smile and hold up the letter. "It says here that the judge has issued a ruling and that neither of us is required to appear. He filed an assault charge against me, but I'm not guilty of that."

"Good."

"And he's found guilty of assault...sixty hours of community service, no prison time."

Dev makes another growling noise. I skim the rest of the document. Nothing about a hate crime. Maybe that's not a law in Boliat, but I was pretty sure I made it clear he assaulted me because I'm gay. Well, anyway, it's over, so I file the paper away. I make a couple quick calls: to Hal, to make sure we're still on for tomorrow night, and to my father, to confirm when he's coming down. Then Dev says he's going to call Gerrard. I go to the kitchen to make lunch.

PART III

Chapter Fourteen: Going Home (Dev)

Gerrard picks up almost right away, as though he were waiting for my call. "Yeah?" he barks.

"Hey, I'm back in town," I say. "Are we working out this weekend?"

"Yeah," he says. "I'm trying to see if we can get the field. If not, the U of Chevali said we could use theirs when their team's not on. I'll get the times."

"Okay. So you'll let me know?"

"Uh-huh."

There's silence. I shift uncomfortably. "So, I heard you aren't living at home anymore?"

"Not for the moment."

More silence. "What happened?"

"Well," he says, calm and reasonable, "I'm at a hotel."

"Yeah, but…"

"It doesn't matter," he says. "It has nothing to do with football. I'll let you know when the workout is, and I'll be there ready to get back to the championship game. Will you?"

"Yes."

"All right, then. I–"

"Sorry I didn't get back to you after your text."

"My feelings aren't hurt. You were busy." He pauses. "How did you find out?"

"Zillo called me."

His tone is nonplused. "Huh. Well, he better be ready to work his body as hard as his mouth this summer."

"You can bother me, you know. If you need to talk about stuff."

Now he sounds amused. "I'll remember that if I need to, little brother."

That bothers me, but it's not his fault that it bothers me, so I change the subject. "Did you hear about Fisher?"

"Yeah." The amusement's gone and he's sober again. "His agent asked me to come to the offices to support his retirement. I assume you're going to be there."

"Yeah. Are we going to keep Pike, you think?"

"All we can control is how we perform on the field. We can't talk to the coaches for another two months, so we can only worry about ourselves."

I pace around, phone to my ear. "Good point."

He's the one who breaks the next silence. "You hear anything about your contract?"

"Nah. I'm talking to my agent on Wednesday. Oh, I switched to Fisher's agent, by the way. So I'll see him tomorrow but we're not going to talk business then."

"Really?" Gerrard pauses. "So no more commercials in the middle of practice, I hope? Or in the middle of a playoff run?"

"That was the least of it. The press conference about being gay? The fake girlfriend?"

"Oh, right. Good for you. You're a professional and you deserve a professional agent." A short pause. "So, see you for a workout Saturday?"

"Okay." I want badly to ask him how Angela found out, but I can't think of how to do it, and so we just hang up there.

Lee's unpacking when I come into the bedroom. "We should go in about fifteen," he says.

I put Gerrard out of my mind and move on to the other call I wanted to make. "I want to call Ty and ask him what he was talking to you about."

He raises his eyebrows, and his whiskers lift as well. "Okay. Let me know what he says."

So I call, but I don't get an answer; maybe he's traveling or something. I grab my clothes just as my phone rings. I put it up to my ear and say, "Hey," thinking it's Ty calling back.

"Devlin." Damian's voice. I straighten up and steady the phone with a paw. "Slight change of plans."

"What? What's happening?"

"I'm at the Firebirds office. Can you go by Fisher's and pick him up? He's being obstinate."

"Obstinate how?"

"He's refusing to come to the offices and Gena can't get him in the car. Locked himself in his den, I guess. Can you go talk to him? I'd go, but I'm working on contracts with Rodriguez and I think you'd have a better shot anyway."

I drop the clothes. "Yeah, I'll head over there now."

"Thanks," he says. "I'll tell Gena. See you here in a couple hours."

Lee gives me a questioning look, so I fill him in quickly. "All right." He fingers my shirt. "Take ten minutes and change. Here, wear one of your new shirts and these slacks. I'll grab a jacket and your Firebirds tie."

It takes a little longer than ten minutes, but I get dressed and we get to Fisher's by quarter to two. Gena meets us at the door. "Is he still in the den?" I ask as we come in.

She rubs a paw between her ears and then fiddles with her shirt buttons. "Thank you so much. I tried talking to him, but he's…he says I don't understand."

Lee goes to talk to Gena while I try the door of the den. It's locked, but Fisher yells, "I told you, I'm not doing it!"

"Fish," I call. "It's me. Come on."

There's silence. Maybe he's coming to unlock the door? No, the next time he talks, his voice is lower, but it's still back at the desk. "Dev?"

"Yeah. You wanna let me in?"

His voice is deep and scratchy. "I can hear you just fine."

"I can't see you, though."

"Don't need to see me, do you? They want me to go make this statement and retire and I'm not doing it. I'm not hanging it up. They can do whatever they want, but Leroy's gonna get me signed to another team."

Shit. "You mean…Damian."

"Yeah, whatever. Look, they're blowing this whole thing outta proportion. Everyone does it, nobody gives a shit, the league'll bury it so they don't get embarrassed, and I'll play a couple more years."

Lee's down the hallway with Gena and I don't have anyone to turn to for advice on how to handle him. What do I do here? "They're not kidding," I say, hoping maybe he's just drifting and I can pull him back to reality. "If you don't retire, you won't get another job. Damian told me."

"Damian. That fuckin' prick. He said…" His voice drops and he mumbles. "No, I talked to a guy from Chevali, he says they'll take a chance on me."

"Fish," I say. "You play for Chevali now."

"I know that," he snaps. "I meant…I meant Kerina. I just said the wrong word, that's all. Don't make a fuckin' federal case out of it."

"You can't talk to Kerina right now." I lean against the door. "That's tampering. They can't make you any promises."

"I know." The words come slower now. "But I talked to them…"

"Recently?"

The pause is longer, dead silence stretching on for seconds before it's broken. "I don't know," he says, finally, and there's something raw and scared in his voice.

"Look, Fish, trust me. Just come down with us and retire. Everyone'll say how much they love you, the team'll take care of you and the family." I look back to where Lee and Gena are now standing with Junior and Bradley. The two young tiger brothers standing together reminds me of me and Gregory again, of being teenagers when we heard that our grandmother had suffered a stroke. We stood in the front room dressed in suits and ties and didn't say anything to each other, as though each of us had lost a different grandparent. It wasn't until Mom came and told us what to expect that we started talking to each other.

I shake Gregory out of my head and turn my muzzle back to the door. "Gena and the cubs will come down too, everyone's waiting for you." He doesn't respond. "Come on, Fish, just open the door and come on out."

Gena takes a step down the hallway. Lee smiles encouragingly. I lean against the door. "Fish?"

The scratch is back in his voice. "Tell Gena and...and the boys to go on ahead. I'll ride with you in the truck."

"You going to come out?"

"I'm getting my suit on," he growls. "Tell them to go on ahead."

When I walk down the hall, Gena steps forward toward me. "What did he say? Is he okay?"

"He's getting his suit on. He told you and the boys to go on ahead in the car and he'll ride with me in the truck."

Lee takes Gena's paw. "I'll go with you guys, okay?"

"Yes." She looks toward the den door. Bradley and Junior don't look at any of us.

My fox gestures with his muzzle for me to go back to the den. "He probably just wants some private time with Dev before he goes."

"Retiring is so difficult. All right, come on, boys." Gena gathers her sons and they file out the front door. Lee gives me a quick kiss on the nose and then follows them.

The den door is still locked when I get back, but when I press my ear to it, I hear movement inside, the creak of a chair. Then there's a sound like a distant car door slamming, and the scrape and thunk of a window closing.

It's quiet for one heartbeat, two, three. Then my head explodes.

Chapter Fifteen: Emergency (Lee)

I've just rolled down the window of the passenger seat of the car when I hear the muffled sound, like a car backfiring in the garage of Gena's house. The tigers in the car look around, but I guess it wasn't as clear to them as it was to me. Gena starts the engine. "Wait," I say. I look back toward the house.

Nothing's moving there. My fur prickles, though, and I *know* something isn't right. "What?" Gena flicks the key back and the engine dies.

The boys shuffle restlessly. Junior leans forward while Bradley looks out his window toward the house. "Did you hear something, Mr. Farrel? I thought I heard like a crash."

I flick my ears and nod. "I'm going to call Dev."

But I've no sooner gotten my phone out and in my paw than it buzzes. *Dev: Come back.*

"Stay here," I tell them, throwing the door open with the relieved thought that at least Dev is all right, and the growing certainty that Fisher probably isn't.

Dev texts again as I'm running up the lawn toward the house. *Can you see into den?*

There's a convenient button to call him back, so I hit it and put the phone to my ear as I get to the house. I scramble through their front yard and around to the side of the house, ignoring flower beds as I go from one window to the next, peering in.

"Hey."

"I'm outside. What happened?"

I find Fisher's den at the second window, the model trains all along one wall, the big desk close to the window. The chair is pushed back at an angle, but nothing else looks out of place.

"Loud explosion. Gunshot maybe. My right ear is ringing. Fisher's not answering me anymore. Lee, is he—"

I get up close to the window, and then my blood goes cold. Fisher lies on the floor, still. Even his tail isn't moving.

"I'm calling 911," I say, and hang up before Dev can answer.

Gena comes up slowly from the car, where Bradley's head pokes out of the open window. She stops halfway up the walk. One of the neighbors, an older cougar, pokes her head out of her front door and asks if anything's wrong.

"911, what is your emergency?" sounds in my ear.

I give them the street address and tell them there's been a gunshot fired and someone may be injured. They tell me they're dispatching an ambulance and will be there shortly, and in the meantime they ask me for more information: do I live there, do I know the identity of the injured party? I tell them I don't live here, and I almost tell them who it is before my fox brain kicks in and I think about Fisher's name being splashed all over the news with a 911 recording. "I don't know who it is," I say. "I was nearby and I heard a gunshot, and I saw someone through a window lying on the floor."

They tell me to be careful, that the shooter might still be in the house, and I don't say anything to that except to tell them that I'm not going inside, which is true. But as I say that, the office door slams back against the wall with a crash and Dev runs into the den. He looks around for a moment and I point to where Fisher's lying, unnecessarily.

After kneeling beside his friend, Dev comes to open the window. I put the phone on mute. Already I can hear sirens getting closer.

"He's alive," Dev says grimly. "But his face is…a mess. I don't see the gun. Don't look in," he says as I start to lean past him.

"Don't move him. Ambulance is on the way. Police, too, maybe." I hold up a paw, because the 911 guy is asking if I'm still there, and I unmute the phone. "I'm here," I tell him. "I can hear the sirens. Thanks so much for your help."

Dev's whiskers are flared and his eyes widen as I hang up. "Police? They're going to think I shot him!"

"Well, I couldn't tell them I knew he shot himself. Don't touch anything," I say, "and don't worry. Is he conscious at all?"

Dev shakes his head. "His eyes are partly open, but he didn't respond when I…" He swallows and looks back into the den. "Jesus, Lee," he says, and now his voice shakes. "Why…?"

"Hopefully we can ask him later," I say, bracing myself. I'm trying not to think about Gena, edging forward along the sidewalk, or the cubs waiting in the car, so big but still really just kids, or Fisher lying on the den floor. I need to keep it together at least until the ambulance gets here, and hearing Dev shake reinforces my determination to shove the rest of it aside. "Just be calm. You did the right thing."

"What right thing?" He flicks his ears back toward the den and then forward at the wailing sirens, closer now, only a couple streets away.

"Breaking in." I glance down to where Gena's waiting. "At least we can tell her he's still alive, and keep her back. She doesn't have to remember what it was like to find her husband bleeding on the floor."

"I do, though."

"You're a tough tiger." I look past him, but keep my gaze above where Fisher's lying. "We have to be tough for a little longer, then the medics will handle it."

The ambulance arrives with a scream of siren and a screech of tires. An armadillo and a raccoon hurry out of it, both carrying big duffel bags of gear. "Stay there," I tell Dev, and hurry over to meet them.

Gena's coming up too, but I reach them first. "He's inside," I say, "and there's no other shooter. Dev—my friend is with him."

"It's my house," Gena says. "It's my husband. Please…"

"You know him?" The armadillo points at me.

"Yes, yes," Gena says. "He and Devlin are friends. Please hurry!"

"He's in the den." I point to the window. "In the house to the left."

The armadillo nods to the raccoon, and the two of them rush into the house. Gena starts to go after them, but I grab her paw. She turns, eyes wide. "Is he…?"

"He's alive," I say. "He's not conscious. Dev's with him."

The wild tension drains out of her and her face crumples. "Alive?" she says, and then she puts a paw to her muzzle and starts to cry. I reach out to hug her and she clings to me, body shaking with tears. After a moment she waves at someone, and I turn to see Bradley getting out of the car. At his mother's motion, he gets back in.

A police car turns down the street, siren blaring, and pulls up next to the ambulance. A uniformed kinkajou comes out and walks up to us. "Are you the family?" she asks.

"She is." I pat Gena's shoulder. She's still crying, shaking.

The kinkajou doesn't try to pull us apart. She asks me if the shooter is still around, and then if we're okay, and I tell her the EMTs and my friend are in the house. She says she'll go in and get an update for us.

Gena keeps sobbing on my shoulder, saying incoherent things like, "I thought he sounded…I never imagined…why would he…" and I don't have any answers. I just pat her on the back and hold her, and review the evening in my head.

I wish I'd insisted Fisher come out while we were there (but he'd refused Gena; he would never have listened to me). I wish I'd noticed how he was acting, had suspected something (but his wife didn't; how could I?). I wish I'd been able to say something that would've made him feel better (like what?). And I wish Dev would come out. I can't imagine what he's going through, sitting with Fisher's body in there.

That last wish gets granted, at least. Dev and the kinkajou come out together, soberly, quietly. The officer stands near us and I release Gena. She clings to me and then lets go after a second, lifting her muzzle and wiping her eyes.

"He's going to be okay," the kinkajou says, smiling reassuringly. I notice her pressed navy blue uniform now, the name "E. Mallory" on a patch on the front. "They're just getting him on a stretcher and we're going to take him to the hospital. Do you want to ride with us?"

Gena nods, and then says, "The boys."

"I'll drive them," I say. "Go with Fisher." Here, at least, is something I can do.

So Gena gives me her keys, and the armadillo EMT comes out of the house to fetch the gurney from the ambulance. Dev and I wait with Gena until the EMTs wheel Fisher down the walk, and then Officer Mallory gestures for Gena to go with them.

"We'll see you there," Dev says. She doesn't acknowledge us, looking down at the still form as she walks alongside. The EMTs say encouraging things to her like "looks a lot worse than it is" and "superficial damage" and "breathing normally" even though Fisher has a tube in his muzzle and the side of his face turned toward us is so matted with blood that I can't tell what's still there.

When they load him into the ambulance, Dev and I walk back to the cars. The police car trundles by us, and Emily waves from the front. I wave back, reflecting that I've met more police in the past six months than probably the whole rest of my life.

Dev doesn't even look at the police car. "You okay?" I say softly, squeezing his paw.

"Not really." He squeezes back. "But enough for now. You?"

"Same."

When the police car and ambulance are gone, everything goes quiet again. Birds chirp and cars drive by, and it could be any suburban afternoon. Several people are looking out of their windows, some standing at open doors. We pass the cougar, who calls out, "What happened?"

"Accident," I say. "He was cleaning the gun and it went off."

She believes that only marginally more than I do, but she says, "I hope he'll be okay. They're such a wonderful family."

At Dev's truck, we pause. "I'll see you at the hospital," I say. "I should get back to the boys."

"Yeah." He pauses, and then grabs me and kisses me, right there in the middle of the street.

I hold him and kiss back. Not for long, but long enough. When we pull apart, he rubs at his eyes. "Be careful."

"I'll follow you," I say.

Bradley gets into the front passenger seat as I climb into the driver's seat of Gena's car, he and Junior chorusing, "What happened? What's going on? Why is there an ambulance? Where's Mom?"

I start the car. "Your dad had an accident," I say. "Your mom's going with him to the hospital and I'm going to drive you guys. That okay?"

"I can drive," Bradley says.

Dev's truck pulls out ahead of us. I release the parking brake and pull my seatbelt on. "It's no problem," I tell them as we pull out to follow Dev. "Don't worry, your dad's going to be fine."

"We heard them talking about a gunshot," Junior says, and I don't know what to say to that. I can't say that it wasn't him, because they'd see right through that, so I repeat that there was an accident. They ask me more about what happened, but hesitantly, like they don't want to know. I help out by pretending to know even less than I do, saying that the paramedics said he would be fine. They stay quiet, and I do too, until we pull in to the hospital parking lot where the ambulance's lights are still flashing. "Go with your mom," I say as we stop behind the ambulance. "I'll park the car."

Junior gets out right away, but Bradley stays in the front seat. "You don't wanna go?" I ask.

He shakes his head. Junior's already at the back of the ambulance. "You sure?"

"Yeah." His voice is rough. "I mean, someone has to tell Mom where the car is."

I could as easily do that, but I'm not going to press him. "Okay," I say. I wheel the car toward the visitor parking. Dev spots me and follows in his truck.

"I didn't want to say it in front of Junior," Bradley says as we park, "or Mom. But...you think...he might've done it to himself?"

I turn off the car. Two spots down, Dev parks. "Why do you say that?"

His tail flicks, and he holds his paws in his lap, extending and retracting the claws. "Just thought it. He never takes that gun out. He keeps the drawer locked."

I stay quiet and Bradley, nervous, goes on. "He hasn't talked to us much, and he's been different, angry a lot. We had a class on depression in school and they said those were some of the signs. But he didn't try giving things away and he didn't seem sad." He bunches one paw into a fist. "He still wanted to fight, and in the playoffs he called us and said things were going great, but..."

"I don't know," I say, "but I know that whatever happened, it wasn't because he doesn't love you guys." Dev hovers outside the car. I crack the door open so he can hear me. "Dev says he talked about you a lot and he's really proud of you."

At the sound of my door opening, Bradley reaches for his, and when we're all outside, Dev repeats what I said. "He talked about you guys all the time."

That doesn't have much more effect on Bradley than my words did. So at the entrance to the parking lot, I stop him for a moment. "Whatever happened," I say, "he's still your dad and he's going to need your love and support. If it was an accident, he'll be really embarrassed about causing you guys all this stress. And if it wasn't—"

"I'm pretty sure it was," Dev interrupts.

"Okay, but if it wasn't..." I look up and Bradley looks back at me, attentive now. "If it wasn't, then he's probably already regretting it. It was probably just a one-time crush of retirement and frustration and he'll still need your love and support. Okay?"

The young tiger nods slowly. He looks toward the hospital. "I wish I didn't have to go in there."

"You want to stay out here for a bit?" I nod to Dev. "Dev can go in and tell them we're waiting out here. I'll wait with you."

"I can wait by myself." He sounds a little irritated, but not much.

"Yeah, I know." I fold my arms. "I know you don't know me, but Dev and I are friends of your mom and dad—"

"It's not that," he says. "I just want to be alone. Forget it. Let's go in."

"You sure?" I ask, but he's already walking to the hospital.

Dev meets my eyes and inclines his head. "Tigers," I sigh.

"Teenagers," he says with a slight growl.

"Yeah." I take his paw, and we go inside.

Chapter Sixteen: Waiting (Dev)

Damian calls me as we walk into the emergency room, and I still can't quite hear properly out of my right ear, so I hold the phone to my left. I fill him in on what happened, and he snaps into efficient agent mode, telling me not to worry, that he'll take care of it with the Firebirds and will meet us at the hospital. "Jesus," I say to Lee as I hang up, "imagine the mess Ogleby would have made of this."

It's another hour before Damian shows up, and by that time Fisher's long been in surgery and my hearing is pretty much back, along with a mild headache. We still haven't gotten any news; the doctors said that once he went in, it could be as short as half an hour. They didn't say how long it could be. Damian takes me aside.

"Keep me updated," he says. "I'm going to take off, because no family wants the agent hanging around at a time like this. I've already postponed my flight back to Crystal City, though. I'll stick around until we get a definite word on him. And let's put off our business call until Thursday."

"Sure. What's happening with the retirement?" I ask.

He pats my shoulder. "Don't worry about it. Fisher signed the papers yesterday."

"He didn't say anything about that." Damian meets my eyes and I curse myself for forgetting his memory loss. "Right."

"We'd drafted a statement; I told the press that he wasn't here to read it himself but I gave them all copies of it. He's retired. It's official."

"Great. Some good news for him to wake up to."

He nods sympathetically. "I told Gena and she'll tell him when the time is right. Obviously not first thing." His paw lands on my shoulder. "This isn't strictly your business, but in case you were wondering, I also told her that I'm not done with him by a long shot. He won't have any more football contracts, but there are things he can do. When he recovers, he could maybe coach, or get endorsements, and I'm there to help those things happen."

"You take good care of your clients." It makes me feel good.

"I'm responsible for them." He lowers his voice even though we're out in the hallway, separated from the waiting room by a closed door, and Gena's talking to her sons and not listening to us at all. "I don't care how it happened, either. I'm going to send a statement to the Firebirds that it was an accident."

"Yeah, okay." An accident? I have no fucking idea how it could have been an accident. He sends them all out of the house and only shoots himself afterwards? Did he want to wait until the family was away before cleaning his loaded handgun?

I want to ask Lee about it, but there's never a good time; we sit with Gena and the boys all afternoon. It isn't until dinner, when we're all hungry and the nurse says she'll come find us if there's news, that he and I have time to ourselves.

I can't help but compare the cafeteria in this hospital to the one in Lake Handerson, the time I was there to see my dad after the fight with Lee, just like I kept thinking about the waiting room the time I had to take Lee to the hospital late at night with a broken thumb. Hospitals now remind me of that family tension, the echoes resounding from weeks ago and making me shift in my seat, tail curling and uncurling. Then I see Gena and her two teenaged boys and I'm reminded that the familial tension here isn't mine. I'm also reminded that Gregory never came to see Dad in the hospital.

Lee and I sit at our own table eating mushy chicken and pasta in cream sauce with overcooked peas and carrots, and we talk about anything but Fisher. At the end of the meal, we look over to the family of tigers. "How long do you think we should stay?" Lee asks me.

"I have no idea." I sigh. "I want to find out what happened, and whether he'll be okay. After that I guess we should go home."

"Should I cancel the flight on Thursday?"

I tap the table. "Not yet. I mean…once we find out what's up with Fisher, if there's a reason for us to stay, maybe I will. But I need to go clear things up with my parents and…" Saying Gregory's name evokes him in a way I don't want to do right now, a tightening of my gut and paws.

He glances over at the family. "I feel like I owe them something."

"Doc." He looks at me, and I take his paw. "You've already done a lot for them. We're not family. Gena wasn't shy about asking for help when she needed it. So let her ask if she wants more."

"You're right." He lowers his ears and his tail swishes. "Maybe they'll be better off alone."

"Of course. I'll call some of the guys, let them know Fisher might appreciate some visitors."

He wrinkles his nose. "Maybe only a couple people. Who were his best friends on the team?"

I think about that. "Me. The line coach. I guess Pike maybe, or Jenks, the other DE. I dunno, he spent a lot of time working with me when I got there."

"Wait a day," he says.

"Yeah, you're right."

He meets my eyes. "Glad we can help each other out."

I keep hold of his paw. "It's easier when it's not about either of us, right?"

"Right." He looks up more intently at me. "How are you doing? You had to be in there with him, see him…"

I try to block out the memory of Fisher sprawled on the floor, blood pooled on the carpet under his head, of the EMTs rolling him over and finding the gun still clutched in his paw. I can still hear his rasping breathing, hear the armadillo say that if he'd fallen onto his back he might have drowned in his own blood, and I can smell the thick haze in the air, gunpowder and flesh, and for a moment I worry that my dinner won't stay down.

But it's not much better to think about why he was lying in a pool of blood holding a gun. I focus my attention on the russet fur and black nose in front of me, on the concerned blue eyes and the tall chocolate-brown ears. "I'm doing okay," I tell my fox. "Being with you helps."

He smiles. "Maybe we were wrong about the universe's capacity for dumping shit on us, eh?"

"Well, if it was all quiet and peaceful, what kind of test would that be?"

Gena raises her voice at their table: "Don't say that!" It draws our attention, though by the time we look, both boys are staring down at their plates and we can't tell who it was directed at. My gaze lingers on her, though, on the curl of her lips showing more teeth than usual, on the tight wrap of her tail around the chair leg, at the tension in the table.

What if that's Lee in ten years, or twenty? Not that I'd ever do to myself what Fisher did, but…but it's a violent game. I'm sure Fisher never thought he'd end up here. He thought he'd play forever, the same way I do.

The cafeteria has some kind of light jazz playing just loud enough to insulate conversations; kind of like Neutra-Scent for the ears. (There is also a lot of actual Neutra-Scent around.) I sneak another look at Gena and the boys, and lower my voice. "You think Fisher will get better from the concussion?"

He sighs. "Let's let him recover from the gunshot first." His voice, too, is low, and his ears flick around.

We both look down at the table. "When you have that passion for the game," I say, "retirement's gotta be like dying anyway."

Lee nods. "I think…there was more to it. It might really have been an accident. I mean, maybe he was thinking about it, took the gun out to look at it, and it just went off."

"While he was…" I check to make sure Gena isn't paying us any attention; she and the boys are eating silently. "…pointing it at his head?"

"Or maybe he was putting it away and looking down." Lee turns his paw over to hold mine. "Until we ask him, we won't know, and maybe not even then."

We finish eating and get up when Gena, Bradley, and Junior do. On our way back to the waiting room, Gena tells us we can go home. "I really appreciate all you're doing, but I don't want to keep you here all night."

"If you'd rather be alone," Lee says, "we'll go, but we don't mind waiting, honestly."

"I want to make sure he's okay," I add.

She smiles and doesn't argue, so we settle down in the comfortable chairs. Conversation is slow because we don't want to talk about Fisher, but he's clearly on everyone's mind, so it's hard to talk about anything else. I'm thinking a lot about Lee and Damian, but I can't really talk about Damian because that leads back to Fisher's retirement.

Lee tries to talk to Bradley and Junior, and finally engages them with one of the sports magazines left on the table in the waiting room, something from about four months ago—basketball, not football. While he's talking, Gena and I sit together and drink bad coffee. I know it's a stereotype. I wish the coffee wasn't bad, but it is.

"Feels like I've been in hospitals more the past six months than the rest of my life." I look over at Lee.

She seems relieved to have someone else to worry about, even retroactively. "What happened in the past six months?"

So I tell her about my father breaking Lee's thumb, about Lee going up there to get in a fight and knocking my father out (I gloss over the particulars of the head wound). "Oh, and he was in jail overnight. Lee, I mean."

Gena looks startled. "That wasn't the time he was in the fight in Boliat?"

"Hah. No, that was a different thing." I rest my elbows on my thighs and lean over. "That wolf got sixty days of community service, by the way."

"I would never have thought he'd be so…fiery." She watches him point at a magazine article and smile, sandwiched between her two large boys. "He seems so nice and sweet."

"Even when he was dressing up as a vixen?"

Her brow wrinkles. "I still don't understand that."

"I'm not sure I do either."

"Is that why you two were having problems? Not the dressing up, the other things."

"Well…" I clasp my paws together, tail flicking around. "Sort of. Maybe. I think it's more that, you know, for the past two years we've only been seeing each other long distance, getting together on weekends, and it's been fun and exciting. Now it's serious, it's full time and we're living together."

"But he's moving to Yerba."

"Right, but we don't want to just go back to long distance if there's not going to be a future in it. You know? If we can't live together then what are we doing?"

She doesn't seem too worried by this. "I know at least two couples, one married, who keep separate residences."

The thought is intriguing: Lee and I with separate apartments in the same building, me going to his place, him going to mine. I file it away to suggest to him. "I think we'll stay friends, whatever else happens. We care about each other too much not to."

"Good." She pats my knee. "I like you both."

We talk haltingly for a little longer, and then a nurse comes out, a short mouse who smiles as she goes over to Gena. "He's stable now and resting," she says.

"He's all right? He's going to be okay?" Gena wrings her paws.

"The doctor will go over all that with you. If you would care to follow me?"

Gena looks down at Lee and her boys, then over at me. "We'll be fine," I tell her. "Go."

So she follows the nurse back into the hospital. I go sit with Lee and Bradley and Junior, but none of us feel like talking much. The sports magazine they were discussing lies open to an article about basketball leagues outside the States, but they're not looking at it anymore.

Gena comes back about fifteen minutes later and walks right over to us. Lee gets up, and I follow suit. "We can go," he offers.

She shakes her head. "He's going to be okay. He's got some damage to his jaw. It's…they wired it shut. Six weeks."

We wait. She breathes. "There was…a little damage…" She touches her cheek, just below the eye. "But they don't think there was anything else."

"It missed his brain?" Junior says.

Gena winces and her ears go flat. "Yes. Well. They said there is a risk of…they want to monitor him. He'll have to stay in the hospital for a day or two."

"Do you want to stay?" Lee asks softly. "Should we take the boys home?"

"If you're staying, we're staying," Bradley says stubbornly.

Gena shakes her head. "There's no use in us staying. He won't be awake until morning. I'll call the school…you can come here tomorrow and we'll sit with him all day." She wipes her eyes. "I left my number, so they'll call me if there's any change, but he's heavily sedated. They said he'll sleep through the night."

Junior looks stubborn, like he wants to stay anyway, but he doesn't say anything. Bradley stares at the floor. Gena turns to Lee. "Can I…talk to you for a minute before I take the boys home?"

"Ah." He splays his ears. "Sure."

They walk off, out of the waiting room and out through the sliding glass doors at the front of the hospital, where they pass out of my sight. I try to cheer up Junior and Bradley. "So your dad's gonna be okay."

"Yeah." Junior doesn't seem all that enthusiastic. Bradley still doesn't talk.

"You know, uh…a buddy of mine in college had his jaw wired shut after he broke it in a game. So your dad's going to be drinking all his meals for a while, but after that he'll be fine. My buddy's jaw was just like new when they were done." I search for anything else I can tell them. "Once he got so desperate for something to eat that he tried putting a Big Mac in a blender."

"Ew," Junior says, looking more engaged.

"Yeah. Don't do that. He didn't enjoy it."

"Okay." He looks at Bradley and then makes an effort to keep the conversation going. "What kind of things do work?"

"Soup, of course. Vegetables puree up pretty good."

"Milkshakes?"

"Well…my buddy tried that, but the cold ended up hurting his mouth. So maybe warm them up a bit."

He sticks out his tongue. "We'll take good care of him. Jeez, I can't believe he had an accident like that. He always told us to be so careful with the guns."

"Just goes to show, even careful people can have accidents." I glance at Bradley as I say that and he curls his tail around his leg, still not talking.

So I ask Junior who his favorite FBA team is, and we talk basketball for a bit until Lee gets back with Gena. Her muzzle is damp around the eyes, but she's got a smile on. "Ready to go home, boys?"

Bradley does look up then, and both of them go to hug her. We all walk out of the hospital together, and I watch the three tigers hanging on to each other as though worried they might fly apart. The hospital rises cool and white behind us, red lettering across the face of it, and we leave behind the smell of antiseptic and Neutra-Scent, walking through the glass doors and into the night.

I put my arm around the fox beside me and I swear silently that I will never do anything like this to him. That, in there, that will never be me.

•

We don't talk much in the truck on the way home, both lost in our thoughts. At one intersection, he says, "What Gena wanted to talk to me about...it was kind of personal. It's not about Fisher or anything. I'll tell you about it if you really want me to, but I feel like she'd rather it be kept private."

"I wasn't wondering," I say, although now I am, a little. But I guess it was probably something she wanted to get off her chest, and she feels closer to Lee than to me. Or else she needed to leave someone with the boys.

He stares out the windshield. "The one thing she told me about Fisher was that the doctor's report said there were burns around the lips and gunpowder residue on the teeth."

"Burns? Like from..."

"From the mouth of the gun."

The words come out clinically, almost emotionless, and the only indication of how much they affect him is how tightly his paws are twined together.

So Fisher had the gun in his mouth when he fired it. "He's a lousy shot," I say roughly.

Now Lee does turn my way. "I think that probably he just wanted to see what it would feel like, or maybe he was going to shoot himself and then stopped. If he only caught his jaw, then maybe he was taking the gun out of his mouth. Maybe he'd reconsidered and it really was an accident."

"Maybe he fired too early as he was putting it in," I snap back, paws tight on the steering wheel. I'm angry at Fisher again, at my friend, for turning his back on me and his family, for being so blind to life outside football that he'd rather die.

"We'll probably never know." Lee reaches over to hold my paw. "But wouldn't you rather assume the best? Assume he changed his mind?"

"What if he tries again?"

"He'll be watched pretty closely. I think once he gets over the retirement and realizes that he still has a lot of life left, he won't want to do that again."

"But you don't know that."

"No." He rubs his fingers through the fur on the back of my paw. "But we have to hope for the best, right?"

"I guess so." I understand what he's saying, but it's hard for me to do it. I keep seeing Fisher's muzzle covered in blood, picturing him putting the gun to his mouth. I keep thinking, this is what he *wanted*. I can't wrap my head around that. Was it so grim, the life without football? I'm looking forward to the off-season, for time away from the relentless practices and feeling sore and beaten up, for time to spend with Lee and time to play video games and watch movies. Maybe I don't want that to be my whole life yet, but I can't fathom the feeling that there's nothing left. Especially when he has a family.

Hope for the best.

Stopped at a light, I turn to Lee, who's quiet and thinking again. "We have to worry about the things we can change, right?"

"Ideally. But we can't always control what we worry about."

"I hope he's okay," I say. "But I don't know what I'll say to him next time I see him."

"Let's worry about that when it happens. For right now I think I want to go home and just hold you, if that's okay."

"That's just fine," I say, and I speed through the light to get to that moment as fast as possible.

•

Wednesday morning, my phone buzzes, startling me awake. I lunge for it and fumble until I can read the message, thinking it's something about Fisher.

Ty: Tell Lee he can tell you. Went okay, not great.

Lee lifts his head from the pillow and looks in my direction. "Fisher?" he asks quietly.

I shake my head and show him the message. He stares and then laughs softly, rolling onto his back and snuggling against me, loose and relaxed. "Ha. Okay, I'm glad."

"What?" I put the phone back on the nightstand and rest a paw on his stomach.

He grins widely and rests his muzzle against my collarbone. "Ty was going to bottom for the first time. That's about what I'd expected him to say."

It takes me a moment to process the words. "Wait, what? The guy who was all worried about who was on top? He was going to let that wolf—wow, he went from zero to gay in like a month."

He flicks his tail under the covers. "It's often the guys who are all obsessed about it who want to try it, right?"

"If you say so." I squint down at him. He doesn't seem particularly concerned one way or another about it, but he's also good at hiding things.

"I'm glad it went okay, though. A lot of guys might freak out about it. Hope he stays in touch with Arch."

"Yeah," I say, still thinking about stuff. "I don't think he wants a long-term thing. He's just messing around."

"That's what he told me. Arch doesn't really want that either," Lee says, resting a paw on my arm, which reminds me that my paw's on his stomach, and I move my fingers around, pressing in on his fur and skin. "Anyway, I think Ty's bi, not gay."

"I've never actually met a bi guy," I say. "Hey, if he's bi, that means there are fewer bi guys in the league than gay guys."

"Yeah?"

"So I'm not the smallest minority." I grin.

"Ty's not out, so you still are." He looks up, sees my whiskers droop, and cranes his head up to kiss me. "Aw, that just means you're special."

"Yeah, yeah." I kiss him back, grumbling.

He runs his claws up and down my arm, but it's casual, comforting. My fingers move down near his sheath, but he's not aroused and neither am I. "Anyway," Lee says, "at least someone's having a good day."

"I'm not sure Ty is. I think he's back home now interviewing wives again." I reach for my phone and send him a quick text, *Glad to hear it.* I pause, wondering whether to send a wink or not, and decide on a joke. *Would you say that visit was hard to top?*

Lee rolls away from me and grabs for his phone as well. "Nothing from Gena," he says. "We're supposed to meet Hal and Pol for dinner today, but…"

I send the message to Ty and meet Lee's eyes over our phones. "As long as we don't say anything about Fisher."

"Okay." He checks his e-mails. "And Father's in town, wanted to know if dinner's still on today. I'll see if we can do lunch, or drinks after."

My phone buzzes. *Ty: Har har. Actually that was the easy part. ;) Like they told us in rookie camp, it's easier to be on top.*

"No word from Gena yet?"

"No."

I hold my phone and lean back. "Let's put off the flight to Hilltown for a couple days. I'll see if there's anything we can do for Fisher. And I can see Gerrard, too."

He nods. "I'll see when Father's going back. If he's here through Friday, maybe we can see him tomorrow."

We lie next to each other working out our schedules with our phones and then get up to shower, because neither of us is quite in the mood for sex. That doesn't mean we can't shower together, and I still enjoy rubbing my paws along his body and through his fur, and it's an interesting, intimate sensation washing each other without either the afterglow of sex or the exciting anticipation of it.

Of course, what's foremost on our minds is how Fisher is doing. We wait for the call from Gena all morning, but the only call is from Gerrard, calling to tell me that we can work out on Friday (the 13th, he notes without further remark) as Carson should be back then. I ask how his home situation is and he cuts me off with a comment to bring Zillo "if he wants to come."

Lee's father replies that dinner Thursday would be fine, and that he's flying back to Hilltown Saturday morning, so I check to see if we can change our tickets to get on his flight. "This off-season is harder to manage than the season is," I grumble, booking two first-class seats on his laptop as we sit on the couch watching sports news.

My fox leans against me and grins, his tail curling along the couch. "You've got all these relationships to manage now. Not like in Hilltown when basically you knew a few guys from the team and you'd go get drunk with them, or come visit me."

"This is only a few guys from the team," I point out. "Just their lives are a million times more complicated."

"Willie and Shaz were what, nineteen? No families—no wives and kids, anyway—and nothing to do but spend the hundreds of thousands they got their rookie years on booze and video games and strip clubs."

"And I spent a lot of time at home, too." While Gregory was starting his successful career, buying his new house, showing off his pregnant wife. "That felt like summer vacation, only in spring."

"Counting the week in San Rojo."

"Mmm." I lean over and nip at the tip of his ear, which is just within reach.

He grins and squirms, and then his phone rings and he takes the call. "Oh, hi, Gena," he says, and both of us sit up straight. He makes a couple of acknowledging noises and then, "I'm glad to hear it. Will he be in shape for visitors?" He meets my eye and nods in response to Gena. "Okay. Keep us informed."

When he hangs up, he puts the phone away and says, "They're bringing Fisher home this afternoon. It sounds like Gena's got a nurse lined up, and we'll be able to go over there tomorrow."

I do want to talk to Fisher, to tell him that if he felt like killing himself, he should have talked to me or Gena or someone, anyone. I have no idea how to have that conversation, but I'm worried that if I don't have it, I'll feel guilty if he decides to try again. And if I've learned anything from three years with Lee, it's to forge ahead if you know something is right but aren't sure you'll have the strength to do it.

We both ask in a half-hearted way if the other wants to go out, and end up sitting at home and watching sports news on TV. It's a slow month; college basketball is heating up, but neither of us really cares about that. Still, we watch, because every so often they talk about the college football draft, and I like to think about who might be new teammates of mine next year.

Lee is already worrying about his job with the Whalers; I can see that when the TV turns to a feature on one of the quarterbacks who's declared for the draft and his ears flick in that direction. He unmutes the TV to listen to the feature, even though he's still looking down at his phone.

I ask what he thinks of that guy, and he looks up at me, ears still swiveled to the TV. "You mean the quarterback or the guy evaluating him?"

"Either."

"Don't know much about the QB. The guy doing the feature is pretty good. We always trusted his judgment." He grins at me and his tail rustles against my back. "You know you're going to sign an agreement that you can't talk about anything I tell you like this with your teammates or anything."

"Yeah," I say, though I hadn't thought we were doing anything but having an innocent conversation. I guess if he said the Whalers like that quarterback and I happen to mention it around the locker room, it could get out and make trouble. So I watch the feature and keep quiet. It's nice to have football be the distraction, for once.

When the sports news cycles around again, we clean up the apartment. Lee's not shedding as much now but there's still fox fur in the corners and floating around, so he vacuums and I do some laundry. Gena calls to let us know Fisher got home okay and is sleeping, and the rest of the day goes by peacefully until we have to leave for dinner.

Chapter Seventeen: Conflicting Reports (Lee)

Hal says Pol wants to go to a museum exhibit and asks if we'd like to meet them there or do dinner later. The exhibit is art by immigrant teens, and Dev's initial reaction is lukewarm, but then we both decide we could use some culture and so we dress up and meet the swift fox at the entrance to the Chevali Museum for Community Art.

He's standing against a dingy plaster wall along with a short, pretty coyote. She comes up to just below my eye level, a nice change from hanging out with the six-foot-plus Dev and Ty, Peter and Jocko, Aran and Jay, even Arch and Jocko's sister-in-law. "Wiley," I say as she takes my paw with a firm grip, "but you can call me Lee. Everyone does."

"Polly," she replies, "but call me Pol."

Dev shakes her paw. "So what's so interesting about this exhibit?" he asks.

She doesn't seem intimidated by his size or grip. "I'm a parole officer for juveniles, and one of my charges has some art in it."

"A parole officer? Hal didn't tell us." I look past the entrance to the first piece of art I can see, a painting in shades of grey of what looks like a post-apocalyptic landscape. "All right, I'm sold."

We go first to Pol's cub, and there's a photo of him beside his three pieces. He's a jackrabbit with a brand of some sort on his shoulder. "He's doing really well," she says. "Been out for a year, he's working at a grocery store, and he got his focus back on his art. It's so easy to get distracted from what's important when life gets in the way, you know?"

I feel the weight of Dev beside me. "Oh, we know," I say, and turn my attention to the lovely charcoal sketches. "Are any of these of you?" There's one canid lady, but the detail is so light that I can't tell whether it's Pol.

"No. His mom is a coyote. It's probably her." Neither Dev nor I says anything, but Pol goes on. "And before you ask, no, not all my charges are adopted. The proportion of adopted cubs who get in trouble with the law is about the same as the proportion in the overall population."

"I had adopted friends in high school," I say, and Dev nods agreement. "And one adopted boyfriend in college."

Pol relaxes, her tail losing the tension in its curl. "Good."

"I guess you get a lot of that stereotype?" I ask.

"Only from the people in state and local government who fund my agency." She shakes her head. "Let's not talk about it."

As we move on, Hal asks about the trip to Yerba, and I talk about the apartments and then about Jocko and his sister-in-law showing us houses. "And," I say, and then stop myself. "Well, there were a couple surprises I can't talk about."

Hal glares. "Then why'd you bring them up?"

I study a textured piece made of burlap bags and pretend not to be very smug about having secrets. "Because the rest of the trip sounds boring."

"I don't think looking at houses is boring," Pol says. "So are you married, or…?"

"Hah," Dev says. I give him a raised eyebrow, and he composes his features into a smile. "I mean, not yet. We're both waiting to settle our careers."

"I told her you're not married," Hal says.

"I wanted to see what they'd say when I asked," Pol says sweetly.

Ah, coyotes. I smile. "I approve of her, Hal."

"You would."

"I don't understand this one," Dev says. "Is it just a bunch of bags stapled to the wall?"

We read the small plaque, which doesn't help much ("Antonio Villareal uses the medium of the bags of coffee from his native country to illustrate the loneliness of coming to the States on his own, along with his gratitude to his parents for sending him.") and Pol points out that Villareal is a zorro, and when you smell the bags, you get coffee, dirt, and some asphalt odor. "The dirt and asphalt maybe contrast his old home and new home."

"The smells are intentional?"

"Oh yes, they have to be." She leans in and smells again. "I get the scent of some kind of fox, too. Probably him."

"Don't see the point of it if not everyone can get it," Dev grumbles.

Farther along, there are more paintings, a couple embracing goats and a desert scene with cacti. Not too complicated. Dev and Pol examine them more closely as Hal and I stand back, and the swift fox lowers his voice. "If you can't answer this, I understand, but…couldn't help but notice that Kingston wasn't at his own retirement speech."

Dev hears, though, and turns around. We'd managed to push the hospital out of our minds for a short time, but I see it come back in his eyes when we look at each other, and if Dev isn't any good at hiding his feelings, I'm not much better in this case. I bring my ears up and wait to see if Dev says something.

He does, though I can see the struggle he has; his ears stay down and he doesn't look Hal in the eye. "Yeah," he says, "he didn't take the retirement well."

The swift fox clears his throat. "Not well like locking himself in his house and refusing to come out?"

"Uh." Dev still doesn't look up, but he does turn his head toward me.

"He thinks he can play another season," I say, desperate to think of something. "The retirement is being driven by, uh, his agent and…"

"Wow," Hal says. "Would've thought his agent would want him to keep playing."

"Well, more the team." Dev clears his throat.

Hal looks between us. "Something else is going on."

"We don't really need to know the details," Pol says.

We all turn to look at the coyote. She's got her gaze fixed on Hal, and he flicks his ears back and says, "Sure, okay."

She turns to me and Dev with a definite "I'm changing the subject" air. "I know a little of your story from him," she gestures to Hal, "but how did you meet?"

I let Dev tell the polite-company sanitized version of that story. "And how about you two?" he asks.

I know they met on a dating site, but I'm interested to hear what they'll say, so I perk my ears and keep quiet. "It's hard to meet people in my line of work," Pol says. "I try to avoid reporters, in general."

"Computer dating," Hal says, shortly.

"You didn't tell me what Pol did, though." I nudge him. "Worried I'd tease you about dating a cop?"

"You had enough trouble with the law," he says smoothly.

Pol raises an eyebrow. "I'm not technically on the police force. I'm a parole officer. I work with the police."

Dev leans forward. "You ever work with, like, gay cubs?"

I perk up my ears, surprised. Hal and I glance at each other and I give him a look that I hope conveys, *Hey, I'm rubbing off on him.*

"Sometimes." Pol taps the side of her muzzle. "This one jackrabbit is. He told me. And there's a wolf, I think she might be from the way she looks at me."

"They live at home?"

"She does. He was on the street but is in an apartment now with a couple other guys." She raises a paw. "I don't ask, and he doesn't tell." Her expression changes as she looks our way. "Um. Sorry if that's offensive."

"No," Dev says, and checks with me.

I take his paw in mine, squeeze, and release it quickly because we're in public. "No, it's fine."

We're at the end of the exhibit and Pol says, "I'm going to use the restroom before we leave."

"We'll wait here." Hal watches her go and then turns to me and Dev. "What's goin' on with Kingston?"

We're both taken aback, but I recover first. "It's kind of a private family thing."

"Yeah," Dev says. "I asked if he'd talk to you for your article, if that's what you're wondering."

Hal swivels his ears to my tiger. "Yeah?"

"He said no."

The swift fox's ears go down. "I know he had two concussions in the last month. I already talked to the Firebirds team doctor about other matters and he said he treated Kingston for concussions, that he was experiencing 'significant' memory problems." He uses air quotes. "So did he forget to go to the retirement? Did he forget about the concussions and believe he can keep playing? How bad is it?"

Neither of us says anything. I'm deferring to Dev and he clearly thinks I should talk, probably afraid that he'll say something he shouldn't. Hal doesn't let the silence linger. "I know it's private," he says. "But you guys can trust me. If you don't tell me, all I've got is the team doctor, and he told me on the record what Kingston's symptoms were. What do you think is going to look better, a frank and sympathetic list of his symptoms or," again with the air quotes, " 'doctors confirmed that Kingston had serious memory loss following two concussions, and Kingston retired the week after the championship but did not attend his retirement and was not available for comment'?"

Dev bites his lip, looking at me. I know we're thinking the same thing: that second one sounds a lot better than "…and was not available for comment because he shot himself and was in the hospital." So I say, "Sorry, you're going to have to go with that one."

Hal's narrow muzzle swings between us. "Huh," he says in a low voice. "Must be pretty bad if you're not going to talk to me about it. I thought it was just concussions." He focuses on me. "And after that call with Gena about winning championships based on ruining lives…"

We stay quiet. He sighs. "All right. Cards on the table. I made some connections with the article. Doctors and therapists, but also other players struggling with injuries."

My ears go up and Dev straightens. Hal goes on. "A lot of them are legs and back injuries. But a few have memory problems. Ace Leffson keeps a little recorder with him all the time. Friese Lowry has a live-in attendant. And the doctor I'm working on the article with is trying to get them into a support group so they can share their stories and lives."

"A support group." I turn to Dev.

He nods slowly. "But he can only join this group if he talks to you about the article?"

"We-ell," Hal says, "I don't necessarily want to put those conditions on it, but you know, the group is going to be part of the article. So…"

Dev shoves his paws into his pockets and his eyebrows descend. "You're blackmailing him."

"Um, no." Hal holds up a paw.

"It's more like extortion, actually." I fold my arms.

"I'm offering something in exchange for participation in the article." Hal flicks his ears. "Not formal payment or anything, I'm just pointing out that allowing me and my friend to interview him would lead to putting him in contact with other players suffering the way he is."

I know that suicide attempts often stem from players feeling alone and hopeless, and support groups are great remedies for those feelings. "You could connect him to the group after the article comes out, though."

Hal glances at Dev. "Reckon I could."

Dev's staying quiet. A small group of people walk past us, talking about the paintings, and when they're out of reach, I respond in a low voice. "We can talk to him again." I curl my tail around to brush Dev's legs and his ears flick at the reassurance. "But if he says no, then it's got to be no, and all we can do is say we'd really appreciate a connection to that group."

"I understand that." Hal leans back. His nostrils widen and his expression changes; his eyes flicks to the side and his ears flatten. "So yeah," he says loudly, "I think next year's team is going to get even better."

He doesn't look toward the corner where Pol disappeared as she walks out from behind it, her ears down and expression stony. "You were asking them to harass Kingston again."

"Not 'harass,'" Hal says quickly. "Just offering some assistance in exchange for some words. Tit for tat." Pol folds her arms, tapping her fingers. "This is part of bein' a journalist, y'know. It ain't all Pulitzers and savin' the world. And how long were you there listenin'?"

"He's their *friend*." She walks toward the exit without waiting to see if we'll follow. We do, and she talks over her shoulder. "And don't give me that old 'no friends in this business' excuse for acting like an amoral shit. Lee is your friend and you wrote an article about him with his permission."

"Yeah, I did," Hal says, hurrying to catch up with her, "and if he hadn't given his permission, I would've written something anyway, and it wouldn't have been as good, but I'd have done it. He's a public figure and his story is public."

We get outside onto the sidewalk, where the air is dry and the heat of the day is just fading into the light breezes of evening. As the door closes behind us, cutting off the air-conditioning chill and smell, I clear my throat. "Technically I'm just dating a public figure."

"That's public," Hal says.

"So you're not going to have any friends?" Pol stops there, nobody moving to end the evening or get dinner or anything. Dev and I stand awkwardly to one side.

Hal's brow lowers and he shoots a look my way. "We still friends?"

"Uh, yeah." I spread my paws to Pol. "I mean, he took me in when Dev and I were having problems, and he listened to me. He bought me orange juice and decongestants and he got me to like Starbucks."

"I'm not sure about that last one." She glances at him. "I mean, being a point in his favor."

"I like them," Dev says as a chinchilla couple walks around us.

"Their tea is good." I smile. "And he helped me and Dev get back together. The point is that yeah, Hal's still my friend. I know he's trying to do his job and I understand the conflicts."

She brings her ears up slowly and then relaxes. Hal reaches out and puts a paw on her arm. "It's part of the job," he says.

"I know that. I want to know if you know how it feels."

"I do." But he gives her a wary look, his ears half-back and the grey fur of his neck slightly bristly.

"Really? What if you were the one who'd been injured? What if your career in journalism affected your mind or something, and then someone wanted to interview you about it?"

"Hey," he says. "I'm not one of your kids who can't grasp the concept of morality."

"No, it's an interesting question." I lean forward. "What if you could've won a Pulitzer but you'd lose the use of your paws? Would you do it?"

We all look at him and he leans back defensively. "What, both paws?" He holds them up and wiggles the fingers. "Like, cut off?"

"No." Pol flexes her own fingers into hooks. "Like…carpal tunnel syndrome from typing. All gnarled up and stuff."

"Do I have to go through with this?" He looks around again and we all stare back. I give him an encouraging smile. "Fine," he says. "Maybe I would, yeah. But I don't know that a Pulitzer'd do it. You know what I'd give up a paw for? To be able to publish something that really makes a difference. I don't give a shit if it gets an award as long as someone comes up to me years from now and says, 'Hey, that article you wrote about the Firebirds, that really changed my life.'"

"Hey," I say. "That article you wrote about the Firebirds…"

"Shut up," he says amiably.

"Okay," Dev breaks in, "but that time you talked to Corcoran and got me flown up to Lake Handerson to visit my folks in the hospital…that really did change our lives."

Hal starts to say something and then closes his muzzle as Pol holds up a paw. "Wait, I haven't heard this story."

So then we have to go through the whole bit where I put Dev's father in the hospital and Hal got Dev flown up there to visit the two of them, and his father kind of acknowledged that I wasn't some fruity spy trying to ruin his son's life. Dev has said that he thinks it was me fighting back that did it, but while Mikhail might have respected me after the fight, he didn't really start opening up until Dev came up to talk to him.

"Ah," Hal says, "he was already out of jail. You guys would've figured it out eventually."

"I didn't say it was the only thing that changed our lives." Dev gives me a nod and a grin. "This fox did a good enough job of turning my life upside down on his own."

"To be fair," I say, "your life needed it. And so did mine. Although it's not so much upside down as…as meeting in the middle, maybe."

"What's that supposed to mean?"

"Well…" I'm not sure we should be having this whole discussion in front of Pol on a public sidewalk in Chevali where anyone might recognize him, but there's nothing really wrong with it, I guess. It's easier if I don't look at anyone, though. "I mean, you were headed toward being a bored suburban father with a job at your dad's garage. I was headed for being an outspoken political activist jerk working at a copy shop."

Hal clears his throat, and I look up to see his eyebrows raised. I turn to Dev. "Anyway, you know, I made you less, um, bored, and you made me less of a jerk."

I watch him process the remark and start to prickle, and then see the prickling subside. "I'm glad I'm less boring," he says.

"Bored, I said, not boring. You could never be boring."

The silence only lasts a couple seconds before Hal says, "But I'd be fine if someone wanted to talk to me about it. And even if I wasn't, I'd understand them asking."

"All right, all right," Pol says. "That story about you getting the two of them together did it. You're off the hook." She leans forward with a smile that shows her fangs. "For now."

Hal meets her muzzle for a kiss, and as we move along on our way, he turns and mouths to me, "Thanks."

We grab dinner at a fancy place nearby, where Dev orders extra portions and complains about the over-attentive service, and we all talk about movies and politics and our jobs. The topics never stray close enough to the personal to let her argument with Hal resurface, and we finish the dinner on a pleasant note, promising to do it again soon.

In the parking lot as we walk to our truck, Dev turns to me. "Let's come back here some night, just the two of us."

"Love to," I murmur, and daringly take his paw. "So you liked the atmosphere, if not the food?"

"I liked the food," he says. "Both entrees and both appetizers. The dessert was a little skimpy, though."

I laugh as we get into the truck. "So what did you think of Pol?"

He considers. "She's smart, she asked interesting questions, and she's nice. Seems good for Hal. I felt a little intimidated at a table with a bunch of canids like that."

I think about where I've felt intimidated lately. "Oh, but not with Ty and Arch?"

"That's different. Ty's a teammate of mine."

"Being a jock makes a difference?"

"To me."

I let him win the argument. "Fair point. And what did you think about Hal's proposition?"

"Uh." He shakes his head. "I guess we let Fisher decide?"

"Yeah." I watch the road ahead of us, stretching ahead with cars and traffic lights and twists and turns. "And if it was you, if you couldn't remember things right, would you want the world and all your fans to know? In exchange for having someone to talk to?"

We stop at a light. He stays quiet as we drive on through. "When you put it like that…" he says finally.

I wait, but he doesn't go on. "If you had to make that decision for Fisher, though." I keep my voice low. "Which way would you lean?"

"I don't know, fox." He sounds tired, and that's my signal to let the conversation go. It's unanswerable anyway. I think Fisher would do well with a support group, but I don't like the idea of him being coerced into it by Hal. Or by us.

Dev's paws look tight on the wheel and he's focused forward. I recognize the street we're passing and get an idea. "Hey." I reach over and pat his arm. "Want to go get soft-serve ice cream before we head home?"

He lights up, with perked ears and a huge smile. "Oh my God. That sounds amazing."

It's messy and tastes of chemicals and we both get it all over our muzzles by the time we're home, and then we lick each other clean, laughing as tongues tickle our whiskers.

Chapter Eighteen: Wired (Dev)

Around eight in the morning, we get phone calls within five minutes of each other, Lee from his father and me from Damian. "Is this too early?" his gruff voice asks.

"No, it's fine." I lie on my back, looking at Lee's naked body as he gets up and moves to the living room, swishing his tail back at me.

"In season, I try to call before practice starts," Damian says. "Hard to break those habits in the off-season."

"It's fine." I close my eyes, luxuriating briefly in the presence of an agent who knows my schedule and cares about it. "What's up?"

"Well," he says, "I'm not allowed to discuss contracts or anything because of the tampering laws. Off the record, posing hypothetical situations, I've gotten an idea of the range you might be able to command if the Firebirds agree to trade you to a team that would give you a new contract: it looks like a four-year contract for five million."

I get over the first surge of excitement that other teams are interested in me and work out the numbers. "That's just over a million a year."

"Right. We could probably front-load that, something like a million and a half signing bonus and 750 thousand a year. And keep in mind that really only the first two years are realistically guaranteed, so you're looking at probably three million."

That's still more than double what I'm getting now. "It sounds good?" I say cautiously.

"It's certainly good to have interest," he says. "But I think if you play another full season at the level you're playing now, you'll easily get four years for ten million, maybe fifteen."

"That's better."

He chuckles. "Yes."

"Which teams were interested?"

"Well," he says, "I can't tell you the names of the teams because then it'd be even less legal."

"It's not legal anyway, is it?" I point out, and then, because Lee's ears perk in my direction, "Is one of them located near a city I might recently have visited?"

There's a short silence. "You know, I really shouldn't tell you any more about it. Let's just discuss the numbers."

Wait, I think, is he telling me yes by not telling me no? I spend a few seconds trying to figure that out and then just give up. "Okay. What do you think Chevali would offer?"

"They aren't committing to anything. I think they're not worried about you leaving, but I've told them they need to come up with a counter in the next week so that you can make a decision. They're busy working out their contract restructurings and dealing with Fisher and Strike."

"What happened with Strike?" I sit up. The guy was a jerk, but he was never really a jerk to me.

"Oh, he made a lot of post-game comments and didn't come back with the team. They didn't say anything specifically but I'm sure they're trying to decide whether to trade him or bring him back."

"Bring him back," I say without hesitation. "Yeah, he's weird, but so am I. He can play, and if we just give him away because he pisses off a few people, then what message does that send the team?"

"That they don't want players who are jerks? Well, I'm not his agent, so I don't really have any say in that." For a moment, he sounds wistful. "But I'm sure you'll hear what happens on the news somewhere. That guy's not one to keep things quiet."

I settle back onto the bed. "No, for sure."

"Anyway, there's this new kid in the draft who's got blazing speed and fewer personality issues. Chevali might do well to draft him."

"Let me guess, he shares an agent with a couple Chevali players."

"Of course he does. Lots of agents have players on the Firebirds." He gives that chuckle again.

"All right," I say. "Anything else?"

"Not right now. In a few weeks it'll start heating up, but until then just enjoy your time off. Say hi to Lee for me."

"Will do. Hey, one question…"

I think about how to phrase it for so long that he says, "Yes?"

I lower my voice. "Of your clients, are there any where their relationship got in the way of their success?"

He doesn't hesitate. "Of course. I've had clients turn down contracts because their wives didn't want to move to a new city. I've had clients accept subpar contracts because their wives did want to move to a specific city. I've had clients whose divorces have disrupted years when they could've gotten a huge contract. I know it's not all about money, but that's the best metric I have. Football's a team sport. There are definitely cases where the relationship kept the player from playing his best and that might've cost him a championship, but there are so many factors that I can't really say that."

"Okay." My heart sinks.

"But," he says, and lets it hang there for a moment. "I've also had clients whose relationships enhanced their careers, wives who provided stability and confidence, who attended the meetings with them and helped them make decisions."

"Oh."

"What I'm guessing is that you're going to ask me next how to tell which kind of relationship you have."

"Something like that."

"Dev, if I could do that, I wouldn't be wasting my time making mere millions in the sports agency biz. Here's my advice for you right now: stay with Lee at least for the next year, because from a business standpoint, you've got a high profile relationship and you don't want to be explaining to the public why you're not together anymore. Or if you really have to break up, do it in the next couple months before the training camps kick in. I think personally if you were single, you'd get a little more play with the ads, but again, I have no idea. So if you're doubting whether Lee will help your career…maybe you should focus on that and not what I think."

"All right." My voice sounds very small.

"If you need a couples therapist, I can look one up in the area."

"No, no. We're fine, thanks. Just…we might be buying a house in Yerba."

"Okay. That's a good investment even if you don't stay together."

I exhale and close my eyes. "So I've heard. Thanks for taking the time to talk."

"Sure. Let me know about the therapist."

Lee's still talking to his father and so I lie back and think. My gut feeling is that I want him by my side. But what's the chance that something he would do might fuck up my career? What's the chance that football or the life I'm living will lead to something that'll make him miserable? What if I don't have as much self-control when it comes to someone like Argonne in five years? What if I see a pretty tigress? I mean, I chased enough females in college…I might miss it.

Argh, I'm going around in circles about it. I just don't know. I love him. I don't want to hurt him. So I focus on what Damian said about the business side of my career. It's nice to have earned at least enough respect that my salary might double, and it's nice to think that if I play at the same level next season—why would I not—I could earn even more. Being gay isn't an issue if you can play. I'm sure Polecki's not suffering from coming out. I wonder if Cornwall will reconsider staying in the closet. I mean, he plays for Yerba, after all, and if they're coming after me to sign there, they'd surely be open to another gay player.

But there, the problem isn't the front office, it's the team, and Cornwall knows his team better than I do. I wonder if he'd want to come play for Chevali. More likely he'd go to Crystal City to be with Polecki, but would that make things worse? Would guys razz them more as a couple? I sort of feel like that's how things would go if Lee were a Firebird. It's already bad enough listening to them talk about the wives and all.

Lee comes into the room and flops next to me, draping an arm across my chest. "Father's staying in a hotel downtown, and he's busy all day, but he's got time for dinner. What was that about other teams?"

I tell him briefly what Damian said, and he nods. "How does it feel to have an actual agent?"

"Pretty good. I won't lie and say I don't still feel bad about Ogleby."

He rolls against me and rests his paw on my stomach. "It's okay to feel bad. That means you're a nice guy. I like that about you."

"And are we going to see Fisher later?"

"I'll call Gena and see if he's in shape to get visitors." He teases his fingers up and down my stomach. "Later."

I kinda want to stay in bed with him, but the need isn't that strong, and if he calls Gena now, then there's no chance she'll call while we're occupied. So I shove him in the chest and say, "Call her now."

He yips and rolls away, and then looks back with mock hurt. "Fine, fine, push me out of bed." And he really does get up all the way out of bed.

"I didn't mean," I start, but he's got a sly smile going. As he stands up, he brushes down his fur slowly, and then up his sheath and his half-hard cock.

Just like that, the need is stronger. I get up on my elbows, making his smile wider. He curls his tongue out over his lips. "I'll just go shower first."

I wait until he's in the bathroom to run in and pounce him.

•

When we get to Fisher's that afternoon, Gena answers the door with a smile and ushers us in. We meet the nurse, a tall cougar who eyes us both with clinical professionalism as if diagnosing us somehow, and then Lee sits down with Gena while I ask what Fisher's up to and if I can see him.

He's out on the patio, sitting in the sun with a small laptop computer and a whiteboard. The first thing I notice is how white the bandages around his jaw and head are in the sunlight. Otherwise, he looks normal, eyes closed as though he's just napping, ears flicking around.

As I come up beside him, his eyes open and he looks up. He makes a noise in his throat, then looks annoyed and writes, *Hi*, on the whiteboard.

"Hi. How you feeling?"

Shitty. Keep forgetting I can't talk.

His paw shakes slightly as he writes. Some of the letters look ragged, but then some of them look fine. "Are you in a lot of pain?"

He shakes his head, erases the board, and starts over. *Lots of pills.*

From the side table next to him, he picks up a glass of water—at least, it looks like water—and inserts the straw into a small space between his lips. I have an odd feeling of looking into my future.

But that's silly. I mean, Gerrard is almost as old and he's doing fine.

And one year ago, Fisher seemed fine as well.

Wind rustles the leaves. I can't figure out a good way to introduce the subject, so I just bull right into it. "Hey, do you think you might want to talk to other retired players?"

He turns in my direction and his paw lifts in a gesture that's hard to interpret. So I forge ahead. "You know, Lee's friend Hal, the reporter…he's writing an article on retired players." I clear my throat. "There's a support group."

Fisher makes the same gesture with his paw, only stronger. This time it registers more clearly as a dismissal. I sit back, but then I think, let me try one more time. "A lot of them are going through injuries, conditions and stuff that their careers left them with. I'm sure some of them are depressed too. It might be good to talk to them."

He finally stirs and wipes the whiteboard clean. *Leave me alone*, he writes. *I'm fine.*

"All right," I say, and turn, getting up from the seat.

He takes hold of my arm, keeping me in place as he scrawls a few words below the others. *What's going on with the team?*

"Don't know." I stare at the word "team" and think of Gerrard. "Lee and I have been in Yerba for the past week."

He asks how that went and I tell him we're going to buy a house, probably, and he wants to know if I'm going to buy one here too, and that leads to a discussion about whether the Firebirds are going to keep me. I tell him what Damian told me that morning, and he says the Firebirds would be idiots to let me go, which leaves me warmer than the sunlight on my knees.

His tone, scrawled in impermanent marker though it is, reminds me a lot of the old Fisher, the one who came up to me in practice nine months ago and told me I should try to move to linebacker. I guess talking about football and listening to other people's news is easy for him, but it's easy to forget when he's having problems that the Fisher I'm friends with is still in there. But it's there in the letters on his whiteboard, however shaky, in his scowl and irritation in having to write them, in the concern I can see in his eyes when we discuss my contract.

So I keep the conversation on football and away from his family and his accident. I don't mention his retirement, and he doesn't either. He does once write that he'd like to play with me again, but I don't know if that's wishful thinking or if he's forgotten that he retired. The question gives me a sinking feeling, so I sidestep it.

The nurse comes out about fifteen minutes later to ask if Fisher needs anything. He shakes his head, but his eyelids are drooping, so I leave him to nap in the sun and follow the nurse back inside.

Lee and Gena are sitting on the couch talking about Gerrard and his family situation. I join them for a little while, and then Bradley and Junior get home from school and the house turns chaotic for a while. They both run out to say hi to Fisher, and the nurse has to go out to tell them not to excite him too much. Then they say hi to us and run off to their rooms. Junior doesn't even look at firing up the FBA game he'd been playing with Lee.

"They've both been worried about their father," Gena says, looking after them. "But they also missed a couple days of school and I told them they had to make up all that work."

We don't stay much longer, because we have to go to dinner. "Social butterflies," Lee says. We both walk out to say good-bye to Fisher, and he stirs from his nap to wave, not even moving to pick up the whiteboard pen.

•

Brenly looks up over his glasses from the shiny plastic-topped table in the colorful flower-riffic hotel restaurant, and a smile curls up the corners of his mouth when he sees us. He's got on a collared shirt, open at the collar, and tan slacks, and he looks like he's been working all day.

Which I guess he has. We sit around the table and Lee lets his dad order wine, and we ask how his day's gone.

"Good, I suppose. I visited with Carson Omba—"

"Carson's back?" I interrupt.

Lee gives me a look, while his father smiles and says, "Yes. And Winston, and Angela Marvell." He hesitates.

"We heard," Lee says. "She and Gerrard are having difficulties."

Brenly looks down at the table, his ears flat. "Yes, well. I think that may be somewhat my fault."

Lee and I both stare at him. "Wha...?" is all I can manage.

"Did you introduce Gerrard to that coyote in Hellentown?" Lee asks faintly.

Brenly shakes his head. "When I took over their finances, I'd gotten their salary info from the Internet to give myself an idea of what sort of packages I'd be proposing to them. They have a lot of options I don't normally get to consider, and I wanted to be prepared. Then when I got the financial records, to be thorough," he adjusts his glasses, "I checked the finances against the salaries. For Winston and Carson and Jorge, they all matched up more or less perfectly." His brow wrinkles. "They don't have a lot of imagination. They've dumped it into savings accounts."

"They're trying to play football," I say.

Lee looks at me. "Didn't the rookie symposium teach you guys about managing money? You called me after that with all these ideas."

"Uh-huh," I say, "and then a week later I was in a minicamp and they got..." The visit to Fisher is recent enough to make me stop myself from saying "knocked out of my head." I adjust clumsily. "I forgot all of them."

"You should be okay," Brenly says. "Especially if you buy the house in Yerba, which is about as solid an investment as you can make. And when you get a bigger contract, we can talk about what else you can do. If you still want to hire me."

"Of course," I say without hesitation.

Lee's tail wags at that. He flashes me a smile and then goes back to his dad. "So what happened with Gerrard?"

"Oh. Well, they were managing their money very sparingly, regular deposits to a money market fund and into the household expenses, but the deposits didn't match the salary; they were off by about ten thousand a month, a hundred fifty thousand over last season. The other guys are off by a thousand here, a thousand there, and that alarmed me at first, but when I talked to Jorge about it, he said, 'Oh, I drop a thousand at a nightclub,' so I bumped up my margin of error. But a hundred fifty thousand...well, Gerrard doesn't seem like the clubbing type, much less a hundred, hundred fifty nights a year. So I, uh."

He scratches behind his ears and exhales. Lee can't let the silence sit for long. "You asked Angela about it."

"I thought she might have another fund she'd forgotten to tell me about, or that they'd helped out a family member."

"Well..." Lee lets it hang there.

"Right. So she said she would check into it and get back to me, and she never did. I asked her about it when I visited her today, and she said she was going to assume that she wouldn't have that money, and then she asked me how much I thought she would get from a divorce settlement."

"Jesus," I say.

"Divorce," Lee sighs. "Already? She knows what athletes do."

"I asked," Brenly says. "As tactfully as I could. I mean, I asked whether she was certain she would be getting divorced. She said that he knew the rules and he'd always promised her that she and her family would come first. She seemed to view that as stealing from her cubs."

We look at each other. "No wonder Gerrard didn't call you," Lee says softly. "He blames me for breaking up his family."

"He blames me," I say, my chest tight. I think about Mike and—what was the other cub's name?

"Poor Mike and Jaren," Lee says. "I wonder how much she's told them."

"The only thing preventing me from feeling like a total shit about this is that Angela said they're used to their father not being around much," Brenly says. "I don't know. I didn't ask her many questions. I talked about my divorce and recommended a lawyer; she didn't have one."

"You shouldn't feel bad." Lee leans toward his father. "Gerrard did the cheating."

"That's not how 'feeling bad' works." His father adjusts his glasses. "Just the word 'divorce' brings up a lot of the feelings and issues from the last few years. It's worse because Angela is trying to shut out her feelings, and I don't know her well enough to tell her that that just prolongs the time it takes to deal with them. So I get to go back through a mini-recital of all my feelings at the time too."

Lee stares down at his plate, and I feel bad for him, so I try to move the subject away from his parents' divorce. "So they're not even going to try to work things out?"

Brenly spreads his paws. "Maybe the divorce lawyer is just a tactic. But she seemed serious about it. She said that she wanted her home and her cubs, and that if Gerrard was going to be a part-time father, then she'd rather that be official."

"Seems extreme." Lee rubs his muzzle. "I bet there's other stuff going on."

"Maybe," Brenly says. "I didn't get that deep into the conversation. It's not really my business. She mentioned calling the Firebirds liaison guy…"

"Elmsley?" Lee's ears go up.

"That's it. She said he told her to do nothing and the team would look into it. That didn't sit real well with her. She told him off."

"Whew." I shake my head and take a drink of the wine. It's a little sharper than the whites Lee usually orders, but not too bad. I roll it over my tongue. "I'm going to see him tomorrow for the workout, so I guess I'll see if he's doing okay."

We go on to talk about our trip to Yerba, and Brenly wants to see the houses we looked at, so Lee takes out his phone and flips through the photos.

It's neat looking through them and talking about them as a couple, but now I'm looking at the kitchen and the staged bedrooms and living room in a flat, scentless way. They're the imagination of some agent who sets them up to appeal to the broadest possible crowd of people, of course. While we were walking through the house, we could ignore that and focus on the space, but in the photos the house doesn't look like ours, and all the doubts about our faithfulness and temptations creep back around the edges of my mind.

I don't want to dwell on them, though. So while we're eating (the food is presented as elegantly as at the French restaurant, though it's not as good), I talk with Lee and Brenly about our visit up to Forester. Lee fills his father in on Gregory and our agenda for visiting, and that's not much better than me thinking about Lee cheating on me. I clench my teeth and chew my food with hard, fast movements. With Fisher's crisis and Ty's surprise, I'd sort of pushed Gregory to the back of my mind, but now he jumps back. He hasn't gotten in touch with me to apologize; my parents haven't called me to arrange anything, and as I finish up my cut of steak, my stomach twists with the worry over seeing them all again. Maybe I will end up cutting him out of my life. Maybe I've already started.

And then my fox drops something I hadn't known, something that shoves Gregory back into the background. "I was thinking about visiting Mother," Lee says.

Again, the table quiets. Brenly says, "Did you want me to come along?"

"Maybe? I promise not to shout at her this time. It'll be easier without that otter there."

"Why do you want to visit?"

Lee scrapes his fork around his plate. "To talk to her. And to try to get some of my stuff out of my room. I don't want all of it—she can keep some of it if she wants. But there are a couple things maybe I'd like to have."

And he wants to know exactly what was burned. He hasn't told me that, but I can read it. I think maybe Brenly can, too. "I think it's a nice thought and I'm sure Eileen will appreciate it."

"I'll give her a call before we come by," Lee says.

Brenly turns to me. "It's nice that you're doing this thing with Forester," he says. "Have you thought about including parents as well?"

"It's open to everyone," I say. I wonder whether my parents will attend. I wonder whether they would've attended something like that when I was a student.

"Right," he says, "but you could reach out to parents specifically. I think there's a 'parents of Forester students' mailing that I still get occasionally."

"Good thought," Lee puts in.

"If there'd been an event like that when you were going," Brenly says to him, "we might have gone."

"Might have?" Lee raises his eyebrows and ears and kind of smiles.

"I would have. I might have dragged your mother along."

Lee shrugs and smiles. "It's nice to imagine that might have helped. I mean," he says, catching my eye, "I'm sure it would have helped a little, and I'm sure there are families it would help more. Like that kit you met at the airport, right?"

"I was thinking of him." I lean back in my chair, not really full, but full enough that I can wait for dessert. Maybe Lee will suggest ice cream again. "I'll ask Damian if the UFL can publicize the event too. And maybe Polecki will come along, which would help a lot."

"I'm sure he will." Lee grins. "He was practically begging to."

"I might get to meet him, too?" Brenly's ears go up.

Lee pats his father's paw. "I think he already has a financial advisor."

"You never know, especially with all that endorsement money he's about to rake in." Brenly smiles, and I see a lot of Lee in him then. "But I'm still a football fan at heart and it would be a thrill to meet him. I don't suppose he could introduce me to McCrae?"

"Last I heard, McCrae hasn't come out," I say gruffly.

That makes Brenly's ears go a little flat, but he keeps his smile on. "You know, the guys in the office keep asking me what you're really like, and they want to know what other UFL players I know. It's always nice to be able to mention one or two new names to them."

Lee laughs. "I could've introduced you to a bunch of the Dragons players."

"When they win ten games in a season, then get back to me." Brenly grins at his son with the bond of shared fandom futility.

"There's some good guys on that team." I feel obliged to point it out, even though I was only a Dragon for about two thirds of a season.

"Of course there are," Brenly says, "but they got rid of their best guy, didn't they?"

I'm not sure what to make of that. Lee agrees with him and I say an "aw, shucks" kind of thank you, but it feels funny in a good kind of way. Like, of course my boyfriend's father should be a fan of mine, but I hadn't expected to actually hear it. And when he says, "Don't shrug it off; you've done a terrific job so far and I'm sure the Dragons are kicking themselves for letting you go. You should be proud of what you've done," I hear again the echo of Lee in an old college apartment lying next to me in bed and saying the same thing, and left unsaid in Brenly's words are that he is proud of me, too.

The gratitude keeps me quiet through dessert, when Brenly starts giving us advice on houses. Mostly he talks to Lee, but he always makes sure I'm listening, and even says, "you both need to be aware of this." I ask him about the financial benefits of paying cash for a house versus a mortgage and he says it's more complicated than Lee said.

I elbow Lee and say, "See, you didn't know best," and he gets a little huffy like he does whenever I point out that he's not a hundred percent right, but before it goes too far, his father laughs and says that generally what Lee said was right, only there are tax breaks that we'd get because the house is considered an investment, and the seller might accept a lower amount in a full cash offer than a higher amount with a mortgage and bank fees and paperwork attached.

The funny thing is that even though I know he's a professional—and not just a professional, but someone I'll be paying to manage my money—the conversation doesn't feel like professional advice. In this small, intimate dinner, taking account of Lee's feelings and knowing how to defuse them and work with the dynamic the two of us have, Brenly feels more like he's giving us advice as *our* father.

CHAPTER NINETEEN: OLD BONES (LEE)

When we get home from dinner with Father, I check my e-mail and find a set of attachments from Clara about one of the houses we liked which is still available, and she wants to know if we want to put down an offer on it. It's 540,000 dollars listed, but she thinks if we can go to 575,000, we'll have a better chance of getting it.

"We can pull that together," Dev says. "I got nine hundred thousand from Strongwell, before taxes, and your dad said that if I buy a first home with it then I get a tax break up to, um." He thinks. "Anyway, he said if I spend up to six hundred thousand on a house, it would work out."

"But he also said the seller would accept less if we pay cash." I start typing out a reply. "Let me ask her if we could do five-fifty cash."

"It doesn't seem like that much less." Dev puts a paw on my shoulder, looking at the screen as I type. "Is it worth it? Wouldn't we rather get this thing settled quickly?"

"If we go to five-fifty, then there'd be more left over for..." I pause. Talking about Dev's brother at the dinner reminded me of Alexi. I understand that Dev doesn't want to just hand money over to him, and I'm sure as hell not excited about giving some of our money to a guy who's betraying his own family like that. Just a couple months ago, I might've said *fuck him* and left it at that.

But I can't think of Gregory without thinking of Mother, how scared she was and how hurt, and how all that turned into her lashing out at me. Is Gregory scared and hurt? Is it fair to punish his cub because he's having trouble dealing with his brother's celebrity and homosexuality? Isn't the right thing to do to be charitable and helpful, to extend love instead of turning our backs? I'm sure it's easier for me because Gregory's not my brother; there's no weight of years of affection to sharpen the betrayal. But still, I'd rather Alexi grow up knowing and loving his uncle, and I think Dev would too, if he'd stop and think about it.

It's also hard because neither of us knows how much Gregory actually might need. Ten thousand? Fifty thousand? If a lawyer, even a junior one, is worrying about money and Dev's parents aren't sure they can help, then my inclination is to guess on the high side. Father drilled into my head that most people don't keep enough savings around, which is partly why I'm still in good shape despite not working for almost three months.

Also, of course, because Dev pays for a lot of my expenses. "For what?" he says.

"For, you know, if…" I type a little more of the letter. "If someone we know needs twenty-five thousand."

"Lee."

He's standing on the side my tail is hanging out on, so I flick it against his legs. "Or, fine, I'll keep the extra twenty-five thousand and I'll show you how much money it is."

He curls his tail against mine and squeezes my shoulder, his fingers digging in. "Leave my family to me."

"Oh, is that how it works now?" I turn to him. "So next time Father asks us to dinner, I'll just go alone?"

His muzzle scrunches up and he glares down. "That's different."

"What's different about it?"

"Wha—?" He lets go of my shoulder and stares. "That's—that's *dinner*. You're talking about my brother calling me out in the national media—"

"A callout that nearly everyone ignored or missed."

"—and being a total shit to me because of my relationship, and accusing me of—Jesus, fox, it's not like we're married and he's your brother-in-law."

I lean back. "No, I guess it's not. So I'm not an important part of your life?"

"Hey." His paw lands on my shoulder again. "No, that's not what I said."

"You implied that it would take a marriage to make me important enough in your life to help make decisions about what to do about your family."

"Doc…" He shakes his head. "How did this start out being about what to bid on a house and end up being about our relationship?"

"Everything is about our relationship. Come on, I drove up to Hilltown and put your father in the hospital, and you're arguing with me about whether I should discuss your nephew's hospital bills?"

I say "nephew" deliberately to stress Dev's relationship to Alexi while taking Gregory out of the equation, and it works at least a little. His frown relaxes and he exhales. "He thinks I'm trying to use that to buy him off or something, and he'll never accept it now. I know him. He's all…he's pissed off that I got famous and he thinks it's because I'm gay, and he's pissed off that I'm gay because he thinks I did it to become famous, and…fuck. You know? Just let me deal with it. Maybe he'll be there when we go up and maybe he won't, but either way, I'll handle it."

"Fine." I think I disguise my resolve, but as I turn back to the computer, Dev grabs my shoulder again.

"Fox." I turn and look at him, and he stares down at me. "I mean it."

"I said, 'Fine.'"

"Uh-huh. I know that 'fine.'"

I nuzzle his paw. "You wouldn't object if I gave Gregory some of my money, would you?"

He laughs. "You can sure as hell try."

"All right, then." I finish and send the e-mail. "I'll put my fox mind to work on it—what?"

The sparkle in his eyes isn't there anymore. He gestures to the computer. "You could at least have waited until we agreed to send that e-mail."

"Why? We didn't make any real decision. I'm just asking if we could offer a lower price with cash." I'm starting to feel a little warm about it, though, because maybe I did over-react a bit. Gregory is his brother and I'm inserting myself into the problem like I did with his dad.

"We were in the middle of talking about it," he says. "You went ahead and asked her. We could at least talk to your dad."

I sigh. "Fine. You want me to forward this along to my father, I will. I'll see what he says, and we'll see what Clara says, and then we'll talk about it together and make a decision."

He stands there while I forward the e-mail, write a quick note to Father with it, and include a thank-you for joining us for dinner. I turn the computer to him. "How's that look?"

"It's fine," he says, his tail flicking.

"Okay." I hold the cursor over the "Send" button. "I'm gonna click it."

"Go ahead."

So I do, and then I shut the computer. Dev doesn't move, so I stand up and put my paws on his arms. "Are you really upset?"

He's tense, but he meets my eyes and his ears are up. "I'm still pissed off at Gregory, and I thought I'd be the one holding you back. But you want to go up there and help, and I haven't worked out shit with him yet. He might not even come to the house when we go up there. Shit, doc, you just went through this with your mom. Would you have wanted me getting all up there in her business?"

"You were playing football," I point out.

"Yeah, but if I wasn't."

I shrug, trying to imagine that. "Sure. I mean, you probably could've helped keep me under control. Anyway, it's academic. It's over now."

He shakes his head. "If we're really in an important relationship, we should talk about things. You can't just do things when *you* think they're right if they concern me too."

"We do talk about things." It's a silly fight, and we've been getting along so well the last week. Maybe there's something else going on with him. Whatever it is, it's not worth getting upset about, and certainly I did act hastily. I sigh, and my ears go down. "I'm sorry, tiger. I'm not going to make the excuse that that's how I am, because you know how I am. But I should've had the discussion with you before sending the message. I know it's not just about the house price."

"Yeah." He stares down.

"But." I place a finger on his chest and he looks down at it, then back up at me. "All I did was ask a question. I didn't make any decisions. So I think you overreacted a little bit as well. Don't you?"

"Hmph."

I press a little closer. "Don't you?"

He shifts. "Maybe."

"Mm." I lift my muzzle to kiss his nose. "How about you apologize to me in the bedroom?"

His eyes stay on mine. "I don't think I overreacted that much."

"Okay, then…how about you take your naughty fox back there and teach him a lesson?"

Now the corner of his mouth quirks, and his ears flick forward. "I don't think you were that naughty."

I step back and look at him. "So…you don't want to have sex tonight?"

"I didn't say that."

"Okay, then." I fold my arms and curl my tail around my leg. "How about you tell me what you do want?"

He eyes me for a moment and then takes my wrist and leads me into the bedroom. Fully clothed, we sit on the edge of the bed. "I dunno," he says. "I'm not really that upset. It was just that I was in the middle of talking to you about something and you ignored me."

"I didn't ignore you," I say, though I'm no longer sure of that. "All I did—"

"I know, I know." He covers my paw in his. "It was a silly thing to fight about."

I lean in closer. "Is this about the decision we're making?"

He doesn't answer right away, but then he gives a noncommittal shake of his head. "Maybe. I didn't think so, but maybe everything is. You know,

I felt so sure about it a few days ago, but…" His eyes flick away. "You're not sure and that's maybe making me think I shouldn't be sure either."

A few days ago. I wonder whether the other events of the last few days are weighing on him. I swing my tail around behind him and press my weight against his side. He rumbles and leans back. "Sweetie," I say softly, "the one thing that I've never questioned is that we love each other, you know? We're gonna have little fights—and big fights too—but I'm trying to see the big picture, which is more than the fights and more than the good times and more than the families. I don't want you to feel something because I might or might not feel it. I want you to feel it because you feel it."

"Right," he says, "like it's that easy."

"Oh, come on. I know I'm a fox, but I'm not some mystical mentalist who can change your feelings."

He lifts a paw up to my chin and holds it while he searches my eyes. "You sure? Because I think you're a little bit magic."

That warms me, and sets off other reactions in me. "Uh," I say, trying to find words. "I think we're magic together sometimes."

"Only sometimes?"

"Many times?"

He chuckles and kisses me, wrapping his arms around me, and when he pulls back I gasp, "Okay, like then maybe."

His gold eyes burn down into mine. "*Now* I want to take my naughty fox to bed."

So he does, and I am duly punished for my transgressions, only not really, because the sex is warm and affirming, like washing away the residue of the fight in the best way possible. I get a little punishment back at him, too, squeezing and tickling him after he's come, and then he pins me to the bed and licks up into my ears, and we go to bed happy.

•

The next morning, he goes off to work out with Gerrard, and given my father's role in that breakup, I don't go along (not like I was invited anyway). Briefly I consider calling Angela, but we were never really that close and I don't want to bother her if she's upset. Although she apparently didn't mind having a meeting about financial assets—but I'm not qualified to talk about those either.

So I call Mother, because I'm going to have to eventually. We exchange cordial greetings, and then I get to the point of the call. "I'm going to be up there in a couple days. Dev has a thing at Forester."

"Oh," she says.

"I was wondering if there's…" How do I say this? "I was wondering if it would be okay for me to look through my room. I don't want to take a lot, but there might be a couple things." My eye lights on the plush dragon my father got me to replace my childhood one, which was locked behind my door when we visited.

She doesn't answer right away, and I say, "If it's too soon, that's fine. I don't really need anything and I can wait."

"We'll see how I feel." She pauses, and then says, "I mean, I think it should be all right. I am sorry about the things that are gone."

"But I wanted to say, too," I go on because I don't want to dredge up all the shit about her burning my jacket and stuff, "even if you don't feel okay with that, I'd still like to, y'know. Get together maybe."

"Yes," she says. "I'd like that."

"And." I inhale, preparing to go on, but she cuts me off.

"I think…just you and your father for now, Wiley."

My ears go down and I kind of sag back, there at the desk. I was hoping to move forward more, but of course it's kind of quick and she's being cautious. At least she said "for now," so there's hope in the future. A distant future maybe, but still a future.

"That case," she says when I don't say anything, "with the cub who killed himself. How did that turn out?"

"They settled out of court."

"Oh. I—I hope the family achieves some peace."

"Yeah. I think only time can really do that."

"Maybe you're right. But people can help it along by accepting the Lord's way. Or," she says, before I can object, "the way of the universe, if you prefer to think of your life as existing in an uncaring void."

"I do. Way less responsibility that way. The only person I disappoint if I screw up is me. And the people I love, I guess."

"It seems far less comforting to me."

I shift the phone and lean back in the chair. "Okay, if you feel like talking about it…how did you end up going to the church? You and Father never took me, growing up, and he's still not going. Was it your family?"

She hesitates. "It's hard to explain."

"I've got a couple hours."

"It might go better in person."

I consider that and find myself agreeing. "All right, then. Let me know when would be a good time." I pause. "I guess not Sunday morning."

"No, that might be nice," she says. "I'd love for you to meet the pastor down at the church."

"Uh." Now I feel awkward. "I was kidding."

"I know." She surprises me with a sly smugness. "I'll figure out a time and I'll call you."

"Okay. Thanks." Maybe things are getting better if she can joke with me like that.

"Wiley?" She pauses. "Thank you. For calling."

"Oh," I say, "thank you for answering."

And after we hang up, I wonder if there's anyone else I should call in Forester. I try Salim, and to my surprise he picks up his cell.

"Allen asked for your number," he says.

I'm more than a little surprised. "When?"

"Yesterday. There was a message on the FLAG alumni list that your boyfriend will be coming to campus."

"Wow, okay. Why didn't he call me directly?"

"You changed your number."

"No, I didn't." I think for a moment he's talking about when I got the new phone from Dev. "Oh, wait…yeah, that first year out of college, I started using the phone the Dragons got me and I stopped using my personal one. I never thought about it because Dev and my parents had the number and nobody from FLAG ever called me."

"You did not encourage us to."

"But wait! You texted me when Dev came out!"

"I have your new number. I do not believe anyone else does. At least, Allen said he does not."

"Ah, jeez. I'm sorry. But I was going through a lot with Dev, and everyone was pressuring me to talk about it. I mean, you know."

Family and boyfriend, for Salim, are separate things. The marriage and children are for his parents and his religion; the boyfriend is for him. "Yes," he says, "but I still talk to my friends."

"So who are you still in touch with from FLAG?" He doesn't say anything for a few seconds, and I chuckle. "So it's not just me."

"The baby made things very busy—she is sick again now—and Jeremy got a promotion, so I can only see him certain evenings."

"It's okay," I say. "I've had a few busy months myself."

I give him the capsule of Dev's season and my struggles, and right before he hangs up, he asks, "Do you hear much from Brian?"

"I—no. I tried to work with him on some charity stuff, but he was very—very Brian about it. We're not talking now."

Salim chuckles. "All people are divided into three classes: the immovable, the movable, and those that move."

"Is that a proverb?"

"Perhaps. Good-bye, Wiley. I will try to make it down to Forester campus on Sunday, if the cub is better."

"Best wishes to her," I say.

It'd been such a nice week, and then Salim had to go and remind me of Brian. Well, I don't need to think of him. He had his moment with Dev, and I've already said my good-bye to him.

So I call Father and tell him I'm getting together with Mother, and he congratulates me on not saying anything that makes her hate me (not his exact words, but close). I'm not sure whether to feel proud of that or not. And he says that Dev and I seem to be doing well together, and that's what I think about after we've made arrangements to meet up that evening.

We are doing well together, and yet I'm still insisting on taking the month to make the decision. Haven't the past four months—let alone the prior two years—taught us enough to know whether this will last long-term? What am I waiting for, what sign will tell me that Dev really is the one for me, the relationship I need to put all my energy into? I keep looking at our friends and family as though there's a solution there: Father, Fisher and Gena, Hal and Pol, Ty and Arch and mystery future wife, Gerrard and Angela. But none of those people are me and Dev, so ultimately I come back to realizing there's nobody I can count on but myself, and that's where it falls apart. Because I love Dev; there's no question about that. I'm just not sure I deserve him.

CHAPTER TWENTY: CONFESSIONS (DEV)

Gerrard got us use of the field, of course. I find it hard to imagine that the Firebirds would deny him anything in their power to grant.

The stipulation is that no team personnel can be around, because we're not allowed to have contact with them. So the locker room is closed and the halls are eerie and vacant. I park in the athletes' lot and then have to walk halfway around the field to find the one open gate, where a few other trucks are parked.

Gerrard, Carson, and Marais are tossing around a football. Gerrard's in a Firebirds shirt and athletic shorts, and every time he tosses a football it's got a crispness to it, like he's trying out for quarterback. Carson, in a plain white tee with a warmup jacket over it, lobs the football carelessly, but when he catches it, his paws are quick and sure. And Marais, the big cougar, looks like he's tossing the football around with a couple buddies, in sweatpants and a Firebirds sweatshirt.

"No Firebirds gear?" Marais asks as I stroll up.

"Shop's closed," I say, holding out my paws. Gerrard fires a pass at me, and I try to catch it as cleanly as Carson has been, mostly succeeding. I hold the ball a moment before tossing it to the leopard. I haven't held a football since the championship game, haven't even been near one, and it's a curiously intense, sharp feeling, like an alarm going off in my head. It's warm, the surface scuffed from dozens of claws so it's easier to grip, and the distinctive leather smell along with the surrounding field transportsz me back weeks, months, years, and I'm a football player again.

I walk over to the group and they spread out to make space for me. "Is Zillo coming?" Gerrard asks.

"I called him on the way over. He said he'd be here. What about the other guys?"

Gerrard whips the ball to Marais, who bobbles it and then drops it. "Nobody else is interested yet."

"Give it a month," I say.

"Or not."

We chat as we wait for Zillo. Marais talks a lot about going back to New Kestle and the school he's helping build there for the children of immigrants. I mention the art exhibit we saw with Hal and Pol, and he's interested; he hadn't heard about it. The others stay quiet; Carson's not a cat of many words, and I don't want to ask Gerrard about what's going on with his life. So when Marais asks what the rest of us are up to, I talk about going to Yerba and looking at houses with Lee.

"Ah," Marais says, and grins. "Buying a house in Yerba. Maybe your agent knows something he ain't supposed to?"

"My agent doesn't know anything," I say. "At least, he's not telling me anything. Lee's got a job there and his job is probably more stable than mine."

I'm starting to feel the throwing motion as I shoot a pass to Gerrard. He gets it easily and looks at me as he tosses to Carson. "You'll be a Firebird as long as you want to be. Least, as long as I'm here."

Carson, unexpectedly, fills the silence in which I can't think of the right way to say thanks. "So you got at least two more years."

We laugh, and that enables me to say, "Thanks, I appreciate it. I want to stay here."

"Hey," Marais says, "This guy gonna be a coach when he's done playing, no doubt. He pretty much a coach right now."

"If they want me to be," Gerrard says. "But I'm not worrying about that right now."

What is he worrying about, I wonder? He looks loose and untroubled, ears up, sharp muzzle keeping an eye out for each of us. With each throw, he shows the grace that makes him a premier athlete, the focus on the present moment that makes him a terrific linebacker. And, maybe, a terrible husband. I wonder briefly whether I could commit to Lee if I could think that way, if I could just understand that he's what I want *now*, and to hell with the future. Then again, that kind of thinking got Gerrard into the mess he's in now. Which, to be fair, doesn't seem to be bothering him.

"Hey," Marais says to me as Zillo walks through the gates. "You got a house in Chevali?"

I shake my head. "Only been here less than a year."

"You buy your boyfriend a house first?"

Zillo hurries up. "Sorry I'm late. The other gate was closed. I parked by you, Dev."

"He's moving now," I tell the cougar. "I'm not."

Carson, again, chimes in. "I bought my grandmother a house before I bought one for me. Family needs it more, take care of them first."

"Yeah, but—that's your grandmother," Marais says. "Boyfriend, it's like if I bought a house for some girl in Hellentown gave me a few blow jobs."

All the rest of us go quiet, trying not to look at Gerrard. I don't even know if his Hellentown mistress has a house or what, but it's just too painful. Marais obviously doesn't know about it yet; he can't possibly be that tin-eared.

He does, however, mistake the cause of our silence. "Hey," he says to me, "look, I'm sorry, he's more than a blow job, right? It was a joke. I didn't mean it really. Hey, Zillo, what you been up to?"

The other coyote (also in a Firebirds t-shirt—where was I when they were handing those out?) gives me a look with splayed ears and then just mutters, "Oh, just playing FBA on the box and chillin'."

Gerrard clears his throat. "Calisthenics first," he says, "and then we'll do sprints and drills. I figure a few hours. No plays this time, but a few weeks down the road we'll start doing some basic movement and practice working as a unit."

"Be nice if we could get one more player to be the other outside line-backer backup." Marais gestures around. "Me an' Zillo can't run plays ourselves. You guys know anyone?"

I wonder if Polecki would want to come work out with us, but he's a middle linebacker anyway, so probably not, even if he wasn't going to be busy being a world champion this summer. I run through the Dragons, but I wasn't a linebacker there so I don't know that group well. Gerrard speaks up. "There'll be more guys here by then. This first one is just to keep us in shape, keep us together."

It's only been two weeks and we're all still in good shape, but even on the best days, most of us couldn't keep up with Gerrard, and he seems intent on proving that. After the jumping jacks and sprints, he does fifty pushups—only Carson and I keep pace with him—and then he points at the stairs of the stadium.

We all hit the base of the stairs in a line, but Gerrard is first to the top. Carson's second, and Zillo and I get up there right around the same time (he wins by a whisker, if we're really keeping track). I think the downhill will be easier, but Gerrard doesn't turn around; he runs across the top of the stadium, and so we all follow him, and that's where Zillo falls back. He might be lighter than I am, but I used to be a cornerback. I'm faster on my feet.

Still can't catch Carson, though, and neither of us is catching Gerrard, five feet ahead of us, then ten, then twenty. He runs with a purity of concentration that makes me wonder whether he's actually thinking about anything but the process of running, his tail streaming out for balance, his feet hitting in a precise rhythm.

When I'm playing football, I can empty my mind that way. When I'm just running, my mind has a little time to wander back to Forester and my family. I tense when I think about Gregory and then I wonder whether he'll even be there, and then I think that I want him there, I want to confront him about this, and then I think that putting Gregory and Lee in the same room is probably a bad idea, and by then I realize that Zillo is right behind me, so I shift my focus back to the hot concrete under my paws, the rhythm of my breathing and the flow of my muscles.

Gerrard gets halfway around the stadium and then runs down the stairs. We all think we're done, but he keeps going, across the field and back up the original stairs. I'm tired but not exhausted, and Carson follows, so I do too. Marais gives up, but Zillo stays with us until Gerrard completes the second circuit, standing on the logo in the middle of the field to welcome the three of us who finished with him.

"Good workout," he says, and pats each of us, and then, like it's a game week and he's going to see us again tomorrow, he heads for the gate.

"Thanks for coming," I say to Zillo as we follow Gerrard.

"I'm gonna be sore tomorrow." He stretches his arms over his head and then stops. "Better get some stretches in. But you know, this was good. Didn't realize until I came here that I miss having workouts, a schedule, something to do." He looks around the stadium. "This gives me somewhere to be. Yeah. I'll keep coming."

Somewhere to be. "All right," I say, and I'm back in the real world, and Gerrard is a friend who's going through a divorce and Zillo is adrift after a breakup and I'm a tiger trying to figure out my own relationship. My legs are killing me and I should probably join Zillo in his stretches, but I want to talk to the other coyote. So I jog and catch up to him about ten feet before the gate. "Hey," I say.

He keeps going, so I walk alongside. "Look, I just want to say, I'm sorry about what happened."

"Wasn't your fault," he says.

"Lee's sorry, too, and his—nobody intended for this to happen."

"It's my fault," he says calmly, keeping a paw on the gate when we reach it. He stops and waits for the other guys, panting slightly from the workout, but his ears and whiskers are up and he doesn't appear to be at all affected by talking about his separation. "I have to lock up. You can go."

"Are you—I mean, are you going to go to Hellentown?"

His eyes narrow and meet mine. "Why would I do that?"

My tongue trips over itself. "You have—I mean, family—there's another—you—"

"My family is here," he says, and whether he means it or not, he sticks out his chest so the Firebirds logo rises out at me.

I hold up my paws. "Okay. Look, if you want to hang out—have dinner or something…"

"I'm fine." He locks the gate and walks over to his truck, parked nearby.

My truck is partway around the stadium, so I stand there feeling helpless while Gerrard drives away.

The emptiness of the stadium area feels weird. During the fall, I wouldn't be able to get a block without running into throngs of fans, stopping to sign autographs. But now the streets are bare of fans, bare of groupies, bare of people selling drinks and snacks and drugs to the fans and groupies. I can look up along the outer wall of the stadium, the tiers of exposed ramps along which people stream before and after games, the cold dark lights at the top.

The morning was sunny; the clouds are gathering but haven't blocked out the sun yet. It's pleasantly warm on my ears as I think about Gerrard and the groupies that line the street during the season. Would I really catch the eye of a tigress, maybe in a few years when Lee's and my relationship has become routine and predictable…?

Then I laugh, loudly enough that a guy sweeping the steps on the restaurant across the street looks up. Even if we buy a house, even if we settle into jobs and families and he settles things with his mother and I settle things with Gregory, how could our relationship ever become predictable?

But maybe I'd want something more predictable? Maybe I'd get tired of the endless bickering, the tension over any kind of gay rights issue, the headstrong attitude…

…the warmth, the passion, the embrace waiting for me at the apartment, the football mind, the courage?

I shake my head and touch the wall of the stadium. I can't see it. I can't see how Gerrard could give up his family life. What could be that tempting? And now he doesn't even want to go be with this coyote and cub that he threw away his family for?

Maybe he's hoping Angela will take him back. Maybe he wants to stick around and see his boys. Maybe he really only cares about the team.

I hope he takes me up on the offer of dinner. I really want to understand what's going on with him. But until then I'll have to settle for driving home and grabbing Lee and telling him I love him. Somewhere to be, Zillo says. That's funny; I didn't feel that sense of being adrift, and maybe it's because I always have somewhere to be.

But as I pull out of the lot and get on the streets to return home, the problem of Gerrard stays on my mind. Did he always mess around? Or was it something that happened because of the life? I've only been starting for half a year and I almost cheated on Lee. What happens in another year, or two, or five?

I obviously can't ask Gerrard, although he's the person I should ask. I could talk to Lee about it, but he wouldn't know any better than I would. And then I think that there is someone else, someone I know who used to play around and stopped. And I have an excuse to go visit Fisher.

•

Lee is happy to go visit the Kingstons again. He calls Gena to make sure it's okay, and Gena thinks it's a great idea. She's doing fine, but she says Fisher would really appreciate the company. So we head over there and Lee goes into the living room to talk to Gena. I head out to where Fisher's sitting on the patio, right where I left him last time.

Trees rustle around the open brick patio, and the grass is brown in front of us, which is really the only reminder that it's winter. A faded, forlorn volleyball, half-deflated, lies in the scrub under the trees, a pale white against the sandy beige of the ground; otherwise the yard is pretty well kept. Only two chairs sit together on the patio, so I take the empty one next to Fisher. His tail curls and his mouth twitches; he looks at least somewhat pleased to see me. He doesn't pick up his whiteboard, but he watches me as I sit down.

A couple glasses half-full of some greenish-brown slop sit with dirty straws on the side table near where his paw rests. The bandages around his jaw are dirtier now, or duller with the sun now hidden by the clouds, and I try not to look at them. "So, how you been?" I ask.

He rolls his eyes and gestures at the glasses. Then he waves a paw at me, and his eyes rise in a question.

"Oh, I just came from…" I pause. Then I think I might as well go on with it. He knows life goes on. "…Gerrard's workout. Linebackers only." His eyes look interested, so I elaborate. "Calisthenics, stair runs, you know."

He nods and looks down at his paw, flexing it. "When can you exercise again?" I ask. "It'll do you good to keep busy."

He shrugs and looks away. "C'mon, Fish. When?"

Three fingers. "Three…weeks?" He nods.

"Good luck."

We sit quietly for a while. Finally he picks up the whiteboard and scrawls, *You gonna talk?* in jagged blue letters.

"What do you want me to talk about?"

He shrugs again and leans back, closing his eyes.

"Okay, look," I say. "So there's this thing with Gerrard. You heard about it?" He shakes his head, but doesn't open his eyes.

So I tell him in a nutshell about Gerrard getting kicked out, about the family in Hellentown, and about Gerrard being so cool about it at the workout.

He opens his eyes and writes, *Gerrard = football.*

"Yeah, but there's more than that. Can I ask you…"

He watches me attentively. I take a breath and lower my voice. "You know, you used to…you used to fool around." He doesn't react. "But you stopped, and you never fathered another cub. That I know of, anyway. Or that you know of. I guess." He still isn't reacting one way or another. "Anyway, I just wanna know. When Gerrard came in…when guys come into the league…I mean, do they come in wanting to fool around?"

His brow furrows. I inhale. "Like, did you mess around in college? Did Gerrard cheat on Angela in college? Do the guys who get in trouble do it because they've always done it or is it something that happens to you?"

He keeps frowning and points at me, his eyebrows raised.

"No," I say, "I haven't cheated on Lee." He doesn't have to know that I almost did, and anyway that was when Lee and I were sorta kinda broken up. "I want to know if I will."

He scowls and scribbles, *How should I know?* and thrusts the board at my face.

I lean back and exhale. "I just want to know if I should watch out for it. I mean, is it—did you get tempted? Did you just give in?"

The scowl deepens. He shakes his head and puts the whiteboard down. "Come on," I say. "It's over, it's in the past, and it could help me."

We wait for a moment and then he points at the whiteboard and then back into the house. "Fine," I say. I scoot my chair closer. "There. Now they can't see, and if we hear the door, erase it."

He sits there and doesn't move. "Fish," I say. "Look, I'll—" I take a breath. "I'll tell you something if you'll tell me. Okay? Look. Before the championship I was really stressed and pent up, and there was this fox…and he really reminded me of Lee. And I almost…" I take a breath. "I mean, I came really close. And I'm afraid I might again."

Fisher looks steadily at me. Then he writes on the board. *Didn't?*

I shake my head. He erases the words, and then he starts to tremble. He clutches the board so tightly the wooden frame cracks with a sharp noise.

That jolts him. He looks at me and I'm surprised to see the shine of tears in his eyes. He looks back at the glass doors and then he picks up the marker and starts to write.

You can never tell Gena, he starts, and he looks at me for confirmation, intently.

"Promise," I say.

He erases the board and holds the pen over it. A breeze rolls through the patio. He scribbles a couple letters and rubs them out with his paw, the blue staining his orange fur.

I wasn't trying to kill myself.

I thought we were talking about cheating, but I don't want to stop his confession, so I nod and lower my voice. "I know that."

He lifts his paw and rubs his eyes, then stares down at the whiteboard, not looking at me. Slowly, he writes, *I was thinking about it.*

I hold my breath, watching the words take shape, my mind skittering ahead faster than he can write. *I took the gun out to see if I could do it. I sent everyone out of the house. I*

He hesitates, and his paw shakes, and then he erases the board.

"You put it in your mouth?"

He shoots me a look, eyes wide. "There were burns." I touch my lips.

His eyes close and his head sags. Then a moment later he lifts his head and looks back at the house. "Yeah," I say softly, "Gena knows."

His paw lifts the marker, scrawls on the board. *I decided not to do it. It was an accident.*

"How did it happen?" I ask quietly.

Don't remember. I. He stops and then writes, shakily, *woke up in hospital.*

So he doesn't actually know if he tried, if in that one moment he did decide to do it, or if his finger slipped as he was pulling it out. Or he's lying and he knows, he's known all along. "Listen, Fish," I say. I put a paw on his arm. "Gena knows it and she still loves you. She's stuck with you. That's not going to change. But she needs to know that you won't do it again. Will you?"

He keeps his head down and slowly erases the board. *Forget my children's names. Sometimes I don't know what year it is.*

"But you know now, right?"

He doesn't respond. "Fish?"

I remember you, he writes. *Remember the games.* Then he erases again and starts over. *It's only going to get worse.*

"You don't know that. There's therapy, there's treatments."

Watched my father die like this. He writes it fast and erases it almost before I have a chance to read it.

I sit and stare at him and I don't know what to say. I've never watched anyone die or degrade. I don't know why this all came out in answer to my question about cheating, but it's good that he's talking.

Easier to hide when I can't talk, he writes. *But still happening.*

"Lee says lingering concussion effects can last for weeks. It might still clear up."

He shakes his head and then below that, he writes, *Started before.*

"Jesus, Fish." I keep staring at the words, trying to process them. "Like, forgetting people's names and shit?"

He shakes his head, wipes the board clean. *Little things.*

"Did it start before you took that serum?"

His head whips around, and I feel like the breeze has gotten chilly very quickly. Slowly he nods, but he doesn't write anything. I decide not to pry into the serum thing. "Look," I say. "Tell Gena. You can get help, you can talk to people."

The patio is quiet, just our breathing and the sound of the breeze through the trees around us. Slowly, he writes, *No help.*

"This isn't like being on the Firebirds. Nobody's waiting to take your spot if you can't remember the plays. There's no shame in it." His muzzle keeps a stubborn set. "Jesus!" I say. "What happened to the guy who shoved me around the locker room, who told me what I had to do to make it?"

Sorry, he writes.

"That's not the point!" I shove him in the arm. He wobbles in the chair, but recovers his balance easily. "The point is you have a family, you have something else to—to be good at now. Are you going to sit here feeling sorry for yourself for the rest of your life?"

He looks very deliberately at me and shakes his head with a resignation that frightens me more than the wires around his jaw. "Fish," I say quietly, "You're not going to try again."

Neither of us moves for a moment. Then his paw swipes the eraser across the whiteboard and he holds the marker there. The fumes rise amid the late winter desert breeze. *Don't want to*, he writes, and then adds, *now*, and underlines it.

"There are people who can help you." He turns away and sets the whiteboard on the table to pick up one of the half-drunk glasses of green goo. With some difficulty he fits the straw between his lips, and I watch the liquid make its way up to his muzzle. He grimaces.

"Tastes shitty?" I ask, and he nods, but he keeps drinking. I lean forward and ask to smell it when he's done, so he gives me the glass. Grass and fruit reach my nose, with an earthy undertone: beans or soy or something. "It doesn't smell that bad."

He wrinkles his muzzle, picks up the whiteboard, and writes, *Gritty.*

"Fish," I say, "listen, that friend of Lee's—no, listen, hear me out, dammit." He makes a pushing-away gesture without touching me. "He's been talking to other players and doctors."

The reporter?

"Yeah, Hal. He's a good guy. He wrote up that profile on Lee. Did you read it?" He shakes his head. "Anyway, Fish, listen, he's trying to get people to talk about former players with memory problems. He might be able to—"

Fuck, I know that closed expression. He's staring out at the yard and patiently listening, waiting 'til I'm done so he can tell me to get lost. I follow his eyes and see the volleyball, and I think about Bradley and Junior. "What about your boys?"

Now he turns and raises his eyebrows, wary. "What if they play football? I mean, they're good, right? Wouldn't you want them to know what happened to you and how to fix it?"

He hesitates. Then he writes, *Doesn't happen to everyone.* His paw hesitates at the end, as though he's thinking about writing more, or about making it a question, perhaps. In the end he caps the marker and puts it on the table.

"What if it's genetic?"

His paw doesn't reach for the marker. He stares down at the whiteboard, and then he sets it down and folds his paws in his lap. I reach for anything else, all the other points Lee and Hal and I discussed. "There's other people going through the same things. You could talk to them instead of sitting out here alone. You're always saying I don't understand. Maybe I don't. But these other guys might."

He turns to look at me, so slowly that he looks sixty years old. There's pain in his eyes, but doubt now alongside it. "I know you're tough. These guys are tough, too. They're all old soldiers. You know how soldiers have groups and reunions and stuff, like the VFW and all? This is like that but for football players."

With a slow exhale, his head sinks again and shakes slowly from side to side. And then he turns his head toward me, just a little. There's a crack in his façade, a glimmer of hope in his eyes.

"Fish," I say gently. "It could help you. It could help Bradley and Junior, and lots of people."

He swallows, and then, after a pause, he nods once, sharply. "Okay," I say. "I'll tell Lee. I'll set it up. Thanks—I mean, you're gonna feel better, Fish. I know it."

There's no relief nor happiness in his eyes, but there is a sort of peace, or maybe resignation. And then he picks up the whiteboard and marker. *About the fooling around,* he writes.

"It's okay, Fish."

In his eyes, there's a little of the old fierce Fisher who pushed me around a weight room once. The look keeps me in my chair as he scribbles, *Gena knows the life. When she tells me to stop I stop.* After a second he stares down at the board and changes *stop* to *stopped*.

"Was it easy? Stopping, I mean."

He turns and looks back over his shoulder into the house again, and then erases the board. Slowly, he writes, *Nothing worth doing is easy.*

And I have to be happy with that. I don't know what to make of it, but at least it sounds like Fisher is willing to move forward for the moment.

When I go inside to tell Lee and Gena, they're both happy, and Gena particularly looks relieved. I sit with them and talk for a little longer, but my eyes keep straying out to where Fisher's sitting on the patio alone, his tail curling back and forth, staring out at the dead yard.

PART IV

CHAPTER TWENTY-ONE: OLD HAUNTS (LEE)

Friday while Dev was at his workout, I looked up some info on the southwestern schools the Whalers are going to be sending me to. I'm not officially on the clock, but it didn't hurt to call up and introduce myself to the athletic directors, to tell them that come summer I'd be replacing the old Whalers guy. Most of them just passed me on to their secretaries to make sure that my passes got the correct name on them. A couple, bored, I guess, talked to me directly, and one recognized me from the Firebirds profile. We had a nice chat and I came away with the impression that he's definitely 'family,' though he couldn't really come out in the job he has. I promised to make time to see him when I visited his school.

We pick up Father at the hotel Saturday morning and cram into a cab with all our luggage. It's been less than a week since we got back from Yerba, but with all that's happened, it feels like forever since we've been in an airport. It also feels like an escape from the problems of Fisher and Gena and Angela and Gerrard, even though we're heading right into the problems of Gregory and Mother and Forester.

When we check in for the flight, we realize that Dev booked himself and me in first class and Father is, of course, flying coach. We can't change the arrangement because the flight is booked, but I go back to sit with Father when Dev takes a little nap. And when we get to Hilltown, Dev and I go to the rental agency and Father goes to pick up his car. "Well," I say, parting at the parking garage, "it was nice flying with you. In separate seats."

Father adjusts his glasses and smiles. "Glad it worked out. I'll see you tomorrow afternoon to drive up to Eileen's. Good luck with your parents, Devlin."

I'm now pretty familiar with the road up to Lake Handerson, even when it's five below zero and the highway's bounded with dirty snow walls thrown up by the plows. At least the snow on the hills beyond is a pristine, gleaming white. "Ah, the north," I say, leaning back and adjusting the heater to stop it from blowing my fur all over the car. "Sorry about the shedding," I say because Dev's been quiet ever since we got on the road and I know he's way deep in his own head about his parents and his brother, and I want to get him thinking about something else.

Dev waves at the air and shakes his head. "How do you grow all that fur? You're just a little fox and you've got enough fur blowing around here to make a whole other fox. This didn't happen last winter."

I laugh. "Sorry. It's going back and forth from the hot to the cold. And it did happen, it's just that we weren't living together so I only shed a little when I came over and I cleaned it all up."

"So every year we're going to have a house full of fox fur."

I pull my tail around and comb through it, pulling out loose fur. "If you didn't want fox fur, you shouldn't have chased after a fox."

"I didn't say I don't want it." He turns, and I'm relieved to see a warm smile on his muzzle. "I prefer it attached, is all."

"Me too, but sometimes you don't have a choice." I pat my tail down and let it fall back beside the seat.

His smile fades, but he's more relaxed now. "Want to talk about it?" I say. "This is only your parents, right? Gregory's tomorrow?"

"Yeah." He sighs. "I just want to tell them I'm upset. I mean, I want to hear what they think too. Do they think it's all right?"

"Did they call you back after you talked to your brother?"

He shakes his head. "I meant to call them, but Fisher and all. Talked to them last night and confirmed that I was coming and they said it was okay. I didn't ask about Gregory. Figured I'd be up here today, no point getting into a fight over the phone."

"I don't think it got out into the media. The AllSports guy didn't follow up?"

"Nah. Nobody else called about it either. I think it sank out of sight." He pauses. "I'm glad, of course, but you know, it's kind of sad, too. I mean, it probably made him even angrier. He wanted to be noticed."

"He's going to have to learn to deal with it. Getting mad at you isn't helping. I'm sure it's making him feel better, but he's gotta grow out of it."

He stares ahead into the white snowscape and the narrow black line we're driving through it. "Great. I'm sure if you tell it to him just like that he'll see the error of his ways."

I lean back into the seat. "I'll leave the talking to you, stud. Don't worry. I'm just along for moral support."

The car is quiet for a moment, and when I glance his way again, he keeps flicking his eyes over at me. "What?" I say.

"Oh," Dev says, "I was wondering if you were also going to promise to change your fur to have tiger stripes, while you're making impossible promises."

I snort. "I can keep quiet. I can totally keep quiet."

"All right, all right. Maybe you can change."

There's not much more I can say to that, so I change the subject. We talk a little about what we're hoping to eat while we're visiting here, about the places at Forester and the burger place he wanted to take me to in Lake Handerson last time and didn't have a chance to. "Butterburgers," he says. "They're awesome."

I put a paw on my stomach. "God, I think I gained a pound just hearing that."

"You'll like them." He grins at me, and I ask if there's a "Saladburger" option as well, and he says I don't appreciate good food.

We check in at the hotel and drop our bags off at the room, where I check my e-mail and find a response from the real estate agent in Yerba. "She says if we can pay cash, then five-fifty will probably work fine," I say. Dev doesn't answer, and I choose not to crow about being right. "But she still thinks that five-seventy-five would cinch it. That's her opinion. So... should we make an offer?"

He sits on the bed with his elbows on his knees. "Do we need to decide what we're doing here..." He gestures between himself and me. "Before we decide on that?"

I'd like to. But I also don't want to jump the gun on anything. "Well, if we wait then this house might be gone and we'd have to look at another one, and I'll have to rent a hotel room for a month. Which is fine, I guess." I take a breath. "I know we still have another two weeks or so in our month."

I'm waiting to feel his calm assurance again. That might be enough to overcome my objections, especially since I'm not sure what's holding me back. Weirdly, it feels easier to buy a house than to tell Dev I want to be with him.

But Dev doesn't say anything, not right away. He sits on the bed opposite me and looks over the laptop screen, and after a while he says, "I guess we can still buy the house."

In the same way that his confidence would have boosted mine, his doubts reinforce my own. I focus on the e-mail. "Let me ask you this," I say. "Would you be okay renting your investment house in Yerba to a friend?"

He rubs his chin. "Can I tell my friend not to have sex with other friends in the house?"

"If we're just friends," I point out, "you don't care about that."

He hmmms. "Can I charge my friend a scent-cleaning surcharge for stinking up my furniture and getting fur all over it?"

Even if we're not going to be boyfriends, our banter feels reassuring, and brings a little smile to my muzzle. "If we're friends, I wouldn't have sex with other people in the house if you didn't want me to. That seems like a reasonable friend thing to ask, I guess, and anyone I'm interested in would have their own place. I mean, unless I hook up with this super-hot homeless guy."

"Then you can afford a hotel room. He'd probably appreciate it," Dev says. He smiles and pushes his foot at mine. "Go ahead. Let's do it."

I nod and type away. "You want to read the e-mail before I send it?"

He comes over to sit on my bed and reads it over. "Sounds good. You want to do five-fifty?"

The proximity to his parents and Gregory makes that question weighty. I don't answer right away. Dev points to the screen. "She says five-seventy-five to be sure, and we can afford that."

I try to figure out how to give voice to my hesitations. "If…"

"Don't bring up Alexi."

"Okay, well…how much do you have in the bank? Right now?"

"Um." He scratches his head. "Forty thousand maybe? I dunno."

"You don't get paid again for months, you know. That's going to have to pay rent, first class tickets…"

"I'm getting a check for making it to the championship, too."

"Okay, so another fifty, something like that?"

"I'll have enough, fox."

I've already got my backup plan, and it's not worth arguing about. At the end of the day, Dev's finances are his own, and this is going to be his house. So I tell the agent that we'll put in a bid for five-seventy-five, and send the e-mail.

Once it goes, he pushes the laptop aside, takes my paws, and kisses me. And I know he wants me to make my decision now. I just can't help thinking about sneaking out of his apartment in the middle of the night because I didn't trust myself around him. What's changed since then? The championship is over, but football season will come around again as surely as autumn, and leaves will change and players will charge each other over a green field and Dev will have only one thing on his mind. Is it cheating to commit now, when we're both free of distractions, or is it the best time to commit, when we're both free of distractions?

I kiss him back and because I have to say something, I say, "I love you, tiger. No matter whether we're friends or more, I love you. I just…"

He holds me against him. "Never mind. We'll figure it out."

"Yeah." I rub a paw over his ears. "You ready to see your parents?"

"No." He sighs. "Can we just stay here tonight?"

I rub his knee. "We can do anything we want. But I'd recommend visiting your parents."

"It's going to be all shouty and messy." He shakes his head.

"Not if you don't lose your temper." I try to be optimistic. He gives me a look and I add, "And your father doesn't lose his temper. Hey, there's a chance it'll just be quiet and tense and awkward, right?"

"Thanks," he grumbles, but gets up and pulls me with him.

The sun has long since set by the time we pull up in front of his parents' house. The maple tree in their yard is a cluster of bare branches against the streetlight, and our paws crunch the snow on the street as we make our way to the sidewalk and the path to the porch. The bite of cold on my pads, the way the snow clings to the fur between my toes, all that reminds me of the last time I was up here in the snow: to see my mother and get my things from her house. This time, I hope, things will go more smoothly.

When we get to the front porch, I stay a step back and watch him ring the doorbell, watch him open the door and greet his mother with a smile. Then any unease is driven out of my mind as Duscha reaches out and hugs me, too, and kisses between my ears. "Lee, how have you been? Come in out of the cold."

We're bustled into the foyer, where we wipe our feet, and then we follow Duscha into the living room. They haven't changed it much, although I do notice that where the photo of Dev previously was the one from his draft, they've changed that to a picture of him from the championship game. It must be before, because he's happy and full of hope. Anyway, it looks a lot better next to his brother's law school graduation picture.

Dev and I sit together on the teflon-upholstered couch. Mikhail, Dev's father, joins us a moment later. He offers us both beers and we accept, and then he sits in his large armchair.

We talk guardedly for a little while. When they ask whether I was at the championship game, Dev opens up about our fight and reconciliation, though he doesn't tell them everything. "Lee thought I should do more to help gay people," he says, "and I thought I should just play football."

"You should play football," Mikhail says.

"We're compromising." Dev smiles at me. "I'm going to do some things during the off-season, and I'll try to stay active."

"It helps to have another player out," I say.

"And Polecki's a really nice guy," Dev adds. "We met him and his boyfriend in Yerba. His boyfriend plays in the league."

I'm a little worried about being indiscreet, but neither of his parents ask anything further about his identity. Duscha says, "I am glad you're happy," and Mikhail nods, and then Duscha talks about the weather the previous week and how lucky we are that we didn't visit when it was below zero for three straight days and the Minkles' pipes froze so they had to go stay in a hotel until they were fixed.

"Good time for the auto shop, though," Dev says.

"Very busy," Mikhail nods. "Frozen locks, one frozen engine." He waves a paw. "Careless people."

Small talk carries us through dinner, another steak and boiled vegetables meal that Dev devours with relish. Comfort food for him, but not for me; my parents didn't serve steak all that often. After dinner, we retire with wine to the living room, where I remind Dev that he has to drive to the hotel later and he takes mineral water instead.

And then, at a lull in the conversation, Mikhail clears his throat. "We wished to talk about Gregory."

Dev tenses visibly. I try not to show how much I feel his tension, although my ears lie flat and I can't really help that. "Yeah?" he says, and his voice is cold.

Mikhail's voice is flat, without judgment. "Your brother was only doing what the company assigned him to do."

"The company assigned him to make a statement about supporting 'traditional families'?" Dev sets down his mineral water, leaning slightly forward, tail tip flicking.

His parents look at each other. I can see from their expressions that they have doubts, and Dev reads it the same way. I keep still and silent. I don't think Gregory was pressured by his company to take the case, but I certainly don't know him as well as his family, so I'm going to keep my muzzle shut.

"You are free to express your opinions about the world," Mikhail rumbles. "Why should Gregory not be as well?"

"Hang on," Dev says. "My opinion is that Lee and I are just as much a family as Gregory and Marta."

"And Alexi," his mother puts in.

He waves a paw in acknowledgment. "Gregory's opinion is that Lee and I aren't a family. You don't see a difference between those opinions?"

I'm proud of him, making it easy for me to stay quiet. Duscha wavers. "He should not be speaking out against you," she says.

Mikhail turns to her. "If he supports his brother, perhaps he does not get this job," he says. "Who will feed Alexi if Gregory is fired for speaking up about a matter of no importance?"

Dev gets more intent, his words deeper and slower. "No importance?"

His father waves a paw. "If he does not argue for this case, someone else will. If it is not a good case, the courts decide."

Duscha watches her husband, and seems about to say something, but then Dev speaks up. "But Gregory doesn't have to be the one out there siding with those assholes."

"Representing is not the same as 'siding with,' " Mikhail grumbles.

"Saying 'I support traditional families' is."

"He has a job and he must sometimes say things in the course of that job—"

Dev pounces on that. "So you think he lied? Is that better?"

His father's voice rises. "I do not believe he hates you. But he was working with these people for many weeks. Perhaps they questioned his dedication because they have heard of you."

Dev and his father are bristling; Duscha and I sit back, shifting uncomfortably at the tension in the room. I wait for someone else to say something, but nobody does, so I point out, "But he made the statement after the case was settled."

Duscha meets my eye and though she doesn't smile, I feel her approval and it drives away some of the worry I felt about speaking.

Mikhail keeps staring at Dev through my remark, but his fur smooths down and he lowers his head. "He cannot speak publicly during a case." He sounds tired; perhaps our objections are wearing him down.

"So," Dev says, elbows on his knees, pressing forward toward his father, "you think Gregory said something he doesn't believe in order to please a bunch of assholes? You approve of this?"

We all watch Mikhail, and he doesn't look at any of us, hunched over, fingers tapping each other as his paws rest between his knees. Finally he looks up. "Gregory must work. He is not always allowed to choose the people he is paid to represent. Everyone deserves to be heard in court, and someone must hear even the 'assholes.' If he represents them, he cannot speak against them."

The tension comes back into Dev's posture. "Dad," he says, "they bullied a kid into killing himself because he was gay. Lee talked to the kid."

My ears warm and my smile breaks out despite my efforts to stay stoic. To hear Dev defending Vince makes me want to hug him right there in front of his parents.

"Gregory did not know that."

"Oh, you've talked to him about it?"

Duscha does break in then. "He has agreed to come over tomorrow morning so you might speak to him. He was very upset after Thanksgiving."

"Yeah, well, so was I," Dev says.

"You left immediately," Mikhail points out.

"I have a job to do, too." Dev points to his picture, where he beams in his white away jersey.

"You will talk with your brother," Mikhail instructs. "We talk to each other in this family."

That is a shot aimed right at Dev's heart, a reference to him not telling his parents he was gay before he came out on TV, and he recognizes it for what it is. He shuts his muzzle and looks sulky, and then I risk a little movement, just a lean in his direction so he can feel my warmth and my weight. His tail flicks behind me, acknowledging it.

"Misha," Duscha says, "Devlin is right. Gregory did not have to take the case. It was free."

"He should not be working for free," Mikhail agrees, "but he told us the company instructed him to take it."

"What difference would it make if someone else represented those people?" Duscha, sitting in her chair on the other side of the coffee table from her husband, commands his full attention now, as though we are only spectators at the family argument.

"What difference does it make if Gregory does? It is a job."

"It is a principle," Duscha says.

"Dad," Dev says, "What if someone brought in a car to your shop that you knew was stolen. Would you work on it?"

His father's eyes crease. "How do I know it is stolen?"

"It—it doesn't matter. Would you do your job? If you don't do it, someone else will."

Mikhail shakes his head. "But if I know it is stolen, I will report it to the police."

"What he means," Duscha says, "is that if someone brought you a car you did not approve of..."

"Why do I not approve of it? Car is a car."

"A foreign car." Dev holds up a finger. "One of those ones you always say is terrible and nobody should drive it."

Mikhail shakes his head. "Of course I fix. We fix foreign cars all the time." He looks, frankly, a little bewildered.

The desire to keep quiet and unnoticed is overwhelmed by the pain of watching ineffective rhetoric. "What if someone had painted on their car," I say, "that all football players are murderers?"

Mikhail frowns, and Dev turns to me with a question on his muzzle. I go on regardless. "And this guy got in an accident and his door is dented and the paint is scratched," I say. "Would you repaint his door? That says that your son is a murderer?"

"Why would…"

I raise a paw to politely interrupt. "Never mind why he does it. He's crazy. People write crazy things on their cars all the time."

He shakes his head. "I would fix door. I would not repaint."

"You wouldn't go out of your way to show you approved of his crazy message," I rephrase, to explain the point.

"You see," Duscha says. "That's what Devlin is saying about Gregory."

The living room is quiet for a bit. I stare ahead at the blank TV, then down at the half-emptied glasses of wine on the table. I'm not sure if I helped, but Dev does reach over and brush my paw with his, so I think that at least he appreciated what I was trying to do.

Mikhail exhales and leans back in his chair. "We will ask Gregory about this statement tomorrow. We do not need to argue any longer tonight," he says. "When you and Gregory have apologized to each other, we will talk further if we need to."

"Apologize?" Dev straightens on the couch and leans forward, resting one paw on the coffee table. "Apologize for what?"

"For quarrel, for not talking." Mikhail stares at his son. "For arguments in the family."

Duscha clears her throat. "I don't think either of them needs to apologize," she says.

"Gregory does." I mutter it softly enough that only Dev hears me.

"They fought at Thanksgiving." Mikhail reaches forward and picks up his wine glass. "They have not talked since."

"Thanksgiving was Gregory's fault too," Dev says.

"They talked on the phone," I say, trying to help, but everyone talks over me.

"Devlin—" Duscha starts, but he keeps talking.

"No, I'm perfectly willing to come back here and talk to him if he wants to talk to me, but if you expect me to apologize for anything—to him— then you're going to be disappointed and I might as well not come back."

I expect Mikhail to explode, but he just drinks his wine and puts it down on the coffee table. "You will come here tomorrow and talk," he says.

Dev stares at him and then leans back on the couch. "Yes," he says. "All right. Talk."

I can see the tension wound up in him, can feel it in the restless flicking of his tail behind my back, and I can even smell it over the wine when I put the wine down. His scent is sharper, the way it gets when he's agitated, and it stays that way through the rest of the evening and into the car on the way to the hotel.

"You okay to drive?" I ask, because I'm still pleasantly buzzed, if only slightly.

"Fine," he says. "It's a mile."

We head off, and I turn the heat up. "If you want, I'll stay at the hotel tomorrow morning. Maybe it should just be you and your brother."

He thinks about that, and for the first time in a while, he relaxes. "Gregory would probably prefer that. So I think you should come along."

His teeth bare in a grin. I hold my paws in front of the vents, waiting for them to warm. "I don't want to be a *pièce de annoyance* for your brother."

"Nah," he says. "You should be there, because otherwise I might punch Gregory, and that'll make things worse."

"Okay," I say. "Peacemaker I can accept."

That makes him laugh. "Fox, you are a lot of things, but I've never known you to be interested in making peace. I do think you'll help me win my argument. You said some smart things tonight."

I smile and lean back in the seat, feeling warm in my chest again. "I do that sometimes."

"Sometimes," he says, and then raises an eyebrow at me. "Even if you did break your promise about being quiet."

"Do you really expect me to change?" I ask. I'm a little annoyed at myself, though I can't tell whether it's because I promised to be quiet or because I broke my promise.

Dev picked the hotel, so it's a big luxury one with fluffy pillows and a fluffy comforter and a completely Neutra-Scented room. When we checked in, they added a surcharge because I'm a fox, for descenting the room and whatever. The cheaper hotels don't bother with that, but when you pay twice as much for a room, I guess they figure you'll pay any old extra charge. So I make a point of going and sitting in all the chairs, leaving my scent and floating puffs of fur everywhere in the room, until Dev tells me to sit still.

By this point I've closed the curtains because the window looks out onto an industrial park, and I've got my shirt and pants off, so I wag my tail at him and tell him to come make me sit still. He advances on me, grabs my wrist as I try to dart away, and pulls me against him, toppling us both to the bed.

I wriggle against him, but now he has both arms around me and he mouths my ear, rumbling, "You cannot escape me," and I giggle and squirm, making sure my rear rubs against his boxers, where I can feel him ready. And when the boxers come off and we get down to it, I'm not all that careful about where we get the lube, or what parts of the floor I get sticky. They're going to use every penny of that descenting fee.

I make sure not to come on the bed, though. I mean, we have to sleep there.

Lying next to him, his breathing regular, his chest rising and falling, one great paw resting on my thigh, my thoughts turn to our month. All this thinking about what makes a family and I still don't know whether Dev and I would make a good one. We fight a lot, but the fights are fun, except when they're not. Maybe this whole month idea was a mistake. After all, it's the off-season, we're both happy to be together again after the two weeks off, and we've been busy with Fisher, with Gerrard, with Ty, and with our respective sets of parents.

The sheets are warm with our shared body heat and the ceiling is patterned in shadow. I imagine lying in a bed in our house in three years, five years, ten years. Isn't that why you stay with someone? Because you see a future with them? I picture Dev lying beside me after I've been with the Whalers and he with the Firebirds another three years, if he takes a contract offer this offseason, or another four or five if he waits until next year. Maybe each of us will have won a championship by then; maybe neither. Maybe we'll have had another big fight. Am I still active in gay rights? Have I lost myself in football again, the way I did with the Dragons?

I know what my heart says. My heart doesn't want to be anywhere else but here. I know how amazing Dev is, how much he's done for me and for himself, and how much he's improved my life. But I keep coming back to my particular talent for fucking things up. Even after three years, more or less, I'm not sure he knows how to deal with it. But that's who we are, right? Me the troublemaking fox and him the focused tiger.

Salim's words come back to me, about the kinds of people in the world. I think neither Dev nor me is immovable, but I don't know if that's enough.

So what my question comes down to is: do I think I can stop myself from fucking this up?

CHAPTER TWENTY-TWO: BROTHER IN LAW (DEV)

I'm yawning and stretching in bed, and Lee's already out of it, sitting naked on one of the chairs by the window—not the one I bent him over the night before. He's got his nose to the break in the curtain, and the bright crack of sunlight in the dark room illuminates the tousled russet fur between his chocolate-brown ears. Where the sun doesn't hit his ears, they turn black and disappear into shadow. Below the curve of his legs and the shadowy outlines of his similarly dark feet, I see the white tip of his tail twitching restlessly. I lift my head. "Taking in the, what did you call it, 'industrial wasteland'?"

He turns so that the daylight catches one of his blue eyes. "It's pretty under the snow. You can't tell how ugly the buildings or the asphalt are. Except where the cars have gone."

"That's one thing I miss about winter." I don't particularly want to get out of the warm bed. "The snow was pretty."

"It melts eventually," he says.

"In Lake Handerson, there's an abandoned train depot where they plow all the snow, and there's a big pile that lasts until June."

"Yeah," he says. "Remember the lot behind the abandoned Ark-Mart? About a mile from Forester?"

I shake my head. "Never went there."

"Ah." His white teeth flash sharp in the light. "We used to go have snow-ball fights there in May. Great fun."

"We should go," I say, and then laugh. "I guess now it's nothing special."

"Now we could probably go sledding down the pile of snow there," he says. "I did that once or twice with…friends."

Brian, I think, but I let it go. "What time is it?"

"Eight." He yawns and looks back outside. "Pretty day."

"I guess we should shower soon." Mom said she'd have breakfast on the table at nine, and Dad was annoyed that it would be that late. Usually he wants to be at the garage by quarter to eight, and even on a Sunday he likes to keep those hours. But I told Mom that I was not getting up at six in the morning while I was on vacation, and anyway it was going to take Gregory two hours to drive here from Gateway.

He wriggles around in the chair before getting up. "Jesus, Lee," I say, grinning. "It was twenty-five dollars."

"It's the principle of the thing. They've got fabrics that are easier to treat now, they've got Neutra-Scent. It's a hold-over from the days when strong-scented people weren't welcome in polite parlors."

He walks over as he talks, finishing up by bending over my side of the bed. I scoot backwards to make room for him to sit. "I know," I say. "I learned about the Great Odor Rebellion of 1881."

"Ha." A smile plays across his muzzle. "No, the annoying thing is that this isn't even one of the places where foxes and skunks and weasels were kept to the 'smelly' parts of town. It's just this hotel chain using a holdover from those prejudices to wring a little more money out of people. It makes me mad, so I'm protesting within their terms."

I reach out from under the covers and rest a paw on his thigh, rubbing the cool fur and the warm muscle beneath. "Didn't you tell me once that protesting on their terms is ultimately futile?"

"Okay," he concedes, "maybe I'm just being spiteful."

He leans over to kiss me, and his nose is as cold as if he'd been pressing it against the glass. "Is it that chilly out?" I sigh. "Maybe we can stay curled up in bed and they can come over here."

He doesn't even respond to that, just raises an eyebrow and smirks, and I say, "You're right, you're right. Give it another few years before we have sex in front of them?"

He laughs. "I'll go start the water." He curls and flicks his tail as he walks away toward the bathroom, and I watch his body, bringing my paw back under the covers to rest my cooler pads on the warmth of my morning erection.

We don't do anything about that, unless you count Lee soaping it up, because it's not really that urgent. Lee offers a quick soapie in the shower, but I'm happy to wait until he's ready too and we can get off together. Anyway, I don't want to chance leaving any stickiness in my fur where one of my family members might smell it at an awkward moment.

I'm waiting for him to finish drying his fur when he says, "There's something I wanted to talk to you about."

I poke my head into the bathroom where he's standing in the big stall, heat lamps and gentle blowers coaxing the water out of his fur, magically silent. That's classy hotels for you. "Is it a magic word to say to Gregory so he'll accept us?"

"I wish." He runs his paws along his tail, fluffing up the fur, and motions with his muzzle toward the main room. "In the inside pocket of my jacket there's an envelope." As I walk out and over to the chair where he draped his jacket, he goes on. "I was thinking about what you said, about me giving my own money to Gregory for Alexi."

I pull the envelope out. "I'm sure he won't take it, but…" My claws find the open flap and the check inside and I stare at it.

"I never did anything else with your playoff check," he says from the bathroom. "I deposited it, so that's off my account, which isn't ideal, but…"

"Lee." I stare at the numbers, the name "Gregory Miski" in his neat writing, and walk back in so I can see him.

He keeps talking, quickly. "If you think it's too much, I won't do it. I wanted to tell you a bunch of times but I couldn't find the right time, with Fisher and all the stuff going on, but, uh." He ruffles the tip of his tail, the fur blowing back and forth and little clouds of it drifting across the bathroom. "I didn't want to give it to him without letting you know."

"This is too much." I wave the envelope.

"It's my money."

"He's my nephew!"

His blue eyes fix mine. "Yeah. And you'd feel like shit if something happened to him that you could've prevented if your brother wasn't being an asshole."

God dammit, he's right. I start to put the envelope back in his pocket, then take it out again. "He'll never take it from you. And stop doing that while we're talking about him."

He's got his legs spread and is rubbing his balls. "What?" he says, looking innocent. "The fur's damp. This is always the hardest place to get dry."

"Gah." I turn away from him.

"Anyway," he goes on, "I thought it'd be better from me, because of him thinking you were trying to bribe him and all."

"If he thinks I'm trying to bribe him, he'll think I asked you to give him the money so it wouldn't look like I was trying to bribe him."

"All right. So…do you want to do it?"

I sigh and look down at the envelope again. The image of Gregory's muzzle snarling at me comes up. What's he going to do? Well, he's practical. He'll take the money if he needs it. He may not like it, but he'll take it. "I could give it to Mom and have her give it to him."

"I'd have to write out another check."

"No," I decide. "You're right, we should give him the money. But I want to do it. I want him to say 'thank you' to me and you both. Can I turn around yet?"

"I'm drying my butt. And if you're giving him the money to get a reaction, it's not the right reason to do it."

"Doc, I know it's not. But right now it's a damn sight better than punching him in the face, which is kind of my other alternative, so I'm gonna go with forcing him to thank us for something." I wave fox fur away from my nose with the envelope. "This shows him that we're family, that we want to help him. And the 'thank you' just means he's acknowledging that. Do you actually have any fur left or is it all in the room now? Should I buy some glue and have you roll around here?"

"Sounds like fun, but I'll pass." The blowers go off and he steps out as I turn around. "If you're sure you want to do this, then okay."

"This is a really nice thing you're doing," I tell him, admiring his fluffy, clean fur and his bright eyes and smile. "Didn't you want to give this to Equality Now or something?"

His tail wags slowly. "Don't really want Brian to have any of it."

"But wouldn't it help a lot of other people? Make a lot of kids' lives better?"

"Sure," he says. "But I want to help your nephew. Besides, Gregory saying 'thank you' to both of us is worth forty grand right there."

That startles a laugh out of me, a deep one from my stomach, and he laughs with me. I hold the envelope in my thumb and one finger and use my other eight fingers to rub down his sides, through his freshly-clean fur. "Hey," he says, "if we get the house, can we install one of those dryers? I kind of love it."

"More than me?" I lean down and nuzzle his ears.

"Well…" He pretends to think about it, his ears splaying. "Get it some attachments maybe…"

I turn the rubbing into tickling and chase him out of the bathroom. "Go get dressed, traitor fox."

He laughs and waves. "You should try it tomorrow. I know your fur's all short but it feels awesome."

"Maybe I will. Maybe I'll love it more than you."

"We can have a three-way with it," he calls.

I adjust the front of my pants. "Stop saying things like that or we'll be late."

It's five after nine when we get to my parents' house, and I recognize Gregory's car out front, an ostentatious luxury sedan that makes my claws extend around the steering wheel of the rental car as I park out front. "He had to get an overpriced *foreign* car," I say.

Lee eyes the car as we get out. "Probably a company car. Maybe he didn't have any say in it."

"Maybe he didn't." I slam the door of our rental car. "But this is a rental and I made sure it was States-made."

My fox chuckles. "Mikhail never said, but I wonder if he was staring at my Civique the whole time we were arguing on the porch."

"I don't think he was arguing because of the type of car you drive," I say, tension winding a knot around my gut as I look up at the house and picture Gregory inside.

"No, but I'm sure it didn't help. What was that word again? Khoo-ee something?"

"Fox." I stare down at him.

Lee looks up at me and squeezes my paw, and then, like he did back at Thanksgiving, he says, "We got this, tiger."

"You're not going to call anyone a cocksucker?"

He raises his eyebrows. "Does anyone else in there suck cock?"

"It's cold," I say, and start walking toward the house.

"Oh, come on." He hurries through the snow, crunching after me until we get to the sidewalk. "That was a little bit funny."

I squint against the bright blanket of snow glowing in the morning sun. "A little," I admit.

"Okay then." He pats me on the small of the back, smoothing down the nice collared shirt I put on, and follows me up the porch steps.

Mom opens the door, so they'd been watching the street or heard the car. We come into the dining room, where an awkward five places are set around the table and the smell of eggs and toast fills the air. I guess Lee and I are meant to take the two on one long side of the table, and Gregory is already sitting across from those places, with Dad to his left.

We take our seats and Mom brings coffee out as we help ourselves from the bowl of scrambled eggs and the plate of wheat toast. Lee takes black coffee and I add cream and sugar. Gregory's, too, has milk and sugar, I note. I look up from the steaming coffee cup to Gregory's face, which is carefully facing forward between me and Lee.

I see myself there, the lines he and I both inherited from our father traced in black fur between our ears and down around our eyes, the set of our eyes around our muzzles. But where my head is rounded like our mother's, Gregory's is wider and square like our father's, his cheek ruffs more full. There are lines in the fur around his eyes that I don't think I have, severe wrinkles that make him look more than the three years older he is.

Mom is good with the small talk, so we hear a lot about our former high school friends and their parents. She alternates: one of Gregory's old friends, and then one of mine. We listen, making small talk, and when Mom throws in a news tidbit about one of her friends' sons who is gay, Gregory throws down his fork on his mostly-empty plate.

"Is that what I'm missing a day with my family to talk about?" he says, still not looking at me. "I could just log in to Locale dot net if I wanted to know who's having kids and whose marriage is broken up and who's…" He glances at Lee, then at me, and then ducks his head. "This is about that Families United case, so let's talk about it."

The table is silent. Gregory lifts his head and looks toward Mom and Dad. "It's over, by the way. They settled, no court, no drama, okay? No wrongdoing admitted."

"I told them," I say. "Also about the statement you made afterwards."

He looks perfectly puzzled, so I take out my phone, where I've stored the statement for Mom and Dad's benefit. "This sound familiar? 'I'm proud to have reached a settlement that reinforces the value of traditional families and the good work done by the Christians of Families United. I look forward to continuing to support them against all the intolerant people who wish to encumber their freedom of expression in this country.'"

It takes me a long time to read it, during which Mom and Dad sit with ears perked and Gregory looks bored. When I set down my phone and look at him, he says, "Oh, that."

"Did you say these things?" Dad asks.

"Probably." He waves a paw, glaring at me. "If you'd followed any of my other cases, you would know that it's very common for me to read a statement prepared by my client at the conclusion of a case."

"One that lays out your feelings on a social issue?" Lee jumps in.

"They're paying for my time, they get to dictate what I say. And look." He raises a paw and points at me. "It wouldn't have been news at all if not for *you*. So if you're looking for someone to blame…"

It takes me a moment to process that. "What—me? You're blaming me for your right-wing bigoted—"

"Devlin!" Dad snaps.

"—hate speech?"

"Where's the hate?" Gregory demands. "Read it again. 'The value of traditional families.' 'The good work done by the Christians of Families United.' I never mention you, or homosexuals, or anything like that."

"Don't act stupid." I snarl. "As the brother of a publicly gay figure, your support of 'traditional' families…" I hope I'm getting the words right, and

I check briefly with Lee, "…implies that you're opposing me and other gay families."

He holds up a finger, smug. "I didn't say that."

"That's what 'implies' means," Lee says.

Gregory rounds on him. "You stay out of this."

"He's here with me," I say. "He can talk if he wants to."

The table is silent for a moment. Then Mom says, "I think Devlin has a point, Gregory."

"What point? That he can bring in some random…fox to be part of our family?" His glance toward her and Dad is a little uneasy, and his voice rises before they can object. "I know what you mean. Listen, this is how the firm works. When I defended the real estate developers—successfully, you know—I wasn't going to make a statement to the press about how I really wanted the two acres of wetland to survive but I was glad I'd won the case. My client was Families United and all that statement did was reflect their values."

"Their 'values'," I growl. "Their whole purpose is to invalidate relationships like mine."

He composes himself again and takes the last bite of his eggs. "It's not their whole purpose. They try to make families stronger, to help cubs make the right choices, to help parents support them."

I can feel the heat radiating off of Lee, but he keeps quiet. I find myself channeling what he wants to say. "The 'right' choices according to what they believe."

"Of course," Gregory says. "Everyone's morality is determined by their own belief system."

"The point is," I say, because the conversation is sliding off into abstraction, "that you took the case. This group drove a gay cub to kill himself—"

"That's not proven." He raises his voice, cutting me off. "The settlement stops the family from going ahead with the lawsuit. It doesn't admit to any wrongdoing."

"We know."

"The reasons a person takes his life, which is a tragic event, are complicated and can't be laid at the doorstep of one or two persons who only communicated positive messages of love and hope that have not resulted in suicide in most other cases." He sounds like he's reciting from a legal brief now.

"For Christ's sake, stop being a lawyer and have a heart for once." My voice is louder, I realize, but that's what Gregory's good at doing to me. We're both tense, like we want to jump over the table and fight.

Dad speaks up. "Gregory, you were told to take the case by the company. Is that not so?"

Gregory takes a breath. "Kind of." We all stare at him. "I mean, they said it would be a good case for me to take, it would be appreciated by the company, yes."

His words feel incomplete, and I'm not the only one who feels that way. Mom says, "Why would it be appreciated?"

"I guess they asked for me." My brother sits up with some pride.

"Who did?" Dad frowns, leaning across his empty plate.

"The Families United people. Someone at their office heard about me, I guess." He doesn't look at me as he says that.

"Because you're Dev's brother," Lee says, and then shovels a forkful of eggs into his mouth, like he hadn't meant to blurt that out.

But he's right, of course. I mean, I know it. Dad says, "Because of all the cases you have argued," but I can tell that even he doesn't believe it.

"Come on," I say. "How many suicide cases have you argued before? How would they have heard of you except as the brother of the famous gay guy?"

Gregory flinches, then growls. "You're saying I'm not a good lawyer?"

"I'm saying you're an idiot if you think whatever cases you won were the reason this religious group wanted you in the courtroom." I raise my voice again, and Mom says my name but I don't stop. "So they didn't mention me at all? Didn't ask your views about gay people? Did you think at all about how your appearing on that case would look?"

"To whom?" he sneers. "To Mom and Dad? To you? To *him?*" He stabs a fork in Lee's direction. "I know how it looked to my company: it looked like I was a professional who could take on a difficult case and negotiate a settlement."

"You're not the only lawyer," Lee says quietly.

"Of course not," Gregory says.

"On the case, I mean." My fox looks up. "They have an in-house lawyer and they had a local legal consultant for the district where the suicide happened. Why were you there, exactly? What specialized knowledge did you provide?"

"I…I consulted…" He shakes his head and then shoots a look at Dad. "Look, why is he even *here*? Isn't this a family matter?"

"He's here because I want him here," I say. "Counselor, maybe you'd like to answer his question? Why were you there?"

His ears go back and his lip curls. "Don't play at being a lawyer. Stick to hitting people."

"You're avoiding the question," Lee says quietly.

Gregory's paw slams the table. "It's too complicated to explain if you don't have a legal background. The point is—"

"Gregory." Mom says his name now, and that does stop him. We all turn to her. "The issue is not what people thought, but how it makes your brother *feel.*"

The table goes quiet. Dad says, "Oh, feel. Why should feelings matter in business? Gregory must do as his company says."

"Yes, Misha," Mom says. "But he can also tell them if he is uncomfortable."

"And then what?" Dad raises his voice. "The next time there is an important case, they worry whether he is uncomfortable, they give it to someone else?"

"Yeah." Gregory looks around. "I can't turn down cases just because... because I feel bad about it."

"Do you?"

We all turn to the fox. Lee has his paws clasped in front of him on the table, and he's looking intently at Gregory. Nobody says a word, so he goes on. "I'm sorry, I mean, I barely know you. But your mom is right. It's about feelings. And maybe this is how your family processes guilt and affection and whatever, but..." He shakes his head.

"You're right," Gregory sneers. "You don't know me."

"But I know the situation." Lee looks steadily at him. "My mom joined that Families United group. Last time we saw each other, it didn't go well. But I felt bad about it, and so did she. We still disagree over how I should live my life. She doesn't think love should be the only reason you're with someone."

I want to hug him. I think Mom does, too; she reaches a paw toward him and then pulls it back. He doesn't seem to notice, going on as my brother stays miraculously quiet. "We love each other, is the point. And I think maybe underneath all of this, you love Dev and you don't understand why he's a different person now than he used to be. It's confusing and scary. But he's not that different. He's just doing different things. And if you feel bad that you defended the people who want to take away his happiness..." He pauses, then, and there's a little sparkle in his eye as he looks at me with a raised eyebrow and a cupped ear.

"Happiness," I affirm.

He smiles and returns his attention to Gregory. "Then you should say so. And if you don't understand why he feels bad, ask him."

The table is quiet. Lee pushes his chair back. "Breakfast was delicious, thanks," he says to Mom, and takes his plate into the kitchen.

"Lion Christ," Gregory says. "I don't feel bad. I did a job, that's all."

Mom stands and picks up her plate as well, following Lee into the kitchen. Gregory says, "Mom," but she doesn't stop.

Dad sits still, his expression pensive. Gregory turns to him. "Dad. Come on, you understand, I have to do the cases they give me."

"Yes," Dad says. He turns his head slowly to me and then back to Gregory. "We may not understand your brother's decisions, but you should always take family into consideration."

"He—" Gregory points at me.

Dad doesn't let him finish. "When your brother did not respect the family, I expressed my displeasure. He has apologized for that."

"He hasn't apologized to me!"

"For what?" I snap before Dad can. "We hadn't talked in years—"

"For how it affected my career!"

He hurls the words at us like a volcano exploding, and even Dad is somewhat taken aback. Gregory turns to him, ignoring me. "Everyone in the office was coming up to me like, 'hey, I heard about your brother,' and 'so did you turn him gay' and shit like that."

"Seriously?"

"That is…not your brother's fault." It takes Dad an effort to say that, and his ears flick. I remember him talking about the guys at the auto shop and my own ears fold back. So many things I'd never thought about while sitting up at that conference table.

"And what about Alexi?"

This strange turn of the conversation stuns me into silence. Dad, too, seems perplexed until Gregory goes on. "He's going to have to go to school, and all his friends who like football, they're going to be asking him about his gay uncle. He'll get teased, he'll get picked on. He's already white, as if this wasn't hard enough."

Oh. "He's two years old," I say. "He won't be in school for another three years."

"He's twenty months," Gregory snaps. "He has friends down the block."

"How is he doing?" Dad asks, softer, and I wish I'd remembered to ask that.

Here is the moment where Gregory would ask me for money, if he needed to. The room is quiet and it's a lot easier to remember that we're a family here, a family with a sick cub. If Gregory would just look at me, would let me see his vulnerability and his need…but his expression remains closed and guarded. "He's fine," he says. "For now. White tigers just need more care. We're doing fine."

"Anyway," I say, "Polecki came out. There'll be others. And in three years, nobody will even remember."

"Right. Nobody will remember the first gay football player. You're even stupider than you look." Just like that the family moment is over.

"Gregory." Dad, in that deep arresting voice that still curls the end of my tail.

Gregory scowls, and then picks up his plate and stands. Neither my father nor I say anything. He walks to the door, and then turns and says, "If Dev was doing a lot of heroin and I took an anti-drug case, you wouldn't be mad at me." He stomps into the kitchen.

I'm up and out of my chair and have already taken two steps after him before Dad waves me down, and even then I take one more step. "He is angry," he says.

"He compared my relationship to a drug habit!"

Dad nods. "It was disrespectful, and I will speak to him about it."

"Speak to him?" I'm still seething and I want to hit something, preferably Gregory's smug muzzle. "When I came here with Lee, you threatened to throw me out of the house. You said I couldn't come back."

He growls low in his throat. "I know what I said. You are here now."

"Why are you defending him?"

"I am *not* defending him!" He sits up straighter and challenges me with a stare. "I understand what he feels because it was not so long ago that I felt the same. Your fox is…difficult."

I open my mouth to argue and then incline my head. "He is, yeah. But I love him."

"He antagonized Gregory at Thanksgiving."

"So did I."

"Yes." Dad waves a paw. "Gregory sees only the fox, blames him for the change in you."

"You know his name, right, Dad?" I ask, resting my elbows on the table and leaning forward.

He doesn't change his expression immediately, but after a second the corner of his mouth lifts. "Lee. Wiley, yes? Farrel. His father is Brenly. All right?"

"You can use his name once in a while," I say.

"Gregory blames *Lee* for the change in you. None of us saw you often after college."

"I was in the UFL, trying to—"

He holds up a paw. "I understand. You have Lee, it is difficult to tell us because you are afraid of how we will react."

"With good reason."

"Yes." He smiles, showing the tips of his canines over his lips. "It is still not something I completely understand. But…" he gestures between me and the seat where Lee'd been sitting. "When we see you together, it is clear that there is something. Something very good for you. So," he nods and his paw falls to the table. "Your mother and I approve of it."

"Then Lion Christ, tell *him* already."

"He is your brother too." Dad hands me his plate. "Maybe you should tell him. Now take my plate in and come to the living room."

I grab his plate and mine and the coffeepot. He gets up as I walk to the kitchen and heads the other way.

Lee and Mom are still in the kitchen talking in low voices. His ears are flat but come up as I come in, and he smiles. "Thanks," he says.

"You could hear?" I say without thinking and then chuckle and brush my nose along the top of his ear. "Right."

"I have been talking to Lee about his mother," Mom says. "Are you going to see her with him?"

I drop the plates in the sink and the coffeepot on the counter. "I don't think so. It would upset her. Last time I did that I thought it went okay, but…"

Lee shakes his head. "She was upset after. But it's okay, she doesn't blame *you* for it."

"To be fair," I say, "it's the sort of thing you would do."

"Uh-huh." He smiles. "Which is why it was so sweet that you did it anyway."

"It was years ago," I say to Mom's look. "He was nervous about them, but I thought that was just about school. They knew he was gay."

"Yeah," he says. "I think they were fine with it when it was theoretical. They weren't ready to actually meet my boyfriend."

"Well," Mom says, "I don't know that we were ready to meet you either, but I am very glad we did."

"Me too." He smiles at her and then at me.

Much as I would like to stay in this room, I have to go out to the living room, where Dad and Gregory are already sitting on opposite sides of the coffee table, leaving me only the couch where I sat with Lee last night. I park myself in the middle of it and sit up straight, reviewing breakfast's conversation in my mind. Gregory is sprawled back in his chair, arm hung over one armrest, phone in his paw; Dad sits relaxed with a cup of coffee. Neither of them says a word.

"Look," Gregory says finally, looking up from his phone, "can we get to whatever you want me to say so I can get back home to my cub?"

I look at Dad, who sits back in his chair. "I want you to say whatever you want to say," he says. "Your brother is here, and you have the chance to talk to him."

"He doesn't want to hear what I have to say," Gregory says.

"Try me." My throat is tight, but I want to know what he's going to say. I can't imagine it will be anything like what Lee's mother has said to him, but now I feel a little more strongly what he must have felt listening to her, even though Gregory hasn't spoken a word yet.

Gregory sighs. "Look," he says, "I know all this stuff is attractive right now. It's hip, it's how society's changing. But there are a small core of people who are pushing it to change faster than it should." He keeps his voice low. "And the people they're targeting are young cubs. Right? Cubs want to do what feels good, so they go along with the whole 'love is all you need' hippie bullshit that we got rid of in the seventies. The rhetoric is compelling—to someone with an underdeveloped mind."

"So," I say, "some people—who? Are trying to turn people gay? Why?"

He waves his arms, more flamboyant. "To cement their own power, to make themselves look bigger and more legitimate than they are. If they fool all these cubs into trying it out, into identifying with them, then they get to make all these laws that you can't fire them, that you have to recognize their relationships…"

"Wait." I hold up a paw. "I'm trying to figure all this out. So I'm only with Lee because some shadowy cult of people talked me into it somehow?"

Gregory looks at me from under my father's brow and rubs his paws down his cheek ruffs, then steeples them together in front of him. "It was tough following me through high school. You wanted to rebel. You were afraid you'd never make it in the UFL. And this…" He waves his paw. "This fox comes along and shows you how to rebel, how to become a celebrity overnight. I can see how you were tempted. I—hey, wait."

He's shrunk back in his chair because I've stood up. My fists are balled and though I don't intend to fight him, I'm sure I look imposing. I'm not sure he realized until that moment how much bigger than him I am now. But as much as I want to hit him, I am aware of my father, of Mom and Lee in the kitchen, and I stick to words. "That's what you really think? You think I'm still your little brother, confused and stupid, trying to cheat at games so I can beat you?"

"Dev—"

"Yeah, I didn't go to law school," I say. "I'm not as smart as you are. But I don't need to be smart to know when I love someone. I don't need to be smart to know that he doesn't have to have tits for me to fall in love. And I don't need a law school degree to know that you're a condescending asshole."

"Devlin," Dad says.

"I'm fine." I turn to him. "I'm sorry that this talk didn't work out. I know you hoped Gregory and I could work things out and walk out of here friends and brothers again. But I don't think it's gonna happen."

Dad looks at me and I'm surprised at how sad his eyes are. Gregory stays silent.

"Lee!" I call back to the kitchen.

He walks partway into the living room, tail swinging behind him, but his tail stills when he sees me standing in front of the couch. "What—er—everything okay?"

"Yeah," I say. "C'mere."

He takes a few steps toward the couch on the side nearer my father, and I walk out to meet him. Without another word I pull him against me and lower my muzzle, crushing it to his.

He freezes. I hold the kiss, and a moment later he brings his arms up around my back, but he's still tense. I don't try to force my tongue through his lips, just stand there kissing him until he relaxes a little. Then I let go and I turn to face Gregory, who's looking toward the fireplace, pointedly away from us.

"Don't you ever fucking presume to know what someone else feels," I say to him in a low growl. "Especially your own brother. And don't treat me like some ten-year-old cub who doesn't know the difference between right and wrong. I don't give a shit who you defend from here on out, okay? I'll expect you to show up defending murderers and shitbag corporations who screw over people, and whatever. It's how you make your living. Dad's right, you don't have any control over that."

The room is quiet. Lee drops his paw from my back. Nobody says anything. I clear my throat. "So, I'll see you at Thanksgiving and Christmas maybe. Depends on how my work goes. Say hi to Marta. Good luck with Alexi."

I grab my jacket, but Lee's looking at me and not moving, and I can't figure out why until I feel the stiffness of the envelope in the jacket pocket. I pull it out and hold it up between us. For a moment I consider putting it back in and walking out. But I know that's not the right thing to do.

"By the way," I say, turning and holding out the envelope, "if you want to know how much Lee considers himself family, here. This is from both of us to help with Alexi's expenses."

Gregory doesn't get up, though his eyes do watch the envelope. Dad finally gets up to take it from me and he opens it. His eyes widen. "This is…very generous."

Mom appears in the doorway to the kitchen and watches Dad walk across the room to drop the envelope in Gregory's lap, the check sticking partway out of it.

We all wait for his reaction, and at first he doesn't do anything, not even look down. Then curiosity gets the better of him and he drops his eyes. His fingers tease at the check and his brow lowers as he reads it. "What is this?"

"I told you, it's to help—"

"Is this to shut me up?" The envelope falls to the floor as he lifts the check out of it.

"No!" My voice rises again. "What the hell is wrong with you?"

He stands up, brandishing the check. "And it's in his name! You couldn't have sent the message any more clearly if you'd written 'shut up' on it."

"Gregory! I have had enough of this behavior." Dad stands up, but his usual authority doesn't stop Gregory—or me, for that matter.

"I thought I was perfectly clear before." I match his tone. "I don't give a shit what you say or do. That," I point to the check, "is for my nephew."

"What," he sneers, "so you can have me indebted to you? So you have a forty thousand dollar chit you can call in sometime in the future?"

"So your goddamn cub doesn't get any sicker!"

"I told you," he says, "we are doing fine." And before any of us can stop him, he takes the check and rips it in half.

The pieces flutter to the carpet in silence. Even Lee is dumbstruck. I can't process all the thoughts going through my head. And of all of us, it's Mom who finds her tongue first.

"You will apologize to your brother," she says, her eyes fixed on Gregory, "*and* to Lee."

He stares at her and then turns to Dad. "Dad…"

But our father shakes his head slowly. "Your mother is right. Family comes first and you are not thinking of family."

"I'm—" Gregory stutters, the first time I've seen him unable to speak in years. "But—you don't understand—that was—"

"Apologize," Dad says, "to both of them. And then I think you should leave."

Gregory looks around the room, skipping over Lee, and then his eyes rest on me. His jaw tightens and he stomps past all of us without a word. A moment later, the front door slams hard enough to rattle the glass in the windows.

Silence drags on and on, and then Dad reaches a paw out to Lee. Lee takes it, looking up into his muzzle. "I am sorry," Dad says.

Lee tilts his head. "For?"

"I am realizing that it sounded as though I did not consider what Gregory did to be serious. And the truth is…" He looks up at Mom. "I

Over Time

did not want to believe that it was. I knew your relationship confused him, but I hoped the case was a coincidence or that he did not really believe it. And now it will appear that I am only apologizing because you offered forty thousand dollars to our grandcub."

"It was Dev's money really." Lee smiles. "He gave it to me and so it made sense to give it back. But," he adds quickly, "thank you. There's no need to apologize for believing the best of your children."

"I have perhaps not always done that." Now he releases Lee's paw and looks at me.

I shuffle my feet. "I haven't made it easy."

"No." A smile flickers.

"I'll write another check," Lee says. "To you guys. You don't have to tell him where the money comes from."

"Thank you." Mom comes up now. "It is a very nice thing."

"And I hope," Dad says, "that we will see you both here for the holidays."

CHAPTER TWENTY-THREE: BACK TO SCHOOL (LEE)

That was about the most uncomfortable kiss I ever had. I couldn't pull away with Dev obviously making a point in front of his father and brother, but I couldn't really forget about them watching, either. I'm just glad he didn't want to make more of a demonstration.

And it ended pretty well for us, at least. I leave the house smiling and waggy from his parents' reception to me and the idea that we'll be able to help Alexi, but my tiger's mind is elsewhere.

"I don't get how he can be that way," Dev growls as he slams his car door closed. "Where the fuck did that come from?"

I watch the puffs of his breath and mine in the car and rub my paws together to warm them. "Let's not forget that after our first, ahem, date, when you came back to my apartment, I didn't know if you were going to hit me or kiss me. And then we didn't talk all summer, and I wasn't sure you were going to come back."

He laughs harshly, but relaxes a little. "What do you mean? You bought a new dress."

"I hoped." I smile. "I didn't know. I thought you might spend the summer denying it ever happened and putting that faggot fox out of your mind."

"As if." He shakes his head. "But still, I didn't think gay people were..."

"Didn't you?" I try to remember the Devlin Miski I met that spring, and fail. "You maybe hadn't thought about it very much. Gregory probably hasn't met anyone he knows is gay, and having it be his little brother, right around the time you're getting to be a big celebrity..."

"He's jealous, I know."

I clear my throat. "Could you start the car? It's a wee bit chilly."

"How long have you lived in Chevali? A month?" He snickers and starts the car anyway, and then pulls out into the street.

"I'm losing all my fur. See?" I wave it all around in the air and he coughs theatrically.

On our way out of town, I keep the conversation going. "Don't you feel just a bit excited that you're more famous than he is? That you're doing better? I mean, you were in the UFL Championship game."

He doesn't answer, and I can see his thoughts going back to the game itself. "While he's taking charitable cases who only want him to be involved *because of you*. That seemed to bother him more than anything else, you know."

His expression clears, and I see the memories of the game fade. "Yeah," he says. "That's pretty great, huh?"

"And who'd have guessed your dad would throw him out?"

"He didn't really…" Dev pauses. "He did, didn't he?"

"I mean, it's not permanent or anything, I'm sure. But it gave him something to think about. And you made a pretty nice speech there at the end, too."

He flicks his ears, and his whiskers lift. "I just thought about what you would say. Well, no, I mean, I didn't even have to take time to think. It came out like that."

Warmth that has nothing to do with the car's heater fills me. "I'm glad. And I hope the words have an effect on him, even if it takes time."

He nods, and when neither of us says anything, he turns up the music.

Two exits down the highway, almost out of Lake Handerson, I can't hold in the question anymore. "Hey, Dev?" He turns his ears toward me but doesn't look away from the road. "Was I okay? I mean, did I step out of line or talk too much?"

That gets him to laugh. "After I pulled you in to kiss you, you ask that?"

"I just want to be sure. You know, your dad might be onto something with this whole 'talking' thing. Maybe I shouldn't worry so much about keeping quiet?"

He chuckles and reaches over to pat my leg. "You were fine, doc. Don't even worry about it. You made good points."

My ears go up and my tail relaxes. "So I can learn, I guess."

"You can. You don't always."

"Fair enough, I guess." I shake my head. "What was with that kiss?"

For a few seconds he thinks about it, and then says, "Ah, it seemed like a better idea than punching him, and I couldn't think of anything else to say." His muzzle half-turns. "You think it was a bad idea?"

"It was a sweet gesture." I smooth down my cheek ruffs. "I don't think I was looking my best."

"I doubt they noticed, fox."

Forester College is much as I remember it, all stately limestone and brick under a blanket of snow. I used to know more of the history than I do now: founded by Jason Keller, a beaver, back in 1894; briefly famous in 1971 for making it ridiculously easy to qualify for an educational exemption to the draft (then-president Mitchell White: "We would rather teach our children to fashion plowshares than bury them with swords."). Famous alumni include Jay Wortham, an ermine who served two terms as Senator; Mariann Morgan, a vixen who fought for female suffrage and the Orwell Acts; and one Devlin Miski.

We meet with a fiftyish pine marten named Rob who is the Forester University Athletic Director, a grey fox named Janine who is the Director of Special Events for the University or else maybe the Director of Marketing, I'm not sure, and a young stallion named Chuck who is the current president of FLAG.

Rob and Janine are dressed in typical Midwestern business suits, but Chuck wears a huge loose flowery silk shirt over a tight t-shirt bearing the design of a rainbow flag, and his jeans barely contain the thick muscles of his legs. The last president of FLAG I remember was a polar bear business major who would have said that Rob and Janine were underdressed; when Chuck takes me aside during the pre-meeting drinks, I am absolutely unsurprised to hear that he is a junior in sociology.

"Hey," he says, "you were in FLAG, right?"

"I was." I don't need to go into how I grew distanced from it my senior year, when dating Dev made it difficult to be part of my gay crew. I was active for three years, and that's not a bad track record. My senior year would have been his freshman year, and I vaguely remember a horse freshman from the few meetings I went to, but I wasn't one of the people he would have noticed either, and he doesn't say anything about it.

"So did you get my e-mail?" He's all excited the way horses get, bobbing his head and grinning at me. "What did you think?"

"Oh," I say, remembering, "I'm not sure I'm on the FLAG alumni list. I might not have signed up my senior year, and I don't check my Forester e-mail anymore."

His head stops moving and his ears go out to the sides. "Aw, that's a shame," he says. "I put a picture of your boyfriend up there and I wanted to get one of you, too, but I wasn't sure you were an alum and by the time I got it confirmed, it was too late. But I mentioned you!"

"Too late?" I tilt my head. "They haven't even decided if they're going to do the day yet."

He waves his drink around so enthusiastically that I'm worried it'll spill. "I know, but I wanted to let people know I was going to be helping plan it so I could bring suggestions from current members and alums. It's cool, though, I'll get your info and put it in the announcement when we go ahead with it."

"If they go ahead with it."

He jerks his head toward the others with a big horsy smile. "I already talked to Janine and she says she wants to do it, she just has to figure out how."

I look over to where Dev is talking to the fox and marten, and perk my ears in that direction. Dev's talking about Polecki and how he'd be willing to come up as well, and Rob responds with enthusiasm about having two players who were in the championship. He suggests maybe they can arm-wrestle. Janine's thumb-typing furiously on a little Blackberry; she breaks in to ask what companies they can contact for sponsorship money. I make a mental note to suggest Ultimate Fit; maybe they can work in the third commercial Dev owes them as part of the event, and he won't have to interrupt his minicamps or training camps or even his next season, if they hold onto it that long.

Chuck is saying something about a dinner that evening, and I focus back on him. "It'd be really cool for the club, be a chance to meet him outside the confines of the event, because he's going to be really busy then."

"Tonight?" I say.

"Yeah. Even if he can only show up for fifteen minutes. It's just a regular meeting. I think for the actual event, we'll organize something too, but…" His head's bobbing again and he's smiling. "I worked with Janine on the first Pride Day last year and she's totally willing to have the students involved, but we were supposed to have time with Marcia Bendinger too and then Janine said they had a chance to meet with some of the local alumni, and it never happened…"

I'm sure the name is supposed to mean something to me, but I have no idea who that is or why the students would want to meet her. I get the gist of it though, and I'm sympathetic to marketing people taking over an event. "I'll see what I can do," I say. "How about coffee at Ketteridge's?"

"We do the Starbucks on Maple," Chuck says, his grin threatening to burst from his lips. "It's bigger and better lit and we can usually all get in upstairs if we go an hour before they close."

"There's a Starbucks on Maple?" I ask, because it doesn't seem like things can have changed that much in two years, but of course they do and apparently they have.

"Oh yeah! It's a block down from the bookstore. They just put it in last year and it's amazing, they're already talking about putting another one in on the other side of campus."

"That's where Ketteridge's is."

"Yeah, but nobody really goes there. I mean, some of the theater majors do. I guess it's usually pretty full when I go by. I don't go there very often, though." His silk shirt ripples as he gestures and bobs. "But yeah, if you guys can show up at the meeting, it's in Harnwell Hall at eight, and we're usually over at the Starbucks by nine-thirty and they close at ten-thirty. That'd be awesome."

What kind of coffee shop on a college campus closes at ten-thirty? I don't ask that; instead I say, "We'll see what we can do."

He smiles and extends a hand to my paw. We shake and then talk about all the gay rights news of the day, the lawsuits coming up over marriage. I tell him how when I started school back in 2003, none of us ever believed marriage would actually come about, and now people are taking it seriously. He says that people like Dev coming out really help because they're reaching other segments of society—people who watch sports aren't generally the ones who have the most enlightened views on gay rights.

It's a nice talk and stirs up those old feelings again. I start to tell him about the Vince King case and then I think it's settled and I shouldn't, and then I think, hell with it, and I tell him all about it. He's horrified at the incident, furiously glad at the lawsuit, and, like me, unsure what to think about the settlement. "I'm glad they had to pay, but I wish it'd gone to trial." He blows a snort. "Send me the info and I'll tell people about it. We have a newsletter."

It's a nice gesture, and I remember when I would've eagerly offered the services of the FLAG newsletter. But the people it reaches are people who already know what kind of shitty things Families United does. They don't need more convincing. Plus, now, I'd be exposing Gregory to the world if I did that. Partly I genuinely feel bad for him, but also I don't want to give him a platform to yell about Dev.

Rob and Janine offer to take us to lunch, but we don't go to Goose's, the diner, nor to P.J.'s, the casual dining restaurant where my parents met Dev for the first time. They take us to this place called Aqua, a smallish restaurant with blue-tinted walls and aquaria all around the entrance. We're seated at white-linened tables with soft light glowing in blue shades overhead and given blue leather menus from which to choose seafood, all caught from the nearby lake.

On the way over, I get a call from Gena. She wanted to let me know that Hal came over and spent some time with Fisher and that he left contact information for some of the other guys he's been talking to. I ask how Fisher's dealing with it, and she says he seems more relaxed, though it's only been a little while. The nurse is working out well and Gena sounds more positive than she's been since—well, since midway through the season, I guess.

By the time I get into the restaurant, Chuck and Rob have taken the seats around Dev, so I sit across from Janine. After we get the "what do you do" out of the way, we end up having a pretty good conversation. Her title is actually Director of Marketing and Communications, and she's a Forester alum (from well before my time, though she's not as old as Rob).

"Okay," I say, "so I need to ask your opinion on a critical matter that I've just become aware of at Forester." Her ears perk my way, and she looks serious—because she doesn't know me yet. "What do you think of the Starbucks?"

The grey fox's first response is a marketing one: "Oh. Starbucks has been really great to work with. They're putting a lot of money into the community and they're respecting our wishes as far as where to set up their shops..." Then she sees my expression and says, "But I'm a Ketteridge's gal myself. Starbucks is fine for an afternoon latte, but if I'm sitting with friends..." She looks past my shoulder. "Don't do much of that around campus anymore. Maybe when my cubs go here."

She has a boy and a girl, eight and thirteen, and I let her tell me about them, and then she lets me tell her about my job with the Whalers and the championship. I can tell she's not that into football, but she admits that she watched the game with her husband and that he was excited about Dev. " 'I watched him play here!' he kept saying," she chuckles. " 'I coulda gotten his autograph!' It was really cute."

"Didn't bother him that Dev's...you know, out?"

She shakes her head. "I don't think it even came up. I mean, when it was announced, we talked about it and then talked with our cubs about it too. Our church doesn't get into politics, so it never came up before. But we made sure to tell the cubs that Jesus preached love, and whatever people do to fill the world with more love you can't fault them for."

"I haven't had great experience with religious groups." I look over her shoulder into memory, and then back to her friendly grey and orange muzzle, whiskers highlighted in blue by the light above us. "It's nice to know that there's a church out there that doesn't care who I love."

"There are a lot of them," Janine says. "You just don't hear about them because they don't yell and get on the news. But I don't think churches should do that anyway. They're supposed to provide guidance, not make spectacles of themselves. Jesus also preached about that, you know, about the 'hypocrites' who 'stand and pray on the street corners so they may be seen.' I think those are important words."

"I wish more religious leaders followed them." I shake my head and perk my ears back up. "Sorry. It gets old being told that you're damned to hell all the time."

She smiles, and as Rob raises his glass to make a toast, she leans over to me and says, "You have more friends than you know."

The food is good: lake trout and open-mouthed bass and farm-raised catfish (catfish are the exception to "locally caught," because they're bottom feeders and I think people would prefer not to think about what's at the bottom of the lakes where they throw all their garbage). Janine gets the lone chicken dish because she isn't a big fan of seafood, and I get a laugh with a joke about the chicken being line-caught at a local farm.

I keep an ear open to Dev's conversation, but they're mostly making him relive the Boliat game—the last one he won—rather than the championship, so he's staying in good humor. I see him miming the strip he had that led to a defensive touchdown, and then even Ty's catch.

When he talks about that, he pauses and looks over at me. Thinking about Ty too, I give him back a smile, and he goes on with his story.

Chapter Twenty-Four: Homeward (Dev)

I'm glad to have the meeting so soon after breakfast with my family, because it takes my mind off Gregory for at least a couple hours. The memory of that conversation makes it a lot easier for me to talk to Rob and Janine about planning an event where I will return to Forester as the "favorite gay son," as Janine puts it. The actual name of the event is going to be worked out, but Rob favors something like "Diversity in Athletics Day," which he thinks can be abbreviated to "DAD" so that fathers will feel included. Janine isn't as hot on that; I stay politely out of the argument, because there's no way to make the day abbreviate to "FUCK YOU OLDER BROTHER."

I really want to get Lee involved when they start talking about who else to bring to the event, because I know Polecki and that's about it. They're talking about some actor and a singer, and it takes me like ten minutes of the conversation to realize that the actor is gay. I never knew. Meanwhile, Lee's talking to that stallion, who is so excited I think he's going to run laps around the room.

When the stallion (Chuck) gets to talk to me over lunch, he keeps asking about my coming out, which annoys Rob. I spend the whole lunch balancing stories between the two of them: first a story about the playoffs for Rob, then a story about the press conferences I've had.

"And what happened at Media Day?" Chuck says when we're finishing up the fish. "That whole 'wish I hadn't come out' thing?"

"Ah, that." I shake my head. "I was under a lot of pressure. Plus the guy who was asking was someone who knows me, who's been trying to get under my skin for years. Well, months. It *feels* like years. A few months back he took a picture of me with a female panther to try to convince Lee that I was cheating on him."

"Were you?" Chuck stares at me.

Uncomfortable images of Argonne rise in my head. "No. But he's the one who published rumors on his blog, and then my idiot agent—ex-agent—blew them all out of proportion."

"All's well that ends well, though, right?" Chuck grins.

"So what was the difference in the two Hellentown games?" Rob asks. "You lose one week, win the next…home team loses both times. How often does that happen?"

I shake my head. "Strike made the difference in the second one. I don't know. We just wanted it more."

The marten nods approvingly. "Coach wants to know if you'll be able to come talk to the football team when you come up for the event."

"Sure," I say. "I'd love to say hi to him. Is he around?"

"Nah, he's out recruiting. He'll be here then, though."

"Hey," Chuck breaks in again. "You can come talk to the FLAG guys tonight, right? Your fox said it was okay."

I glance at Lee, who's talking to the grey fox. "If he said okay, then okay."

"Cool." Chuck gets a big smile showing all his square teeth that reminds me of Charm when he's talking about the bunny he just had sex with. I wonder if Chuck likes to play around as much as Charm does, but that's probably not a horse thing. It's more an athlete thing. Like Gerrard.

After lunch, we shake with Rob, Janine, and Chuck, and the three of them go off in separate directions while Lee and I stand in the chill snow and look around. "Anything you want to visit again on the campus?"

"We could walk by the stadium," I say. Without the distraction of planning the event, I'm starting to think about my brother again, and I want to head that off.

I remain quiet as we set off across campus. It's Sunday, but the lack of classes doesn't mean the students walk without purpose along the snow-covered paths, ears perked, tails wagging or curling, some hurrying intently, others making their way more leisurely in small laughing, chattering groups. I get distracted watching them and turn to Lee. "When did college students get so young?"

He laughs. "I was just thinking that. Were we this young?"

"Someday, I guess." I watch a skinny ferret running after a deer whose backpack must outweigh her. To our right, on the green, a couple tigers lob snowballs at each other, and in front of us, paws clasp together, muzzles turn toward each other, backpacks jostle and shift, and the babble of the crowd grows.

A block later we turn, expecting to see the stadium, but it's a huge brick building that greets us, closer than the stadium should have been. "Right," I say. "They tore down the old one. Forgot about that."

"Still want to see the new one?" Lee keeps walking.

I can almost smell the newness of it, the bricks gleaming even in the overcast cold of winter, bright maroon against the glittering white snow. "Sure." Silver letters topped with snow spell out "Forester Field" (I assume—I can see "Fores" from where we are) and the Forester flag flies atop it, snapping crisply in the wind next to the state flag and the Union flag.

We get up close enough to put our paws to the cold bricks. "New stadium and a Starbucks," Lee murmurs. "This place is going to hell."

"Don't forget Diversity in Athletics Day," I remind him.

"Oh, right. Is that what they're calling it?" He chuckles. "You'll get the Jesus protestors for sure."

I wonder whether Gregory will help organize those, and my paws tighten to fists. I'm being ridiculous, I tell myself, forcing my paws open. "When are you meeting your mom?"

"Tonight. Father's picking me up."

"Where?"

"Wherever I tell him. I didn't know where we'd be."

I nod. "You're coming with me to the FLAG thing though, right?"

He rubs his whiskers. "I'd like to. Let me see if we can do dinner and get me back here by nine. I don't want to rush things, but if we have an early dinner…oh, and I should call Salim and ask him to show up there, too." He leans back against the brick wall, the lighter fur inside his dark brown ears vivid against it. "What are you going to do for dinner?"

"Haven't really thought about it. I guess I could see if any of the guys are still around. My old roommate, teammates…"

"Girlfriends?" Lee grins and elbows me as he takes his phone out.

"Hah." I snort. "Maybe I'll just grab some fast food and call Charm. Talking to Chuck made me miss him."

Lee's tail wags. "Say hi for me. You'll have more fun than I will." His ears go down and his smile vanishes. "I wish Mother'd meet you."

"I like your father," I say. "We can work on your mother. Well—you can, at first. I'll be on my best behavior when you do re-introduce me."

"I know you will." He looks up at me, and I think he wants to kiss me, but we're both aware that we're out in the open on a big visible stretch of pavement against the brick wall, next to a street where cars are going by at a swift rate. I remember a night when we kissed on the street without caring who was walking by, but that was when he was in a dress and it didn't matter so much.

Now we both acknowledge the moment silently, smile, and let it pass. And then Lee says, "You're not the one who has to worry about misbehaving," and he takes a step toward me, up on his toes, grabs my muzzle, and kisses me right on the lips.

It's startling, but I lean into it and wrap my arms around him. We don't hold the kiss for long, but we don't cut it short because we're in public. Cars go by, slow down, maybe, but nobody honks, nobody yells. And when we break apart, nobody is staring at us. A couple people are approaching, but they just smile and hurry on past to whatever their destination is.

"You're a bad fox," I murmur.

His blue eyes sparkle up in the crisp cold air. "You like it?"

"You already know the answer to that." I land my paw between his ears, which splay out above his silly grin. "Come on, let's go get somewhere warm and see what we're doing next."

We go to the student union, where the bustle of students makes me more nostalgic than I want to be. Back when I was on campus, I didn't have to worry about agents or contracts, about friends who might be losing their minds or their families, about other people's families accepting me. I just had to pass the classes my dad picked for me and play football. And I wouldn't trade this life, not for anything, but I also don't feel like I can sit here among the students happily chatting over open notebooks and laptop computers, drinking coffee and smoothies and eating the greasy pizza from the student union food court. I'd feel like a voyeur somehow, like an old guy coming back to relive the good old days.

"Let's go to Ketteridge's," I say to Lee, but he raises a paw to me. I wait as he threads his way through the tables to where a small arctic fox sits alone, bent over a book. Lee touches his shoulder and the fox looks up, then smiles broadly and stands to hug him. They talk, words I can't hear over the noise of the room, and then Lee waves in my direction and they both turn.

I give them a smile as they both walk toward me. "Dev," Lee says, "this is Jason, my TA from that English class I didn't pass."

The arctic fox shakes my paw. "Real pleasure to meet you," he says. "My boyfriend and I have read a lot about you."

"Ah," I say, and look at Lee.

"I didn't know!" Lee laughs. "I suspected, because he has that vibe…"

"You do too," Jason says. "I was pretty sure, but you can't really ask those things. Then I saw you in the news. I sent you an e-mail, but you never answered."

"I'm hearing that a lot recently. I should probably reactivate that account." Lee shakes his head. "Glad I ran into you, though. We're getting together with FLAG tonight if you want to come. Bring your boyfriend, too."

"Maybe." Jason looks evasive. "I don't usually get political, you know? Angling for a tenure job, you never know if the head of the department is going to be a homophobe or what. We talked about getting married, but it probably wouldn't be good for either of our jobs."

Lee nods. "All the time I was working for the Dragons, I stayed in the closet, and when I was outed I got fired."

I keep quiet during this talk because it feels like a throwback to Lee's old activist days, and I don't know a whole lot about it. When I came out, I got a million-dollar commercial deal, so I don't feel like I have a lot to say here.

They talk about some professor Lee used to have and Jason used to work for, and Lee tells Jason about his job with the Whalers. The arctic fox doesn't understand football or follow it much, but he understands that getting a job with a pro team is a big deal for both of us.

Lee makes him promise to try to come to the meeting tonight before we part ways. "Seems like a nice guy," I say.

"He tried to help me graduate," he says. "Schruft is an asshole and to be fair, I wasn't doing really any of the work anyway. But Jason was cool. Be interesting to meet his boyfriend."

"For years I didn't have any gay friends and now I'm sort of overflowing with them. Well, he's not a friend yet, I guess, but I'm meeting more of them."

"And we'll see Salim tonight, too." Lee's tail wags. "You remember him, right?"

"Vaguely? He was the guy who was with you during the playoff game?"

Lee nods. "After Brian, he was my best friend here. Though that's kind of like saying that after Strike, Ty is the second-best receiver on the Firebirds."

"Really? You think Ty's better than Zaïd?"

"Maybe not right now, but if he keeps working. He's got a great burst; what he needs to learn is how to shake corners. He's good and elusive from the slot because it's easy to run picks off assignments, but when you've got a corner shadowing you—you know, like you did in college—it's harder to get clear in the open field. Strike's got great speed, but that's what he's really good at. He disguises his routes and he's got a stop-and-start like I've never seen anywhere else ever."

I stare down at him. "You said you don't watch the wideouts."

His tail wags more. "For Ty, I don't."

"I guess I should get all those opinions from you now, before you're working for the enemy." I narrow my eyes at him.

He fluffs out his cheekruffs and his eyes glint. "Just picture yourself pinning the enemy down to the bed."

I clear my throat. "Uh-huh. When are you meeting your dad?"

He laughs. "We don't have quite enough time. Unless you want to do a quickie on campus. I used to know a couple places…"

"What? Really?"

We're strolling past Vickers Hall, a building I think I had one class in, and Lee points to it. "Fifth floor, there's a closet at the end of the hall that had a broken lock, so the janitors never kept anything in it. But the door closed just fine."

"Seriously?"

We pass a cluster of students, and he waits until we're clear of them. "Twice. I blew Misha in there and got a blow job from, um…" He scratches his head. "What was his name?"

I shake my head. "I shouldn't ask about your college days, should I? And did you really date someone with the same name as my father?" But the story is enticing and kind of hot.

"It's not short for Mikhail, as far as I know," he says. "Anyway, I had sex with you in the Dragons stadium."

A couple foxes ahead of us flick their ears back. But they keep walking, and we keep walking. "Yeah," I say, lowering my voice. "And Polecki and Co—his boyfriend do that a lot too, I guess. How, uh…how many places do you know?"

"Well." He waves up ahead. "The best spot is up there, by the Tri. In fact, if we walked over during a change of classes, there was about a five percent chance we'd see someone go in. Used to be, anyway."

"Why so many places on campus? Didn't you guys have dorm rooms?"

"Sure," he says, "but sometimes you don't want to go back in the middle of the day. Sometimes you've got a roommate and you don't have anywhere else to go. Sometimes you just want to do something a little dangerous."

"Ever get caught?"

He laughs and bumps his shoulder into my arm. "I didn't. Brian did once. It was actually on the roof of the math building with his World Cultures TA."

"Figures," I say. "Anyone else ever get caught?"

"It was mostly me and Brian and Allen who did it." He flips his tail against mine as we walk by a newer addition to the campus, a bright red brick building with an angular glass roof. "There's a back hallway in there that almost nobody goes in. Last chance."

"I can wait." I return his grin. "Cause I don't care if my roommate catches me with my boyfriend."

We kill another half hour in the Bookstore looking for Forester souvenirs before his father comes in and meets us. We exchange a few words and then I bid the two foxes good-bye.

I spend another twenty minutes looking around the store, but I'm not sure I want any of this. It feels like holding on to the past. Then I check the sale rack and find a t-shirt that says, "Forester Football 2006 – Division II

Playoffs." It's in Lee's size and I'm not sure he ever got one, so I pick it up for him.

On my way to find dinner, stomach starting to growl, my phone rings. I glance down and see Hal's number. Weird. I pick it up.

"Hey, Dev," he says.

"Hey. I heard you spent time with Fisher today."

"Yeah. That's what I'm calling about." I wait for him to say more, but he's quiet.

"Did it go okay?" I search for what he might be calling about. "Was he absent-minded?"

"Yeah." The swift fox sounds cautious. "That's part of the problem."

"What, you can't use what he gave you? I don't know anything about his injuries or—or anything else, if you're asking me to verify that."

"No." Hal pauses again. "Look, I'm gonna tell you this in confidence because you're a friend and I think you should know. I don't think it's anything you can take action on, but…you should know, that's all. If you don't want to tell Lee, I'll understand."

"Lion Christ, Hal, what happened? Did Fisher murder someone?" I try to make it jokey, but it falls flat.

"No. He was a good interview. I got a lot of stuff out of him about his concussions, about the way all the teams handled it—don't worry, I ain't gonna nail the Firebirds on anything, this is bigger than them. I got to experience his memory loss and include that as part of the article, I talked to Gena, got her perspective…it's good stuff. Er—useful stuff, I mean."

"Okay." None of that seems relevant to his tone.

"It was toward the beginning of the interview. I asked him about retiring, and he said something like, 'I'd still be playing if it wasn't for that goddamned Leroy.' I asked who Leroy was—"

"His former agent."

"Yeah, Gena told me that later." Hal breathes in again. "But Fisher just said, 'Leroy's the asshole. He said it'd be okay. He said I'd heal faster, said nobody would care about it.'"

The significance hits me right away. "Holy shit. So it was Leroy who got him the stuff?" And then I can't remember whether Hal knew about the serum, but I'm pretty sure he didn't. "I mean, something illegal to make him heal faster?"

"Don't worry," the swift fox drawls. "That ain't the hornets' nest I'm pokin' at. Don't know what it was, and I'm assuming you don't know nothin' about it either."

"Right." My heart slows. "But it was Leroy?"

"We-ell." Hal draws the word out. "I asked Gena about that. Not in so many words, mind you, just asked the last time Fisher talked to Leroy."

Another possibility is taking shape in my mind, the way I can see a play developing on the field, and I have the same kind of dread I have when I see a play that we're not ready for, that I'm not in the right position for. "He got the names of his agents mixed up when I was there last week."

"Yeah. Gena went and got his phone, and Leroy's number ain't even in it. I just got off the phone with Leroy and he says he ain't talked to Fisher in more years'n he can remember. Might be lying, of course. If there's illegal stuff involved, he probably would be. But he didn't feel like he was worried about talking to a reporter."

"Shit." I think about Damian's smooth voice, his assured manner, his confidence in telling me he would do whatever needed to be done for my career.

"Like I said. I don't think you can do squat about it. But thought you'd like to know."

Would I want to do anything? Damian makes me feel so much better about my career than Ogleby did. I know I have other choices, other agents I could call, agents who have called or written me in the last few months, but how do I know whether any of them would be better? "You think there's any danger he'll be arrested or something?"

"Always that danger if you're into something illegal." Hal sounds amused. "Sorta what that means, you know? But if you're worried about Fisher letting something slip…I don't think his testimony'd be worth much until he's over the concussion." He stops long enough to let us both wonder whether that will ever happen. "But if your guy's doing that with Fisher, he's doing it with other players, and yeah. Something to be prepared for, I guess."

"All right. Thanks for the heads up." I break out of my self-concern for a moment. "You gave Fisher the support group number? Is he going to go?"

"I think so. Gena's going to make him, and Cara's on board with it."

"Cara's the nurse?"

"Ayup." When I don't say anything, he goes on. "Don't know if this'll make you feel better, but in one of his lucid periods, I asked him whether he regretted it. If he would change it, would go back and not play football."

Over the trees, the top of the new stadium shines in the sunset light. I think about all the boys who can't wait to have their turn on the field there. "What'd he say?"

"He said, 'What would I have done? I'd be working construction like my dad. We wouldn't be living here. We wouldn't have the championships. No, I don't like the ending, but I wouldn't change the story.'"

"Not all players end up like him, right?"

"Right." He answers quickly. "Then he asked me not to tell Gena that he said that. Didn't think she'd understand. I don't know if he remembered I'm writing an article, but…" I can almost see his shrug. "Eh, I'll talk to her later. I think she'll understand better than he thinks she will."

"I think so too. I don't know her that well, but…yeah, I think so."

"So I asked if he would change that last game, if he'd sit out the championship, all other things being the same."

Of course he wouldn't, I want to say, and Hal goes on, affirming that I know my friend well. "He said no. He said odds were he wouldn't get hit again in that game, and it was just a fluke. He thinks if he played the whole game, the Firebirds mighta won, and I couldn't say no to that." He sighs. "Then he started talking 'bout the Rocs again."

It's sad, but I'm glad Fisher still has those championship memories. And I know he loved those years and that he loved the time he spent with me, too, even if it was just one year that he has trouble remembering. That doesn't change the experience we both had.

I thank Hal and hang up, walking through campus to a small collection of restaurants that's grown two new ones in the two years since I left. I think about Fisher and what'll happen if in fifteen years that's me, and Lee's playing Gena's role, fretting, mourning the loss of the partner he knew.

But Fisher still loves Gena, and he still knows me. He's still the same person. A lot of the anger issues might come down to using the serum, and I'll never do that. Never. Even if Damian says it'll miraculously cure me, add three years to my career. He says I can make forty-five, sixty, seventy million—who needs more than that?

Though now I wonder if that includes years added by taking illegal drugs. Shit, what am I getting myself into with this guy? What if he's busted and all of his clients fall under suspicion?

I'm being paranoid, I tell myself. When was the last time anyone cared about performance enhancing drugs in football? This isn't baseball, for fuck's sake, where reporters write huge long articles about how horrible it is that players tainted the game. Here, you get caught doing steroids, you're out four games and then you're back. Yeah, that serum shit is worse, would probably make some headlines, but I'm not doing it and nobody will ever be able to prove I'm doing it.

I don't have to decide about Damian right now. Of course I'll tell Lee, and he'll help me figure out what to do the way he always does, the way he'll help me with decisions—and I'll help him—through the rest of our lives.

The rest of our lives. As I think that, it feels right. Because if I am left with only the best memories of my playing days, I realize, I'll want him to be in them.

I'd been thinking that it wouldn't be fair to Lee to saddle him with a broken-down player in fifteen or twenty years, to put him through what Gena's going through now. I'd been worried that committing to me now isn't fair to him. But what Hal said rings true to me. Gena would understand Fisher's answer. She knows how much football meant to him. And Lee knows how much it means to me.

We share more than just football, too. For so many years we had only each other, afraid of what exposure of our relationship would bring. I look back and forth at the students I pass, snow crunching under our paws. How many of them are gay? How many of them are closeted like Jason, worried about how their sexuality will hurt their career? How many are like I was, wondering why sleeping with girls isn't quite as exciting as their friends say it is? How many will be helped by my appearing here to tell people it's okay?

It feels very noble. And yet I know that when June rolls around, my mind will be one hundred percent back on football, on trying to get back to that championship game and win it this time. When I'm on break, like now, it's easy to think about that kit I met at the Chevali airport, about that poor bear who killed himself, about Jason and his boyfriend and all the other people I don't know. But I know it won't last.

Lee probably knows that too. Maybe that's why he's been so supportive and yet subdued, not fiery as he often is about the subject. Enjoy the time while it lasts, I guess, and don't push me to do more.

So am I staying with him just because it's easy (ha)? No, I'm pretty sure I'm not. For one thing, it's *not* easy, but that's okay. Like Fisher said, nothing worth doing is. The fact is, I don't really want anyone else, and I don't want him to want anyone else. But he's the one who insisted on this month, which makes me wonder if he's talking himself into being with me.

How easy would it be for him to find another boyfriend, one who cared about gay rights and didn't put life on hold for two thirds of the year? Look at him, he walked into the student union for two minutes and came out with a gay guy. A committed one, but whatever. And he's going to that meeting tonight, and he has all his friends from the old days. If he wanted someone else, if he's trying to make me prove that I'm the one for him, then what have I done in the last two weeks?

More importantly, what more can I do?

Chapter Twenty-Five: Old Home (Lee)

Father and I talk on the way to the house about what to expect. I tell him about the last conversation I had with her, and he tells me that he's talked to her too.

"She's certainly feeling differently," he says, "but you should still watch what you say."

"Father," I say, "I am always watching what I say."

He shakes his head. "Then you should watch what you say and also stop yourself from saying certain things before you say them."

"We'll be fine." I slouch back in the seat and stare ahead at the snow-covered road. "How did the rest of your meetings go?"

"Fine." He taps the steering wheel. "Nobody else was sending money to their mistress without his wife's knowledge. Any news on him, by the way?"

"Dev says he's putting his mind completely into football. He wasn't even going to go to Hellentown to visit his other family."

"Sometimes that's the choice you make."

I've thought about it a little since Dev told me Gerrard's attitude. "I wonder if he even cares about that family."

"Enough to send them money and lose his legal family." Father shakes his head. "I still feel bad about that. I told Angela that she should consider doing what she can to make sure the cubs have a father."

"Huh." I turn and look at him. Wonder if his own divorce affected that. "What did she say?"

"She said her brother is going to come stay with them for a bit."

I chuckle. "She has an unmarried brother?"

"Divorced."

"Well, not everyone can be gay." I smile. "So an uncle is an okay substitute for a father?"

"For some people." He looks at me.

"Hey," I say, "I wanted Uncle Roger to adopt me because you threatened to cut my tail off and sell me to the gypsies."

"I'm pretty sure I didn't say anything about cutting your tail off. But you ruined an expensive suit."

I flatten my ears. "I was ten. How was I supposed to know that chocolate syrup doesn't come out? I was playing..." I pause. "What *was* I playing?"

"Hamlet, I think." He takes a turn slowly in the snow and looks over his glasses at me. "You had just been stabbed by Laertes."

"I was playing Hamlet at ten? Oh, we saw the movie, didn't we? Why was I using chocolate syrup?"

"That one you'll have to answer. I assume your mother hid the ketchup." I shake my head. "I've done a lot of dumb things in my life."

"Speaking of which, how are things with you and Devlin?"

"You think he's one of the stupid things I've done?" My tail bristles.

"No; I think he's one of the people who's suffered from the stupid things you've done. But also one of the people who's benefited from the good things, so smooth your tail down and don't give me that attitude. You guys were apart for a while and now you're together. It seemed to be going well at our dinner in Chevali, but I didn't get to talk to you there. So…is it?"

It's a question I've been asking myself for the last two weeks, and especially now that we're here in Forester and the month I'd given us is half over. More than half over; in about ten days I'm going to have to start getting to work on the players on Yerba's board, packing to go to the combine, moving into a new place… "I think they're going well," I say, checking the mail on my phone. "The agent put in our offer on the house. No word back yet. She said we might hear tomorrow or Tuesday."

"Good. I hope you get it."

"It'll be a good investment for Dev, if nothing else." I sigh. "I don't know what to think. I keep thinking I'm insane for putting off a decision, for considering we might be better apart, but then I think maybe I'm thinking with my—you know, not my brain. I mean, we'd barely been living together a month when I snuck out in the middle of the night after having a huge fight." A fight where he was trying really hard to be understanding and I couldn't tell him what was bothering me; that might be the worst part of it.

"You didn't tell me you snuck out in the middle of the night." We turn onto less-plowed streets and skid slightly; Father corrects automatically and keeps going. "I would've expected you to storm out after a screaming match."

"I can't do that to Dev," I say. "I've walked out on him twice, once because I hurt him, and once because I was afraid I was going to hurt him. I wasn't ever yelling at him."

We go a little farther down the road in silence, and then Father says, "Does that tell you something?"

"Besides the fact that I don't want to yell at him?" Well, I have yelled at him a couple times, I guess, but never as angrily as I did at Mother a few blocks from where we are now. "I don't generally yell."

"You're worried about hurting him."

"Right. I'd sort of figured that out."

He sighs. "It means you care. There are a lot of people you don't care about hurting. Not that," he holds up a paw, "you go around hurting people. But you often say things, and your tongue is pretty sharp. You get that from your mother, by the way."

I laugh. "You've said some sharp things too. The point is, is it good that I'm worried about hurting him or bad because I think I have the capacity to? Do I want a relationship where I'm constantly second-guessing myself?"

Father shakes his head. "If you find a relationship where you're not, then tell me."

"There was Misha." I wonder if the arctic fox will be at the meeting tonight.

"Who's that?"

"I dated him for a year in college. He graduated and we broke up rather than try to keep going out long distance. I didn't really worry about what I was saying around him because we were mostly on the same page."

We stop at a red light. Down the road, semi-anonymous in the row of houses but always distinctive to me, is Mother's house—that's how I have to think of it now. Father flicks his ears toward me as the light turns and we crunch forward over the pressed snow. "And why not try to keep going out long distance?"

"I don't know." I push my memory back into the mists of Before Dev. "There were other guys in FLAG, he was moving back home to Mt. Royal… it didn't seem worth it." Plus, not as discussable with Father, Misha and I were both bottoms, and while the sex was good, neither of us was very enthusiastic about topping. There was that one time when we picked up a guy who did both of us…I stop that train of thought and try to adjust my pants discreetly.

"You're moving to Yerba and Dev's staying in Chevali. And you made it work long distance for years. Maybe with Misha you didn't challenge each other. Are you good for each other?"

"That's not the point." Misha and I did challenge each other, but again, not in ways I can discuss with Father.

"So…yes?"

I nod. "We are. I really believe we are."

"Then is it worth trying to make that work?"

I reach down and pick up the end of my tail and hold it in my lap. "It's not that simple," I say, but I follow that up with a question to myself: *Isn't it?*

"All right," he says as we pull in to Mother's driveway. "I'm glad you're at least making an effort to make *this* work."

Mother doesn't have things boxed this time, although I do catch a glimpse of empty boxes in the hallway upstairs. She greets us at the door in a pair of jeans and a red sweater. "I was cleaning," she says, picking at dust clumps on the arms of the sweater. "Hello, Wiley."

"Hi, Mother." I clear my throat, trying to shake the memory of the last time I saw her. It's been a month and a half and I already know the bad part is behind us, so I don't feel any tension, only a kind of emptiness that I didn't expect. The house is so familiar and yet different, even the scent. No matter how often we'd redecorated in the past, the scent had always been the three of us, but now as I stand in the foyer and breathe in, it's her and nobody else. There's a roasting chicken, but I'm sure it's not a permanent resident.

At least there's no church-going otter. Mother stands alone in the hall-way and keeps her muzzle lifted so that her eyes meet mine and Father's. "Do you want to go look at the room before or after dinner?"

"How long until dinner's ready?" Father asks.

By the smell, I'd say probably about twenty minutes, and when Mother confirms that, I say, "Let's do it after."

So we sit around the living room with wine (red wine, but I don't say anything) and make uncomfortable small talk. "What brings you up here?" she asks.

"Paying a visit to the old college before I start my job," I say. It's a little early to mention Dev, so even though I'm tempted to see how she handles it, I refrain.

Father gives me a grateful look and compliments the house and what Mother's done to redecorate it. She takes the compliments with a little bit of grace and makes a somewhat snide remark about his own tastes, which causes me to jump in.

"His apartment looks really cool," I say. "It's comfy and I really liked it there."

"Well," she says, "of course bachelors would love a bachelor pad. Are you seeing anyone?"

This is to Father, who shakes his head, his ears going down. "Are you?"

She shakes her head as well. "There's someone at church…Mr. Davette. Do you remember him?"

"I think so. The carpenter?"

"Furniture craftsperson." She sniffs. "He lost his wife to cancer last year and I'd spent some time with him, but I didn't want to let things go further." She pulls up and stops the discussion there, but her ears flick toward me. "But recently he...he heard about some of the problems and he's been very kind. So I was thinking I might go to dinner with him."

"That's great," Father says.

"Were you ashamed of me?" I say, and then take a drink of wine. I shouldn't have blurted that out.

They both turn to me, and Mother says, "Why would you say that?"

Because she said she didn't want to let things go further. Then when he heard from somewhere else about her "problem," which I'm translating as "gay son," and didn't shun her, she offered to have dinner. I don't want to explain that, or sound paranoid about the way her ears flicked toward me, so I just say, "Sorry."

I do notice that she doesn't deny it as she goes on to talk about this carpenter guy. He's a fox, of course, because Mother's not that experimental. Father keeps his tone neutral, not letting me know what he thinks about either Davette himself or the prospect of Mother dating him. Neither of us is very encouraging, but she goes on. "He keeps track of his whole business himself. He has goals and plans for the future and he's working toward them. His daughter just graduated from Whitmore. She's got a degree in architecture and a job with a prestigious Port City firm."

"That's great," I say, echoing Father. It's not necessarily a dig at me not graduating, of course. It might be an attempt to get me to meet this intelligent, no doubt beautiful, vixen who would make me forget Dev and my love of cock. In fact, I'm tempted to ask, *Does she have a penis? Because then she'd be perfect.*

But I'm being good, I'm trying to make this work, so I keep my lips shut around my fangs and I smile and nod. At least Mr. Davette doesn't seem to be a crazy fundamentalist nut job, so he's a step up from Mother's previous friends.

Like me, Mother hates being alone. Father's doing well with his solo apartment, but Mother has to keep talking about the people in her life. When Dev and I were apart for a couple weeks, that was one of the things I thought about a lot. I've rarely been alone for any length of time. I got to college and within a month had latched onto Brian. When he left, there was FLAG and then Dev. And that's my life.

"Oh, the chicken's ready." Mother gets up at a shrill alarm and hurries into the kitchen.

Father looks across at me with a smile. "Hang in there," he says, low enough so his voice won't carry to the kitchen.

"I dunno." I keep my voice pitched in kind. "This Violet Davette sounds like the whole package. I should just call Dev and tell him I'm going straight."

He shakes his head. "Go on, get it all out before dinner."

I glance toward the kitchen. "I don't have time to get it all out. Don't worry, I'll behave."

I make the statement with more confidence than I feel. It helps, though, that dinner is good. Whatever else changed about Mother in the years I was growing up and at college, she's not wasted the time spent in the kitchen. I can vaguely remember complaining once when I was six or seven about a dinner I didn't like, but rarely since then. And anytime I brought high school friends over for dinner, they raved about it.

Tonight, even though I've been eating in fancy restaurants with Dev, the dinner is as good as anything I've had in the last six months. The roast chicken is moist and sprinkled with rosemary, while the cooked carrots and peas retain some snap, and the light maple glaze (that's a midwestern trick) adds dimension to their natural flavor. There's also a square loaf of bread, obviously from a bread machine that Mother must have gotten in the last two years. The meal is delicious, and I make sure to say that several times because it's true and easier than talking about anything else.

Mother clears the table and Father helps. I offer but there isn't a lot for me to do, so I wander out to the hallway and put a paw on the banister, looking up the stairs. My paws wore the carpet bare: running down those stairs as a young cub with the eager anticipation of getting to play outside or running up those stairs to the privacy of my room as a moody teen. Mother's replaced the carpet since then.

Father comes out and stands at the base of the stairs with me. I think about the time I fell down them and he stood here where we are now, picked me up and rubbed my tail where I'd fallen on it, told me I would feel better soon. I remember Mother vacuuming up the stairs, me skipping up ahead of the vacuum and her playfully chasing me with it; later in life, I would be given that responsibility. The vacuuming, not the chasing.

"Your mother will be out soon. I think we should go up together."

I eye the empty boxes in the hallway above. "Probably right." I feel uneasy, worried about what I'll find missing from the room. She wouldn't have burned any of the things I want: my plush dragon, some of my favorite books, the poster of All That Jazz—no, that's probably gone, come to think of it. I clench my fists. At least I can get another one of those easily enough.

Most of the things I really value and want I took with me to my apartment in Hilltown when I moved there. What I left behind, largely the things I didn't take to college or the gay clothing—like my pride jacket—were things I didn't want to risk wearing in my closeted environment or hadn't had a use for in college.

"I'm not in a hurry," I say, and lean against the wall, trying to hide my worry. "It'll go quickly anyway. There's only a few things."

"You're doing well so far," he says quietly. "Just remember that this is hard for her, too."

"How are you doing?" I think to ask him. "The Davette guy doesn't bother you?"

He tilts his head. "It's strange, sure. I don't think it bothers me all that much, though. I'm glad Eileen found someone to be happy with."

"Do you miss that?"

He smiles at me. "If you meet someone eligible, go ahead and introduce me, but I'm not unhappy to have a little time to myself."

"I don't meet many eligible ladies, sadly," I say. "Dev knows this actress."

Just then Mother comes out of the kitchen and takes a breath. She smiles at both of us. "Shall we go up?"

We follow her up the stairs and past the empty boxes in the hallway. The lock she put on my door is still there, hanging open. She walks past it and into my room. I follow.

Here, as nowhere else in the house, my scent hits me. A younger, bitterer, more idealistic me sulking on the bed in my pride jacket after being told not to wear it to family gatherings, sitting with the acceptance letters from Forester and Javister College, looking up the gay rights groups at each for the fiftieth time, sitting here with my best friend from high school and pulling out the Abercrombie catalog to point out a parka I hated just to see if he'd comment on the underwear model on the facing page (he didn't); speaking of that underwear model, all the nights spent huddled under the blanket with a flashlight staring at him and jerking off into a tissue—now I feel like Mother must certainly have been able to smell that when she changed the sheets on my bed, and my ears go back, but that scent, at least, has faded from the room.

My All That Jazz poster is gone from the wall, as are all of my movie posters. The wall is mostly blank, as a matter of fact, a uniform reddish beige; either the posters weren't up long enough to leave marks or the wall's been freshly painted. The bedspread is new: more colorful, more juvenile than the simple sea-blue one I had in high school. I head over to the bookshelf, not saying anything, and check the titles there. It looks more spare than I remember, and as I go through, searching for those titles I want, I notice several of them missing. The thought of books being burned gets my throat tight, especially when I figure out some of the ones that are missing: Oscar Wilde (yes, very gay, even though I picked up that book in ninth grade before I realized what was different about me), and the plays of Berthold Brecht and Molière (not very gay, but theatrical, I suppose, and French), and the Gore Vidal book (okay, he is gay and I didn't really like him that much anyway), but also my Pynchon and Eggers and even the Harry Potter books? What the hell?

I grab a bunch of books and throw them into a pile, not really caring what they are, just desperate to get them all out of there. Next I check the closet, but there's nothing there I really want: I spot an old hooded sweatshirt and remember the comforting warmth the hood made around my ears, so even though I don't really want the old thing, I grab it. Then there's Hothead, the old, worn plush dragon my father bought for me back in middle school, before I liked football. He's sitting on the neatly made bed in the center, and I reach for him, but then stop.

Mother's not watching; she's gone back out in the hall with Father. They're talking in low voices I choose not to hear. I stand there and look at the dragon.

The placement on the center of the bed means something. The room is staged, a display about the early years of Wiley Farrel, and Hothead there is one of the key pieces of that, the only plush toy I kept through high school.

I sit on the bed next to him. I've got a new one that Father got me when we couldn't retrieve this one, and that one goes along with my new life. Do I want this one that badly? Couldn't I leave him here as part of Mother's museum exhibit, so she can come in and look at the memories of when she had a cub who didn't bring scary gay tigers into her life?

Ah, shit. I reach out and rub Hothead between the horns. "You going to be okay here?" I ask. "I think you'll be happier here. I mean, I'm going to Yerba, and remember how they beat us in '94? You wouldn't want to be thinking about that all the time. Just hang out here and think about '89."

Father pokes his head around the door, holding a box. "You okay, Wiley?"

I slide off the bed. "Yeah. Just got..." I point at the books and sweatshirt. Taking them won't disturb the neat order of the room. "A few things."

He looks around the room, his eyes lingering on the blank spaces on the wall, then on Hothead sitting on the bed. "Not bringing him?"

"I'll hold on to the one you got me." I force a smile and pick up the pile of books. He holds out the box. "Thanks."

All the books I want to take and the sweatshirt and a couple other odds and ends barely take up half the box. Father looks down, then up at me. "You sure that's all?"

I take another long survey of the room. It's been over a year since I set foot in it, and though it had seemed important to me a couple months ago to get in and get my things, now the room doesn't even feel like mine anymore.

I'd like to be angry at Mother again, to feel that clean, consuming rage at the lacquer preservative she's placed over her idea of my childhood, but when I see her in the hallway, she's looking down the stairs and her ears are down, her tail curled around her legs, and she's rubbing her paws together aimlessly. She looks lost in her own house, and it strikes me that as uncomfortable as I feel walking into a room I no longer recognize, I get to leave in a few minutes. She's trapped here alone in this house that she can never really remove the past from.

But no, she doesn't want to remove the past. She wants to return to it. And she can't do that, either.

I don't have much to say to her. She looks up as I carry the box into the hallway, and glances into it. Her ears lift slightly. "That's all you're taking?" she asks quietly.

Maybe she was expecting I would take more of her museum exhibit. She seems relieved, whatever the reason, and I don't want to press. "Yeah. Thanks," I say.

And then we stand there awkwardly until I say that I promised to meet some people at Forester around nine, and as it's eight-thirty, we should probably be going.

Mother nods and says, "The streets will be getting icy." Four years ago, she would've asked who I was meeting, whether I'd be getting my work done, and so on. Now she just follows us down the stairs and stands while we slip into our coats.

"It was nice to see you," she says as I heft the box again.

I don't know what I can say to that that's truthful, not right now, so I say, "Yeah," as Father embraces her, a dry, chilly version of the kisses I've seen them share in the past.

And then we're outside, and the cold bites at my ears and nose. I walk down the steps, and all the times I've walked down them are faint echoes behind me. My feet now are real, the gritty stone is cold but not slippery; Mother's too careful for that. Father's car is the same as it's been for years, but I'm different, sitting in the passenger seat rather than in back.

"Thank you for handling that maturely," Father says as we drive off.

"I mostly just feel sorry for her." I don't look to either side as we leave my old neighborhood.

He exhales with the faintest puff of white—the car is warming up quickly. "I guess that's a good change from being angry."

At least I've proven I can change, which Mother would prefer to forget, and she can change too, if not as much as I'd like to see. She'd love to have 1999-Wiley permanently there in the house, or maybe 1996-Wiley if she wants to be more motherly, but at least she's recognizing that there's something of him in me. And if I can sit through a dinner with her and not get annoyed at her talking about her new boyfriend and his perfect daughter (who is definitely not gay), then I'm still changing, still growing, and maybe somewhere down the line, she and I will find that our changes bring us back closer together.

Of course, I'm sitting here thinking about changing as I'm going back three years in time to a FLAG meeting. But I'm attending as an alumnus, and I don't expect to see most of my old friends there. Salim said he'd try to make it, and...ha, do I think Brian will show up? Only then do I remember Chuck saying that he'd sent out an e-mail to all the alumni. I guess I ought to brace myself for Brian's inevitable appearance, then. Pity *he* can't change. In Salim's catalog of the three kinds of people in the world, there's no question which one Brian is.

Are Dev and I also unable to change? Come football season, of course, Dev's focus will go back to the game, and rightly so. Brian will probably go back to hectoring him. What about me? Will I push him during the season again? Will I worry about being a distraction? I'll have a job, and the likelihood of all the crazy shit that went on this fall happening again next fall—or anytime in our lives, really—is pretty slim. But if it does, or if something else happens...that's what's been worrying me. I don't know if I'll go back to the same old behaviors, threaten the relationship again.

So am I trapping myself at a point in the past? Am I unwilling to let go of 2008-Lee? Since I came here last December and had to be dragged out of the house, yelling, I cut ties with Brian and my activism career for the good of my relationship, walked out on my relationship for the good of my boyfriend, and got myself a job in the field I want to work in.

If I can sit through dinner with Mother and not yell at her, then maybe I have the strength to change how I handle my relationship with Dev, too. If it's something I want badly enough—and apparently I do—then why am I shutting myself off from it? Shouldn't I be open to change in myself? Isn't that exactly what I've been upset about Mother not recognizing? Maybe I'm not one of those people who can't or won't move after all; maybe it took an evening with someone standing still for me to see my own movement.

Father's saying something about shipping the box to me in Yerba, and I say, "Yeah, hold onto it until then," absently, because my paws and tail are uncurled and relaxed and I think I'm ready to talk to Dev.

Chapter Twenty-Six: Talking It Out (Dev)

I end up at P.J.'s mostly because Lee would never go back there. I get broccoli cheese soup and a big steak with non-fancy vegetables and a side of potatoes with cheese and the meal fills me up nicely. I spend the broccoli soup worrying about Damian and then in between courses, I decide that I'll talk to Lee and we'll figure it out together, and by the time the steak arrives, I'm not worried anymore. I shift my attention to the FLAG meeting where I'm supposed to show up and…I'm not sure what. Talk? Just smile and wave?

The chirpy vixen in the red and white striped apron comes back with the credit card slip and then hovers at the table, and I know that hover. It's the "now I know who you are and I want to ask for an autograph but I don't want to be rude" posture. So I smile, sign the check, and keep my pen out. "Is there something else?" I ask.

She pulls out a blank paper. She only realized who I was when she saw the credit card, her boyfriend is a big football fan and went to Chikewa State to see us in the playoff game his freshman year, and could she get an autograph for him please?

I sign the paper and add the "#57" before I wonder if he'd prefer I write in my Forester number, but by then it's too late, and anyway, I'm fifty-seven now. She doesn't care, just takes the paper and stares at it, then thanks me profusely. A few of my neighbors look curious, so I get up and walk out before more people start asking.

It's gotten dark outside in the time it took me to eat dinner. I wander under streetlights and pass a street where Lee and I had a shouting fight once, and then we grabbed each other and went back to his apartment and ripped each other's clothes off. The memory makes me smile. In those early days, we were so passionate, so devoted to discovering each other and being together. Now our passions run just as strong, but maybe not quite as close to the surface. Is that what time does to passion? Was it the secrecy? Is the relationship less exciting now that everyone knows about it?

I try to leave these thoughts at the door of Harnwell Hall. Game time, I tell myself, breathing in. Even without Lee, I can do this.

The meeting is easy to find: it's the room bustling with activity and noise. Chuck spots me when I poke my head in the door and waves me up to the front. "Dev! Can I call you Dev? Come on up!"

Heads turn and the room goes quiet. I raise a paw and smile out at the thirty-strong group as I walk up to Chuck. Wow. They're all about Lee-height, smaller than I am, except for one polar bear in the back. There's a pair of arctic foxes, several ermine and weasels (when they have their white winter coats, they're hard to tell apart if you don't look at their tails), a couple skinny wolves, a puma, a raccoon...no red foxes, though. Wait, there is a silver phase red fox, bushy silver winter coat showing over his black fur, talking to the otter next to him.

"All right, let's settle down," Chuck calls as I get up to the front next to him, even though nobody's really talking anymore. "Devlin Miski, Forester alum and gay football player, has been nice enough to agree to come chat with us. He's going to star in a Diversity in Athletics Day here at Forester in a month or so..." He looks to me for confirmation and I nod, and in that space there's a smattering of applause. "And he's dating another Forester alum from our very own little club, a Wiley Farrel. Anyone here remember him?"

One of the arctic foxes says, "Oh, I do," and the ringtail next to him nods with a smirk.

"Cool," Chuck says. "Anyway, I'll, uh, I'll turn it over to Dev now."

"Oh." I look at him as he sits down, then at all the people staring at me. "I thought I was just going to answer questions."

"Sure," he says, "you can do that too if you like. But if you have something you want to say...I mean, you're gonna have to do a speech for Diversity Day, so you could look at this like a test balloon if you want."

"But I don't have anything prepared." He's still looking at me expectantly, and I remember a conversation with Lee from a long time ago. "Well, hang on. Let me..."

He steps back. My heart pounds and I look out at the sea of faces, all eyes fixed on me. My tongue dries up. How is this harder than tackling two-hundred-pound football players?

I think again of Lee. I imagine him out there watching me with that smile, telling me I can do this. *We got this, tiger.* I take a breath and the knot in my chest eases.

"I feel awkward saying this," I start. "Because you guys are all out and proud and you're fighting for gay rights. My boyfriend always talked really fondly about this group and it's cool to see everyone here." I breathe in again. "A lot of people view my coming out as a part of a movement, a blow;

or an accident, a corner I was forced into. But…" Looking at the faces in front of me is a mistake, even though they look interested, worried, amused, concerned. In the back, a couple are whispering, ignoring me. I imagine Lee again and go on. "But it wasn't those things. You guys know there were rumors, that—" Shit, Brian was part of this club, too, right? Better not mention him. "That my agent let them spiral out of control and I had to hold a press conference about them. But nobody was forcing me to come out. Lee wasn't forcing me to come out. He didn't even think I should.

"I told everyone I was gay because I love him. And it didn't seem right to lie about it. That's all."

Nobody says anything. I don't know what reaction I'd hoped for, but I go on, a little awkwardly. "So, you know, what you're doing here is great, but for me, and I think for a lot of gay people—a lot of us—it's about love. Have things been difficult these last few months? Hell yeah. I've been harassed, Lee lost his job. But…but we can be honest with the world about who we are and that we love each other. And that's—I mean, that's what you—we—should all be remembering."

I look back to Chuck to make it clear that I'm done, and the room applauds politely. I don't know what I expected, but as the stallion steps back up, I catch sight of that silver fox and otter with their arms around each other, kissing, and that makes me smile. That's enough, I think Lee would tell me.

Chuck pats me on the back. "Nice work. If you want help polishing that before the day, let me know." He looks out at the club. "Any of you guys have questions for Dev?"

I'm prepared to treat it like a press conference, but the first question I pick, from an ermine up front, is, "Do you look at your teammates in the shower?"

Okay. It's going to be one of *those* Q&A sessions. "I don't hide my eyes," I say. "But I don't stare at them, either."

"Who's got the biggest…equipment?" the ermine wants to know.

"Let's keep it classy, people," Chuck says, saving me from having to answer, though I think later that I should've just told them it was Charm. He wouldn't have minded and they would've enjoyed hearing it. But a season full of press conferences has made me wary of everything I say in a public forum.

They ask about my boyfriend, about whether I've introduced him to the team, about the behind-the-scenes reception my sexuality has gotten, lots of questions I've already answered in press conferences, but I guess these guys probably don't watch a lot of sports reporting. It's okay; I'm good at answering inane questions politely, and these guys aren't asking if I regretted coming out or why I don't think any other players have—well, Polecki has now, so that's not a valid question anymore. But mostly they want to know about my life on the team and outside the team: how people treat me, where I go for fun.

And then the ringtail who said he knows Lee asks if I knew the guys who beat up the gay person a while ago and if I was afraid of them. I say that was before I came out, so I wasn't afraid. I thought it was stupid at the time, and hateful (that last isn't strictly true; I didn't think about it much at all), but I didn't really understand how it applied to me. The ringtail follows up by asking how I'd get straight people to understand how it affects them, and I say that's why I'm doing this Diversity Day. He lets it drop there, seemingly satisfied.

The arctic fox beside him asks how my boyfriend deals with my life. "You guys know Lee," I say, because I think he's the one who said he did. "He's kind of passionate—strike that 'kind of.' We have fights, but we've been together three years and things are still working. He loves football too, and in fact he's been working as a scout in the league, so we do share the same world, pretty much."

Where is he, they want to know, and I say he's visiting family and will be joining us afterwards. "Were you in FLAG when you were here?" the puma asks.

I shake my head. "I wasn't out then. I mean, I…I wasn't out to myself until my senior year, and then I thought that being gay would mean I'd get blackballed from the team."

"How did you find out you were gay?" a female raccoon asks.

Wow. How do I answer that in ten seconds? "Well," I say, "I saw this fox and fell for him, so that kinda did it."

They laugh in a knowing way, and though there are a couple followup questions, I deflect them. These guys aren't as good nor as persistent as professional reporters. They actually have a sense that some things should remain private, or they're too polite to go to those places.

After about forty minutes, the questions die down. Chuck stands up again and conducts the official club business, which I'm allowed to remain for, though I sort of space out without listening. I'm more focused on sitting in a room of gay people. I keep looking around at pairs sitting together, same gender, and thinking, "they could be a couple." Especially the two arctic foxes, but their fur is so thick that their gender is hard to tell when they're not talking, and then they hold paws partway through the meeting, so that takes the guesswork out of it.

But just being in a room full of guys who have boyfriends and ladies who have girlfriends is strange, and it feels good. Here, the thing that sets me apart is that I'm a football player, not a college student. I can talk about Lee, and nobody here thinks it's strange or a curiosity that I'm dating a guy. Nobody will ask if I'm not attracted to girls, or treat me like a museum exhibit or an ambassador. Everyone here understands about being gay, and they've all gone through their own trials. I think that I would like to hear some of their stories, too.

The meeting winds up quickly. Chuck takes me by the arm right away and leads me out in a casual exodus of people, out into the hallway and to the cold air of a campus street. All the way, he keeps talking about the club and how great it was for me to come and talk to them, how inspiring I am, and how much he enjoyed talking to Lee.

At this, the arctic fox couple comes up alongside us and the smaller one, the one who raised his paw, says, "Yeah, how's Lee been? He hasn't exactly stayed in touch."

"Up and down," I say. "Had a great job, lost it, got another one. He starts in a couple weeks."

"I tried to e-mail him when that article about him came out, but he never responded."

"He doesn't have his Forester e-mail anymore," Chuck puts in helpfully. "He said he didn't get the alumni mailing." Then, to me, "This is Misha Cameron."

"Ainsley-Cameron." Misha smiles at the fox next to him. "This is Parlon, my husband."

"Misha," I say, and the name rings a bell. I glance up at one of the buildings we're passing, an engineering school, I think. It's not the English building Lee pointed out, but it's similar. "Wait, are you the one Lee—uh, I mean, did you and Lee—"

He laughs. "Parlon knows about my past. Yes, I didn't want to mention it, but Lee and I dated for a while. And yes, whatever he told you is probably true. What was it, out of curiosity?"

I try to bring my ears up, without success. "He said he and you, uh, in the bathrooms of…the English building, I think…"

"Oh, yes." Misha grins, and his partner—husband—rolls his eyes. "There and about a half dozen other places on campus. He was never really worried about getting caught. Of course, we were all younger then."

"Yeah," I say.

"So fair's fair. Where has he blown you?"

The fox's dark amber eyes glint under the street lights. I smile. "Uh, we had sex in an empty equipment room in the Dragons' stadium. Other than that it's been not really adventurous." Then I feel like I have to explain myself. "See, it was hard for us to worry about being caught. Mostly for me, but he was working in football too, and that—well, it sort of ended up being why he got fired, when it came out."

Misha nods. "I read about that." His long white tail curls back and forth, and brushes his...his husband's (I force myself to use the word, even in my own head). "I'll be honest," he says. "I'm surprised he's been with the same guy for so long. I think I was the longest relationship he'd had at the time, and that was, what, six months?"

"Six months was his record." The ringtail who asked about the football player has come up behind us. "Hey, I'm Allen."

I reach back to shake his paw. "Lee's mentioned you, too."

"I'd hope so." He laughs. "If he talked about anyone at FLAG besides Brian, I mean."

"Fuck, is *he* going to be here?" I say, not even thinking about it.

But Allen just chuckles, and Misha smirks. "I see you've met Brian," Allen says.

"A few times too many." I clench my fists and try to stop my tail from lashing, unsuccessfully.

"He and Lee." The ringtail shakes his head. "You either loved 'em or hated 'em."

"Put me down for one in each column." I don't really want to think about Lee and Brian together.

"Wait," Misha says, "so those two don't hang out anymore? Who came between them?"

Allen glances at me, and I see his deference. "Couple guys on the football team," I say, and while I'm trying to figure out how to say more, the arctic fox's eyebrows rise. Chuck, on my other side, murmurs something under his breath, so I know he knows the story. "Not like that. I guess he—Brian—was in a bar on campus—still don't know which one—and he was mouthing off at them about something, and they beat him up."

I hate to make it stark and bare like that. I didn't know the guys, a couple of the offensive line backups, but for months after that I heard from friends of theirs that they'd gotten railroaded, that they hadn't deserved to be kicked off the team, that all they did was shove the guy outside so he'd shut up.

Unfortunately, the guys in the bar could see what happened after they shoved him outside, when they followed him and threw several punches, and that's why the team acted quickly and didn't protest.

Not that I cared about all that. Not at the time.

"Oh." Misha turns back to Allen. "That was what you asked about."

"Yeah. We were all hit by it, but Lee was worst. Brian went to some hospital and then transferred schools. Lee was just…quiet after that. And the next year, he disappeared."

I clear my throat. "I think that was my fault."

They all look at me. "It was his choice, I mean. But we were dating, and he didn't want—he was worried that if he hung out with his gay friends, that he would keep getting into conversations about his boyfriend and eventually he'd spill the secret. So he sort of closeted himself away."

There's silence until Allen says, "You must be a hell of a catch."

I feel warm and flushed and can only think to say, "I guess Lee thought so."

"Hah." Allen elbows Misha and points at me. "Look, his ears have gone all back."

The arctic fox grins. "Adorable," he says. "I'm starting to see what Lee sees in him."

"Only now?" Chuck says across me. "Have you looked at his butt?"

"Hey," I say. "Come on."

"I like arms, myself." Misha glances at mine. "But also, you know, that thing you said about love…that was really sweet."

"It didn't seem to go over well." I step on a smaller footprint in the snow. "I guess you guys know that already and didn't need me to come in and say it."

"Nah." Chuck pats my arm, maybe a little more familiarly than is warranted since I just met him today, but I let it go. "I think it just wasn't what they expected. You know, you're a football player and they didn't think you'd get all mushy like that."

"There was something of Lee in that speech," Misha says, still smiling warmly.

"More than a little," I admit. "Basically he told me that a couple years ago."

"After we'd been dating." Misha takes his partner's—dammit, his *husband's*—arm. "I guess we each had to find that out somewhere else."

"It was sweet." Parlon, with a deeper voice, looks across him and smiles at me. "And it needs to be said every so often because it's easy to forget."

We've gotten to Maple Street at the edge of campus, alight and alive even on a Sunday night in winter with shops across the way and the familiar green Starbucks logo half a block down to our left. I don't remember a Starbucks ever being there, but enough here is familiar that for a few steps, I'm twenty again with no more worries than classes and practices where I didn't have to exert myself to do well. Life was no more challenging or interesting than kicking piles of snow and avoiding patches of ice. And then, down that side street two blocks up, there's a semi-underground bar where I once picked up a fox I thought was a vixen and changed my life.

At the Starbucks, we crowd in, the cougar and raccoon rubbing the cold from their ears as the sturdy badger behind the counter says, "There you guys are."

Parlon walks up and hands a credit card to the barista. "I'm buying for everyone tonight. Whatever these guys want."

I should be doing that, but I didn't even think of it, and now I feel like a heel. I mean, maybe Lee and I are buying a house, but I probably make more than everyone in this group combined.

Misha puts a paw on my arm and I look down into a warm smile. "Don't worry about it," he says in a low voice. "Parlon's young, but his family's money, and he made ten million last year when he sold his business."

Maybe I should have guessed from the cut and smell of his clothes, but honestly they're not much different from what my teammates wear when they're not playing: fancy shirts and slacks, less jewelry, more fur conditioner and scent, I can tell now that I'm up close. Compared to the college students in their jeans and loose shirts, they're a world apart, but I'd taken them for people with jobs, not necessarily with lots of money.

So I say, "Cool, that's great."

"It's nice to be able to talk to someone who isn't blown away by the numbers," Misha says, again in that confidential voice. "I guess ten million is nothing to you."

"It's a lot to me. I'm on my rookie deal, which is, well, considerably less than that." I chuckle. "My new agent promised me more on my next deal, though."

"Do you get raises when you do well?" The fox's ears flick out to the sides. "Sorry, I don't really know anything about how it all works."

"Well…" I explain a bit about rookie pay scales, put into place so teams couldn't give massive deals to unproven talents who hadn't played a single game, and about the way the new contracts work, basically sky's the limit but it can depend on who else at your position is also out there this year and so on.

Parlon joins us partway through that with two Starbucks cups and gives one to Misha. "Vanilla latte," he says, "nonfat."

"Thanks, hon." Misha leans in to kiss him and then sniffs the cup. "Dev was explaining about how he gets paid. It sounds complicated."

"You have an agent, though, right?" Parlon's gaze is sharp and shrewd.

I nod and wrap up the explanation as Allen and Chuck join us again. It's after nine and I wonder when Lee's going to get here, so I apologize and take my phone out to text him.

While I'm doing that, Allen and Misha chat, and Allen says something about how he can't believe Lee and Misha lasted six months. "I mean," he says, "did you have a double dildo or something?"

Misha laughs and looks sideways at me. "He's asked me this before. He's only bringing it up because you're here."

"I never!" Allen protests.

"Please." Misha waves him aside with a paw and turns his attention on me. "I'm sure he doesn't do it much these days, but Lee was a good little top fox when he wanted to be. Or I guess I should say, when I wanted him to be. I doubt he ever liked it as much as he liked the times I topped."

"Wait," Parlon says. He places a paw over his heart and his ears slide back. "Hold on. Dear, you told me you dated this guy, but you actually topped? Like, insertive-partner-role topped?"

"I am capable, darling." Misha looks at me, then at Chuck. "Shall we go upstairs before poor Devlin here gets completely embarrassed?"

"Little late," I say, and they all laugh. Some of the other FLAG members have their drinks now and are heading upstairs, so we follow them up.

"It's just that Lee was always real open about his sex life," Allen says. "Until he met you, I guess."

"He's still…heh." I feel more comfortable with them now. Comfortable enough to tell this anecdote? Let's see. "He was trying to, y'know, blow me while I was on the phone with my mother."

They chuckle, but it's a patronizing chuckle. "Well, who hasn't done that?" Misha says.

"Despite being asked to stop." Parlon glares, or maybe mock-glares. "Now I know where you got that from."

Misha smiles sweetly. "Maybe *he* got it from *me*."

We array ourselves around a bunch of square tables, and as we sit, the raccoon and the puma both tell me they're really happy to meet me and are glad that I came. Other people echo the sentiments, and Misha, Parlon, Chuck, and Allen are all engaged in their own conversation by the time I respond to the last one, trying to make everyone feel like I'm paying attention to them.

My phone buzzes with a message from Lee: *On my way up. Had to pick up Salim.*

"Lee's here," I tell the others as I put the phone away.

Misha and Allen perk their ears up. Parlon grins. "Finally, I'll get to meet this local legend." He catches my eye and inclines his head. "Not that it hasn't been a pleasure meeting you, but you're more of a national legend."

"I'm not sure I'm more comfortable with that," I say, "but thanks."

"I didn't really tell him that much about Lee until that article on him came out." Misha rests a paw on the table near mine. "I'm not carrying a torch for him or anything."

"I believe your exact words were, 'I used to date that guy,'" Parlon says.

"'Date,'" Allen makes air quotes.

Misha sticks his tongue out. "I'm not this crude at home."

"He's not," Parlon confirms. "It's only when he's around you lot, I suppose."

"Good." Allen grins widely. "Do you good to get back to it once in a while."

I wonder if Lee is going to revert to that sort of form again. In about fifteen seconds, I'll know, I realize, as I see his familiar russet muzzle spring into view at the staircase. He scans the room and hurries over to me as I stand.

"Hi," he says, wrapping his arms around me and tilting his muzzle up. I don't even think about where we are because I know we're surrounded by friends, so I lower my muzzle and kiss him. Just like he did once on this campus years ago, he pushes the kiss deeper, and this time I hold him and don't resist.

Applause breaks out around us and still we kiss, neither of us wanting to break it until we have to. Some people whistle, and finally we slide our tongues apart and then let our lips break as well.

"Well!" Misha says. "He never kissed me like *that*."

Lee turns and his eyes light up. He squeezes me and then lets go to hurry around the table where Misha is getting half out of his seat. Lee hugs him and then says, "I assume this hunk is with you?"

"Parlon Ainsley-Cameron." Parlon rises and extends a paw.

"My goodness." Lee shakes, a broad grin across his muzzle. "Misha, you married money. Good for you."

I've no idea how he can tell so quickly, but Parlon laughs as he and Lee brush muzzles. "And it's a pleasure to meet Mister Farrel's Wild Ride," the larger arctic fox says with a twinkle in his eye.

"I thought you were living in Freestone?" Lee turns back to Misha as Allen stands up for his hug.

"We are, but I've wanted to bring Par back to Forester, and I work half-remotely anyway, so we took a couple days off."

"Yes," Parlon says as Lee hugs Allen, "February in the Midwest. It's a holiday."

It's only then that I notice the weasel standing shyly a step back from the table, dressed in a neat white shirt and blazer with a tie loosened around his neck. He meets my eye and gives a smile of recognition, and though I wouldn't have picked him out of a crowd, I'm sure I know who it is.

"Salim, right?"

He comes over and holds out a paw, which I grasp. "It has been almost two years," he says.

"A little more than that, I think. The quarterfinal game."

"Yes." He smiles. "I am glad you have had more success since then."

"Thanks."

Allen spots who I'm talking to and fairly runs around to hug the weasel. "Salim! So it took Wiley to drag you out of hiding?"

"Oof." Salim returns the hug. "I am quite busy, sadly."

"He's got a family, a job, and a bit on the side," Lee says.

The weasel fixes Lee with a baleful stare. "My private life," he begins, but Allen ruffles between his ears and disrupts his protest.

"Is a lot more interesting than anything I've got going on." The ringtail curls his long tail around the weasel's legs familiarly and keeps a paw over his shoulders. "Come on, I want to hear all about it."

While the weasel weakly objects, Lee squeezes in between me and Misha. Parlon offers to buy him a drink, and Allen laughs. "Lee hates Starbucks. Probably offends his sensibilities just to be in here."

"Their tea's okay," Lee says.

Allen and Misha stare at him. The ringtail turns to me. "If you got Lee to like Starbucks, sir, then I will believe you can do anything."

"When I was sick." Lee sticks his tongue out. "There wasn't anything else and Hal kept getting me their chamomile..." His ears go down. "But I'm not in the mood for tea right now, thanks."

"Hal?" Allen's ears perk.

"Friend of ours," I say.

"I was sick and Dev was in Crystal City for the championship." Lee gives Allen a long look.

"Their coffee isn't bad." Parlon raises his and takes a drink.

"We don't have to have this discussion right now." My fox smiles and settles against me.

With my arm around his shoulder, I feel the excitement humming through him. Allen drags Salim to the table, now seven of us crammed around it, and they all reminisce about the old days while Chuck tries to participate and Parlon and I mostly listen, except for the time when Lee and Misha start comparing partners and techniques, at which point Parlon leans in and says, "Dear, let's save some secrets for our bedroom, shall we?"

"Oh," Lee says, "he's shy."

I clear my throat and nose at his ear. "I happen to agree with him." The comment falls into a lull around the table, and everyone laughs.

"All right, all right." Misha grins at Lee. "Give me your new e-mail address. We'll catch up privately."

"Yeah." Allen leans in. "No more disappearing, right?"

Lee spreads his paws. "I'm out and proud now. I'm not going anywhere."

The ringtail turns to Salim. "That goes for you, too. You live right around the corner."

"I am very busy." The weasel keeps his smile but looks slightly uncomfortable. "I have many obligations—"

"You can answer an e-mail, right? I'm not asking you to write essays or come to weekly meetings."

Allen seems to be losing his good humor, and Chuck steps in with his phone. "I want to get all your contact info to make sure you come back for Diversity Day. I'd like to get more FLAG alums and maybe do a reception in the evening, something nicer in a University hall. If any of you guys want to help out with that…"

"Of course," Misha says.

"Def." Allen perks his ears. "Maybe you could get Brian to show up, too?"

I tense, wanting to say something, but I leave it to Lee, who flattens his ears and then brings them back up. "I don't think that'll work." He shakes his head. "Brian got kind of obsessed with me the last year or so."

Allen snorts and starts to say something, but Lee cuts in. "He stalked Dev and posted rumors about him being gay until he had to call a press conference…"

"That was him? The guy you talked about?" Misha shakes his head and his ears dip. "Poor Brian."

Lee bumps my shoulder. "When did you talk about him?" So I have to tell Lee about my speech, and Allen and Misha and Chuck all chime in and make it sound way better than it was.

Then there's a moment of silence, and Allen says, "Sooooo? Brian?"

"Yeah." Lee leans back against me and rests his paw on the table, chocolate brown against metallic brown. "I didn't want to give him any more publicity than he'd already gotten. And then…well, I got this voicemail from him tonight, about half an hour ago. I guess you can all hear it."

He takes out his phone and calls up the voicemail, then puts it in the center of the table. "Fancy," murmurs Allen when he sees the phone, and then everyone cups their ears to listen.

"Hi, Tip," comes Brian's high voice from the speaker. "I sorely hope thou'rt not disappointed tonight when you fail to spot my spots at the FLAG alumni gathering."

"He's doing a Shakespeare play," Lee murmurs.

"He's always doing a Shakespeare play," Misha says back over the next part.

"Alas, I should expect by now that you'll not pick up the phone when you see my number. This breach betwixt us shall not be healed easily…" Lee makes a "get to the point" gesture with his paws. "…but I suppose I bear some of the blame for it. In any case, I called only to tell you that as much as I would love to see some of the old gang, I have been following this local politician around Chevali. You'd recognize his name, but I don't want to give away any secrets just yet. He's a fascinating fellow. His opposition to gay rights is equaled only by his attraction to cock. We just need some pictures or other proof to shame him into changing his positions or resigning, and I'm delighted to volunteer my experience. Give my best to all the old gang and tell them I am still fighting the good fight."

Silence descends around the table as Lee reaches out his paw and takes his phone back. "So there you go," he says casually. "Athletes are passé now, I guess."

I mock-bristle. "Well, there's two of us out. No more work for him to do."

"That doesn't work, you know." Parlon nods at Lee's phone with his muzzle. "Outing politicians. The problem is the people they represent. Either they'll forgive the guy, or they'll elect someone worse to replace him."

"Brian never saw a windmill he didn't want to tilt at," Allen says.

I try to process all the things I'm feeling about Brian's message. Relief that apparently he's going to leave me and Lee alone, finally; annoyance that he's still calling Lee; some measure of sadness, because in looking around at Allen and Salim especially, I see the absence of Brian not as he is now, but as he used to be. It feels like when we lost Fisher in the locker room, like thinking of him now. I wonder briefly if Brian got a concussion when he was beaten up, but that's probably being too charitable. He's just an asshole, and maybe Lee used to be one too, but he's grown out of it. Still, I hadn't realized how much Brian had meant to him, how much this whole group of friends meant to him, until tonight. Sitting here and watching him laugh with Allen, gently rib Salim, exchange affectionate reminiscence with Misha, I feel like I'm being introduced to his team.

"Why don't we have friends like these in Chevali?" I ask him at one point in the evening.

Lee turns to me and smiles. Misha says, "It's so hard after college to keep in touch. Life takes over and you get busy."

Salim nods, but Lee looks around the table and now speaks. "There aren't any other friends like these anywhere," he says.

Smiles widen and tails wag, and Allen says, "You should've remembered that senior year," but when Lee starts to protest, he waves it off and says, "*Amor vincit omnia*, right?"

"You liberal arts majors," Misha snorts. "Can't you just say, 'people in love do dumb things'?"

"Well," I say, "I'll be playing in Hilltown and Freestone, and you guys are all welcome to come visit Chevali. But you have to root for the Firebirds."

"Will you teach us football?" Misha bats his eyes at Lee.

My fox chuckles. "If you want to go to a game, sure."

"Of course we want to go to a game." Misha turns his gaze to me. "We want to see your boy perform."

"Then you'll have to go to a game," I say, "because we are not releasing a sex tape."

There's a moment of silence where I wonder if I gauged the mood right, if this joke is going to bomb, and then everyone laughs. Lee leans back into me, shaking his head in mock disappointment as I wrap an arm around him. "I've tried and tried to convince him," he says, "but he says the videos are just for us."

"Selfish," Allen says.

I murmur into Lee's ear, "So are there videos of you with other people out there?"

"Nah," he says. "I'm not that dumb."

"Mmm." I squeeze his shoulders. "Too bad."

He arches an eyebrow, and I grin. He shakes his head. "I don't know if exposing you to this crowd was a good idea."

"It took a few years, but I'm glad to meet them." I am, too, slowly getting used to my relationship with Lee being something normal, like Misha and Parlon, like Polecki and Cornwall. I mean—look, I always knew it was *okay*, being with him, I always knew it was *right*, but I couldn't see it as *normal*. Even here, somewhere in the back of my mind, I know that this coffee shop is just an enclave, that out there not too far away, maybe not in Forester University, but not far beyond that, there are people who think we're a curiosity at best, unnatural at worst, who don't believe our relationship should be approved by the state or the church or any other authority, who think we're a bad influence on children.

A lot of my teammates were like that at first, but few have remained that way. Maybe Gregory is traveling that same arc, but slower, the same one Lee's mom is on, the one his dad completed, the one my parents are well on their way to following. Maybe different people just take different paths to the same places.

Hey, look at that. I thought about Gregory without unsheathing my claws.

"We are glad to meet you as well," soft-spoken Salim says. "You are doing good work."

"Work?" I shake out of the reverie.

"Changing people's minds." Chuck leans in, cutting off my view of the weasel. "That's what all these campaigns are about. Like Parlon said, the problem is the people, and what we're all trying to do is get the kind of people who vote for homophobic politicians to realize that we're no different from them." He gestures to my arm around Lee. "Like we know, like we're all sitting here talking about. Over time, people's attitudes change based on what they see, what they're exposed to."

"I know," I say. "Lee told me, people who know a gay person are more likely to favor gay rights. But I can't go meet everyone. I mean, my team have mostly gotten used to it. Polecki's team will. But that's a hundred guys."

"But you're encouraging other people to come out." Chuck's big horsy eyes shine. "And they change the minds of the people who know them. By setting an example, you're helping thousands."

"Like the kid you met," Lee says softly, and I nod. Chuck asks to hear the story, but it still feels too personal and I don't want to share it right now, so I tell him I'll save it for Diversity in Athletics Day.

Sex and civil rights and coffee. I lean back and listen, respond to Chuck when he tries to make conversation with me, but I don't really engage. It's not that I don't want to talk to him. It's more that I'm enjoying the evening, the presence of my fox, and I want to watch him be himself with these other friends.

After a little while, Chuck does drag me away from the table because some of the present FLAG members are hovering and an ermine and raccoon, in particular, want to talk football. That seems a little odd to me, but it turns out they're pretty knowledgeable. They say they were both rooting for me in the championship game, which I know is what everyone who talks to me says (except Polecki and Cornwall), but they also mean it. The raccoon assures me there wasn't anything I could've done, that Crystal City was just executing great and that if anything, our offense let us down. I start to bristle, to defend the guys, and he backs down.

He wasn't there, I think, and he doesn't know. But he and the ermine both keep on about how great I played, and the team, and they say they're Chevali fans now. "What about Crystal City and Polecki?" I ask.

"Yeah," the raccoon says, "but you were first, and you're from here."

And then we talk about next year, and whether I'll be back with Chevali. They both want me to come back to the Dragons, but the ermine says with a laugh, "I wouldn't want you to waste your career here."

That turns into a general discussion of how teams will do next year, which becomes an in-depth conversation that Lee has to drag me out of.

"Hey," he says, "people are heading out. You want to get back to the hotel?"

I raise my head and look around and see people shrugging on jackets, shaking paws. "That time already?"

"They're going to close up soon," Chuck says. "Actually, they're already closed, but we try not to stick around too long past closing so they don't have to wait to clean up. They have classes in the morning too."

The raccoon and ermine I've been talking to shake my paw and say how nice it is to meet me, and I say the same. And then the ermine kind of hangs around, so I grab a napkin and scrawl my signature on it, and do one for the raccoon too. As an afterthought, I scribble my personal e-mail address on them. "I'm not great about checking it, but if you guys want to talk football again, drop me a line."

They both play it cool, tucking the napkins away and saying genuine thanks, but as they leave, I see the ermine's huge grin and the raccoon's tail wagging.

"So it went well?" Lee asks as we hurry down the stairs. Outside a cluster of people waits: Misha and Parlon, Allen and Salim, and Chuck.

"Yeah." I hug him around the shoulders. "Real well. Good guys."

"They are." He smiles fondly at Misha, holding the door. "Thanks."

"Good to see you again. Write me!" The arctic fox lets the door go, wagging a finger at Lee. He and his partner are wearing only loose jackets over t-shirts, unlike the rest of us who at least have fastened our jackets against the weather. I keep my fur short, but I've also got an Ultimate Fit undershirt on, which insulates pretty well. There are times, though, when I envy the thick fur I used to grow in winter.

As Lee and I walk together back to the car, I put an arm around his shoulder. He leans into it and looks up. "Not worried people will see us together?"

I shrug. "If people see a big football-playing tiger and a little scrawny fox walking around together, they'll assume it's me anyway, so I might as well get to hold you."

"Ha," he says. "Scrawny, now?"

"I meant it as a compliment," I protest, unconvincingly I'm sure. "You have a lovely physique."

"Right." He snorts.

The night is cold and still, and the shadowy buildings of the campus are familiar and strange both, silhouettes I remember but whose associations are long in the past. I used to walk around this campus thinking that being a football player gave me lots of privileges, that I didn't have to worry too much about my classes because they'd be taken care of if I had trouble (I never did, though), that I could always find company any night I wanted. Forester might be a liberal arts college, but it's still in the upper Midwest, college football country, and the football players here have a certain amount of swagger.

Now I'm back as a professional football player, and I know that that job gives me exactly as much right to set myself above other people as any other job, which is to say, none. It's taken me a while to learn that, but I started to learn it here.

I squeeze Lee's shoulder at the car and release him. When we're in with the doors shut, I ask, "So how'd it go with your mom?"

I'm guessing it can't have been too bad, because he was in a good mood the whole night, but he hunches his shoulders and stares forward. "It was... fine," he says finally as I pull out onto the street. "I didn't snap and yell at her."

His voice is distant and neutral. "But?" I prod.

"But." He sighs. "I feel sorry for her. She's stuck in the past and really struggling to get to a future she can be comfortable with."

I stay quiet, and he turns to look at me. "Sort of like me," he says.

"You?" I frown. "Come on, you're all about the future and what comes next and all."

"Yeah." He leans back and clasps his paws in front of him. "I hadn't looked at it that way before either. But it's something I thought about a lot on the way back. I'm afraid of moving forward because of how I've spent the last six months. I was feeling like I can't change."

"Based on tonight," I say, "you haven't changed all that much."

He shoots me a look, and I follow up with, "Okay, in some ways you've changed a lot. Like, you don't try to blow me in public restrooms."

That gets a little grin out of him. "Would you like me to?"

"No," I say. "Well. Maybe? No. I mean, if we get caught, the headlines…"

"Right." He grins. "So we won't get caught."

I shift in the driver's seat. My pants feel tighter. "We can talk about that, I guess. But right now we should wait until we're at the hotel."

"We are at the hotel." Lee looks up and out the windshield. His ears perk up.

"Yeah." I park in the garage and we grab the elevator up to the room. On the way, I notice his empty paws. "Didn't you get anything from your mother's place?"

"Father has it. He's going to send it on when my living situation's settled."

"Right, the house." We walk back down the hall and to the room, where Lee opens the door and gestures me inside. I shed the jacket and toss it onto a chair. "When do you think she'll write back about it?"

"Soon." He drops his jacket as well and grabs my paw to pull me over to the bed, but he doesn't hug me or start any kind of foreplay. He just sits down and pulls me down beside him. "So I was thinking about us and our month and all that."

"I was too." I pull one knee up onto the bed so I can face him, and I can't keep the smile off my muzzle. "I really saw another side of you tonight."

"I…really?" His ears go askew and he raises his eyebrows.

"Yeah. But what did you want to say?"

He relaxes and smiles. "It can wait a second. Now I'm curious what you were thinking."

"Well, uh." I rub my paws together. "I talked to Misha for a bit."

His eyebrows crease together. "I thought you said you don't want me to blow you in a restroom."

"Nah, but…" I take a breath. "Look, I know I've kind of driven this re-lationship and all. You went into the closet for me, you lost your job because of me, you left because you were worried about my career. And I've been listening to your friends talk about all the stuff you used to do, so I want to promise you that…going forward, I'm going to listen to you more and I'm going to try harder to let you express the passion and stuff…" I take one of his paws. "In the bedroom and out of it."

His ears stay up, and so do his whiskers. "I'm almost afraid to ask."

I'm nervous as hell, but I make myself go on. "Misha said you used to top him."

Now he laughs. "When two bottoms get together, someone has to be on top. Not all the time. You know, you can blow each other, but it's not the same."

"If you want to do that again…"

His laugh dies down and he searches my eyes. "With you?"

I nod. He squeezes my paw and leans forward, still smiling. "Well, let me ask you something. Do you want to be a bottom?"

"I, uh…"

"Honestly."

"Honestly?" I don't know what to say to that, so I answer honestly. "Not really. But I'd do it for you. At least once."

"Okay." He lifts my paw and kisses it. "I have no fucking desire to be on top. So thank you for the offer, but I think I will respectfully decline."

I laugh and hug him, then sit back. "Thank God. But I meant the rest of it. I don't know what else I can do. I don't know why you need so long to commit."

"Let me try to tell you," he says.

Chapter Twenty-Seven: Talking It Out Two (Lee)

The call from Brian wasn't the only call I got after leaving Mother's; in fact, Brian's came in while I was on the phone with Hal. I'm sure Brian thinks I simply ignored his call, and I would have anyway, but Hal's was genuinely more interesting.

"I just had a big fight with Pol," he says.

I'm standing on the corner where Father dropped me off, against the frosted glass of a coffee shop. I could go inside, but it's rude to do that. Anyway, the bite of the cold air on my nose and ears is refreshing, not so bad yet that I want to forget again what it's like. I watch my words puff white breath across my phone mic and wait for Salim to show up. "Big fight like you need to get her flowers, or big fight like you're breaking up?"

"Could go either way, I guess. Didn't exactly make plans to get together to finish the argument."

"What happened? She asked if she looked fat and you hesitated?"

"I was married for ten years. Give me some credit. Nah, it was about Fisher."

My ears perk up and then I flatten them again as the wind bites at their tips. "Oh, she didn't like you interviewing him?"

"Kinda that. Invasion of his privacy, causing hurt to the family, bothering a guy who just tried to kill himself and should be left alone, my article would be fine without him."

I sag back against the wall. "You know about the gunshot."

"First clue was when Gena asked me not to write about the 'accident.' Second was the bandaged head. Come on, I've been a reporter longer'n I've been married."

I exhale again, fighting a sinking feeling. "Would your article work without Fisher's stuff? Not the gunshot, but the rest."

"Wouldn't be as good, that's for damn sure."

"You got a lot of stuff you can use?"

"Ayup."

"Glad Dev convinced him to talk to you."

"Ah, he wanted to anyway. They all do. It's just whether you can get a little bit of trust from 'em. First thing he wanted was to know who else was having mental problems, so I gave him a couple names and contact numbers. Then he talked."

"About what?"

"I guided him to talk about the cost of his career. Once or twice he thought I was talking to him after his championship wins. Talked for about fifteen minutes about the Rocs' chances to three-peat. Which was interesting, and I s'pose useful in a high-level way. I didn't stop him."

"Jeez." It clutches at my heart, this unmooring of Fisher's memories, how he is floundering around in time and trying so hard to figure a way back to his family. "Still, huh?"

Hal's voice is soft. "I talked to his nurse real briefly too. She only had a couple days with him, but she said she's tryin' to prepare Gena. She doesn't think it'll get better."

The glass of the coffee shop is cold against the back of my head and ears. I close my eyes. "But it won't get worse, will it?"

"Hard to say."

"Fuck." I don't want to have to tell Dev any of this. Across the road from the coffee shop there's a bar, and I wait for the light and then start crunching through the snow in that direction.

"I talked to Dev, earlier. Didn't tell him that part, though."

I don't want to think about Gena and Bradley and Junior, but at least they have each other, and they have part of their father, if not all of him. For better or worse, they all knew that football is a violent game, that people get hurt. I don't think anyone realized the danger to someone's mind, but that's what Hal's article is trying to bring out.

Warm air and the smell of beer wash over me with the babble of conversation and music as I open the door to the bar. It's a loud campus bar; even on a Sunday night, there are students planning to sleep in on Monday and students who arranged their schedule to have no Monday classes (I never managed that). Some trashy 90's song is playing as I order a Leiney. I make sure I can see through the windows to the corner where Salim was supposed to be ten minutes ago. "What did you tell Dev?" I ask, raising my voice over the music.

"Where are you?" Hal asks.

"A bar. I have to go see some old friends, and after hearing about Fisher, I need a beer to relax myself." I glance down at the coasters, and then sit hard on the barstool and laugh.

"What?"

"I'm in the Fang. I'm sitting at the bar where Dev walked up to me, when I was..." The bartender comes over with my beer.

"When you were the charming Ms. White?"

"Yep." I lean on the bar and look to my right. There aren't any football players there, not tonight. I do let my gaze linger on a grey fox sitting alone in a salmon silk shirt, and when he lifts his muzzle and catches my eye, he frowns and looks away. Straight boys. I chuckle and down a couple gulps of my cold, malty beer. "Maybe you should hit a singles bar tonight," I tell Hal.

"Relationship advice?"

"Life advice. I don't know, it sounds like the thing with Fisher went okay, and if Pol's going to get upset any time you have to push at people's privacy to do your job…"

"Thinking that m'self. When are you back?"

"Few days."

"Want to grab lunch?"

I get down to halfway through my beer, set it down, wipe my lips. The cold turns warm in my stomach. I glance over at the grey fox again and he looks away. So he was looking at me. Amusing. Maybe I should drag him along to the FLAG meeting. "Sure. I've got a week or two before I need to start work."

He makes an exasperated noise. "When you come down to see Miski, you better not forget about me, y'know."

"I won't. I'm getting together with some old friends tonight. I don't want to let people go anymore."

"Good *ma'e*."

"Ha. You can come up to Yerba, too. We've got a football team."

"Planning on it."

"And hey, the thing with Pol…good luck." I check the window. Salim's wandering around outside. "Speaking of old friends…I gotta go, my friend's here."

"All right. Take care. Best to the tiger."

"Yeah. Thanks for the info." I hang up, pause to consider whether I'm sufficiently buzzed for the FLAG meeting, and decide I should probably finish the beer. So I gulp down the remainder, leave the bartender a tip, and hurry out.

It's not easy, but I push the Fisher stuff to the back of my mind while chatting with Salim. I haven't gotten a chance to see him in forever, so I ask how his various families are. His legal one is going well: one kit and a second on the way, everyone healthy now, his wife a wonderful mother and a good companion. They live with her mother and her aunt, so the kits are well cared for and the elder weasels do most of the cooking. Salim insists on bringing in hired help to clean. "It's expected," he says, "but it's also considered very nice of me to do. If I did not, then Nonna and Tanta would clean the house, and I don't feel that's right."

"All right. And how's Jeremy?"

He smiles. "The promotion means more work, more hours. But it is good."

"So he won't want more of your time."

Salim shakes his head. "You know how cats are. He does love his time alone."

"I think tigers are different from bobcats," I say. "At least, Dev isn't big on crowds, but he likes spending time with me."

"Jeremy appreciates the time we have and appreciates the time we do not have," Salim says with a chuckle.

"Sounds like a good arrangement."

He points to the street we're crossing. "This looks new. Was there a hole there that Brian tripped into one night?"

"Yeah." The street's been paved over, smooth black asphalt. "Oh, he called while I was talking to Hal. I guess I should listen to the message."

So Salim and I listen to it together. I shake my head. "One crusade after another."

"That was you once, too," Salim says. His dark eyes meet mine. "But no more? Are you happy?"

"I'm happy." I swish my tail. "The crusades haven't gone away, not by a long shot." I tell him about Vince King, about my Yerba job and my confrontation with Jocko and how scared I was to push the gay tolerance thing with him.

"But it worked out?"

"Yeah." I remember his and Peter's reaction. "Some guys who come off as homophobic really don't know any better. It's like if I told you that all tigers are...well, no, I'm not going to say anything that'll get me in trouble later." He laughs. "But if I told you that all people in the football world are dumb jocks. And maybe you meet one player and he is a dumb jock. And you read in the papers about how dumb some football players are. So you're not, like, biased against football players. You just have a small sample size and a whole bunch of media bias. So then say you meet Dev and you expect him to be dumb. I guess that's what this guy was thinking."

"Still, he should be open to understanding people," Salim says.

"He is, I hope." I look ahead at the street we used to walk up years ago, familiar and yet new, and spot the Starbucks logo. "At least his boss likes me."

"That is good. Oh, when did this Starbucks come in?"

We make small talk all the way to the green mer-otter. By this time, I am done with the cold, so we hurry inside, wipe our feet on the mat, and head right upstairs.

I'd intended to get to know some of the younger FLAG members, to give them advice and listen to their stories. But right away I hug Dev and kiss him, and then Misha's there, and Allen, and we get talking about the old days and the time skips on by. Brian's name comes up once, so I play his voicemail for everyone, because nothing in it is particularly private, and it's good for everyone to hear where he is.

Before I know it, people are exchanging e-mail addresses and pulling on jackets and getting ready to leave. Misha and his adorable husband hug us warmly, as do Allen and Salim, and Chuck too, a little over-enthusiastically. But it's all good, and to me it feels, more than dinner tonight, like coming home.

I'm trying to figure out how to tell Dev what I've decided about us, but he forestalls me with his own thoughts. We're in sync there, too, although spurred by different experiences. Forester is where we met, and maybe for both of us, going back to the beginning of our relationship helped us more clearly see the path to the future.

When he asks if I want to top, I have to hold back a laugh. I'm going to have to e-mail Misha later and tell him about that because it's just too cute of Dev. I wonder if he was really thinking that for all these years I've wanted to push myself inside him and was too afraid of how he'd react to ask. Honestly, he never really wanted to talk much about our sex life, and after I insisted on him at least learning to give blow jobs, I was happy enough that I didn't think we needed to. But maybe we should talk a little more than we have been, at least.

So then he asks the very reasonable question: "I don't know why you need so long to commit."

And I try to tell him.

"You know that when I left, when I walked out, it wasn't because I don't love you, right?" He nods, though his ears go back. "I love you so much it scares me sometimes. But I scare myself more. Because I feel like I can't go for more than a year or so without screwing something up. First with Brian, then my parents…"

"Hey," he says, and reaches across the small span of bed between us to squeeze my leg. "None of those are your fault."

"Not mine alone, I know." I take a breath. "But when you're involved in three major relationship disruptions in such a short span of time, you have to ask if it's something to do with you. I think that's partly why I left, because I couldn't stand staying around with all the shit that was going on and taking the chance that you'd kick me out. Worse, that I'd ruin your chance at a championship and then you'd never forgive me. If you'd lost that game the way you did and I'd been hanging around you talking about gay rights, you'd blame me for it. Maybe not out loud, and maybe not consciously, but—"

"No," he says firmly, holding my eyes with his. "There's so much that goes into a game, I know that it's at least fifty percent luck. We could've won that game, and maybe if you had been there, I'd have been a little more inspired."

"All right." I smile and take a moment to savor the warmth those words suffuse me with. "I have things to learn too. But the point is, I've been worried I'll do or say something that will ruin things between us. And I worry about that because of what past me has done. But look, I've changed just in this past month, haven't I?"

"Maybe a little." He pretends to examine my face. "I'll have to do a full inspection later."

"I'm okay with that." The humor relaxes me. "The point is, I didn't believe that I *can* change. That I can tell you we'll talk about things and we'll do our best to understand each other, and we'll still have fights, but we'll also make up. So the question for me tonight became: Am I willing to work to make this relationship work?"

"Just tonight?"

"I thought about how Mother views me, refusing to move past the point in our lives when things weren't complicated. I don't want to stick myself in a box the way she's doing. Only she wishes I hadn't changed, and I wasn't believing that I could." Salim's voice comes back to me. "Salim told me there are three kinds of people in the world: ones who can't change, ones who do change, and ones who can but don't. I don't *want* to be that last kind. And I think, if I work at it, I don't have to be."

He nods, his paw rubbing up and down along my leg. "So what was your answer?"

I lean forward, bringing my nose an inch from his. "What do you think?"

His eyes, bright gold, stare into mine. "I know what I think. I want to know what *you* think."

Laughter bubbles up from my chest, and I lean forward to kiss his answering smile. "I'm rubbing off on you."

"Not yet," he rumbles, "but maybe soon, depending on your answer to that question."

I scoot closer. "Well, I was thinking about the last few years. Tonight especially, you know, it was nice to see all the old guys again, but in the back of my head I was thinking that as cool as all those guys are, and as much as I missed them, you know, they never really came after me when I disappeared. They let me go. The only people who have really come after me have been Father and you."

"Uh-huh." He clears his throat. "Your chances of sex after this conversation go down the more you mention your father, you realize."

"Last time." I hold up one paw and then rest it on his chest. "The point is...the point is that I love you. And for some fucking strange reason, you love me too. I've thought that I had love a lot of times in my life, and I never wanted to chase it down so badly as I do with you. And here's the thing: no matter what happens in the future, this is special now. The things I'm worried about are things we can control, and I'm scared of what I'll do, but you...you make me a better person. So I think you can make me the kind of fox who will be brave enough to talk to you, who will trust you and himself enough to work things out. I mean—I don't want to put this all on you. I mean that I can make myself that kind of fox, with your help. And besides all of that..." I take a breath. He's listening intently, not revealing anything really. "Besides all of that. This, what we have, this is worthwhile. And I was losing sight of that because of how scared I was. I'm sorry about that. However long it lasts, I want to be with you every minute of it. If we break up in a year, or five years, or ten years, then the time until then isn't wasted. That's a year or five or ten that we have together."

"Do you think we're going to break up in a year or five or ten?" he asks.

I start to answer, and then he says, "Honestly."

"Honestly? I don't know. I don't have a fucking clue." I take a breath. "We're both passionate and we sometimes fight. But if we both love each other and think that what we have together is worthwhile, then I think we're both smart enough to figure out how to keep it working."

"Uh-huh." He allows himself a smile, and the happiness behind it lights up the room, lights up *me*, like the sun is rising in my chest, and Jesus Fox, it's almost too much to take. "So that means yes?"

Just yes? It's not enough, none of it is, to tell him how much I love him, to tell him that whatever happens with his brother, whatever happened with my parents, with Hal and Pol, that they aren't us. That I believe in him, I trust him, and maybe more importantly, I trust myself. "That means..." I kiss his nose and before I know what I'm doing, I drop down off the bed, onto one knee. I have no idea what to say, but fortunately, a lifetime of books and movies have made the words rote. I hold his paw and look up at him. "Will you marry me?"

Chapter Twenty-Eight: Into the Future (Dev)

My brain short-circuits. I'm staring down at him and he's staring up with eyes like a clear sky and he's kind of smiling, but the longer I stare at him, the more he strains to hold that smile there. After a little while, he coughs and says, "Okay, you can say 'no' if you want. I know this is sort of a surprise."

"Sort of," I choke out. "God dammit, fox, can't we have one conversation where you don't spring one on me?"

He laughs and his eyes sparkle. "It was spur of the moment." He looks down. "I'm still down here."

"Yeah." I rub my whiskers. "Look, I…we haven't even talked about marriage or anything like that."

" 'Spur of the moment' sort of implies a lack of foresight." He starts to get up. "I understand, it's—"

"Don't get up." I push his shoulders back down.

His ears flick to the side and his smile returns. His tail swings from side to side. "Okay."

I take a breath. "Let me think about this for a second." Lion Christ, this fox. What the hell am I going to do with him? And yet it's thrilling, the edge every time something happens, the wondering what he'll do next.

When I first met him, I didn't think he'd be any good for me. It turned out he was maybe the best thing to happen to me in my life. No, scratch that 'maybe.' I'd be an idiot to let him go.

"Hey," he says, and I turn my attention to him. "Maybe you can talk it out with me?"

Makes sense. I take a breath. "Marriage is a weird thing, and it's still— I'm sorry, it's still hooked up in my mind with a guy in a tux and a gal in a dress and a church and all that. Honestly, I don't know if I'm ready for it yet."

I catch the flick of his ears even though he tries to keep them up. "That's okay," he says. "Honestly? I'm a little scared by it too. But I figure if we're doing it together…it's less scary."

"Yeah," I say. "But…" I lift his paw to my muzzle and nuzzle his fingers. "It feels like something we're jumping into." I don't say *you're jumping into* because I'm in this with him. "Like, trying to go from our twenty yard line to midfield just because we feel like we should be there, not earning it."

"You think marriage is midfield? Not the end zone?" His eyes sparkle and he smiles.

Three years ago, I don't know if I'd have been able to think fast enough to answer. "I think the end zone is walking off into the sunset together. At the end, you know?"

"All right." He inclines his head to me to go on.

"Football is what brought us together, y'know? And we're still deep in the football life, both of us. So I think maybe an engagement ring isn't the ring we should be thinking about right now."

His eyebrows go up as high as I've ever seen them. "If I could get you a championship ring, stud, I would. But that's not just jumping to midfield, you know?"

"No, no, I know." I reach out and take one of his paws. His fingers close around mine, warm and confident. "But I feel a lot more confident in the football world with you. And I think when I have a championship ring, there'll be a lot less pressure on football, and…"

His eyes are serious and his gaze unflinching. "So…when you win a championship, we'll get married? What if you never win one?"

"You think I won't win one?"

"Of course you'll win one."

"All right then." I see his lips part and I move my free paw to them. "Hush, I know the odds. I know the teams that got there once and never again. So maybe if I have a little extra motivation…maybe that'll be a bit of an edge. You know, over all those guys who don't have a fox they need to make sure they keep around."

His smile grows. He licks my finger. "You don't have to win a championship to keep me around."

"I know." I squeeze his paw. "I figure waiting for the championship will keep you around for a while. After that we have to get married."

He laughs and rubs his head into my paw. "So we're engaged to be engaged?"

"Yeah. I like that." I relax. Everything's going to be okay. No, better than okay. "And with another one or two or three years, we'll both be more ready for it. So are we good?"

He nods, holding my paw. "We're going to stay together and we're going to work on talking and making this work. I mean…" He takes a breath. "I promise you, tiger, that I will remember that I love you. I promise I will do my best to be worthy of you."

Warmth closes my throat. I say, "Oh, fox. I love you. I'll remember that, and we'll talk about stuff and work on things and…"

He's up by then and in my arms, and I squeeze him tightly against me. The warm strength of his embrace, the twisting of his lithe form against mine as we roll back onto the bed, the passion with which that pointy muzzle pushes against my broad one and the shifting of his hips as his tail wags, all of these bring that warmth back to my throat and chest, and I want to hold him as tightly as I can because I don't want him to get away. I want to be inside him because that's as close as we can get; I want to share the buildup and release of our passion, to make him yelp and moan just as I do and then lie next to him and fall asleep in a haze of his scent and the feel of him.

And because God is good and the universe loves me, that's more or less how the next twenty minutes go. We both want it badly, but once our clothes have been thrown to the floor, we delay, teasing each other with fingers. "I can't feel it like this once it's in me," he murmurs, rubbing a finger along my shaft.

"Haven't you felt it enough?" I do the same to his, finding the smooth contours and familiar knot already growing.

"Never enough," he says, and later, when I'm inside him and we're both panting harshly from the release of sex and my stomach is warm and smelly from his release, I move to lift his hips off my shaft, but he settles down firmly. "A little longer," he says, and leans down to kiss me, and I know why he wants to stay that way.

"Engaged to be engaged," I murmur against his tongue.

"Words," he says back, and licks at my whiskers, a caress that makes me shiver. "The promise is what matters, the intention."

"Mmmf." My paws slide down his naked back, fingers pushing through the thick fur. "Wasn't the promise made of words?"

He pulls his head back slightly, one eye on mine. I nuzzle at him and try to clear up the slight confusion I see there. "I'm not being…whatever. I just want to make sure I understand what you mean."

"Mm." He kisses my whiskers, my nose, the whiskers on the other side of my muzzle. "We can call it engaged to be engaged or whatever; the words just frame what we intend. Which is that we're promising each other to try our best to understand each other and be together for the rest of our lives." He wiggles his hips from side to side and reaches back to rub a finger up my slick shaft to the point where it enters him. "That we're joined together more strongly than this."

" 'This' is pretty strong." I push my hips up and his down.

His ears flick and he brushes his lips against mine. "Yep."

"But you're saying…" I bring my paws up to circle his ribcage. His pulse throbs against my paws. "You're saying that we just got married?"

He kisses me. "More or less. Someday we'll stand in front of a bunch of people and say lots more words. Someday we'll have a piece of paper from some government that says we legally share our lives. But…well, I mean, do you feel that? I guess I shouldn't assume."

I chuckle. "I hadn't thought about it like that. I was just trying to make sure you don't run away again." I play-growl and push his hips down again. "Maybe I should just keep this in you all the time."

He squirms. "I think that'd make football a little more difficult. Though we'd have four arms to catch interceptions with."

The image makes me laugh and bounce him on my stomach, and I slip out of him without either one of us intending it. "So much for that," I say.

"You can always put it back in again." He stretches out, no longer confined by our coitus, and lies half atop me on one side. "And again and again..."

"Oh, I will." I lick the bridge of his nose.

"And if you really do want to put this," he reaches down to his own dripping shaft, "in you one day, we can try it."

I look down my white fur at his pink length and the mess it left on my stomach stripes. "Misha spoke highly of your topping abilities."

He presses against me with a laugh. "Misha's a sweetie. He's also the only lover I've had who was more of a bottom than I am. I came over to his room once and he had a toy stuck up under his tail because he couldn't wait fifteen minutes for me to get there."

I rub down his back, pressing into the muscle. "Do you have a toy? Do you want one?"

"Oh, god. No, I guess..." He thinks. "I could've bought one when we were living apart, but I liked keeping myself for you. And back in college, I never had a problem finding someone..." He clears his throat. "I did sometimes use Misha's toy when I was topping him. If you want me to top you, we can start with a small toy or something, but anyway that's a long way away and we can do other stuff if you want to play around, too, like cuffs or blindfolds or shaving."

"I can't shave," I point out. "My teammates see me naked in the shower."

"Ever see any of them shaved?"

"Uh. Okay, actually yes. But you know, I'm the gay one, so..."

He laughs. "It's okay. Shaving's not one of my things."

"Things? You have things? What are your things?" I feel like I should know this already.

He reaches down and cups my sac, rubbing a thumb along the still-hard base of my shaft. "These are my things," he says, and gives them a light squeeze.

"Oh." I roll over onto him and pull him against me, rubbing his sticky mess into his own fur and trapping his paw between us. "Well, I only have one thing and that's this handsome fox I happen to know."

"Mmmf." He squirms, but can't shift me. "Sounds like we're a good match, then."

"Yeah." I lower my muzzle to kiss him. "And it only took us three years to figure it out."

When I lift from the kiss, he says, "Actually, our three-year anniversary is in April, if you mean the night you picked me up at the Fang. We should go there for a drink. I stopped in by accident earlier tonight and it's—"

I silence him with another kiss, and this time when I lift my muzzle, he just looks into my eyes and hugs back tightly, and I cling to this fox who makes me crazy and content and fulfilled and terrified and I feel as happy as I can remember being ever.

•

Monday morning, we wake up with fur still sticky and matted; the bed smells strongly of Lee's musk and to some extent mine. We get out of bed to shower, but Lee flattens his ears as he leans over and sniffs the sheets. "And this hotel doesn't surcharge for foxes," he sighs.

I turn him around and hug him against me. Even dirty and smelly (like me), he feels good and warm, our mutual connection still resonating from the previous night. "I'll leave them a big tip. Come on, let's shower."

In the shower, we talk about the flight home, about going to Gerrard's workouts and going to see Fisher, and I remember what Hal told me about Damian. My mood takes a downward shift. "I have some advice to ask you on the way to the airport," I say, "but not right now."

"Okay." He nods, scrubbing through my fur. "Serious? Your ears went back. Is it about—" He cuts himself off with a shake of his head. "Never mind. I'll hear it when you're ready to tell me."

"Yeah. I just have to make another choice, you know? Right thing, wrong thing, hard thing, easy thing." I close my eyes and let his paws clean me off. "Except there are no easy things. Why does everything have to be difficult? Why can't my friends just be my friends and my agent just be my agent and my family just be my family?"

"And your boyfriend just be your boyfriend?" He steps back so he can work shampoo into my chest and stomach fur.

"I don't think you could ever *just* be my boyfriend." I hold him tighter over his protests, trapping his paws between us. "No. I don't want you to stop challenging me."

"That's what the world is doing, your friends and family and agent and team: Challenging you. When you have the opportunity to do the wrong thing, or to avoid doing the right thing, that's how you become the person you are. Like you said, you don't get to jump to midfield or the end zone just because you want to be there. You get there over time, by making those decisions every day. Big choices, small choices; the choices you make become your habits, and your habits define the person you are. You're the accumulation of your past, both good and bad, and the only way to change is to begin making different choices today." He clears his throat. "That didn't start out being about us, but you know, it sort of ended up that way."

"Uh-huh. Like how we're choosing to talk to each other and think about each other and our future."

"And not to walk out on difficult situations."

"And not to keep things inside."

"Well," he says, stepping back again to cup his lathery paws around my sheath. "Maybe we can keep *some* things inside. Sometimes."

"As long as we do it together," I say, and I pull his muzzle up to kiss me, and he doesn't resist.

•

My short fur dries pretty quickly with the blow dryers, so I've got the towel wrapped around my waist as I search through my suitcase for clothes. This hotel doesn't have a full blow-drying stall, so Lee stands naked at his desk, checking the computer while his damp fur air-dries. I admire the light on his body and abandon the suitcase for a moment to take a picture with my phone.

"Don't post that on the Internet," he says, grinning.

"Why not? Everyone should see how hot my boyfriend is."

I play at using the phone to send the pic to the Internet. I know that he knows I have no idea how to do that, but I still expect him to run at me and try to get the phone away. Instead, he sits in the chair and pulls his tail into his lap, though I can still see his sheath and balls through the fur. He just looks at me with a wide smile and runs claws through his tail.

"Okay, if you don't object…" I press some random buttons on the phone. Then it dials Carson, and I hurriedly hang it up before it can connect. Lee's still watching me, grooming his tail, with a restless energy as though he's waiting to tell me something. "Any good e-mail?"

His muzzle lifts. The smile brightens. "Oh, maybe."

Just as thinking about Damian depressed my mood, this perks it up. "What?" When he stays silent, I advance a step. "Do I have to come over there and tickle it out of you?"

He indicates the laptop screen, getting up as I walk over. I only process the name of our realtor and the word *Congratulations* with a parade of exclamation points after it before Lee, fidgeting from foot to foot, says, "Our bid went through. You now own a house in Yerba."

It takes a moment for the words to sink in. Then I match his smile and wrap him up in my arms. "You mean, '*We* own a house.'"

"That too." He grins and nuzzles against me, craning his muzzle up for a kiss, which I gladly give him. While our muzzles meet, his paws tease nimbly at my towel until it falls to the floor and our bodies press close.

"Mmmmf." We pull apart from the kiss. His paws slide down my hips, down my rear and tail. "I think we should celebrate."

"We just showered," I point out. "And we've got to be at the airport in, uh…"

He kisses me again and brings his paws up to my cheek ruffs. Again I see a clear blue sky in his eyes, stretching on and on and on. "Don't worry, tiger," he says. "We've got time."

Epilogue

Epilogue: Home (Dev)

I jog out onto the field between Gerrard and Brick. Pike's gone to the Devils, but we signed a new defensive end, a tiger from the Tornadoes named Robi. Seems like a nice guy from the couple times we've been out for drinks (he told me about a friend of his who has a gay cousin; everyone wants to tell me about their gay friend or relative now). Every time I look at him, though, I think of Fisher, still living with the in-home nurse, still slipping between years and forgetting the names of his children. Gena's adapting, though, and Fisher seemed to be too, last time I saw them. Junior quit football to try out for baseball, and Gena says that was his idea, not hers.

I never talked to Damian about the serum he got for Fisher. Lee and I decided it was worth the risk to stay with him; Lee agreed with my assessment of it and suggested I talk to some of Damian's other clients to see if drug use was common among them, in which case it might be better to bail. But the Diversity in Athletics Day at Forester went great, and Damian was very helpful when we talked about whether to take a contract from the two interested teams (Yerba was one of them; Gateway, to my surprise, was the other). He and I (and Lee) concluded that it was best not to leave the situation in Chevali: a good young team with lots of promise. What's more, I have a lot of friends here, most of whom are still here: Ty and Zillo and Carson, Gerrard and Steez and even Coach Samuelson. Vonni's gone; Colin stayed. I wish I could reverse that, but you can't have everything.

Haven't gotten a chance to talk to Ty without a hundred other people around, but he seems pretty happy. Rodo asked him about the TMZ article while I was around and he said that the wife hunt was over, but she couldn't come around to meet everyone. I'll have to find out what the deal is, but there's a whole season for that.

The sun is shining and the grass is a brilliant green. My teammates are dazzling in our away jerseys, white with red numbers; we're scrimmaging against our own offense, in the home red with white numbers. Grass and earth, crisp uniform smell, and the scent of sixty thousand people wash over me as I stand in the huddle.

"Standard play," Gerrard says to us. "Running down. Plug your gaps."

We disperse to our positions. I keep in mind the lessons from the summer, the special seminar I and a few others attended on safe tackling to reduce the risk of concussions. Gerrard and many others didn't go, but Vonni and Zillo and Carson and I did, and Gerrard doesn't care how we tackle as long as we stop the guy. When it comes right down to it, some of us are still going to get hit. Football's a physical game, and with the rewards come a whole pile of dangerous risks. But if you're smart, and you have someone helping to look at it in the right way, you can figure out how to get the most out of it.

The offensive line sets. I crouch down behind Robi and Brick and listen for the snap, every muscle ready, every sense alert. They snap the ball and drop back to pass, but Gerrard and I annihilate their protection and swarm our backup quarterback, dropping him to the turf with the ball clutched to his chest.

We trot back to the bench and here, in an intra-squad scrimmage, the sideline is much more casual. A few of the special teams players stand near the fans in the first row having conversations. Gerrard, of course, keeps his attention on the game, but I turn around and look along the stands.

Hal, whose article inspired the seminar, isn't with the press. The league won't issue him a pass for the games anymore, but that doesn't stop him from attending as a fan. And some of us who appreciate what he's done to help us still give him interviews. I pass his phone number around where I can. I don't see him, but really I'm not looking for him.

To my left and ahead of me, a few rows back from the Firebirds bench, is a fox in a Firebirds polo shirt. He's walking up the aisle toward me, smiling and applauding, and I see our history and our future. For a moment, my heart feels too big for this fragile chest of mine.

Life changes you and everyone around you. You can pretend it's not coming or you can brace for it or you can welcome it with open arms, but whatever you do, it's going to come at you like a pair of three hundred pound boars. The best you can ask for is a partner to stand at your side, friends and family and co-workers to surround you, a team to face the on-slaught. You'll never learn exactly how to prepare, but you'll all be doing it together, and you'll never have to face it alone.

I head to the front row and meet Lee there. "Nice sack," he says. "Even if you had to share it."

"It was a team effort," I say.

A couple of my teammates along the line glance my way. Charm, chatting up a couple well-endowed female rabbits, winks at me. Lee nods back at the big horse with an answering smile. "Go get ready. Looks like you'll be back out there in a minute."

He leans forward and kisses me lightly. When I open my eyes and step back, he does the same. Nobody around us grimaces or turns away. None of my nearby teammates says anything about it as I make my way back to stand among them, ready to go back on the field with my fox's kiss on my lips.

This, I think, this is what life is all about.

AFTERWORD: A LIFETIME IN A DECADE

In November 2004, across nearly a dozen states, voters overwhelmingly approved the notion that two men or two women could not enter into the institution of marriage. Whether they meant only to preserve the religious institution of marriage without commentary to the validity of same-sex relationships, the message received by those of us in such relationships was loud and clear: you are not worth including in our community. Only months earlier, Massachusetts had become the first state in the U.S. to allow same-sex couples to marry, though that right was limited to residents of the state (it would later be expanded). In November, that historic advancement looked as though it would stand alone for a very long time.

In November 2004, I was living with my then-boyfriend Kit and working at a high-tech market research firm in the Bay Area, on about the third reboot of a career that had so far been guided by opportunity more than passion. I'd briefly worked at things I loved but could not build a career out of; the work I could build a career out of, while I liked it well enough, was not what I loved. It was somewhere around this time that I was finishing the manuscript of my first novel, "Volle," which I had written with the dual intention of showing a gay character who was comfortable with his sexuality and whose relationships were not looked down upon, and showing that one could write a novel with both a good story and explicitly sexual scenes.

"Volle" appeared in 2005 to just enough enthusiasm to encourage me to write another novel. Soon after its publication, I was laid off from one tech job and stepped immediately into another. And sometime in the following year, as I was stepping out of the shower, a scene flashed into my head, bright and compelling, a scene in which a tiger had come to a fox's door to scream at him that he could no longer sleep with girls. "You've ruined me for women!" he cried, and I heard the fox's reply: "You were never for women."

I wrote the story, "In Between," which was promptly rejected for publication the only place I sent it, and so I posted it to my LiveJournal. But the fox and tiger, Lee and Dev, remained in my head. A year later, I wrote "Secrets," and then I knew there was a novel to be written. I started to write it.

In 2008, I left my tech job for what would be my last one. My novel "Waterways" came out and eclipsed my other novels almost instantly, building on the popularity of its first part, "Aquifers," which had appeared on Yiffstar (now SoFurry) and gained a great following. I was deep into writing "Out of Position" at this point, and early in the year I talked to some friends who happened to be immensely talented furry artists. Thinking that a football-based book would need quite a boost to sell to the fandom (I had, it turns out, greatly underestimated the love for sports in the furry fandom), I asked if they would illustrate the book, and they accepted, though they knew nothing about football.

In May, the California Supreme Court ruled that 2000's Prop 22, asserting that "marriage is between a man and a woman," was unconstitutional. Same-sex marriage immediately became legal, and within weeks, Prop 8 was placed on the November ballot, altering California's constitution to prohibit same-sex marriage. A virulent, expensive fight for public perception followed, with the projected vote hovering around 50%. And in November, Barack Obama was elected, and Prop 8 passed in California. We cheered Obama and mourned Prop 8, feeling rather disgusted at not only the people who'd been "taken in," we thought, by the ridiculous anti-gay propaganda, but also the people who hadn't bothered to cast their votes. Again, marriage seemed far off, despite a slow trickle of states including Iowa and most of New England approving it (with, in some cases, voter initiatives to repeal it again).

"Out of Position" debuted in January of 2009. As I'd hoped, Blotch's art drew many more eyes to it, and the story did a good job of keeping them there.

A little later in 2009, Kit proposed to me.

Still later in 2009, "Out of Position" did an admirable job of reaching out to the gay romance audience, even the non-furry ones. I already knew there would be a sequel, and I was glad that the book was doing well enough for Sofawolf to approve one. Blotch, too, loved the characters enough to ask to return for the sequel.

In 2010, Kit and I got married—in Boston, since our home state was still reviewing challenges to Prop 8. We were hopeful that it would be overturned, but too impatient to wait.

And at the end of 2010, my tech job informed me apologetically that due to a reorganization, they were going to have to pay me not to work there for several months and then stop paying me. My husband sat me down and said that if I wanted to make a career out of being a novelist, then I would have to do it full time, and largely due to the success of "Out of Position," we both thought it was worth a shot.

In 2011, "Isolation Play" came out, and the state of New York became the most populous state to allow same-sex marriage. You all calmed my fears that I could not continue Dev and Lee's story with as much power as it had begun.

In 2012, voters went to the polls in four states (Maine, Minnesota, Maryland, and Washington) and voted to allow same-sex marriage, the first time popular vote had come down in favor of marriage equality. Meanwhile, Lee and Dev's saga had grown from a projected four books into five, as the third book sprawled over 200,000 words in the first draft. I split it into "Divisions," released in 2013, and "Uncovered," released in 2014.

In 2013, the Supreme Court of the United States overturned California's Prop 8 and the Defense of Marriage Act, citing no reasonable reason to prevent same-sex couples from enjoying the benefits of marriage. For the next two years, marriage restrictions toppled like dominoes around the country. I went from tracking every court case and vote that might result in a marriage decision to being surprised on a nearly monthly basis. "Wait, Utah? Indiana? Kentucky?" Court decisions and legislatures made same-sex marriage legal in thirty-eight states.

And in 2014, a highly regarded college football player came out to the world. He revealed that his team had known all season that he was gay and had kept it out of the media. Michael Sam, a defensive end for the Missouri Tigers, was drafted by the St. Louis Rams that summer, and famously kissed his boyfriend Vito on national TV when he got the news. He would later credit his boyfriend, a swimmer (with, dare I say, a foxy build) with pushing him to come out (he also said that they first met when he saw Vito throwing up over a balcony, so let's not take the parallel too far).

"Uncovered" came out that summer as I was already writing and planning this final volume. In the meantime, I'd begun another series of books, less gay-rights focused, and written a bunch of novellas. With this last volume on the horizon and my other series finishing up, I started planning future books.

On June 26, 2015, the Supreme Court of the United States ruled in Obergefell v. Hodges that state-level bans on same-sex marriage are unconstitutional. Couples of any mix of genders are now free to marry anywhere in the United States. There are still places in this country where this change is not welcome, but there are no longer places where it is in dispute.

In January of 2016, the "Out of Position" series came to an end.

•

When Dev and Lee first appeared in my head, none of us could have imagined how quickly and thoroughly our society would have embraced change. I wrote at the beginning of "Waterways," in 2008, that I expected attitudes to change in perhaps the next ten years and that I hoped the book would one day be a quaint reminder of how closed-minded we used to be.

In many ways, Dev and Lee's journey from discomfort to acceptance to joy has been echoed in the world around me, and like the world's, their journey is not over. They like it in my head and have made it clear they intend to stay. Many of you reading this have told me stories of how they've affected your lives, touching, beautiful, happy stories and difficult but necessary stories. You may not know how much they have also affected my life.

As of the end of 2015, I have been a full time writer for five years, the longest I have held any job, or indeed continuously undertaken any activity, including college student. It has had challenges, but I have never had a single moment in which I wished I were doing something else. I am happier in this job than I have ever been at any other work, and I still find it difficult to believe how lucky I am to be able to do the thing I love every day.

My husband Kit deserves all the love I can give him and ten times more besides, for his patience, his unswerving belief in me, his love for me (which all my stories are attempts to communicate to you), and all the support he has provided over the years. These books would not be in your paws right now without him.

But both of us would also like to thank you, all of you reading this right now, for taking this journey with us, for opening your hearts to us at conventions and in e-mail and online notes, for sharing your stories, for becoming our friends, for telling your friends about Dev and Lee, for loving them as much as we do, for your support of this series and of my other books. Without you, these books would not have been possible; without you, all the books to come would never be (or at least, would appear much more slowly); without you, I would still be stealing time wherever I could to write more stories and dreaming of quitting my tech job. You have all given Kit and me a wonderful gift, and you continue to give that gift every year. From the bottom of our hearts, thank you, thank you, thank you all so very much.

Acknowledgments

There have been many, many people who have contributed to these books along the way, and if over the course of the last ten years I have forgotten any of them, it is not intentional.

My college roommate, who will here remain nameless because I fear embarrassing him, introduced me to football and sparked my interest in it. I cribbed a large part of Lee's Guide to Football from conversations with him.

My post-college roommate, who will here remain nameless for similar reasons, fanned the spark into an enduring flame.

Ned, my best friend from college, has shared many phone conversations about football, religion, gay relationships, and a thousand other topics that at one time or another have influenced this book.

Buck Hopper told me a valuable nugget of information about offensive linemen and has been a fellow sports enthusiast and good friend throughout.

Rukis introduced herself to me as a fan of these books and stepped in when art was needed for the last one, doing a fantastic job working with myself and Kenket.

Jack DeVries has been a sarcastic fan, a friend, a reviewer, a publicist of sorts, and a morale booster.

Savrin has loaned his voice to the audiobooks of Dev and Lee, having read through about eight novels to get five recordings down. He's brought humor and passion and life to the narration and done a wonderful job.

foozzzball, at great personal cost, read through the last four manuscripts and offered his usual hacksaw-sharp suggestions, improving the book in each case. His discussions on writing philosophy and technique have made me a better writer.

Ryan Campbell, David Cowan, and Watts Martin have been the best writing group a furry author could ask for. Their advice and observations have been invaluable to these books, and they also have vastly improved my writing.

K.M. Hirosaki, also a sometime member of the writing group, has offered insight, enthusiasm, and friendship through the years, far beyond what I deserve. He has probably influenced the salacious portions of these books more than he realizes, and has been one of my favorite people to show each new book to.

BlackTeagan and Kenket have breathed life into these characters with their brilliant imaginings and renderings, not only in the illustrations but in the presentation of the stories to the fandom and the world. Their artwork has enhanced the books very nearly as much as their camaraderie and friendship has enhanced my and Kit's lives.

Brer and Alopex have been greatly supportive friends over the years; they and the various staff of Sofawolf have taken the "small" out of "small press" (disclaimer: I have done some editing work with Sofawolf and have tried to live up to their standards; I am here talking about everyone else in the organization). With Sofawolf, they have created an organization that treats its creators and customers with equal professionalism, while never losing sight of the passion we all share for these furry critters, no matter who writes or draws them. I have been surprised and delighted by their ideas and support more times than I care to count, and any time you admire one of my books, you are admiring their work.

Brer deserves special mention for all the work he's done specifically on these books, layouts and cover designs most notably. He was the first to suggest a hardcover edition, which I love and I think many of you do too. It's hard to believe that we've been friends for nearly twenty years now, not because it doesn't feel like that long, but because I can't remember a time when I was writing and didn't have him to talk to.

And of course, my husband Kit Silver has stood by my side, both figuratively and literally, for sixteen years and counting. All the good parts of Dev and Lee's romance have their roots in ours, and his spirit is in these books nearly as much as mine is. I write them for him to read first, and even before he reads them I write them as though he is reading over my shoulder. I have read the books aloud to him on car trips, have engaged in hours of discussion over plot and character points, have gotten from him invaluable feedback on structure and character, and that is just the technical aspect of writing. As I mentioned above, he has supported me both financially and spiritually in this writing endeavor; he has been my partner in so many ways and so many adventures that I can no longer count them; he has been my First Reader and my lover and my husband and my best friend and is still all of those things and more. He is Best Wolf, and I am Luckiest Fox, and I could write another three quarters of a million words thanking him for being by my side all these years and they would not be enough. I love him dearly, and if you can see even just a little of that in these books, then maybe he was right and I can make a go of this writing thing after all.

Preview: Ty Game

*Just to reassure you that your friends are not gone forever, here is a sneak preview of the first chapter of an upcoming novel about Dev's friend Ty Nakamura. While writing **Over Time**, I realized that Ty had an interesting story that I wanted to write. I planned it as a novella, but as I got to know some of the other characters, I realized it was going to be a novel. Expect to see more of this in the near future.*

It was weird at first, dancing without any girls around, and Vonni couldn't dance for shit, but after a couple songs, Ty just lost himself in the music and didn't let it worry him. That's what everyone else was doing, and who cared if it was a gay club? While he was dancing, guys didn't bother him, or they assumed he was with Vonni, a couple tall athletic foxes cutting it up on the floor. The stuffy air filled with hundreds of scents, the flashing lights, the pounding trance music: he loved it. Here he could forget about football (with a little assist from whatever those cocktails had been) and just move with the music.

When he opened his eyes, Vonni had been replaced by a wolf half a foot shorter than him. Ty lost a step to surprise, then picked up the beat again and watched this new guy. He looked to have plain brown and ivory fur, though who could tell under these lights, and he wore a tank top that showed off what were probably considered pretty nice muscles outside a football locker room. Heck, they were pretty nice muscles, and the tank top hung straight down from his chest, so no gut. He wore jeans, like Ty, and he had a glittering bracelet around his left wrist.

As his scent filtered through the haze, Ty looked around for Vonni. The fox danced a couple feet away, still awkward, his tail jerking behind him rather than flowing like Ty's did. The wolf wasn't hitting on him and he smelled nice, actually, no heavy perfume, no dominating scent of arousal, so Ty just smiled, and the wolf smiled back, and they danced on.

When he took a break, Vonni was talking to some leopard chick and looked really into her, so Ty let him be. He pushed his way through to the bar, ordered a club soda, and turned to see the wolf standing right there.

Then he did feel the need to raise a paw and say, "I'm straight."

The wolf grinned and shrugged. "I won't hold it against you."

Ty blinked. What was that supposed to mean? He watched while the wolf ordered a cosmo, and then said, "I thought you'd care."

"Oh, I do, but it doesn't mean I'm gonna walk away. You can sure as hell dance, and you're here with a bunch of big muscular guys, so I'm a little curious. Athletes?"

"Football players."

"Oh!" The wolf turned, and there was Dev on the dance floor. "Firebirds, right? That's Miski, the gay one."

"Right. He and his boyfriend just brought us here to dance." He sipped his club soda. Definitely didn't want to get any more buzzed than he already was.

"Cool. How you liking it?"

Ty surveyed the room, lifting his nose. "It's loud." He grinned and rubbed up the side of one of his big triangular ears. "But I'm used to that. Smells good and I love the music. Also I gotta say it's nice just dancing, you know?"

"Sure." The wolf paid for his drink and lapped at it. "You got a name?"

"Uh. Ty."

"I'm Archie. Arch for short."

"Hey, Arch." Ty extended his paw and the wolf took it, with a warm, firm grip. "You can sure as hell dance, too."

"Two years ballet." Arch grinned. "I don't use the moves, but the coordination comes in handy. So you play football, huh? You any good?"

"Yeah." Ty couldn't help grinning.

"Cool. I never watched much football, because that's what my dad made me watch with him. You know, to counteract the ballet lessons. So when I got kicked out, I swore off it. But I gotta say, between you and Miski, I might pick it up again."

"You should." It felt like the club soda was spiked, like something in it was making him feel warm and happy. "We're going to the championship this year."

"That a fact?" Arch raised an eyebrow and finished his drink. "Well, Ty, I'm gonna keep an eye on you, then. And if you're ever back in Yerba and you wanna go dancing…" His paw was outstretched again, and a card reflected the club's rainbow lights from between his fingers. "Look me up."

Ty reached out and took the card and clasped the wolf's paw at the same time. "You taking off?"

"Just heading back out to the dance floor. It is loud here and I'd rather dance than talk. Maybe I'll see you there?"

"Maybe." Ty took the card as the wolf released his paw and then saw Dev coming up. He shoved the card hastily in his pocket and followed the wolf's tail out to the dance floor as Dev took the empty seat.

Dev was worried about Vonni, and after that Pike came up and said it was time to go, so Ty didn't see Arch again that night. But he took the card out in his room, sitting in his bed. *For a good time call Archie Collins*, it read, and listed the phone number below it.

It was tempting to say that the guy had the wrong idea about him. But he hadn't really hit on Ty at all. Couldn't a guy just have a guy friend to go dancing with? Even if one was straight and the other gay? Some of Ty's friends could dance, but there was something about Arch that was different. Maybe it was that the wolf had walked away from him. That hadn't happened with anyone, male or female, since—jeez, high school maybe.

Ty curled his tail up on the bed and looked at the card again, then put the number into his phone.

•

After the game, he sat at his locker and looked around. Pretty much everyone was down after the loss: tails drooped and ears were flat everywhere he looked. The rest of the wideouts grumbled around him about the new guy coming in, Lightning Strike, and they hadn't even had a chance to say good-bye to Ford. So nobody was really in the mood to go out.

But Ty'd caught a touchdown, and even though he was pissed about Ford and Strike just as much, he was already envisioning being traded to a team where he could be the number one wideout, or else hanging around a couple years until Strike left this team just like he'd left all the others and taking over the top spot here. Whatever happened, he was sure he'd come out on top. And he'd caught a touchdown. He felt like going out.

Dev had a date with his fox, which was cool that they could go out together here and people wouldn't care as much. Ty'd never really thought about it much, apart from the college jokes about staying away from the hookers in Yerba (because they were usually males in drag). It was cool, though, having seen the stress on Dev, to see him more relaxed. Or at least to think of him more relaxed, because he'd still looked a bit stressed even on Korsat Street.

The tall fox took his phone out and thumbed it open. There on the first page of his contacts was the name: Archie Collins. He rubbed his whiskers. Ah, what the hell. It didn't mean anything.

So he texted: *Sorry about your first game as a Firebirds fan.*

He'd gotten dressed and was just chatting with Rodolf when his phone buzzed. Archie had replied: *What makes you think I watched? ;)*

He grinned until Rodolf snapped his fingers, and then he looked up at the deer. "Sorry," he said. "Messages."

As they talked, he typed back: *Aw, I thought you liked me.*

Rodolf started telling him about the terrible things this guy he knew on the Hellentown Pilots had said Strike did while he was there, while Ty listened absently. And a couple minutes later, he flipped open his phone when it buzzed with the response.

"Oh, you think that's good news?" Rodolf snapped. "You think you won't come in for some comment about how much better he is than you?"

"Sorry." Ty wagged his tail. "I'm sure it'll be fine. I'm gonna head out. See you on the plane."

He looked again at the message that said, *Nice touchdown :)*, and then called a cab.

•

Korsat Street wasn't nearly as crowded on a Sunday night, and the music in the club wasn't quite as good. Arch wasn't anywhere he could see, but then again, he was about ten minutes earlier than he'd said he'd be. So he got a scotch at the bar, savored the flavors, and then raised his arms over his head and sauntered out onto the dance floor. He'd been tackled pretty hard a few times, but he ignored the soreness in his hip and danced anyway.

He'd been dancing for one and a half songs when the smell of wolf tickled his nose. There was nobody in front of him, so he turned with the music and saw Arch grinning, holding up a paw. Ty slapped it, and they danced as if they'd just taken a break two nights ago and come right back to the floor.

It was just as good, too. Ty hadn't really thought much about it, but it was nice to know it hadn't just been a fluke, or something that he'd been remembering wrong because of the drinks. Arch could move and shake, and maybe he swiveled his hips and flipped his tail up more than Ty wanted to do, but damn he looked good doing it.

They danced until they were both panting, and then Ty pulled Arch over to the bar, grabbing the wolf's paw casually just like that. "A scotch and soda," he told the bartender, "Glenlivet if you have it, the best thing you have otherwise. And whatever he wants."

"You don't have to buy my drink," Arch said. "In fact, you lost your game. I should be buying you a drink."

Ty laughed. "Don't worry about it. Normally I'm out at a club with a bunch of guys and I drop a thousand bucks."

Arch raised an eyebrow. "Cosmo," he told the bartender, and then, to Ty, "You go out with a bunch of guys?"

"Friends from college and home. Four of them moved down to Chevali when I got traded there. I got them a house to live in, they support me."

"Ah." Arch's grin widened. "Around here, 'going out with a bunch of guys' means something else."

Ty flinched inside, but not as much as he would've thought. "That's not my scene," he said.

Their drinks arrived, and as they were sipping, a stallion came over to them. "You guys look great together," he said.

"Thanks." Arch raised a paw, and the guy headed off.

"We're not…" Ty called after him, and then shrugged. "Ah, hell with it."

The wolf grinned at him. "You and I know it. Who cares what they think?"

"Well, if they take a picture and publish it, I'd care."

"Nobody's gonna take pictures in here. It's not cool."

Ty looked around, but nobody seemed to have a camera or even to be paying his tall, athletic body any attention other than the kind that didn't care what his name was. "I guess," he said. "But if I get 'outed' in the paper, it's on you."

"I'll deny it if they talk to me." Arch finished his drink. "How's your scotch?"

"Enh." Ty gulped the rest. "It's fine. I shouldn't get too buzzed, though. You ready?"

Arch nodded, and then put his muzzle closer to Ty's ear. "You ever get high?"

The words came across clearly even though the wolf had spoken softly and the music was going at full volume. Ty turned and caught rainbow sparkles flashing in the wolf's dark eyes. "Back in college," he said. "Been a while. My friends don't have a source in Chevali so we mostly get drunk."

"Do they test you?"

"Yeah, but they tell us when it's coming. I already had mine this year." He waved a paw. "You got some?"

Arch chuckled. "I get these migraines, see? I really do. So I got a prescription. Got some cookies at home. You want some?"

The fox narrowed his eyes. "I don't get experimental when I get high. I just get mellow."

"Settle down." The wolf put a paw on Ty's. "Just offering. No strings."

The fox grinned. "In that case," he said, "lead on."

When Arch pulled out his keys in front of a narrow three-story building on a misty street, Ty started to reconsider. The gate was rusted in spots and the place smelled like urine; Ty could count about ten different people who'd pissed nearby just in the last couple days. The cars on the street, though, were not old beaters; there were a couple BMWs and a whole lot of mid-range cars. So junkies might walk around on the sidewalks, but people with money lived in the buildings.

And inside, everything was nicer. The urine smell disappeared when he walked through the door into a brightly-lit foyer with mailboxes along one wall, a lot of mailboxes. Arch didn't stop at any of them, just headed for an old marble staircase at the back of the building, only wide enough for one person at a time.

Arch led him up to the second floor, down a narrow hallway. "This looks like a college dorm," Ty said, looking at all the numbered doors and down at the worn carpeting. "Smells better, though."

"Still crowded." Arch's nose wrinkled just as Ty's was. "Used to be a small hotel, then a rabbit family bought it. Sold it off in the Depression and homeless people lived here for a while. Then a tech millionaire fixed it up to rent." The wolf turned his key in the lock of a door with number 225 on it and opened it, letting Ty in.

The room was a little larger than a hotel room, but not much. To the right, a small wooden table and two chairs bumped up against a small refrigerator and a stack of plastic crates that apparently served as a pantry, filled with cereal boxes and instant dinners. There was no sink in this room, but behind the table, an open door gave onto a bathroom, and Ty saw that at least there was a sink in there.

To the left, a double bed filled most of the space of the room against the wall, sheets untidy, a collared shirt in a pile at the foot. A brightly colored pressboard dresser had been wedged between the bed and the window, and that was all the furniture the room held. There was no TV, no couch, nothing else, and no other doors apart from the bathroom. Mail and laptops cluttered the wooden table, and clothes dotted the floor.

"Home sweet home," Arch said. "Sorry about the mess."

Ty shook his head. "Reminds me of my dorm room. You live here…" He sniffed the air. "With a wolverine? Your boyfriend?"

Arch laughed. "Roommate."

"Okay…" Ty definitely smelled sex in the air. Stale, but unmistakable. "So he's not gay?"

"Oh, we jerk each other off sometimes. Sometimes more than that." Arch stopped, cocked his head, and grinned at Ty. "Depends what we're in the mood for."

"Okay." The fox turned his attention to the fridge. "No kitchen?"

Arch stepped closer to him. "Tell me," he said. "If there was a vixen you could hang out with and sometimes sleep with, and she wouldn't ever want the relationship to be more, would you do it? If it was all just about being friends and sex was just one of the things you did?"

"Look," Ty said, "I told you, I'm straight."

The wolf laughed. "I'm talking about me and Justin. You're getting all tight and judgy, so I'm just putting a hypothetical to you. If Justin was Justine and we were both straight and I told you I had this female room-mate who was a good friend and sometimes we had sex when we both wanted it, what would you say? Something like 'way to go,' right?"

"I guess so." Ty grinned, felt the brush of his own tail against his legs, and realized he had been getting a little tense. Nothing to be tense about, he told himself, and anyway, it wasn't like him to get worked up. He usually just let the world come to him and he dealt with it as he dealt with it, a coping mechanism to survive in the uptight worlds of his family and football.

"So?" Arch stood with paws on hips, grinning.

Ty laughed and clapped the wolf on the shoulder. "Way to go," he said.

"There you go." Arch turned from the taller fox and walked over to the fridge. "Have a seat on the bed if you want."

Ty started toward the chairs by the table, and Arch caught his motion. "Not the chairs. I mean, they're okay, but what are you going to do, sit at the table and get high? Trust me, the bed's better. You can sit on the floor if you don't want to sit on a gay guy's bed with him."

What was he afraid of? "No, it's okay. I mean, I'm a fox…"

"So? You going to rub your musk all over my sheets?"

Ty shook his head, grinning, and went to sit on the bed. This was weird, but it was also fun in a way. Here he wasn't Ty Nakamura, highly touted wide receiver prospect, Chevali Firebird. He didn't have to keep thinking about the passes he'd missed in the game they'd just lost or worry about running his routes or about linebackers and safeties smashing into him (despite his hip). He was just Ty, a fox who liked to dance and who'd been invited by a new friend to come chill for an evening. "What if Justin comes in?"

"Then he can have some," Arch called from the fridge. "But he won't. He works graveyard, so he'll be gone 'til nine. That's why the bed works well. I sleep until he gets home, then he wakes me up and goes to sleep while I go to work. Sometimes we hang out in the evening."

"What do you do?"

"Data entry and customer service for a small startup downtown. It pays the bills, and I have a job, which is more than a lot of my friends can say. I can just about afford this place, a gym membership, and a little savings."

"How much does this cost?" Ty scooted back against the wall and curled his tail around his hips. A couple cracks ran from the corners of the ceiling, but overall the place was in pretty good shape, and it was a good sign that mostly what he smelled was fox and wolverine—no mildew, no rot, no garbage. In that, it wasn't like a college dorm. Maybe gay guys were more fastidious.

"The place is twelve hundred a month. Justin and I split it, so I pay six."

"Holy shit!" Ty sat up and stared around. "Twelve hundred a month? That's almost as much as I'm paying for my house."

"In Chevali, right?" Arch walked over with a paper plate that had two small cookies on it. "Middle of the desert? This is a highly desirable neighborhood here. Walking distance to Korsat, walking distance to the financial district, short bus ride to my job and thousands of other jobs. Also walking distance to about fifty amazing restaurants."

"My house has six bedrooms." Ty grinned as Arch sat on the bed and put the plate between them. "But yeah, this location is pretty cool. Apart from the piss-stained street."

"And these," Arch tapped the plate, "are legal."

The smell of cannabis hovered around the cookies like a cloud. Ty picked one up in his fingers. "Sugar cookies?"

"I'm not a great cook. I basically know this and chicken casserole."

"Where do you cook chicken casserole?"

Arch jerked his thumb toward the door. "There's a shared kitchen. Most of us keep a fridge and a hot pot in the rooms. I have to be careful when I'm baking these because if anyone else smells them, they come running and then cookies disappear. I usually melt some peppermint candies at the same time to cover the smell."

Ty laughed. "A guy in my college used to put Neutra-Scent over the oven vents when he made them. Once he forgot to insulate them and they caught fire. Nothing smells worse than burning Neutra-Scent."

"That's ironic." Arch picked the other cookie up. "Your health, sir."

It was a good enough cookie, the sugar cutting the sharp cannabis taste. Ty crunched and swallowed, and closed his eyes. It was like college again. He leaned back against the wall and waited for it to kick in.

Movement brushed his whiskers. He opened his eyes and saw Arch pulling his shirt off. "Whoa," he said.

"Don't freak out, I'm not going down to fur." Arch dropped the shirt off the side of the bed. "I'll even keep my pants on for you. I just don't like chilling in so many clothes, y'know?"

"Sure." In a couple minutes he wasn't going to care anyway, he thought. "What do you do when you're high without a TV?"

"Movies." Arch got up and walked over to his laptop. While he opened it, Ty watched his back move. The wolf had a pretty good slender body, which made sense if he had a gym membership and went out dancing a bunch. And when he bent over and grabbed a DVD, Ty watched the wolf's tail wag. He'd looked at a lot of guys' butts—naked ones even—but he'd never thought about them sexually. And he wasn't really thinking about Arch that way either, only he knew the wolf was gay. So the wolf wanted guys to appreciate his body, right? Anyway, it was a tight, slender butt, almost like a girl's. Ty still didn't want to fuck him, but he could maybe see where other guys did.

The wolf brought the laptop over, trailing a cord, and set it on the floor near the bed. His chest was pretty well defined too.

"I put in this dragon-fighting movie. The dragons breathe fire and talk." Arch started the movie and sprawled out on the bed on his stomach. "It gets more dragon-y about forty-five minutes in, which is perfect timing."

"Our go-to movie was 'P.W.'s Big Adventure,'" Ty said, stretching out on the bed and letting his tail relax atop his legs. "But that's pretty much insane all the way through."

As the movie started, Ty grinned to himself. Lying in a dorm room watching a movie—if someone had told him that's how he was going to spend his Sunday night, he would've laughed and told them to fuck off. But it was nice, it was chill, and he was starting to get used to the smell of the wolf.

The first part of the movie was a lot of setup: a nation of weasels was trying to attack a nation of deer using magic, and the deer were desperate for some way to retaliate. About a half hour in, when the young buck had reached the desert and found the dragon's egg, Ty got up on his knees and unbuttoned his shirt. He didn't really process why he was doing it; he just felt warm. Getting the shirt off felt good and cooler.

Arch turned his head, but didn't otherwise react. And it was around then that Ty started really noticing shit, like how pretty the dragon's egg was, and then when the dragon itself appeared on the screen, he said, "Holy shit," out loud. The camera seemed to linger on it, the sparkling scales and rainbow glitter around the long neck and reptilian head. When it breathed fire and the young buck only barely dove behind a rock in time, the fire danced and cascaded around the screen and looked freaking amazing.

And it turned out that the young buck had met a sarcastic dragon, but it wasn't even the dragon's lines that were cracking Ty up. It was the fact that it was talking at all. He couldn't explain it, but he just kept thinking, like, what if it wanted to talk and then accidentally breathed fire? Because that'd be hysterical.

He tried to cover up his giggles, but Arch was giggling too. "I told you this movie is fucking awesome," he said.

"Oh shit," Ty gasped. "The dragon is amazing."

"Just wait."

And it did get better. There were more dragons, and they actually set fire to a weasel army, which wasn't really funny, so they stopped laughing at that part. Arch actually wiped his eyes a couple times.

"Dude, are you crying?"

"Shut up," the wolf said.

"No, seriously, it's cool." On the screen, the weasels were retreating. "I mean, those weasels are assholes, but they shouldn't be, y'know, uh." He searched for the word. "Made to be on fire."

"Yeah. Can't they just talk about shit?"

Ty thought that was a sweet thought, and it seemed like he'd known Arch for ages. At least, the movie had been going on forever. So he put a paw on the wolf's back. And it was cool, they stayed like that until the end of the movie.

Arch turned and smiled at Ty, then rolled off the bed away from his paw and put the laptop away. "I guess you probably want to get back to your hotel."

His hotel. Oh, shit, right. Ty looked around for his shirt, and then imagined coming in and waking up Rodo. "I don't know if I should. I mean, they'll know I'm high."

The wolf came back to the bed and grinned down at him. "They won't know."

"No, I'm serious. I could get in deep shit for this. If they find out..."

"How will they know?"

Ty inhaled. "Because I'm slurring. No, I'm talking too precisely. See, I can't tell! I'll screw up, and then..."

He sat up with his back to the wall again and gripped his tail in his paw. Arch knelt on the bed in front of him. "You're not that high. You'll be fine."

"What if I'm not?"

The wolf laughed. "Well, the alternative is that you sleep here. You wanna sleep here?"

"I kinda just want to crash." There was some reason he wouldn't want to do that, but Ty didn't remember what it was right away. Then he pulled the bedsheet to his nose and sniffed. "Wait. You're gay. And you have a gay roommate."

Arch kept his smile on. "You can keep your pants on. I promise I won't molest you."

"What about your roommate? The wolverine?" In Ty's imagination, he was a seven-foot tall hulking monster in rainbow suspenders. Suspenders?

"Justin's cool. He's found me in bed with guys before. He'll just assume we hooked up."

"But we didn't. We won't."

Arch shook his head. "This might shock you, but I don't just fuck any guy I meet, even if he is gay and wants to. Sometimes I just want to be friends. Sometimes I want to make sure the guy isn't crazy."

"Oh, shit." Ty dropped his muzzle into his paws. "I'm acting crazy, aren't I?"

"No, you're high is all." Arch put a paw on Ty's shoulder, and the fox looked up. "What time do you need to be up in the morning?"

"Uh. We're supposed to leave the hotel at nine-thirty." That, at least, he remembered.

Arch went back to his laptop. "Okay. I'll set an alarm for eight. That'll give you plenty of time."

"You sure?" Relief overwhelmed him. Arch was a great guy.

"It's fine. But *I* am going to take off my pants. You don't have to, but it's my bed, and I don't sleep in jeans."

"Okay." Ty just sat and waited, calmer now that the situation was handled. He hadn't gotten high since the week before the draft, because even though he was a great believer in the general benevolence of the universe, he was also a great believer in not tempting fate, and besides, he wasn't even allowed to drink legally then. Months into the UFL routine, with his twenty-first birthday safely in the books, he had felt more confident that one night would not result in his expulsion from the league (mainly because three of his teammates had offered him pot)—until he'd actually taken the drug.

Now, his memories of how to handle it came back. He still felt the paranoia, but he was able to distance himself from it. It helped that Arch knew he was high and that he'd already been lying on the bed; it was strange but not too strange. He turned himself around and reclined on the bed on the side against the wall.

Arch walked back to the bed. Ty followed his movements with his ears, heard the steps on the carpet and then the scrape of claws against the fasteners on his pants. The jeans slid down, making a shushing against the leg fur, and then he stepped out of them. Then the bed creaked and the wolf's weight settled onto it.

Ty braced himself so he wouldn't roll toward the weight and rested his head back. Arch pulled the covers over himself, but Ty stayed on top of them. He had his pants on, and even though he was shirtless, winter in Yerba wasn't so cold that a thick-furred red fox would so much as shiver in this apartment. He was aware of the weight of the wolf next to him, but he was unworried by it. Arch was cool. And Ty was cool, too.

•

He came awake in a dim room, disoriented. Wolf smell filled his nostrils and the air on his nose was cool. He turned his head and saw the sleeping wolf next to him. Arch's muzzle was peaceful in rest, smiling and handsome actually. Ty thought about waking up next to some of his college buddies on road trips, but this wasn't exactly like that. Dev was used to waking up next to a guy, but this wasn't like that either. It was feeling comfortable with someone, comfortable enough to share drugs and a bed with on a second meeting, but not wanting to have sex with.

Although he did have a pretty good morning wood going on. He reached down and rubbed it through his jeans, and then imagined Arch reaching over to rub it. The idea was…interesting. In the sleepy haze of morning, when he didn't want to reject the idea just because he was straight, it didn't disturb him so much. He touched his own junk all the time.

So maybe not have sex with, but play around a bit. He'd had friends in high school who told him about skinny-dipping parties in the ocean, and one had admitted that after drinking, when there were eight guys and only three girls, some of the guys jerked each other off. Wasn't a thing, didn't mean anything.

Ty hadn't had time to do that, with football and studying, even if his parents would've let him go out to the ocean late. But he'd gotten erections imagining it.

Yes, but he'd also dated girls and gotten erections from that too. And gotten erections from thinking about breasts and looking at naked vixens.

So…what? He reached out a paw experimentally and rested it on Arch's hip. The wolf stirred but didn't wake. His body felt warm and solid beneath Ty's fingers. It felt…nice. If Arch had been a girl, that touch would've been a prelude to morning sex, but here it just felt friendly.

And then, with a shrill ring, the alarm went off.

Ty yanked his paw back and sat up, and a moment later Arch did the same, rubbing his eyes. "Hey," the wolf said.

"Hey." Ty scooted down and off the bed without climbing over Arch. He found his shirt on the floor. "Thanks for letting me crash."

"No problem. You want to grab coffee on your way over?"

"Uh." Ty pulled his shirt on. "You have coffee here?"

"There's a coffee shop on the corner, open at 5. Pretty good. It'll probably take fifteen minutes for the cab to get here anyway."

Coffee would probably help him wake up. And fifteen minutes for the cab, and the ride to Korsat had been only fifteen…he had plenty of time. "Sure."

So Arch swung his legs out of bed and stood, and Ty saw clearly what he hadn't seen the previous night, which was that the wolf was wearing tight briefs, and also that his own morning wood was at least as prominent as Ty's, and more noticeable as it was only concealed by a thin, stretchy layer of fabric, and…

And the very tip of it was poking out of the top of his waistband. Ty was standing here looking at the tip of another guy's cock. And Arch saw him looking and didn't seem to care, nor did he smirk or offer to show Ty more, or anything like that. He just yawned and stretched—maaaaybe showing off a little, but hell, who wouldn't if he had the body to?—and walked over to pull on his pants.

They got coffee, which was as good as promised, and while they were waiting for the cab, Ty said, "Hey, so thanks again. It was a fun night. Next time I'm in town, we should do it again."

"The pot and the overnight stay?" Arch smiled.

"Sure." Ty laughed. "I mean, if I freak out about being high."

"You didn't mind sleeping in bed next to a gay guy?"

Ty shook his head. "You didn't, like, fuck me in my sleep or anything, did you?"

Arch snorted. "Even if that were really possible, I don't just paw or blow or fuck any old guy, I told you that."

"Yeah," Ty said, "I know. But would you do me?"

He'd meant it as playful, kind of the football player with an ego needing to be stroked. But it didn't quite come out as playful, and Arch gave him a sidelong look. "You asking seriously?"

"Just hypothetically. Anyway, I thought you didn't need things to be serious."

The wolf breathed in his coffee steam and then sipped from the cup. "I don't," he said after a moment. "But I'm also not interested in being some straight guy's experiment, y'know?"

"No, no." Ty sipped his own coffee, confused now, aware that he'd made he situation awkward without meaning to. "Look, I was just messing around. I had a good time—I had fun."

"It's cool. Sorry, I just had…you know, in high school there'd be guys who were like, 'hey, you like cock, wanna blow me?' and a couple times I did. I was a cub, I thought they'd like me after, y'know? But they just…they treated me worse than the girls. So I'm done with that."

"I didn't mean—"

"No, I know you didn't. You're a good guy. Here's your cab." The green car was coming around the corner.

"Thanks." Ty held out his paw, and Arch took it, then pulled the fox into a hug. Which also felt good, again in a non-sexual kind of way.

And as he got into the cab, Arch held the door for a second and said, "Hypothetically? Maybe." And then he shut the door and stood there grinning at Ty as the cab pulled away.

About the Author

Kyell Gold took up furry erotica writing after high school, making the team at his small liberal arts college as a walk-on. He was drafted late by Sofawolf and blossomed in the professional league, earning four Ursa Major awards in his first three years as a pro for his novels and short stories. He has since won eight more Ursa Major awards, including one for "In Between," the first Dev and Lee story, one for *Out of Position*, which also won two Rainbow Awards for gay fiction, and one for *Isolation Play*, the second Dev and Lee book.

His various online presences are linked from *www.kyellgold.com*, and you can follow him on Twitter at @KyellGold. In the off-season, he lives in California with his husband.

About the Artists

Rukis is a freelance illustrator and writer who grew up in the Appalachian region, working with animals and on farms from a young age. After earning a Bachelors in Traditional Animation, she started a career in freelance art, writing and illustrating a small collection of comics and novels in the Anthropomorphic fandom. You can see more of her work at *www.furaffinity.net/user/rukis*.

Kenket aka Tess Garman aka Kenket has a degree in illustration and paints animals for a living. She has collaborated on the award-winning *Across Thin Ice* and on the previous books in the *Out of Position* series. You can find her work at *www.furaffinity.net/user/kenket*.

About Sofawolf Press

Sofawolf Press was founded in 1999 to provide a venue to showcase great writers of anthropomorphic fiction and to promote the genre to a wider audience.

Since the debut of its flagship publication, Anthrolations, a literary anthology of short stories, the Press has added to its lineup other magazine-length anthologies, novels, shared-world anthologies, and other novel-length collections, comics and graphic novels, artists' sketchbooks, and calendars. The Press continues to seek out new and creative ways of expanding its offerings of printed creations. Sofawolf's publications have won twenty Ursa Major awards, and in 2012, Ursula Vernon's *Digger* gave Sofawolf Press its first Hugo Award.

Please visit their website at *www.sofawolf.com* for a full list of titles available from Sofawolf Press. Thanks for reading!